Prai...

'An uplifting and wonde... ...le
friendships, love and self... ...ft

'Thoroughly entertaining. The characters are warm and well drawn. I thoroughly recommend this book if you are looking for a light-hearted read. 5 stars'   Sue Roberts

'Full of humour, poignancy and ultimately uplifting this is an absolutely gorgeous read. We loved it! Highly recommended!'
Hot Brands Cool Places

'A warm, funny, uplifting writer to celebrate!'   Katie Fforde

'A pleasure to read ... A summer breezes treat'   *Devon Life*

'Warm, humorous and full of friendship; an ideal holiday read'
Georgia Hill

'Uplifting'   *Woman & Home*

'A lovely, heart-warming story ... I was hooked!'
Christina Courtenay

'A delightful tale of friendship, family and love'   Jenni Keer

'Laced with the warmth of friendships and the possibilities of new beginnings ... The author has the knack of making her characters spring off the pages so real that you'll care about them'   *Peterborough Telegraph*

Erin Green was born and raised in Warwickshire. An avid reader since childhood, her imagination was instinctively drawn to creative writing as she grew older. Erin has two Hons degrees: BA English literature and another BSc Psychology – her previous careers have ranged from part-time waitress, the retail industry, fitness industry and education.

She has an obsession about time, owns several tortoises and an infectious laugh! Erin writes contemporary novels focusing on love, life and laughter. Erin is an active member of the Romantic Novelists' Association and was delighted to be awarded The Katie Fforde Bursary in 2017. An ideal day for Erin involves writing, people watching and drinking copious amounts of tea.

For more information about Erin, visit her website: www.ErinGreenAuthor.co.uk, find her on Facebook www.facebook.com/ErinGreenAuthor or follow her on Twitter, Instagram, TikTok or Threads @ErinGreenAuthor.

By Erin Green

Summer Dreams at the Lakeside Cottage
Christmas Wishes at the Lakeside Cottage
Retreat to the Lakeside Cottage
Reunited at the Lakeside Cottage

A Christmas Wish
The Single Girl's Calendar
The Magic of Christmas Tree Farm
New Beginnings at Rose Cottage
Taking a Chance on Love

From Shetland, With Love series
From Shetland, With Love
From Shetland, With Love at Christmas
Sunny Stays at the Shetland Hotel
A Shetland Christmas Carol

Reunited
at the
Lakeside Cottage

ERIN GREEN

REVIEW

First published in 2024 by
HEADLINE REVIEW
An imprint of Headline Publishing Group Limited

2

Cataloguing in Publication Data is available from the British Library

ISBN 978 1 0354 1769 8

Typeset in Sabon by CC Book Production

Printed and bound in Great Britain by
Clays Ltd, Elcograf S.p.A.

The authorised representative in the EEA is Hachette Ireland, 8 Castlecourt
Centre, Dublin 15, D15 XTP3, Ireland (email: info@hbgi.ie)

Headline Publishing Group Limited
An Hachette UK Company
Carmelite House
50 Victoria Embankment
London EC4Y 0DZ

www.headline.co.uk
www.hachette.co.uk

Dedicated to the two smiling faces
always missing from my life. xx
2002

To err is human; to forgive, divine.

ALEXANDER POPE, 1688–1744

Chapter One

Friday 27 December 2024
Midday

Paisley

I stand alone beside the old dry-stone wall surveying the quintessential cottage beyond. I'm liking what I see. A giant doll's house with large leaded windows in a symmetrical frontage, the windows flanking a front door painted moss-green, which is currently decorated with a festive wreath and luxurious red satin bows. A traditional thatched roof hangs low like a heavy duck-down duvet with the upper-storey windows sleepily peering from beneath. There's an abundance of bare branches, rampant but knotted with age, growing against the rustic brickwork and tiny porchway. I won't pretend to know what plant it could be, but a rambling rose or wisteria would look lovely in full bloom.

It's a welcome sight after my long drive in this, the bleakest week of mid-winter, the one falling between Christmas and New Year. But I have high hopes for the coming year, relating mainly to personal growth and better lifestyle choices, leading to a healthier, happier me. And lots of much needed change, given the dismal year I've had. Sadly, such hopes skitter around my head dodging the niggling doubts that remind me that my resolve is weak and that reality will waiver between 'more of the same' and 'much of a muchness' by the fourth of January. However, for now, I need to commit to enjoying our mini-break and focus on living in the present.

We've certainly landed on our feet with this rental cottage, despite there being nothing else available given the time of year. Our last-minute booking now feels like fate, as we've clearly nabbed ourselves a fairy-tale cottage, complete with picket gate, cobbled path and an overwintering garden, at a bargain price. Oh well, one woman's sorrowful cancellation is another woman's win! Mind you, that little lesson isn't lost on me in more ways than one . . .

I quickly check my phone for the precise time. I'm five minutes early for our midday check-in. But surely that conveys manners? Somewhat of a rarity nowadays or so it often seems. In recent months I've admittedly learned more about human nature than I'd care to mention.

I push open the white picket gate and enter, the metal latch giving a satisfying 'click' behind me. I tentatively pick my way along the worn cobbles, wary of the uneven path underfoot, dragging my faithful wheelie case. Not that it gets much use nowadays, as proven by the thick layer of dust I had to remove before I began packing. Unlike in my previous life, where surprise mini-breaks were a regular occurrence – we'd think nothing of packing essentials and jetting off on a Friday evening. Boy, how life has changed! Never mind, there's a brand-new year around the corner and I intend to hold tight to my high hopes with a 'New Year, new me' mindset.

Arriving at the doorstep, I gingerly tug the old-fashioned bell-pull. I've never seen a useable one in real life before, and it adds a certain something to our rental experience. Experience and memories – that's what we're after on this girlie break and, boy, are we each in need of some TLC and chilling.

A smiling face appears in the door's tiny bevelled window, before the door itself opens wide.

'Hello, and welcome to Lakeside Cottage ... I'm Josie, the housekeeper – keeper of the keys, so to speak,' announces a mature lady. I like her floaty scarf in autumnal colours: it matches her hair and adds flare to her simple cotton jumper and tweed skirt combo. I always admire how my mum's generation accessorise in often understated ways.

Her warm smile and spritely manner is edged with a slight hesitancy, as her flickering gaze takes in my casual but comfy outfit: boots, leggings and an oversized fleece – quite different to my working attire of pale blue neonatal uniform.

'Hi. Paisley Morris. Nice to meet you,' I say, quickly extending my hand, which lingers for a fraction of a second, before being firmly shaken. The lady's hand is freezing cold, but I assume the old proverb is correct given her bright but faltering smile.

'M-Morris?' A twitch flashes across her brow.

'Uh-hmm,' I confirm, my gaze seeking hers, but she's distracted, deep in thought.

'Sorry. Excuse my manners ... l-lovely to m-meet you. Do c-come in,' she stutters, stepping backwards, freeing the doorway. 'Anyway, w-welcome to Lakeside Cottage, I'm J-Josie ...' she pauses, shaking her head before smiling apologetically. 'I've already said that, haven't I? Apologies, you must think me so rude ... but the surname again was?' She inclines her head, listening intently.

'Miss Morris. The other two guests will be arriving shortly – we'd planned to arrive together. They've been delayed by motorway traffic. Each lane is snarled to a complete stand-still apparently. Thankfully, I came from a different direction, so didn't hit the holiday traffic or tailbacks, unlike my friends.' I fall silent; Josie seems confused – I don't think she's listening to me.

'So sorry, Miss Morris ... but would you excuse me for just one moment?' asks Josie, raising an index finger and double blinking at her own request.

'Sure.' This isn't the welcome I was expecting, but she seems pleasant enough and it's only a key handover. It'll probably take all of five minutes.

Josie hastily trots off along the hallway, leaving me to stand beside the front door, my wheelie case parked upright at my feet. To my left is a side table with a fancy guest book and a pretty ceramic dish containing various keyrings. There's a huge central staircase before me, wider than standard; its notchity newel post looks ancient, given the gouged marks of age-old wear and tear. It complements the wooden beams overhead and the adjacent panelled doors beautifully. The sturdy banister and picture rail are swathed in a garland of holly and ivy, matching the festive door wreath. An historic, homely cottage, tastefully renovated to retain its original features. It's the sort of place I always dreamed of owning. It must date back a couple of hundred years, though I wouldn't hazard a guess beyond that.

I turn around to peer through the small bevelled window, hoping to see a familiar car drawing up to park behind mine. Nothing. The flower borders might look crusty brown and twiggy right now but I bet they're a riot of colour come the summer. I imagine a garden this size once supplied endless home-grown vegetables for the original family. And they were big families in those days. Unlike nowadays, when most families have two or three children at best. Other folks have none, of course. But I quickly rein in my thoughts, pulling my mind back from that particular beaten track before it can upset me. It's an emotional path, that one, littered with potholes and debris, that will most definitely flatten the birthday fizz, throw my mind into overdrive and put the kibosh on me enjoying what should be an incredible few days alongside my two best friends, Selena and Kate, who also happen to be sisters. Selena deserves only the best for her thirtieth birthday celebrations; matching the joy and energy that she put into my own special day back in September.

I turn around, switching my view and hopefully my thoughts. Selena's the main name on the rental booking; maybe I should have mentioned that to Josie, but surely my name is listed as a guest? Though, given Selena's lack of enthusiasm and decision making about how she wanted to celebrate her special day – hence the late booking just three days ago – she's probably made a blunder on the website's booking form. Who leaves it until Christmas Eve to book a rental cottage for their birthday celebration less than a week later? Worse still, for her thirtieth! Selena, that's who. It's not as if it was a surprise entry in her calendar. Or a moveable date, like Easter or Whit Sunday. Or that we hadn't continually been prodding her, ever since my own thirtieth celebration back in September, asking what she wanted to do for hers. The loveable bloody idiot that she is, *of course* she decides last minute. She couldn't have left it any later if she'd tried, keeping us all on tenterhooks, until its almost too late to book anything decent. Not that I'm saying that this isn't decent – this cottage is more than decent for us three. Too big, if anything. Then, in the space of an afternoon, her decision is finally made and its full steam ahead, planning and booking like a crazy fool to ensure it actually happens. Always the way. There was nothing else vacant in the local area, though. Good job this place had had a last-minute cancellation, otherwise where would we be? Probably glamping in the New Forest with no phone signal and outside amenities situated halfway across a muddy field, and some prank-crazy guys reliving their youth in a neighbouring yurt. Good job Selena didn't decide on a week in the sun or a big family party instead – neither of those would have even been feasible at this short notice. What *is* she like? Just wait until she gets here. I'll be giving her what for – in the nicest way.

How exactly can one person mess up time after time when booking stuff on the internet? In fact, I wouldn't be surprised if she's entered my previous name – my married one. I bet she has.

Typical Selena, with her last-minute slapdash manner. That's it! That's what she's done. A year after my divorce and she's used my old name. Now Josie's in a tizzy as Morris doesn't match with the booking sheet, which probably lists McLoughlin. Bless her. No wonder she looked utterly confused. She was trying to be so polite too.

Which door did she go through? The end one or one of these side doors? I stare at the four panelled doors lining the hallway, each with their traditional brass doorknob. I'd have kept original features too, given the chance to renovate a property like this. Though I bet these polished floorboards are a bugger to keep waxed and polished with guests traipsing through. We'll have to be mindful with our heels, otherwise we'll dimple the surface in five days. That's most definitely not something I wish to rectify with a hefty deduction from our deposit money.

That poor lady. No wonder her introduction went to pieces and she was stuttering after I gave my name, but it would do, given she's expecting to hear something entirely different. I'll correct the situation the second she returns. I'm certain it was the far end door she slipped through. I bet she's busy checking the booking details, her heart all of a flutter, not knowing what to do or sure of what to say without causing offence. This wouldn't have happened if Selena and Kate had arrived first, as planned. Typical. Why does everything go wrong for me?

If only the housekeeper would return. I've got my driver's licence and bank cards as proof. Proof that Selena is a prize muppet for causing such confusion in the first place. I love her to bits and all that – she's my oldest and dearest friend – but, despite her savvy ways, her intelligence and creative flare, that woman can't do the simplest of things right. No common sense, as my dad would say.

The far end door opens and Josie returns, her brow still furrowed, clutching a folded piece of paper.

'Now then, on here it states . . .' she says, in a hushed tone.

'I'm so sorry. I bet my friend has caused confusion by giving my previous surname . . . McLoughlin, as was. She probably did it without thinking.'

'McLoughlin. Yes, McLoughlin. For a minute there I thought there was an error.' The tension drains from Josie's face and her warm smile returns. 'Phew, you had me there for a minute. I was thinking: what on earth has happened? This never happens. McLoughlin, yes, that's on the booking sheet.' She gives the paper a little wave before continuing. 'Sorry. You have to be so careful nowadays. You hear of such scams and whatnots, don't you?'

'You certainly do. Please don't apologise. It was our error, not yours. I'm so sorry.'

'It's perfectly fine, dear. All sorted now. Anyway, let's start again . . . welcome to Lakeside Cottage.'

Chapter Two

Selena

'What's he doing?' I mutter, watching the gleaming black BMW in front draw up alongside the picket gate, pull in and park directly behind Paisley's Golf. 'That's where I was going to park!'

'Who parks in front of the actual garden gateway?' says Kate, glancing at me disapprovingly.

'Me and that guy, by the looks of it,' I curtly reply.

'A bit selfish, don't you think?'

'This car wouldn't have blocked the gateway – it's shorter than his. Come on, mate – change your mind, consider the guests and park further along the lane,' I plead aloud, even though he can't hear me.

'Selena, just move along and park in front of Paisley's car. The guy's got a right to park in front of his own property – please don't rile the owners before we've collected the keys.'

The BMW driver, who clearly isn't moving, kills the headlights and opens his door.

'Phew! I'm the least of his worries given that he's thirty minutes late. Has he kept Paisley waiting all this time? Is she sitting in her car?' I say, easing my car past his BMW, bobbing my head as we drive by to peer inside Paisley's vehicle. Empty.

'Where's Paisley?' asks Kate, looking around the quiet lane as if our friend will pop up from behind the neighbouring hedgerow.

'Don't ask me,' I say, pulling my car in front of her parked Golf. 'Can you get out your side or are you stepping onto grass verge?'

'Verge but it'll be fine. I'll manage, as always.'

I don't wait for my older sister to change her mind. I kill the ignition and jump from my seat, allowing the blood to rush to my legs after such a long drive – made longer by the snail pace caused by the motorway snarl up. I vigorously stride along the middle of the desolate road to get the feeling back, taking in the surrounding view.

'Bloody gorgeous, though, wouldn't you say?' I call over the car roof as Kate's blonde hair swishes back and forth as she navigates each step. She's probably wearing her loveliest boots, which she won't want to dirty, let alone scuff. My big sister doesn't do imperfections; the standards by which she lives her life are high. In recent years, she appears to be becoming ever particular and fussier, as if striving towards absolute perfection. Which I certainly am not!

'The cottage or the bloke?'

'Don't start, Kate. You know I meant the cottage, the location, the quietness of the area.' My heart plummets to my own scuffed boots. Why does everyone think that my conversations always revolve around men? Involve men? Must mention men?

'It's my birthday bash and I'm officially excluding men,' I declare. Which won't be difficult seeing as I can't keep hold of one for longer than a quiet drink on a Sunday lunchtime, as my sister is well aware.

'Fair play! Though I'm not starting – I have your best interests at heart, little sis. I'm not looking for myself, am I? Just stating the obvious . . . a bit of chit chat during introductions and we might get a small reimbursement on the rental price,' observes Kate, appearing from her side of the car to shake out her lean legs in much the same manner as I had mine. She takes after our father, so has beautiful shapely legs like a racehorse. I take after our mother, so have sturdy legs like a pit pony – built for stamina, some would say.

'Leave the suitcases in the car boot – we'll grab them later,' says Kate, which was my thought too but of course she said it first. Much like everything in life; Kate does it first and then I bring up the rear, by repeating everything a few years later, be it school exams, driving lessons or home ownership. Well, nearly everything – I haven't followed suit with her engagement, marriage and painful divorce. This birthday I'm hoping for a little extra and to be a little different – which is pretty much guaranteed, given the stunning dress I've packed. There's no way anyone can steal my thunder on this occasion, my thirtieth, not that kith or kin would try to. I need this milestone to be a defining moment, more so than my previous big birthdays.

'Come on then, let's hear what Mr BMW has to say for himself. And find Paisley – wherever she's got to,' I say, heading towards the cottage, which is somewhat more chocolate box in style than I remember from the website. As a successful marketing exec, employed by the number-one ad agency in Europe, I find I'm rarely surprised when presented with goods and services in real life. I know all the tricks of the trade, but the photographs displayed on this rental's website didn't do it justice. I remain schtum, though – no work chat allowed. Though I rarely switch off entirely, as my current ad campaign tends to linger and haunt my thoughts. My downtime can be when my best ideas are born. Though I doubt my current product will be so amenable, given that it suffers from consumer misconceptions and 'bad-press'.

There's a low stone wall with a white picket gate, which the two of us navigate in single file and by turning sideways, given that the BMW has parked so close to the gateway. The owner is now standing before the front door, and his blond man bun and matching beard are the first details I clock as he inquisitively looks at us before impatiently turning to view the front door. His mottled denim jeans, white sports-style top and broad frame are a close second in my observations. A successful career in marketing has taught me to evaluate everything for purpose and meaning.

'Are man buns still a thing?' whispers Kate, as we pass through the gate.

'Clearly so,' I say, as my heels detect the uneven surface of the cobbled path, forcing me to carefully pre-empt each step to stop myself from falling over or twisting my ankle. 'Don't knock it, Kate. He owns a rental cottage in addition to his home. Do you?'

'Ha bloody ha, you're so funny,' retorts Kate, elbowing me as if we were youngsters still. Not that I meant to remind her of her recent troubles back home, but fact is fact. Having divorced three years ago, I live in hope that she starts to show an interest in other men soon. It was sensible for her to hibernate from the dating scene, to heal properly and grow as a person. But when does growth become a bit too much introspection? I'm hoping the New Year delivers a braver Kate.

'Sorry,' I muster, focusing on my heel placement and balancing act. Why I wear such hideous fashions when I'm not going 'out-out' is pure vanity, but definitely the only answer I've ever come up with for short-leg syndrome. Especially when accompanying leggy Kate anywhere. 'Anyway, shhhh. I'm more bothered about where Paisley is – it's not like her to wander.'

'Hello. Nice to meet you. I'm Affie,' says Mr BMW, turning around to face us from the doorstep as we approach. Nice of him to wait for us, but you'd have thought he'd have opened up or even arrived at the designated time, as promised. He extends a broad hand in Kate's direction and energetically pumps her arm. Not that he'd know who was who by the booking sheet, so theoretically I can't be miffed that he chose to welcome her first. Most people do when we're together, to be fair. This feels like those arrival moments at family weddings, when you hope to spot your tribe of relations on arrival but you only ever spy the other families' guests first. And despite the bright smiles and effort to converse, it always feels awkward.

'Hi. I'm Kate. This is my sister, Selena – she's the main one,' says Kate, in reply, gesturing towards me.

'Hi. Yes, Selena ... the main one, as she said.' I shake his hand, smile warmly and my eyes meets his. A strong steady gaze of royal blue, slight flecks of yellow, which are overshadowed in a heartbeat by the effect of his full blond beard and man bun.

'Right, nice,' he mutters, stepping backwards from the doorstep, shifting from foot to foot. I politely drop my gaze and notice he's not wearing socks with his lace-up leather shoes. My ick factor flares every time I spot it. I pray Kate doesn't notice, as she'll nudge me when she does, and she *will* notice. She always notices and always nudges.

We sisters stand shoulder to shoulder, sideways along the path facing Mr Man-bun-no-socks, politely waiting for him to proceed. This is weird – why's he not organised, unlocking the cottage door and walking us through a tour? And where's Paisley got to?

A quick glance at Kate's expression confirms she's thinking exactly the same. Our gaze meets and her eyes widen in a questioning manner, as if the guy's gone blind and won't notice.

'Will it take long?' he asks.

'You'd know, not us,' says Kate, in a bemused tone.

A ripple crosses his heavy brow before a smile slowly emerges.

'I get it: that's funny. If I don't ask too many questions it'll be over in no time – before it's even began – is that it?' he jests, briskly rubbing his beardy chin.

'Err, surely it'll be us asking questions, not the other way around? The booking form was fairly detailed – I didn't miss any of the sections, as tempted as I was,' I quip, joining the conversation, given that I'm the lead person for this party booking.

His furrowed brow appears again, along with a sideways flash of those piercing blue eyes. 'Sorry. I'm not sure that I'm following you—' he begins, as a jubilant shout goes up at the picket gate.

'Yay, Affie, mate! Are we not in yet?' calls the new guy, stepping over the picket fence, his arms cradling a white box emblazed with the words Stella Artois.

'A bit of a hold up, Carlos,' replies Affie, glancing at us before addressing his mate again. 'I see you've been shopping, but that's nowhere near enough, mate.'

'The back seat is stacked to the roof – don't you worry, lad. Hello, ladies, I promise we'll clean up after ourselves, no damage and no partying – cross my heart and hope to die! My mother brought me up better than that.' Carlos' olive skin creases deeply at the corner of his eyes and he flashes us a toothy white smile. His leggy strides deliver him to the doorstep in a blink of an eye, quicker than we sisters can exchange a questioning arched eyebrow. What the hell is going on?

'Who's got the keys, then?' asks Affie, staring at each of us in turn, as if getting down to business now his liquid refreshments and mate have turned up.

'You have, haven't you?' I retort, gesturing between him and the cottage's front door.

Affie's bottom lip protrudes from his beard and his chin shoots backwards as Kate grabs my forearm, bringing my attention towards the wooden door. Through the small bevelled window, distorted by the blown glasswork, is Paisley.

I sigh with relief, despite the unflattering effect it has on her delicate features. Thank God, she's safe, but why, then, are we standing out here? And who are these guys?

The cottage door opens wide, revealing our best friend looking incredibly pensive, with an older lady, wearing a pretty floaty scarf, peering over Paisley's left shoulder.

'Hi, my lovelies – you'd better come in … we've got a slight problem,' she says to us, before turning to the two guys. 'Hi fellas, do you want to come in too? It'll make it easier to discuss things.'

Chapter Three

Kate

I take the lead, stepping beneath the thatched porch and entering a huge hallway – not what I was expecting for a cottage. Though, since arriving, nothing has matched my expectation. Paisley and the lady remain beside the doorway, so I move along inside, positioning myself beside a wide wooden staircase, the natural colour of which matches perfectly with the overhead beams, a series of closed doors and the polished floorboards. I wait while the others shuffle inside and arrange themselves within the hallway too. There's an uncomfortable silence as we cautiously eyeball each other, awaiting 'the discussion'.

Beside me stands Selena, silently chewing the inside of her cheek – which is never a good sign. Affie ducks slightly on entering the door, which must be a nuisance in life, and Carlos boldly enters behind him, before carefully depositing his 'shopping' on the floor. A distinct rattle and clink of beer bottles comes from within. Nice, if that's your main priority in life.

The lady, who's yet to be introduced, remains at Paisley's shoulder, her head slightly bowed, wringing her hands and sporadically muttering, 'This never happens. Never.'

Paisley slowly closes the door, securing the quaint little latch, before turning to face us. I'm not liking her expression. She's got that 'this isn't my fault but . . .' look in those hazel eyes of hers and now she's raking her hand through her curls, clearly stalling for time. Once she's prepped and primed those unruly auburn curls, Paisley never usually messes with her hair, as the frizz factor can go through the roof, as she likes to remind us.

'Come on, spit it out,' says Selena impatiently. Obviously, she's seeing what I'm seeing of our dearest friend – her nearest and dearest friend, actually. I was initially just the big sister, putting up with my little sister's best buddy. Thankfully, our friendship has grown year on year, despite a medley of mishaps and sibling-like squabbles, so we've grown to love and admire each other as if we were all three of us sisters. Our bonds blossomed during the hilarity of teenage sleepovers, camping holidays to Dorset and late-night drunken chats fuelled by rounds of hot buttered toast in my parents' kitchen.

'I'm sorry. There appears to have been a mix up with the bookings. Josie here . . . how rude of me! So sorry. This is Josie Adams, the housekeeper – she's very kindly shown me around the property,' explains Paisley, gesturing towards her as she gives us a small embarrassed wave.

'Honestly, things like this never happen. I can't understand it,' says Josie, before resuming her head shaking and hand wringing.

'Shall we say certain things didn't add up as we were chatting . . . It appears there's been a double booking. Our group . . .' Paisley nods to me and Selena before turning towards the fellas, 'and their group.'

'Bloody hell!' sighs Carlos, his boot nudging the cardboard box at his feet.

'Sorry, but what?' says Affie, his blue gaze widening at Paisley. Her complexion is pale on the best of days, but now is looking ghostly.

'Paisley, this can't be,' hisses Selena, shifting her stance, with her hands on her hips.

I remain mute; I need more information.

'Look, I reacted in the exact same manner, but listen . . . this can be easily—'

'I'm not sharing, if that's what you're about to say. I'm not! I refuse to! This is supposed to be my birthday treat and I'm not having it ruined by two blokes and a beer box . . . complete strangers—'

'Three, actually. Our other mate's stuck fast on the motorway,' adds Affie.

'Selena, hear me out – please,' asks Paisley, looking more fraught by the second.

'No!' comes Selena's sharp reply. 'No offence, fellas, but I didn't plan to spend near on a week with guys. Girls only.' Her hands lift, offering a waving gesture, which comes across as non-aggressive, but her tone – boy, my little sister, she has a tone.

'Fair play. Neither did I,' says Carlos, again tapping his boot against his beloved beer box. His pout is beginning to form, matching my sister's.

'I'm so sorry . . .' mutters the housekeeper.

'Josie, I'm sure we can work something out here,' says Paisley tenderly towards the lady, before turning to address us again. 'Look, I can't believe I'm about to say this, but the cottage is huge. Too big, in fact, for just three guests, but it was worth the rental price for us to secure something at such short notice.'

'We had an unexpected cancellation, so the owners republished the advert, with a reduced price, hoping for a last-minute booking,' explains Josie, her eyes glistening as she speaks.

'Exactly. A last-minute bargain is what we nabbed too,' offers Affie.

'No doubt I'll get the blame for this error, given that it took me so long to make up my mind about what I wanted to do . . .' says my sister.

'Selena, please,' says Paisley, a little louder and more forcefully.

'Sorry, fellas, but you'll have to find somewhere else to stay because I'm not sharing my birthday cottage with strangers!'

'Where, lady? This was the last place available in the area,' says Affie, and we know this is true, as we had the exact same situation.

'Don't think you can pull the wool over our eyes. You blokes can simply mosey off elsewhere and find something a little less chocolate box-ish for your festive break. As you're not gate-crashing mine.'

'Selena, you know they're right,' I interject, not wishing for my sister to embarrass herself further.

'Are you siding with them?' Selena turns on me.

'No. I'm trying to be fair. This was the last vacant rental – which is why you snapped it up. Give him a break. At least he's being honest.'

'No way, Kate. I'm not sharing my birthday break with a cottage full of blokes. I've got confirmations as proof of our booking. Snooze you lose, fellas.' Selena adjusts her stance, oozing defiance and attitude while tapping her handbag. I wish she wouldn't. It never ends well when Selena looks this smug.

'Selena!' Paisley never usually raises her voice; her tone makes us all turn to look at her: eyes closed, her fists clenched and the sinewy tension showing in her neck. Slowly Paisley opens her eyes to stare at her best friend. 'I knew you were about to say that . . . did it not cross your mind that we . . . you . . . were the second booking, the additional one – which has gone through by error?'

'Us?' Selena's smirk fades. Both men shuffle and change stance at the realisation that the ball is clearly in their court.

'Now, that's a turn up for the books, eh, Affie?' jests Carlos, bending down to retrieve his beer box. 'Is there a fridge I can unpack these into?'

'Sure. Straight through into the kitchen,' answers Josie, pointing past me towards the end door. 'In two years of renting such a thing has never happened before – computers, banking apps and modern technology – a glitch has occurred somewhere.'

Carlos takes a stride forward and Selena bursts into life again.

'Hey, where are you going?'

'To put my beers in our fridge. And then I'll collect the other boxes from the back seat of my car, then I'll probably fetch my holdall. And this lovely lady will no doubt show me to my room – is that OK by you?' he says, his chin jutting forward, before he continues on his way towards the kitchen.

'Hang on a minute ... a second ago ...' musters Selena, attempting to stop him in his tracks. She fails. The kitchen door swings closed behind him.

'Sorry, lady. Just ignore his remarks, he's always acting the fool in one way or another,' says Affie, apologetically, to Selena.

'Nice one, sis,' I whisper, shaking my head. Where the hell are we going to find accommodation now? We'll be back in our cars before we know it, fighting our way through the motorway traffic.

'How was I supposed to know?' she hisses, under the watchful gaze of Affie.

'I was trying to handle the situation, Selena,' offers Paisley, before biting her bottom lip. 'But you've blown it. It's our booking that's the error, not theirs.'

'I now understand the confusion outside,' I say to Affie, purely as a softener.

'Likewise. I thought you two were the owners, arriving in tandem as a security measure,' he replies.

This is not looking good. Paisley is stressed, Josie downcast, Selena's bloody fiery and, by the distant sounds of the rattling bottles, Carlos is happily stacking the fridge with beer.

'I don't know where else to suggest. The young man is correct .... all vacant properties around these parts will be taken, given the holiday season,' offers Josie apologetically.

'It's not your fault,' I add, feeling sorry for her.

'Josie has phoned the owners to check ...' says Paisley.

'Check? Check what – that we've all paid our deposits. Have

you guys paid your deposit in full?' snaps Selena, turning quickly from person to person to arrive at Affie.

'Of course. That's how we got the confirmation slip and booking number. Did you?' says Affie, his lip curling into a smirk.

Please, mate, I beg you, don't laugh at her, as she'll morph into her worst version and I'll have to wade in to save your life. Even then, you might still need an ambulance if you rattle her cage.

'Hi, Affie, is it?' says Paisley. 'Is there any chance . . . in a nine-bedroom cottage, which you've rented for what – three guys? Any teeny tiny chance that us three could occupy just three of the bedrooms?' This is where Paisley's good nature comes into play. She's the softest of us three, but still no pushover. I'm next in line on the softness scale. As PA to a psycho-boss CEO, I'm used to being conciliatory and making sure things run smoothly behind the scenes to ensure said psycho-boss has a fuss free day. A true people-pleaser – that's me. And then there's my little sis, propping up at the extreme end of any softness scale. A real go-getter if ever there was one. Brash, bold and brave when it comes to her marketing campaigns, though a little over the top when it comes to real-life situations.

'The front three rooms, I'd imagine,' interjects Josie, coming out in support for the idea. 'The décor's too feminine for a man's taste.'

'Please?' I add, knowing begging is never a good look but necessary on occasion.

Affie shifts uncomfortably.

'Nine bedrooms, you say?' he asks.

'Nine. The cottage can accommodate sixteen adults,' confirms Josie, in a reassuring manner, before glancing towards Paisley.

We watch as Affie looks about him, as if sizing up the vast hallway as an indication of available bedroom size.

'Would you like a tour before you decide? Josie is very obliging,' says Paisley, as if they were old pals.

'The front and rear bedrooms are actually separated by a corridor and there's numerous bathrooms, so no one would need to share,' says Josie, quickly adding, 'I'll doubt you'll know the other party are even here.'

Please, Affie. Please say yes. We'll stay out of your way, you boys can enjoy your break and we'll do our birthday celebration thing, separately. In this big, sprawling, vacant nine-bedroom, beautiful chocolate-box-type thatched cottage – which is surely no man's dream destination but perfect for my little sister's birthday bash week. Please. Would you? Kindly? Come on, just say yes, mate! You know you want to!

'I'll cook a full-English breakfast in the mornings, if that helps you decide,' I offer, without thinking.

'Ah Kate, perfect suggestion! She does cook a cracking fry-up brekkie, Affie,' confirms Paisley, offering me a head tilt in appreciation like a true wing-woman. I'm hoping Selena stays out of it while we work out this situation between us.

'I'll see what Carlos thinks when . . .'

'Does he truly care about such things?' asks Paisley. 'He's happy with a fridge to himself, surely? I can arrange that.'

Affie shrugs. I wink at Paisley – good point.

The kitchen door opens and Carlos reappears.

'Still here?' he says coyly to Selena.

'Ha ha, very bloody funny. Your beer chilling, is it?'

'Nicely, thanks. Affie, you need to see the space in there, double frontage fridges and I bet it'll take all the bottles I've bought.'

'Carlos?' says Affie, nodding in our direction.

'No,' replies Carlos, before turning to me. 'You two . . . seem like nice polite ladies, but this one . . . she's feisty.' I can't argue with his assessment, so say nothing.

'Come on, Carlos – it's Christmas,' says Affie. Bless him for trying to sway his mate.

'You do what you wanna do, man, but I don't think J will

be happy when he gets here. He told you he wanted a boys'
break, "chill with no shrill" – are you remembering that? He
said kicking back with the sports channel and TV schedule, a
cold beer and a table filled with nom-nom! Are you remembering
what he said, Affie?'

'Yeah. I'm remembering,' sighs Affie, before addressing Paisley.
'We just wanted a guys' chill before the new year . . . which won't
happen if—'

'It will, I promise. I can guarantee you a chilled boys' break.
I'm begging here, Affie. Carlos, I'll keep this one in line. Kate
will deliver the biggest gut-buster breakfasts you've ever seen
each morning – you won't be able to eat it all, honest. Can we
just have the three front bedrooms – we'll stay out of your hair.
Out of your fridge, even. You can have the wide-screen TV in the
lounge – it's massive, with sleek remote controls and booming
surround sound system, I imagine. Turn the whole lounge into a
sports arena, if you wish – just for you and your guys.' Paisley's
on a roll, pointing across the hallway towards the closed door
behind him and bigging up the technology as needed. 'You won't
hear a peep out of us. We'll be quite happy with the little snug
lounge just along the hallway. A teeny tiny TV, incey-wincey
remote control – that's all we need.' Finally, she draws breath.

Affie's expression suggests he's considering it. 'Carlos?'

'I really don't know, mate. J being J and all!'

'Well, he's not here! In fact, you won't know we're here either.
Consider it, fellas – please?' says Paisley.

'So, what do you say, Affie – yay or nay?' I pipe up, feeling
we're near to closing this deal, as long as Selena stays quiet.

Affie's face breaks into a smile. 'Go on, then. It'll make it easier
all round for us, you and Josie here.'

'Thank you so much!' says Paisley, rushing over to give him an
impromptu hug. Which takes us all by surprise, though I'm glad
she did it, otherwise I'd have felt obliged – despite not feeling his

man bun styling. Plus, he's wearing no socks with lace-ups, but that's the last of our issues – I can certainly ignore such quirks when faced with a long drive home. Though given that I appear to have landed myself with breakfast duties, Paisley can definitely be the one to step up to the plate with his thank-you hug.

'OK, but you can explain when J gets here, because I'm not!' mutters Carlos, side-stepping Affie and Paisley to open the front door.

I give a huge sigh of relief. Selena mellows, sliding back into her shell, and simply watches from the side lines. She's beginning to know herself well enough to realise that when crunch time occurs she needs to zip it. Nice to see she's learning from previous experiences, such as girls' nights out of the past when her steely attitude has caused us issues when queuing for the ladies' or lost us a vacant taxi – maybe that's her maturity finally appearing?

'In fact, bang on cue. Here he is, the main man himself. J, my man! Has Affie got news for you!' says Carlos, gesturing towards the manly frame filling the doorway.

Paisley withdraws from her thank-you embrace, and Affie straightens up as his impromptu-hug dissolves, while we sisters stare, wide-eyed and open mouthed, at the new arrival.

'Holy crap!' slips from my mouth.

'Affie, my bearded buddy . . . great to see you, mate. It appears you've met my ex-wife!' says Joseph McLoughlin; his suave manner never changes, nor his smouldering good looks, for that matter. Paisley steps sideways, making way for the two men to back slap each other and perform a fancy handshake-grip-fist-bump routine.

'What the hell?' mouths Selena towards me. I simply shrug, because I know what's coming.

Chapter Four

Paisley

'That's it. We're out of here!' I announce, much to Josie's astonishment. 'Come on, ladies – grab your handbags, your keys and what nots . . . we're off!'

'Paise, long time no see – can't you spare just . . .' pipes up Joseph.

'Nope! I can't spare anything where you're concerned.' I side-step Joseph's open arms and head towards the door. 'And don't call me Paise – you've no right, after what you did! Josie, thank you so much for everything you've done. We do appreciate it and, well, it nearly, very nearly, worked out well for us all.' I warmly clasp both of Josie's hands in mine and give them a reassuring squeeze before stepping through the open door. My head held high, shoulders square and my dignity firmly set in place. I pause, waiting for my friends to follow, though they don't appear to be moving.

'Sorry. Your what?' asks Carlos, taking in the scene unfolding on the doorstep.

'My ex-wife, Paisley – I've mentioned her before,' explains Joseph, delivering a casual nod of greeting in Kate and Selena's direction.

'Ooooh, this is the one . . .? Oh, man, shame that. She seems nice,' says Carlos, staring at me before bypassing Kate to glare at Selena, his silence reinforcing the comparison.

'As tactful as ever, Carlos,' jests Joseph, shaking his head while trying to supress a wry smile.

'I don't think that's funny!' snaps Selena.

I don't see or hear any more. I'm off. Striding along the cobbled path at pace, causing my ankles to wibble-wobble as my heels find every crevice between the stones. Hardly a serene departure but I really couldn't give a flying frig what impression I leave behind or how their conversation develops; I won't be hearing it. My only regret is Josie. She was so lovely on realising the error, she couldn't apologise enough and was only too willing to support me in finding a feasible, workable solution. And we nearly did. We were definitely on the verge of everyone having a roof over their head, resulting in a happy girl group, a happy boy posse, a relieved housekeeper and even an inflated rental income for the owners! The universe had a moment of alignment when all was right with the situation, but then ... boom! Joseph McLoughlin walks in. The story of my life. Can. Open. Worms. Everywhere!

I forcefully grab the metal gate latch – the final stage of my dramatic exit. I release the catch and apply enough force to wrench the gate open, but the catch hasn't quite released, and I simply shake the picket gate violently but futilely.

That *wasn't* the exit I was hoping to deliver to my audience. And, worse still, I appear to have left my wheelie case behind.

I dare to glance over my shoulder, confirming a sea of faces watching from the doorway.

'Paisley, please. Come inside and we can talk,' calls Kate.

I pause. I have two choices: continue on my war path, making a second attempt at my exit, or take a slow and embarrassing walk back inside. One will deliver me to my waiting car, the other ... to the snug? A warm kitchen? A bloody nightmare? Is a luxurious double bedroom, with feminine décor and a fancy dressing table worthy of a rethink? Maybe. Should I do this? Could I entertain the idea of spending another night of my life under the same roof as Joseph McLoughlin? There was a time in our lives when I planned to spend every night beside him, but once he'd ... cheated, that put an end to that dream. And now, twelve months after our divorce, do I stay or do I go?

'Think about it, Paisley. Where else can we go? There's nothing vacant in the area – this cottage was our only option!' hollers Selena, from behind her sister.

Someone's changed their minds pretty damned quickly. I suppose I can hear them out, if nothing more. I slowly retrace my steps, which seems like the longest walk of my life.

'Atta gal, you know a little chat makes sense,' mutters Carlos encouragingly.

'Plus, you forgot your wheelie case,' says Joseph, gesturing towards my abandoned belongings.

'After which I'll still leave – if I choose to!' I snap, re-entering the hallway. I notice the men have stepped backwards, giving me far more floor space than I physically need but which I definitely want.

'Let's go straight up the stairs and have a chat, eh? How does that sound?' asks Kate, her voice taking on an overly attentive motherly tone. Efficient, as always.

Without saying a word, I'm unceremoniously bundled up the staircase by Kate and Selena one either side, each clutching my underarms, in the same unsavoury manner which I've previously adopted for manoeuvring a drunken buddy on a messy night out. This time I'm the evictee playing piggy-in-the-middle, attempting to squawk in protest.

'I can leave anytime I choose,' I repeat as we head up, purely for Joseph's benefit.

'And please do if it means we get a quiet week to ourselves,' Carlos whispers, a little too loudly.

'Oi! I heard that!' I snap in reply.

Carlos has the decency to blush and Joseph sends him a warning look.

'What, J?'

'Give it a rest, Carlos,' mutters Affie. 'Why don't you empty your backseat, because it looks like us three are staying put.'

'Not necessarily,' says Joseph, as we reach the top stair, causing us to pause for a split-second.

'Why don't you lie down and roll over, man – I'm sure she can walk over you just a fraction more!'

'Cut it out, Carlos!' says Affie.

'I'll fetch my belongings while you pair figure out which rooms we're allowed to occupy,' is the last we hear from the hallway below.

'In there,' I say, meanwhile, pointing to the first panelled door situated on our right-hand side. I recall Josie's tour-guide talk: 'all double rooms here at the front – with a selection of doubles, twins and singles at the rear of the property. Some have en-suites while others share the main bathroom. Use all the storage areas and cupboard space. You'll find fresh towels, bath robes and toiletries in the linen cupboard here, bed sheets in the one over there.'

Kate pushes the door open, revealing the feminine bedroom I'd taken a fancy to earlier. And which I never in a million years imagined being bundled into like this by these two.

A beautiful boudoir stands before us, tastefully decorated in subtle shades of pale pink, a paradise of slumber with a billowing duvet, an array of satin cushions and delicate painted furniture.

'I'm not stopping! Not now, not ever. I know what you're both thinking, but no way, José. It's not happening, ladies. Absolutely not!' I say, shrugging off their hold.

'This is nice,' exclaims Selena, looking around.

'The master suite is larger, with a canopied bed – I assumed . . .' I begin, hoping she knows I wouldn't bagsie what should rightfully be her room, given it's her big birthday week.

'Really? Mine, I'm calling it!' says Selena, as if her sister would ever do the dirty on her.

'Selena, first things first, please,' mutters Kate, raising an eyebrow and gesturing towards me.

'Yeah, course,' mutters the younger sister.

'I'm so sorry, but I can't. You heard them. They're wanting a week of sporting events and blokey beers – if it had been three strangers then maybe. But with Joseph here – how am I supposed to cope?' Gone is my buoyant mood, the jubilation I felt driving here, looking forward to a girls' week of celebration and bubbles. Instead I've got a face like a wet weekend in Blackpool, as framed in the room's beautiful three-winged mirror.

'Paisley, hear us out,' says Selena, taking control as if I were a rag doll and sitting me in a wicker chair. 'If he can be civil, then surely you can be too?'

They both stand over me, reminding me of our childhood days.

'We're divorced!'

'We know that, sweetie. We were present for each and every moment, but this, this is a doable situation, Paisley.' Kate's tone has reverted to her usual, no-nonsense tone. I shake my head.

'Not even for me?'

My mouth drops open; Selena of all people knows what I've been through these last eighteen months.

'How?' I demand, regaining some of my initial angst. 'I chose to end my marriage to him after what he did and now you two are expecting me to enjoy a relaxing break in his presence? Again, how?'

'Negotiations were going well until Joseph appeared. You were content to share the house with strangers – think of it this way, you know one of the strangers better than the other two!' says Kate.

'We were married. He cheated and ruined everything. If it wasn't for him and some trollop, I'd be . . .' My voice cracks and I suppress the sob that is threatening to erupt. Selena remains close, reaching for my hand to offer comfort, while Kate straightens up to look around her.

'To be fair, I'm not sure I could be in a property alongside Joseph either,' says Selena. 'But surely, if Joseph stays out of our way, we can stay out of his?' Selena glances between us both, awaiting an answer. 'No?'

'It was purely his fault, so *he* should be carrying the can rather than all this equal this and that business,' observes Kate. 'I thought you were both pretty mature about the whole situation, though.'

My thoughts are racing at a hundred miles per hour. He looks so well, which doesn't help matters. I feel like I've been through the mill several times over during the last eighteen months. What with our divorce, the house sale and my mum's sudden illness and subsequent death, and only recently have I started to feel like I'm finding my feet. Yet Joseph looks well. How does he look so well? How has he breezed through and come out looking unscathed? He bloody caused it. Well, not my mother's demise, but still. And as for calling me Paise. Christ almighty – that'll need to stop if I'm to survive the next five days. Never did I think I'd need to suffer another night of my life under the same roof as him. Never. Well, as they say, never say never!

'I'd feel deeply uncomfortable.'

'It's doable, Paisley – we're here to support you,' says Kate. 'Joseph is just one person. His mate, Affie, seems a likeable fella.'

'But Carlos – urgh! He might be good looking, but he seems a right bolshie git,' interjects Selena.

'You heard him say that the backseats are loaded to the gunnels with booze. It's one thing dealing with tipsy girlfriends, holding back hair and mopping up sicky accidents, but when complete strangers . . .' I groan.

'They're not our responsibility,' says Kate sternly.

'How on earth did this happen?' I ask, exhausted by all the panic and stress. 'You make plans, you travel, and the one person you would never dream of inviting is the one person who turns up unannounced. How?'

'That's the universe for you – delivering the unexpected in an unexpected fashion,' says Kate, wandering around the bedroom to check everything out.

'It's like that time I travelled all the way to Australia for that rebranding conference only to step into a lift and come eye to eye with my next-door neighbour on his month-long holiday. It happens.'

'The one whose car you bumped?' asks Kate.

'Yep, him.'

'But it's not supposed to happen to me, Selena. I've been through enough.' I want to say a lot more, but realise I'll sound like a self-proclaimed martyr. And that's never a good look.

'Babe, it's happened. Could you not muster a little courage for the next five days, for Selena?' asks Kate, venturing towards the window to inspect the view. I anticipate her reaction, as it'll probably mimic mine of twenty minutes ago. A luscious green landscape dominated by rolling hills with a vast open sky.

'We know they're not lying. There's nothing else available in the area,' adds Selena.

'So I'm supposed to roll over and accept this all in the name of . . . of what?'

'Me,' comes Selena's weak reply, offering me a doleful expression. 'But I completely understand. I get where you're coming from, Paisley.'

My heart drops. In my haste to flee, I'd forgotten the true reason we were here.

'Oh, Selena. I'm sorry. Is there any chance that we could rearrange?' I cease talking, as my best friend's features fall.

'You only get one thirtieth birthday, Paisley,' mutters Kate, turning around from the windowsill. 'Or so you've been telling her since September.' Her words weigh heavy as I replay the countless times I'd begged Selena to organise her birthday break in recent months, and more so in recent weeks. Now is not the time to retract all that. Selena stands in the middle of a beautiful bedroom, looking every inch the best friend I've needed and relied upon in recent times, her expression growing more pensive with each moment of silence. From my wicker perch, I glance around the bedroom – it really is beautiful. The rental cottage is stunning – exactly what us three ladies need to celebrate Selena's big birthday and end this year on a much needed high.

'These things happen, Paisley. I'm a big girl – what I don't want is for you to feel so uncomfortable in his presence that it pushes you backwards ... in any way,' says Selena. She means emotionally, and I love her for that thought alone.

Who matters most to me in this moment? Joseph? Or Selena and her happiness?

'I suppose I can be the bigger person.' I hear both women exhale deeply. 'Though he'll need to keep out of my way, because I have no intention of opening old wounds. He made his bed, he can lie in it.'

'Thank you, thank you, thank you!' cries Selena, dashing across the plush carpet to enfold me in an all-consuming bear hug.

'We'll make sure he is under no illusion – he'll be invisible as far as you're concerned,' says Kate, striding across the floor to join our embrace.

'Of course, it means I get to claim this bedroom as mine,' I mumble, under the smothered weight of two excited sisters.

'Your wish is granted, even if it turns out to be the best bedroom,' quips Selena, releasing her hold of me, followed by Kate.

'Would I do that to you? Never. The one directly opposite is the master suite – which I believe has your name written on it, birthday gal!'

Kate steps backward and views her excited little sister

performing that stupid wiggle dance she does when a decision goes in her favour.

'Woohoo! Quick, then, let's go and tell them before that guy fills the fridge with beer boxes!' wails Selena, heading for the door.

'Thank you,' says Kate, touching my cheek as an excited Selena disappears across the landing. 'That was a tough decision, but I promise I'll do everything I can to make sure you're comfortable during our stay. I'll be having a quiet word with Joseph, if needs be. I wouldn't be happy if Cody, *my* ex-husband, turned up with his mates.'

I take her hand, giving it a squeeze – she understands. 'Thank you, Kate – I'm not sure how I'm going to manage this.'

'You've got this.'

'I truly hope so.'

Chapter Five

Selena

Opening the door of the master bedroom before we head downstairs, I'm greeted by luxurious furnishings, including a huge
canopied bed. The bath tub even has gold taps.

Paisley's not wrong – this room is gorgeous. Probably too
good for the likes of me.

I instantly remove the mountain of plump pillows, a mix of
decorative, satin and functional cotton, barring one on which
I'll sleep, creating a pillow pile in the nearest corner. A necessary
habit adopted to ensure a decent night's sleep. I can't abide
by this obsession with hundreds of pillows. Having stamped
my own personality on the décor, I stand back and survey the
bedroom.

'Not too shabby!' I say aloud with satisfaction, before a
wave of guilt washes over me. Am I being selfish? Asking too
much of my friend? Could I be so resilient if the boot were on
the other foot? I agree wholeheartedly with each of the reasons
Paisley had listed for us retreating down the M6 motorway
towards home. But love the gal as I do, this is supposed to be
my big birthday bash trip, and I'm not allowing the likes of
Joseph McLoughlin and that brash git with his beer box to
spoil it. Admittedly, the third guy seems nice – despite the man
bun and no-socks combo.

Swiftly returning to Paisley's bedroom, I poke my head around
the door jamb to witness our Kate doing her best to offer comfort.

She's a compassionate sort. Her strengths certainly make up for my weaknesses. But that's how we roll as sisters; I've accepted my place in life – in Kate's shadow.

'OK, I'll slum it in the master suite with the extra-large bathtub!'

'Are you sure you can cope?' asks Paisley, glancing up at Kate with a smile.

'Don't worry about me, I've kipped in much worse!' I jest, sensing the drama has truly passed. 'Can we get this show on the road? It's supposed to be all about me and so far . . .'

'My God, will nothing ever quell your selfishness streak?' snorts Kate, in mock disgust.

'Hey, did I say that to Paisley back in September? Or you, some *seven* years ago? No. I don't think I did. Stop wasting time and let's announce to these three lucky fellas that they have our delectable company for the next five days – absolutely free of charge! Bargain!' I head downstairs, not wanting to waste another minute on this debacle. Then double back on an after-thought: 'Kate, grab the other front bedroom before the guys get a whiff of it. I've no doubt it's as gorgeous as our two!'

'Cheers for that. A moment of consideration, was it?' chunters my sister.

'Ha bloody ha,' I retort, before returning to my mission. I gallop down the staircase two at a time, to find the hallway unchanged, and beer guy still absent, though it's hardly difficult guessing where he'll be.

'Hi folks, sorry to keep you waiting. I'm sure you're as eager as we are to sort out this confusion. But all is sorted now. These things are sent to test us. Right?'

'Right,' repeats Joseph, cautiously eyeing his mate Affie.

'Josie, we'd be grateful if you could convey the new situation to the owners, as we're happy to remain,' I say, spying the housekeeper still twisting her hands beside the front door and watching the proceedings unfolding like some sort of soap opera.

'Are you sure? Mr and Mrs Campbell will be most upset to think this has happened to their guests. Things like this *never* happen. I'm sure they'll offer some kind of reimbursement due to the circumstances.'

'We're sure . . . aren't we?' I say, as Paisley and Kate make an appearance, descending the stairs. Though a goodwill gesture wouldn't go amiss, however small.

Paisley nods, while my sister gives a thumbs up, which is not really her style, but these aren't her usual circumstances. Things don't tend to happen that are out of Kate's control. She either organises it, in which case everything is bloody well perfect, or she saves a sinking ship at the last minute by pulling a metaphorical rabbit out of a top hat. Organising is Kate's forte, whereas, sadly, a debacle such as this is frequently mine. I'm more the arse-about-face kind of gal, all gung-ho regarding life plans. I'm used to dealing with the shambles that frequently occurs but then adapting and responding as quick as a flash. You could say it's my speciality in life. Which is why I love the cut and thrust of the marketing world – plans change, projects are erased and genius ideas arrive in the blink of an eye. Our Kate would have a meltdown twenty times a day if such events happened to her. I like high-energy situations. But then it wouldn't do for us all to be alike.

'That's settled, then. We're nabbing the front three bedrooms too – I hope that's OK?' I ask, hoping the guys don't object – I'm more than ready for round two if not.

A muttering of 'that's fine' and 'suits me' escapes from the two males present. Typical men, they're never that fussed about the details but rather the bigger picture, which probably needs to be in hi-tech colour with Dolby surround sound.

The kitchen door swings wide, revealing the third guy rejoining our hallway party.

'We're wasting valuable drinking time, lads,' he croons, pulling a comic expression and bypassing the rest of us en route towards the front door.

'Excuse me,' I call, forcing him to stall and turn, acknowledging my presence. 'We were just saying that we're happy to compromise and so we're expecting you fellas to do likewise, to ensure this week is as pleasant as it can be for all concerned.'

'Really? And here's me thinking you were the one making the most fuss. As I said earlier, those two ladies seem very nice, but you, you're one contrary woman, lady. I'm thinking you need to be having a quiet word with yourself rather than the rest of us. Guys, I've got one more trip to the car and then I'll need showing to my room to unpack. I'll leave you to communicate with this one.' In a flash he's gone, and the tiny bevelled window shows a distorted view of his retreating frame.

'Contrary? Me? Has he taken a look in the mirror lately?' I repeat, noting that no one corrects him and everyone avoids my gaze.

'Josie, would you mind showing the guys around upstairs so they can choose their rooms?' asks Kate, her comforting tone returning. 'We'll make a start by collecting our luggage and unpacking – it'll help to settle us all, I think.'

'Of course. The ceramic bowl on the side table has various sets of door keys – use what you will. All we ask is that they're all returned before you leave. It seems a bit rude of me to mention adding a memory or two to our guest book, given the circumstances, but see how you feel,' says Josie, indicating the nearest table. 'Gents, if you'd care to follow me.'

We three girls wait while Josie and two men traipse up the staircase, a definite creak occurs at the top step before their voices quieten to a whisper as they arrive on the landing above.

'All good? It's going to be OK, I promise,' I remind Paisley, only to receive a curt nod in reply. 'Come on, then, what are we

waiting for? Let's get the kettle on, then we can empty our cars.'
I turn to make my way towards the kitchen.

'Selena!' calls Kate.

'Yep.' I turn in response.

'I'm all good too, thanks for asking.'

'Kate, you're always good – it's a given if you're standing upright.' I continue on my way, but I swear I hear my sister's voice mutter: 'not all the time.'

Phuh! Who is she trying to kid?

Chapter Six

Afternoon

Kate

'Now, I'm not saying we can't compromise, but I do think we need some ground rules,' announces Selena, as we gather in the kitchen, having said a grateful goodbye to Josie.

'Here we go, lads,' mutters Carlos, leaning against the double-fronted fridge as if guarding his domain.

It's a lovely big farmhouse-style kitchen, with an adjoining scullery and additional storage rooms, with a bright yellow Aga, a scrubbed central table and my favourite feature: a split stable door leading to the garden. Not to mention every chrome gadget you could imagine lining the counter tops.

'Quiet, please.' Selena raises an open palm in his direction, clearly taking no interruptions or questions at the moment. I've nothing to say and Paisley's blank expression suggests she's lost in her own world. 'We've all agreed on a sensible solution for the next five days. Us girls occupying the front bedrooms and you fellas have the rear bedrooms, though having not completed the tour I'm unsure if you've got the better deal.'

'Believe me, you have,' offers Affie, glancing at Joseph.

'Not that we're that bothered about such details,' adds Joseph.

'Very gallant of you, mate,' jests Carlos.

'Anyway, moving on . . . us girls will stick to our promise, and we'll take the cosy snug room, freeing up the lounge and big TV for you guys. Kate will happily cook full breakfasts but only at a designated time – I'm not having her tied to the kitchen for three hours each morning because you can't get up for eight.'

'Eight?' blurts Carlos, shaking his head. 'We're supposed to be chilling.'

'Happily?' I mutter. I tune out as Selena takes the backlash from Carlos.

I'd been promised a puppy, so I wasn't impressed when a baby sister arrived, wailing like a banshee. I felt I had every right to sulk. And did so, pretty much non-stop, until I reached sixteen. I can't say I enjoyed the transition from solo child to big sister – the road was bumpy, noisy and often verging on outright war, with my frequent battle cry being 'stay out of my room!' The constant task of staking claim to all my belongings, be it curling tongs, jewellery or clothes – as Selena rarely asked, but just snuck in, and was often accompanied by her little friend, Paisley. I thought having one little sister was bad enough and soon figured that this inseparable pair were near intolerable. But now, watching my little sis masterfully taking charge, she makes me dead proud. This friendship she has with Paisley hasn't changed that much over the years: Selena upfront, Paisley quietly following along behind.

They met aged six, in the dinner queue at primary school, and agreed a childish alliance over mint green custard and chunky chocolate cracknel. Their mutual delight at having found a partner in crime became my 'double trouble', as my dad fondly referred to them. Our Selena has many faults, and I've witnessed and called her out numerous times over the years, but her unwavering support for Paisley is admirable. Having gone through a divorce myself, I know how tough it is to come out the other side and attempt to find your feet. Our Selena was there for me too, though maybe not like she has been for Paisley. I'm not jealous, though. Jealously doesn't or shouldn't come into a sisterly relationship, but I suspect Selena learned a thing or two from witnessing my experience. Not that I shared every detail; I have some self-respect. We all know we're here for each other, however, come thick or thin. If anything, their relationship proves you can form bonds and strong loving attachments without the need for blood ties. It seemed easier for me to adopt Paisley as an extra sister in the end than to object to her being present at every family gathering, camping holiday or Sunday lunch. Not that I would now object, but in my younger days she did seem like an utter pain in the arse, as it always felt like two against the one.

'What do you say, Kate?' asks Selena, breaking into my thoughts. I refocus to find five faces staring at me.

'Sorry. I zoned out,' I admit, knowing it's obvious.

'Hallelujah. I'm glad one of us has,' quips Carlos.

'I was saying that this kitchen is the only communal area, so some consideration is required to make sure our week goes without a hitch,' repeats Selena, clearly narked by my lack of attention.

'Mmmm.'

'Precisely my thoughts, lady. My week hasn't started as I imagined,' offers Carlos. 'I thought I'd be on my second beer by now with a remote control in my hand and a match on the TV, but no, I've got some woman squawking her expectations, which I already know I'll probably not be delivering on or adhering to. Sorry but not sorry, lady.'

Affie and Joseph smirk at this. Selena bristles, knowing that arguing would only confirm his earlier remark but that remaining silent suggests he's won. Game over. Power shift. My sister doesn't play the underdog in life.

'Anyway . . .' I say, unsure how to proceed but not wishing to rock the boat further.

'Exactly. Anyway,' repeats Carlos, before adding, 'I think its beer time. Excuse me, if you would.' He indicates the fridge door, which Selena is currently blocking from swinging wide open.

'But I haven't divided up the fridge shelving yet.'

'Ahhh, well, teach the others and they'll inform me of the necessary. There's a pre-match commentary starting in a minute.' He pulls open the one fridge door, revealing three shelves lined with glass bottles stashed on their sides. We all watch as he grabs, offers and hands a bottle each to the other two guys, before busying himself looking in various drawers and finding a bottle opener. 'Phew, for a minute there I thought my planning had been truly scuppered – though maybe it has, in some respects.' Selena's mouth drops wide. Paisley double blinks, appearing to have woken from her own planet too. Carlos pops the lids on each beer bottle, before returning the bottle opener to the drawer and reaching for an A4 folder propped against the empty bread bin. 'Is this the folder Josie mentioned containing the emergency phone numbers and takeaway menus? Because I'm starving, fellas.' He flicks open the blue cover, seems satisfied by the contents, and thrusts the whole thing under his arm before taking his leave of the communal kitchen.

'Well, I never,' mutters Selena, clearly miffed by his actions.

'At least he tidied up after himself,' says Paisley.

'Is that a knock at me?' asks Joseph, abruptly.

'No! But if the cap fits,' mutters his ex-wife.

'This could be a long week,' sighs Joseph, glancing towards Affie, a polite and patient observer.

'And that's a knock at me, I suppose?' retorts Paisley.

Here we go – hold on tight, as we might be in for a bumpy ride. The bell-pull chimes in the hallway.

'Who's that?' asks Selena, her eyes wide, looking surprised.

'Shit! I forgot to say. That's Waitrose. I ordered a food delivery, expecting us to be settled by now,' I say, making for the front door. Why would anyone not opt for a food delivery at a rental property? 'Sorry, my error – I should have remembered. The last thing I wanted was a staycation living off leftover turkey-based cuisine.' I open the door wide to the delivery guy. 'Hello, welcome, thank you so much.'

'No worries, lady. There's no substitutes.'

'Perfect.' Everything's in order regarding this at least, which is comforting to know, given the current mix up occurring between people, though I doubt substitutes are as readily available.

Chapter Seven

Paisley

I venture into the rear garden in search of solace. I cross the patio area that consists of dry-stone walls and slabbing, passing the built-in BBQ and arrangement of dormant ceramic pots that are over wintering, much like my love life. A flight of stone steps leads me to the upper terrace where there's a huge expanse of lawn, dotted with a higgledy-piggledy path of stepping stones leading past the sturdy park bench on which Joseph sits. It's too late to double back inside, so I might as well brave the conversation.

'New haircut?' I ask, searching for something to say. I want to retch the second the words leave my mouth; I sound so dumb. Is complimenting his appearance something I needed to say to my ex?

'You know how it is,' says Joseph, giving a nonchalant shrug.

'I know alright – change the simplest thing first, hoping it makes you feel entirely different.'

'It doesn't, though, does it?'

'Nah. That "new me" haircut feeling lasts four days tops. The sting to my bank balance lasts much longer.' I'm talking but not actually looking at him – beyond him, in fact. To a pleasant border consisting of evergreen shrubbery and a sculpted hedgerow in dark purple that creates an attractive archway, leading to a secluded section. Eye contact is difficult – I can't be that vulnerable.

'Total tosh really.'

'I don't know why we do it.'

'To make ourselves feel better,' he says, stating the obvious. My gaze flickers to meet his on hearing his honesty. A surge of something zaps through my body, reminding me of the connection we once had, despite not seeing him for so long. Does that not fade or die?

I want to utter 'I suppose', but don't because that might be admitting too much to the one person who caused my tsunami of hurt. The one person I never thought would pull the rug from under my feet. Or hurt me like no other ever has. Or will again. And who now sits staring at me and is probably still able to decipher my thoughts.

I take a seat, at the furthest end of the bench.

'Have you passed our old house lately?' he asks, filling the silence.

'No. You?'

'Yeah. The new people have ripped up the block paving to lay a shale driveway, plus your landscaped shrubbery, and stuck a hideous side-angled garage on to the front aspect of the house.'

'No way!'

'They have. It's as ugly as hell – all garage door and no actual turning space. Lord knows how you swing a car in from that angle.'

'That shrubbery cost us a small fortune. She made a point of saying how much she loved the front garden. Kept banging on about it throughout their viewing, apparently.'

'Or so the estate agent said. Unless that was her way of ear-marking it for removal once they were settled.'

'Why would you build a garage that isn't functional? What a waste of money.'

Joseph shrugs.

I can't bear to drive anywhere near our old home, our beloved three-bedroomed starter home – it would only bring back painful memories of us. The front bay window I'd earmarked as the one through which our excited toddlers would eagerly await their daddy's arrival home, for example. I can't bring myself to acknowledge that the tiny upstairs window never bore Disney-print curtains suitable for a nursery, never threw morning sunshine upon a wicker crib, that the window ledge never held an annoying baby monitor.

Our silence lingers a fraction too long.

'I accidently drove by one night on autopilot and took the wrong turning after a long day at work,' offers Joseph solemnly, before hastily adding, 'I laughed when I realised – thinking what the hell brought me here?' His voice catches before he gives a jovial chuckle. I nod, acknowledging his tale while doing my utmost to ignore the hurt. I'm glad he can take it so lightly. I can't. I'll never drive past there again. Thankfully it's pretty easy not to, given it was situated in a cul-de-sac.

'Did you get to the Galapagos islands for your thirtieth in September?' he asks, clearly sensing the mood.

I look at him askance. Is he taking the mick? Does that warrant an answer? Or will the penny drop without an explanation?

'What? I'm only asking. You were pretty much set on the idea during the seven years we were together. You'd got the travel brochures, the hotel chosen – I imagine your itinerary was all set.'

'It was, but . . .' Surely I don't need to explain myself? He must think I'm one cold-hearted bitch. How could I pack my bags and enjoy a dream holiday destination that he was supposed to accompany me to? Yet another dream squashed. 'It doesn't matter. Anyway, I didn't go.'

'Shame.'

My gaze snaps upwards to meet his – was that sarcasm or sympathy?

'Did you have a nice time anyway?' he continues.

'Not really. It wasn't the birthday I'd hoped for. It turned out to be just another birthday like any other, but with more drink involved and fewer friends.' My words spill out as my head lowers, knowing it'll sound like a knock at him. Which is probably why I don't feel thirty – I feel as if I'm lingering on the edge of being thirty, counting down and still waiting for my big celebration to actually arrive. I suppose the big birthday plans inside my head need to die for that to happen. Though nagging Selena about her big birthday every week since has helped to distract me a bit.

'We did have big plans, didn't we?' he says, with the decency to sound embarrassed.

I daren't look up; I sense he's staring at me. I feel vulnerable now my defences are down, flattened by this conversation. 'Paise. For what it's worth, I am truly sorry for how things turned out. Honest, I am. Of all the people in the world, I never intended to mess this up and hurt you. That was never the plan.'

I give a tiny nod. I can't answer as my voice will give me away. And I don't want that. I don't want Joseph to witness the hurt he has caused me. Not now. Though eighteen months ago I'd wanted him to witness every teardrop. The impact that his behaviour had and the blank canvas that my life had become. A total contrast from the life we had once had. All the big life plans I'd lovingly folded and stashed away within my memory loft. To be treasured for ever, like unused baby clothes in an airtight box, rarely unpacked, for fear of derailing my emotions for the hour, day or forthcoming week. I'm mesmerised by the nakedness of his ringless left hand. How dare his hand continue to function – gesturing, holding that mug – existing without that band of gold. My ring finger is also naked but my band remains fixed, like an invisible mark upon my skin. I'd cried with joy as he'd slipped the slender gold band over my knuckle – a moment I've watched a thousand times on our wedding video. Joseph had been choked, but an awkward cough had sealed the deal. It broke my heart to remove it after our divorce, though it was no mean feat to do so as it had never been off my finger. Joseph had wedged it on during our vows and I had then begrudgingly removed it, alone and tearful, with the aid of some soap and a drink or three. I didn't recognise my own hand afterwards, and the raw-looking pale band of flesh acted as a daily reminder for months. Will I ever trust another lover to get close enough to suggest a second wedding band? I doubt it. I drop my left hand into my lap as if ashamed of my failure in life. Even though the breakdown of our marriage wasn't my fault but solely his. His and hers.

'Dating?' he asks.

'Me?' I sound shocked, even to my own ears. A giggle threatens to escape me at the very thought.

'Like that, is it?' He gives a slight laugh.

'I'm sure you know how it is out there.' I bluff, repeating Selena's favourite phrase.

'Yeah, "out there" – that's funny. It's the pits, if my recent experience is anything to go by.'

'That good, eh?'

'Things have definitely changed – it's not like it was in our time.'

Instantly, I'm taken back to 'our time'. Of long summer evenings, nervous butterfly sensations, stolen glances and welcome kisses between coffees, fancy meals and leisurely walks. Our time was spent tiptoeing through each other's daily lives as we slowly drew the two together and finally bound them into a joint existence via a family wedding. I remember how, on waking most mornings, I'd watch him sleeping for those final few minutes. His long lashes laying soft against manly skin, his fading battle scar from childhood gracing his temple – strangely revealing itself each summer when it didn't tan. Listening to his breathing before the hustle of the working day altered its rhythm and his placid expression became animated was probably my favourite moment of the day – or definitely in my top three.

'You OK?' His voice breaks into my thoughts.

'Sorry.'

'You drifted off someplace just then.'

I give an apologetic nod. I never dreamt I'd hide a thought while in Joseph's presence, especially not on those quiet mornings before his alarm sounded.

'All good, thanks,' I lie.

'Are *we* good, Paise?' he asks, his casual tone as free and easy as I'd ever heard it.

I answer within a heartbeat, without putting my brain into gear. 'Us? Yeah sure . . . we're fine.'

Chapter Eight

Kate

It takes twenty minutes for me to unpack the shopping, re-organise the fridge and cupboard space, and stash our extras nibbles on the counter tops. My hands are busy while my mind drifts, finalising last-minute celebration tasks. There's not much more to arrange for Selena's birthday bonanza – I've simply been distracted elsewhere, but now it'll be full-steam ahead once I get a minute to myself. I create a to-do list in my head – I love nothing more than a task list, as they're one of my great pleasures in life. Bubbles. Cake. Birds. Clown. Four simple tasks to confirm or arrange, ready for Monday. All should be done and dusted within an hour, if I knuckle down in a quiet spot such as the snug or my bedroom.

'Let's officially start this birthday break,' I announce, grabbing champagne flutes from the cabinet, knowing it'll help to put our arrival mishap behind us.

A unanimous 'yes' comes from the other two, as expected.

'This cottage literally has everything you'd need – good choice, Selena,' I say, filling each glass to the brim, allowing the fizzing bubbles to leap just a little higher than each rim.

'A definite fluke, Kate,' says Selena, as we huddle around the kitchen table lost in our world of sisterly love.

'May this week be filled with love, laughter and birthday memories to last us a lifetime. To Selena, the cutest baby sister a girl could have wished for!' I say, raising my glass in her direction.

'To Selena,' agrees Paisley, before we each take a sip.

'Oooooh, this is going to be good . . . despite—' sings Selena, as the kitchen door bursts open and Carlos strolls in. He takes one look at us gathered, glasses in hand, and smirks.

'Your birthday today, is it? Oh, happy birthday.'

I swallow swiftly to answer him, before she can. 'No! Monday, actually. This is simply the opening drink of our week.'

'I'll take back my many happy returns, then,' he says, opening the fridge and audibly groaning before whipping around to glare at us. 'I thought we agreed on halves! This . . . is not halves. Who's moved my beer bottles?'

'I was about to mention that,' says Selena, before I have a chance to answer. 'We couldn't get all our chiller supplies on the shelves you'd left so had a little jiggle about with your booze stash.'

'It's a double-frontage fridge – surely there's space here, and here and, oh, what about here, for your other chiller supplies?' Carlos waves his hand at the vacant compartments.

'Because our stuff didn't fit – it needed to stand up or be piled up or was too tall to fit. Unlike your beer bottles, which we've carefully arranged here, here and here. See?' says Selena, gesturing wildly with her free hand. 'We haven't removed any – you've got Kate to thank for that, because I wanted to.'

'It's a bloody joke. We agreed to share on the grounds that you played fair – this is not fair!' Carlos grabs two bottles of our white wine, pulling them from the shelf.

'Oi! No, you don't. I've been fair in rearranging your bottles. You wouldn't have drunk all that beer today, surely?'

'You're not going to drink all this wine today either. I'll move these out onto the countertop before returning my bottles to their rightful place,' he says, twisting his body to avoid Selena's poor attempt at grabbing two wine bottles with one free hand.

'Carlos!'

The wine bottle smashes before any of us can pre-empt or

move fast enough to save it from hitting the kitchen's red tiles. We stand and stare in horror as the wine flows into the grouting and spreads in all directions.

'Now look what you've done!' shrieks Selena in dismay.

'Me? It was your grabbing that did it,' replies Carlos, waving the second bottle, as if proving his secure grip.

'Me?' Selena looks towards us for support. 'You think it was me!'

'Whoever's fault doesn't matter – there's spilled wine and glass everywhere, so can both of you—' starts Paisley.

'Are you suggesting it was me, Paisley?' asks Selena, her tone lifting by a pitch.

'No. What I said was . . .'

'You are. I can tell. Kate – was that my fault?'

'I'm not sure whose fault it was, but does it really matter?' I add.

'Ladies, back me up here. Have I ever in my entire life spilled, dropped or wasted an entire bottle of wine?'

'Nah,' mutters Paisley.

'Nope,' I answer, unsure where this might be heading.

'So please, some credit . . . *he* dropped the wine bottle and wasted a decent Chablis,' says Selena, pointing at Carlos.

'Yeah, you girls stick together, as always,' he says, returning the intact wine bottle back to the fridge.

'No. No. No! They're being honest, mate.' Selena's tone is yet again developing into an attitude. I'm unsure if my sister can resist becoming stroppy and therefore pushing this guy's buttons further.

'How about we clean up this mess rather than argue the point, Selena?' I suggest, putting my bubbles down and making for the utility area in search of a broom or a mop.

'I've done nothing wrong!' is the only reply I hear, as I trot along the scullery's corridor towards the other storage rooms.

One is decked with metal shelving reaching from floor to ceiling, stashed with store-cupboard essentials, the other with white appliances and laundry baskets, an ironing board and the mop bucket. This is first-class accommodation, that's for sure.

I can still hear Selena's stroppy tone as I drag the mop bucket towards the kitchen.

'That means our stuff stays put, *mate*!' Selena's in full flow. Carlos is leaning against the countertop, his arms folded, staring at my sister as if mesmerised. It's not the first time I have seen people speechless while observing her. I half expected such drama from Paisley and Joseph, given their circumstances, but it appears I chose the wrong pairing. All I wanted was a happy little toast – a few sparkly bubbles – and then to collect my bags from the car and unpack. After which I'd have time to swiftly complete my final few tasks. Then I too would be free to enjoy a holiday chill.

'How about we clean up so we can continue with our break, Selena?' I say, returning to the kitchen to find Paisley has found a broom and has made a start picking up broken glass. I sense that food prep will be in order very soon, given the culinary treats stashed on our side of the fridge. I will bide my time regards mentioning that the guys need a jaunt to the local Co-op, however, if a proper gut-buster brekkie is required tomorrow. I didn't anticipate their needs when ordering for us ladies.

Selena falls silent, swigs her bubbles and stands back for Paisley and I to step in and clean up.

'Thank you, ladies. I appreciate that,' says Carlos, finally moving from his spot and heading for the door.

'Carlos!' I call over my shoulder while running the hot water tap.

'Yeah.'

'I believe you were collecting a beer,' I remind him.

'I certainly was. You're good.' He doubles back, whips a bottle from the fridge, swiftly uncaps it then takes his leave.

Selena frostily stares at me.

'What?' I say, sensing I know her answer.

'Carlos,' mimics Selena, clearly imitating me, before sipping her bubbles.

'Well, Lady Muck. Don't you worry about the mess – we'll sort it,' I retort, knowing she's fuming about the enforced truce rather than a wasted bottle of wine.

Chapter Nine

Early evening

Selena

'Enough about us. How about you guys? Where do you come from? What's your line of business?' I ask, pushing aside one of several giant pizza delivery boxes littering the oak dining-room table, not that this sixteen-seater, possibly antique table was crafted for take-out. A shared lunch consisting of freshly baked sourdough, lashings of stringy cheese and more jalapenos than there should be. A surprise purchase by the guys, between big matches, which now feels like a team-building away-day exercise that your boss truly believes will be a sure-fire turnaround for office moral. I notice Paisley is less than chatty, sitting out on a limb in our line of three, the furthest she can be from Joseph at the head of the table.

'I'm an accountant,' says Affie, selecting his next piece of pizza.

'Really?' exclaims Kate in surprise, hastily adding, 'How interesting.'

'It pays the bills,' says Affie, smiling at her attempt to correct her surprised tone.

'She's not backpedalling at all, are you, Kate?' I say, stirring the pot, knowing she's too polite to openly comment on his appearance, which doesn't quite match his occupation.

'What I mean is . . .' She glances around the dining table before changing tack. 'Fair play. You surprised me there.'

'Accountant for a rugby club.'

'Where?' I ask, collecting the conversation baton.

'Bath.'

I immediately sit up tall, taking in his bulky frame – makes sense.

'What does an accountant do at a rugby club?'

Affie shrugs. 'They still have finances to deal with behind the scenes. I used to play in my youth, but not now.'

'Do you get free tickets?' asks Paisley, coming to life.

'Of course he does. Why do you think we're friends with him?' jokes Joseph, giving his mate a friendly backslap, before selecting yet another slice of pizza.

'Isn't that the truth!' mutters Affie.

'And you, Carlos – what's your line?' asks Kate.

'Does it matter?' His licks his fingers, uninterested in our chatter.

'Errr, no. If you'd rather not say that's fine, but sometimes I know people seeking other people – that's all. I pass on contacts where I can, if I can. I'm not judging,' says Kate.

'You're not judging? Right,' replies Carlos, throwing a glance towards the boys.

'She does come across that way, but she probably isn't,' I say, backing my sister, who always means well.

Carlos nods but remains silent. We three sit and stare, while the other two guys continue to eat. Carlos looks up, surprised to find we're still waiting.

'No judgement?'

A series of 'no's flow across the table in response.

'I'm a performer, as such.' His steady gaze travels between us, before continuing. 'Organised events, private parties, the odd cruise ships when the going is good, but mainly bookings based in the London area.'

There's silence. I'm determined not to ask for details, but I'm glad when Paisley does.

'What's your act?'

'Stripping.'

There's a moment of silence as we assess the faces of the other two guys before we respond. No smirking, suppressed laughing, teasing looks – nothing from his buddies.

'Clothes stripping?' asks Kate, her expression void of judgement.

'Yep. Not wallpaper, if that was your meaning. Adult entertainment is big business.'

'I bet,' I mutter, taking in his size and bulky shoulders. I should have guessed given his cocky attitude and his love-myself vibe. If he can perform as well as he can dish out banter, I bet he's employee of the month, every month!

'Possibly not what your parents hoped for,' says Kate, letting that judgement rein run loose.

'That's a bit rude, Kate – aren't we each free to make our own choices in life?' asks Joseph, po-faced, clearly sticking up for his mate. Kate shrugs and blushes in response.

'Point taken. But then I do own my own home, am mortgage free and financially independent at the age of thirty-two – they didn't expect that either. I don't think their plans would have guaranteed that at this age.'

'Impressive,' mutters Paisley, while Kate appears dumbstruck by the details.

'And how far do you take your performance . . . your act?' My question is met with four startled faces, though Carlos is unfazed. 'What? Are you telling me you lot weren't thinking it?'

'Only you would ask that!' jests Kate, her po-faced expression finally cracking.

'Depends on the gig, the venue, the event, the ticket price charged. I'm part of a troupe so the choreography and routine can determine certain aspects.'

'Fair play to you. See, folks, he gave an honest answer,' I say, turning to address the others.

'Is that it? You seemed more surprised about me being an accountant,' scoffs Affie, wiping his hands on a paper serviette.

'That's because of . . .' Kate stops mid-sentence, but us girls know what she was about to say.

Affie and Joseph exchange a glance, while Carlos simply smirks, before saying, 'I fit the profile for my role. Whereas you . . .'

'That's exactly it,' says Kate, 'you don't look like an accountant. Sorry, Affie.'

'Don't be sorry, I take it as a compliment,' blushes Affie.

Paisley's looking from man to man, her brow furrowed, clearly puzzled.

'How's this come about then – Bath, London and Birmingham?' she says pointing at each.

'Mountain rescue,' says Carlos, in a heartbeat. 'We volunteer.'

'You don't!' blurts Paisley, expelling a surprised laugh, looking at Joseph.

'I do now . . . or rather have done since we . . .'

'Yeah, right. Pull the other one, Joseph,' she adds, distracted by the nearest pizza box.

Joseph says nothing but turns to the other men for support.

'He does, actually. That's how we met and got to know each other – this boys' break has sprung from that,' says Carlos, a little defensively.

'No,' whispers Paisley, shaking her head in disbelief. 'It was all I could do to peel you away from your football, rugby, golf, darts, snooker or any other form of sport showing on the TV, yet now you're willing to go searching for a missing person halfway up a mountain?'

Joseph gives a nod. I'll give him his due, he does look slightly embarrassed.

'Mountains, woodlands, moorlands, caves – you name it, we'll be called to assist in a rescue or recovery.'

'Recovery?' I say, unsure of his meaning.

'Yeah ... not everyone survives their misadventures,' says Affie softly.

'I see,' I mutter, embarrassed by my outburst.

'I wouldn't have thought it your scene, Joseph,' says Kate, re-airing Paisley's initial thoughts, which sounds as if we're colluding to gang up on him. I neither care nor am I interested in how Joseph spends his weekends. And there's only one way to prove that detail. I keep my trap shut.

'You're right, Kate. It doesn't sound like the me from back then, but it's how I spend my weekends now,' explains Joseph, a slight flush appearing in his cheek. 'Paise is right. I rarely moved out of the armchair at home unless I was attending a match or playing in one. And I apologise for that. There must have been many things you wanted to do after a long shift at the hospital, whereas back then I wanted to stay at home.'

'Watching the TV,' adds Paisley, driving home her point.

'I probably could have played things differently back then,' says Joseph, stunning us ladies into silence.

'Mate, don't apologise for who you are ... were ... back then,' says Carlos.

Joseph gives his habitual nod. It all sounds very earthy, new-man-ish, and unlike the Joseph we know.

'Seriously, he should. Because I'm the one that has had to cope with the fallout of his behaviour and it has ripped my bloody life apart in every single department. So, go ahead, Joseph. Be my guest if you feel the need to apologise!' announces Paisley, her cool deserting her.

'I get it, Paise. I behaved abominably. And, yeah, it affected you. I have no excuses, no jokes to crack – I'll own it.'

'I never thought I'd hear you say that,' mutters Kate, 'Where's Joseph McLoughlin disappeared to?'

'I get it. The guy back then is not the guy I am today. You could say I've grown up, Kate. I think that sums it up.'

'Pity it was too late,' mutters Paisley, pushing her chair back from the table and standing tall, frustration etched upon her features. Joseph McLoughlin doesn't utter another word, but gives yet another of his usual head nods in silent acknowledgement.

Chapter Ten

Kate

'So, how's life been treating you?' I ask, entering the kitchen soon after and finding Joseph uncapping beer bottles.

'I'm sure you've heard the sorry story enough times, Kate,' comes his reply.

'Sadly, I have. But since then . . . how's life been?'

'New home, new job, new friends – shed the old skin and created a new start for myself.'

'Oh, is that an acknowledgement that your past actions were pretty snake-like?'

'Funny, Kate.'

'OK, I'll let you off, Joseph McLoughlin. I've known you for years and only ever had an issue with you over you-know-what. I'm guessing you've paid the price ten-fold for that episode, so I'm willing to let bygones be bygones as long as you don't upset our Paisley over the coming week.'

'Good to hear it, Kate. It was never my intention to do what I did.'

'That maybe so, but you ripped the heart out of my girl, so I won't be standing by if you cross a line. Do you hear me?'

'You don't change, do you, Kate? Big sister to everyone, always organising someone or something.'

'You can say that again,' mutters Selena, stashing the empty pizza boxes into the kitchen's recycling bin as she joins us.

'And you, Selena?' asks Joseph.

'Me? Why are you asking me?' she says, clearly narked.

Joseph seems taken aback.

'Because Kate had plenty to say on the subject, so I thought you might too.'

'Nah. Nothing to add – other than what she said.'

'So, a new home – nearer to your parents?' I ask, attempting a change in subject.

'Closer in some respects but not too close,' he smiles.

'I'm with you on that one. Our parents are a nightmare for accidently dropping by, driving by, passing by unannounced, purely to see whose unknown car is parked outside. A sodding embarrassment some days,' I say, feeling our bridge of friendship starting to rebuild.

'Exactly. They've been supportive. I'm starting from scratch, which isn't easy. So things are not as comfortable as the home I left, but it's getting there.'

'I know how that feels. And new buddies too?'

'These guys have been great. I needed to get out of myself and explore interests further afield. I'm as surprised as anyone that I signed up to volunteer, but it's proved worthwhile and fills any spare time I have to offer.'

'It's not regular hours, then?'

'No. You sign up for duty whenever you're free to commit and attend call outs. Of course, it's an entire weekend spent at our base camp, as anything can come through at any time during a shift. But that's the point, isn't it – being there in an emergency when people need you?' His words linger. I'm unsure whether to point out that his explanation fits both his mountain rescue duties and what he was supposed to owe his marriage, but something tells me he already knows.

'Sure does,' I add.

'Christ, man, are you seeking approval from all females or just those present?' asks Carlos, entering the kitchen as well.

'You know how it is, Carlos ... stomping boots on thin ice never mix well, do they?' offers Selena, before Joseph can answer.

'Yeah. What she said. Anyway ... back to it,' mutters Joseph, gathering yet more chilled beer bottles and accompanying his mate back through to the lounge.

As much as I want to rant and rage for what he did to my friend, Joseph Mcloughlin has still got that way about him. I'm not sure I should admit this to myself, and I certainly wouldn't mention it to Paisley, but I kind of get why he'd turn a stranger's head on a night out. He's got that vibe of attraction that definitely pulls you in closer.

'Thanks for ordering the pizza, Carlos!' I yell, hoping he hears my appreciation.

'You're welcome!' comes his retreating voice.

I wait for the door to fully close before turning to Selena.

'Are you actually OK with Joseph? It seems so long since we all last saw him.'

'Am I hell! I'll just show willing until he upsets her and then the gloves are off,' says Selena, balling her fists and raising her guard. 'She's been to hell and back while he swans in looking a picture of health. She's carried the can physically, mentally and emotionally.'

'I thought that too. I tried to make light of the situation, but he's got some bloody nerve, if you ask me.'

'It's Joseph McLoughlin – he always has had,' says Selena, raising her eyebrows to emphasise the point.

'You're not wrong there,' I say, with a nervous giggle, knowing this week isn't going to be easy. 'Well, if you're OK, I'll grab some time to unpack my things.'

'Oh sure, no worries. I was going to suggest a brisk walk to check out the surrounding area but we've got all week. We can't have you being rumpled and crumpled, can we?'

I make a swift exit, knowing that unpacking will take a matter of minutes, but those final few tasks may take a little longer, despite my cover story.

It feels wrong to be shaking off my little sister and side stepping her invite to explore the area. We've only just arrived and I'm seeking 'me' time already. Not that I'm up to anything suspicious as such, but she wouldn't approve, which makes me inclined to be secretive. Not that I need to be secretive with my to-do list, as half the tasks relate to her birthday, but needs must.

My bedroom isn't unlike Paisley's across the landing. A large double room at the front of the cottage, tastefully furnished with an ensuite. The prospect beyond the lattice window is a breathtaking landscape of rolling hills and open sky. No telegraph poles, no vehicles, no building sites or cityscape but a backdrop of purple-headed mountains that dip and curve against a clear sky. An assortment of rich greens and deep purples that stretches for as far as the eye can see – a wilderness created by Mother Nature that needs to be explored and appreciated. But only after I've finished my to-do list.

I reach for my mobile and tap the screen, knowing there will be a multitude of text messages, all from the same number. His number. Not that others don't text me too, but my friends respect the fact that I'm on a break with my sister for five days, and am probably enjoying myself away from work. Sadly, my psycho-boss doesn't understand the concept, because then it would affect his day. His life. His to-do list, which is ultimately my other to-do list. The one that I complete in the tiny gaps left from completing my own task list.

Ten text messages, lined up one after the other, some with literally minutes between them. Each as urgent as the one before, each a little more demanding in tone and nature than the previous one. His curtness has its own Richter scale that I've devised purely for him.

My fingers nimbly select, open, flick and close each text message in order. What the hell – ten messages for one subject! I can imagine him pacing his office, muttering and firing them off in rapid succession before yet another point that he failed to mention comes to mind, forcing him to send yet another. The man is a fool, and here is the proof confirming it. Why do I stay and put up with this? Others ask me this all the time. They never grasp my point that, given my skill set, I can do both the job and deal with him by overlooking his erratic behaviour. I don't try to understand his psychological game playing or egocentric manner. I simply follow orders, complete my task list and receive a salary in exchange. Though Selena and Paisley joke that I don't get paid enough, but actually I do. I get paid way over the odds for my role. Rumour has it that his previous PAs before me didn't stay very long, so HR upped the salary accordingly. It might not be the right incentive, but it works for me, especially after my ex and the financial trouble he caused. But even after a decade spent working for this guy, I've failed to train him in any way during that time. My colleague Janet, on the floor above, has managed to train her boss to hang his own mac on the coat stand. My psycho-boss, meanwhile, still drops his on my desk each morning, come rain or shine, regardless of my subtle hints, clear requests or suggestions otherwise. Probably even today, even though I'm on annual leave.

How many times have I confirmed in recent days that all is in hand? Bubbles. Cake. Birds. Clown. I have four simple tasks – the man must think I'm deranged if he feels the need to keep reminding me. I'm hardly likely to forget the date, as it's also my sister's thirtieth birthday.

I settle at the dressing table, creating a makeshift desk, and begin to collate the information necessary to complete and confirm the four tasks. I know what I'm doing. I've had long enough to think about the details for each, the cost, the carriage, the delivery requirements and necessary signatures for each and payments. My double-barrel surname, Allen-Smythe, graces each of the online forms – not that I'm emotionally hanging onto my old marital status but just the convenience, as it's simpler when there's an element of continuity in one's life. Not that I'm proud of his surname like I once was. I've made it my own, though, by disassociating it from him, especially after his gambling caused us nigh-on financial ruin. I owe him nothing: morally or financially. I know what I'm doing. I've had long enough to think about the details for each, the cost, the carriage, the delivery requirements and necessary signatures for each and payments.

I'm actually 'double-booked', planning two events for Monday, 30th December. Sadly not both for my little sister. I'm a little embarrassed to admit the other is for my psycho-boss' eldest daughter, who has decided to hold her long-awaited-and-dreamed of engagement party on the very same day. Who in their right mind gets engaged on New Year Eve's eve? But thankfully it takes all of twenty minutes to complete the four outstanding tasks. Two for my sister's thirtieth birthday and the other two, annoyingly, in celebration of the forthcoming engagement party.

Chapter Eleven

Evening

Selena

Finally, we girls are all unpacked, fed and sufficiently composed after our stressful arrival to dart into the snug, armed with a selection of nibbles, for some well-earned downtime. I was hoping our first night could be spent unwinding in this cosy, modern room with its squidgy marshmallow-style couches and low-level coffee tables without interruption from the guys. Not that I'm spying on them, but it's difficult fighting the urge to stay away from their sports lounge, so I succumb. On poking my head around the door, I'm greeted by an impressive open hearth festively decorated with a garland of holly, and a TV more than adequately sized to impress any red-blooded male with a passion for sport. Each guy has pitched his spot in a different seat with an array of essentials parked within arm's reach. I duck back out and scurry back to the snug.

We ladies recline in comfort and then, despite my best efforts to sway the topic of conversation, it doesn't take long before the chat revolves solely around my love life, as always.

'I'm sick of that age-old one liner: "I'll give you a call". I hear it all the time and yet my phone fails to ring,' I moan.

'That's because you've become a bloody taxi service for any guy in the village who wishes to have a quiet drink on a Sunday.

What do I keep telling you? Stop doing what you're doing and know your worth!' says Kate.

'I know my worth, thank you! I don't accept dates via text message, do I? I delete those.'

'Righto, Selena. You might as well fit a meter to your dashboard and charge by the mileage – it would earn you more than the price of a diet Coke without the waste of three hours getting ready beforehand.'

'I do not take three hours to get ready!' I argue.

'You so do,' insists Kate.

'You do, Selena – you take ages,' mutters Paisley, joining our sisterly squabble.

'Not on a Sunday morning I don't,' I say, miffed that Paisley would side with my sister. Surely that goes against our girl-code?

'Phuh!'

'Phuh yourself, Kate. You wouldn't know. I don't see you on Sundays, but having done my hair the night before it simply falls into place, so it's just make-up and that takes me . . .'

'Bloody ages,' says Paisley, giving Kate a toothy grin.

'Thanks a bunch, Paisley – side with her why don't you?'

'I'm not siding. I'm just saying – you do. But it's worth it because you always look beautifully presented when you leave the house: hair, make-up, clothes – you can tell that you're a marketing gal through and through.'

'Can you?' I ask, all buttered up by her compliment. 'I never feel like I give off that kind of image. Whereas Kate here . . .'

Paisley nods in agreement.

'I love my work. Though it's hard to market oneself, as opposed to a product, especially when it comes to marketing oneself as a worthy mate, especially with the dating scene as it is,' I say, not wishing to sound too woe-is-me.

'Selena, don't you dare compare yourself to some commodity left on the proverbial shelf!' says Kate, horrified by my suggestion.

'I don't, but no one's interested in getting to know anyone any more. Everyone's seeking trust, respect and undying loyalty without offering a hint of exclusivity or commitment in return. I'm sick of being asked if "all my eggs are in their basket?" only to find they have more baskets than the Easter bunny dotted around the city, with weekly deliveries to each!' The other two giggle but I mean it, and they've no idea. So many are only after so-called 'friends with benefits' set ups, but without much friendship yet demanding a whole host of sexual favours. My last 'FWB arrangement' ended up being more like a repeated one-night stand, all with the same mystery guy named Gregory. To be fair, he was generous with his efforts when engaged, but I receive Royal Mail deliveries more often!

'I never clock off entirely – if you're a creative type, there's never an off button, is there? Much like you, Paisley, with . . . the babies. The premature babies and their special care.' The words slip from my lips and instantly I want to kick myself, as our Kate attempts to silence me with a well-timed glare. My faltering sentence draws attention to so much more than her dedicated work. Gone is the rapid-fire banter of five minutes ago, the feisty interaction between true friends – I've just stomped my size sixes right in it by reminding her of the one thing she probably wishes to forget this holiday: babies.

'Oh, you've got a gob on you!' says our Kate, politely filling the silence while Paisley recovers from my blundering reminder and finds her voice.

'But she's not wrong, is she, Kate?' Paisley sends me a weak smile, as if signalling she knows where I was coming from but that *ouch*, it sodding stung. 'I have spent a lifetime looking after babies, seeing babies, wanting babies. I'm as much all about babies and toddlers as Selena is marketing. We each follow our path in life the best we can by chasing our dreams, don't we?' Paisley's voice is as weak as her smile. I silently will the universe into taking our conversation back to the subject of my faltering love life – it might be flatlining at present, but I'd rather take one for the team than hurt Paisley any further.

'Sorry. Sending you a squeeze,' I mutter, making a sympathetic face. She knows I meant nothing by it. She knows me better than anyone, possibly better than even Kate. On second thoughts, maybe not.

Kate shakes her head in my direction before speaking, 'Blabber mouth over there never puts her brain in to gear before speaking, does she? It's a bloody good job she spends her days yapping about products and inanimate objects, because she's no sodding tact with human beings and feelings.'

'Ooooh, look at Queen Frosty dishing it out. You're only so measured with every remark because you've spent too long working for that psycho-boss of yours, Mr Hart. Or Mr No-Hart-Nor-Brains, as the rank and file at your place call him. If you were PA to anyone else, you'd be less uptight, less guarded and slightly less super-human.'

'I doubt it,' says Kate, sipping her drink.

'Is he still as psycho as ever?'

'God, yes. He'll never change. If anything, he's getting worse as he's getting older.'

'Don't they all?' I mutter.

'Oh Selena!' groans Kate, defensive as ever.

'It's true! He thinks he's Derren Brown – all mind tricks and behavioural analysis. Tell Paisley about last week's antics with his dictation – go on, tell her. I swear he gets off on it.'

Paisley adjusts her legs by tucking them up beneath her body, readying herself for story time. She knows it'll be a tale and a half, having heard as many as I have over the years, and she shares my opinion about Kate's work.

'Last week, he handed me his dictaphone, instructing me to type and prepare the necessary letters and documents. Nothing out of the ordinary there, you'd think—' Kate rolls her eyes towards the ceiling. Paisley leans forward in anticipation. 'Anyway, I start the recording and his voice comes through loud and clear, but in the background there's the noise of trickling water.' Kate pauses.

'Water?' Paisley's brow creases in confusion.

'Then I hear a gush of water followed by the blast of a hand drier.'

'No! He was in the toilets?'

'Actually, at the urinal, given the initial sounds,' says Kate. 'Though I've no proof. I'm assuming that's where he was.'

'No way! There's your proof. You should report this particular tale to HR.

'I suppose at least he washed his hands!' I joke.

'Small mercies, given the circumstances,' mutters my sister.

'And then what did you do, Kate? Tell her, tell her that too,' I urge, knowing that every detail adds to the story but also that each sentence distances Paisley from my blunder a few minutes ago.

'Give me chance!' snaps Kate, irritated by my interruption.

I zone out as Kate continues and I hear it all for the umpteenth time this week. I know she's honest when she says she finished her task efficiently, as always, and then spent two hours fretting how to broach the subject with him to prevent a repeat occurrence.

'Are you kidding?' asks Paisley, 'Surely that's a form of intimidation. What did you say to him afterwards?'

'Lunchtime arrived. I'd delivered the completed letters and documents, as requested. I was sitting there in the communal kitchen, when he enters clutching his empty coffee mug and says, and I quote, "Can you refill that for me. Given that your typing skills from dictation aren't what they used to be!" Well, that was the final straw—' says Kate. 'Without thinking, I said . . . maybe it was the Niagara waterfalls in the background that I found off-putting.'

'What did he say?' asks Paisley, engrossed by the horrors of having a psycho-boss like Kate's.

'Nothing. As always, he simply does that annoying smirk, as if he's enjoying the power of changing your mood – that's how I see it. Bloody mind games and messing with people's heads.'

'Gets off on it, more like,' I mutter. 'I'd have walked.'

'Yes. You probably would, but that's not me, Selena. It's what he pays me for.'

'He doesn't pay you – it's not out of his back pocket. Though you'd think it was the way he acts up and demands personal errands.'

'Kate that's not right. You must say something?'

Kate shakes her head slowly, her demeanour remaining stoic and strong.

'I'd be leaving – I couldn't put up with games like that. Bosses aren't supposed to treat you like that. It's degrading, Kate. I'd be looking for another job come New Year. I don't know how you do it. I'd have been contacting HR by now and complaining.'

'Come off it, Paisley – this is Kate. How long have you been his PA?' I say, turning to my sister, not that I couldn't work it out if I wished to.

'Nine and a half years,' answers my sister.

'How do you keep doing it?' asks Paisley.

Kate shrugs.

'Don't shrug, Kate. And don't say your salary more than covers your efforts either! With your experience you could secure a better position, a decent boss and receive better healthcare and holiday entitlement elsewhere,' I say, having heard her defence too many times.

'So why ask, then?' she says, 'I'm never going to leave when I can cope with his antics. What's the saying . . . better the devil you know than the devil you don't?'

Paisley shakes her head; it makes no sense to either of us.

'Tell her about your errand to buy Christmas gifts for his wife,' I urge. I turn to my friend, 'This is the best one ever, Paisley.'

'Her lingerie?' Kate asks, wearily.

Paisley grimaces.

'I forgot what I was doing once I was in the store. I was so stressed. My head was swimming with other things; organising the Christmas party, a farewell present for a co-worker – not to mention my own Christmas worries – and I completely forgot who I was buying it for. Anyway, I selected my size instead of hers.'

I crease up laughing, while my sister dies once more from remembered embarrassment in the corner.

'No way!' exclaims Paisley.

'And then, would you believe he accompanied her back to the store to return the goods and collect replacements?' I say, adding, 'All very creepy. Frankly, I'd have asked to be allocated elsewhere as soon as I spotted his managerial style. It's way too stressful, Kate.'

'Sometimes.'

'Not sometimes – all the sodding time. Though full marks to the guy – he's playing to your strength in a sad little man kind of way.'

'Selena?'

'He is. It comes down to your "Leave it to me, boss" attitude for sorting stuff out as quick as a flash. It makes it easy for folk to shove their crap in your direction,' I say, knowing my sister prides herself on her ability to cope.

'What? Like you do?'

'Nope. I don't. Not like that. If that was the case you'd have had this big birthday break booked months ago, arrangements made and surprise stuff happening every hour of the day. I'll remind you I booked this on Christmas Eve!'

'Don't we know it?' laughs Kate, as the door of the snug opens and we all turn in unison.

'Sorry to interrupt, but we were wondering if we could borrow some of your white wine from the fridge?' It's Affie, his head and shoulders emerging around the edge of the door.

'Good God, have you drunk all that beer already?' gasps Paisley.

'No. Joseph and Carlos just fancied something a bit . . .' his bottom lip rolls forward, suggesting he's not quite sure what.

'And you're the poor messenger? Bless you, Affie,' I say, sussing the mood of the other gals. 'I reckon you can borrow one – write an IOU and stick it to the fridge door.'

'Yeah, sure. We'll replace it, first thing.'

'What's the score?' asks Kate, showing more interest than I'll ever muster for sports.

'Nil-nil but it's half time. Which is why I've been sent to ask,' smiles Affie. 'Does it matter which I take?'

'No. Here, let me get it,' says Kate, jumping up from her seat. 'I'll grab a round of refills for us too.' As quick as a flash, Affie disappears and Kate follows suit, the door closing behind her, as ever full of eagerness to please and accommodate others.

'What is she like? "Here, let me get it" – that's what her problem is at work, you know? She's too quick to take charge of a situation, too eager to please others and wave her magic wand to complete a request.'

'She's never been any different, though – I'll doubt she'll change now.' Paisley looks wistfully at the closed door.

'More's the pity,' I say, noticing her expression. 'And you? You holding on OK?'

'It's a little unsettling with Joseph being here and, well, you know – not the best timing for me. For the majority of this year I've battled with one thought and one thought only, and now, with the New Year fast approaching, it doesn't help break the pattern, does it?'

'I get it.' I pause before quickly adding, 'I didn't mean to put my foot in it earlier. I know how raw things can be for you regarding the subject of babies.'

Paisley nods. She knows it wasn't meant badly; just me running my mouth on autopilot. Again.

'Selena, it's fine. All things being equal, if our marriage had continued we'd have been hearing the patter of tiny feet in the next few months. But it didn't, did it? It went belly up, hit the skids and ended as it has because he ruined the "us" we'd been planning with the help of some drunken floozy,' says Paisley, adding, 'Since my divorce, those tiny babies have become even more significant to me, though, as they may well be my only experience of nurturing. It's as if my dreams of parenthood faded with the arrival of the decree nisi. Potentially there'll be other partners in my future, but when you've connected with "the one", surely that's meant to be your future sorted?'

'You've been so brave, my lovely,' I say, knowing few have seen her bad days as much as I have. Not that I'm expecting praise or a medal in recognition of my efforts, but we all have our own issues too – none of us are perfect.

The snug door opens and Kate barges in, juggling another open wine bottle and two large bags of popcorn.

'Floozy, I hear. It can mean only one person,' she says, bumping the door closed with her bum. 'Not that you're interested, but Joseph's half cut in there, sprawled across the sofas and not looking his best.'

'My days of caring are long gone!' announces Paisley, retrieving her glass, refilling it, and toasting herself.

If only that were true, I'd sleep easier tonight. Instead I've a feeling I'll be constantly monitoring my friend's mood throughout the next few days. I only hope she can ignore his presence or at least squash down any painful reminders. Maybe she'll even leave here a stronger woman than when she arrived? On second thoughts, that wouldn't be a bad idea for all three of us.

Chapter Twelve

Paisley

I take my time readying for bed. Carefully removing my make-up in the en suite, having lined up my toiletries along the glass shelf as if I'm going to be judged by housekeeping. My hands busily massage my familiar features while I mentally have a quiet chat with my reflection in the vanity mirror. Literally the bare-faced truth, a habit formed in response to all the tough days of the past eighteen months.

I'm content with how the day has panned out, our conversation in the garden, and our evening interactions. Though probably not my initial reaction, but I got through it at least. Thanks to the girls. How many times have I uttered that line in recent times? How many times have I cleansed the day from my face with a renewed promise of tomorrow? And yet here I am, repeating it tonight. Surely those days are behind me?

I was lost. I'm not afraid to admit that I allowed myself to become dependent upon him in every way, other than financially. But the other stuff, the day-to-day dependency that naturally evolved ... He had strengths that I didn't. You can't both be responsible for checking the utility bills payment, that the mortgage remains at a decent percentage, and keep an eye on the latest tyre deal at the local garage. My talents lay elsewhere – providing our household with the best of both worlds. Sadly, none of my roles proved to be vital when we separated.

I brush and floss my teeth as my mind continues to download and tidy the inner muddle of my day.

All of this proved to be major stumbling blocks for me after his departure. Departure! Who am I kidding? I kicked him out. There was nothing amicable about his swift exit from our three-bed semi-detached. I had no idea how much anything cost; he oversaw the flow of the joint bank account. It's embarrassing phoning around utility supplies asking if you have an account with them. Those initial few days were spent learning about the minutia of the life we'd been living – the various accounts, the endless subscriptions, the constant flow of transactions from the current account – half of which I had no idea about. I felt so foolish, and that's before we get to his admission of guilt.

Not all my anger was aimed at him, though. It takes two to tango! How do you get off with someone else's husband, even if it's just for one night? It's a thought that has kept me awake time and again. I couldn't. We ladies are entitled to our jollies as much as the fellas, but still. A married man is out of bounds, surely? If nothing else, I simply wouldn't experience what I need in relation to intimacy, enjoyment or pleasure that way. How does whispered pillow talk with a stranger even begin?

Back then I found myself avoiding other women. I had this ridiculous notion that I was maybe unknowingly standing behind *her* in the supermarket check-out, dry cleaners or lunching at the next table. I tortured myself imagining overhearing a woman discussing my husband and her night of passion while attending my hair appointment. I had this faceless image of femininity from which I wanted to distance myself. And him. I walked around half expecting 'her' to appear from nowhere, wishing to talk to me. Explain. Excuse herself by bringing me up to speed on her growing relationship with Joseph. Whether that be maliciously or by accident. What lies had he told her? What cliché had he used? Was I unloving or uncaring towards him? Neglectful of my husband's needs, desires, his stresses, his emotions, his live-lihood? My brain loops around and around, just as it did back then. Churning over the same details, remarks, worries, only to finally return to the one point that brings all my self-sabotaging to a crescendo: we were trying for a baby! A planned baby. When you're embarking on that journey, you like to think you're intrinsically connected, that all is well!

I finish my nightly routine, step back from the vanity unit and stare at the reflection before me.

'Joseph reappearing had to happen at some point,' I mutter aloud. 'It might as well be now, when support is readily at hand.' I yank the pull cord, plunging the en suite into darkness as if dropping the curtain on today's performance.

I scurry towards my bed and playfully jump between the cotton sheets. I brave the initial hit of cold cotton on bare feet before snuggling beneath a weighty duck-down duvet, resting my head on the plump but soft pillows, all of which are sure to guarantee a decent night's sleep.

But a rap-a-tap-tap sounds on my bedroom door.

'Yes,' I call, hoping this interruption doesn't need me to get out of bed again.

The door slowly opens, allowing Selena's head and shoulders to appear around the edge.

'Only me. I just wondered if you were OK, that's all.' Her expectant face is etched with concern.

'I'm all good, Selena. I'm over the shock and happy with where we're at. A good night's sleep will see me right as rain.'

She audibly exhales, and smiles with relief. 'Good to hear. If you want or need anything, you'll say, right?'

'Of course. But I'll be fine.'

'I'll leave you in peace, Paisley. Night!' Her voice softens to a whisper before she blows me a kiss.

'Night, babe,' I say, snatching the winged kiss from the air and smiling.

Selena disappears and the door closes again softly. Bless her. Lord knows what I'd have done without her constant support, morning, noon and night, throughout these long lonely months.

I switch off the bedside lamp, lie back upon a nest of billowing pillows, and slowly exhale. I'll be fine, whatever this week brings – I'll be fine.

Chapter Thirteen

Saturday 28 December 2024

Kate

I head down the staircase in my dressing gown with little enthusiasm for the task ahead: cooking breakfast. I pride myself on being the most domestic one out of us three, not that its rocket science, but it reminds me of our younger days, when I'd dish up beans on toast for my little sister and her bestie during school holidays. I groan remembering the accolade awarded by Paisley – 'a gut-buster' breakfast – because I doubt our grocery order has the capability of delivering on that promise. Regardless of how much bread and butter I spread, I can hardly feed the proverbial five thousand! I'd need much more produce: sausages, bacon, black pudding, flat mushrooms, steak tomatoes, hash browns for starters. In an ideal world, I need half a dozen different breads to offer a decent selection of toast. And eggs – I only ordered a dozen! We have a multipack of baked beans, though, which instantly reminds me of Cody's refusal to accept Heinz as an essential of an English fry-up. He'd argue for England while quoting Trip Advisor, popular TV programmes and numerous weekends away with his mates. At least us girls will eat them if these boys think likewise and refuse. Why didn't I think about this last night? Probably because I had other more important tasks to focus on, such as birds and clowns. Hopefully today we'll be free to enjoy ourselves. There's no point relying on my sister to get the ball rolling on this week's break; she dallied around making the rental booking and look where that got us. I suppose I'll find something fun for us to do today and . . .

Pushing open the kitchen door, I stop dead in my tracks. The kitchen is spotlessly clean, which is fabulous but also weird, given that the guys stayed up much later than we did. Plus, they had used countless mugs, glasses and dirty plates, which had been scattered around the lounge during day one of their sports fest. To be honest, I half expected to see the sink overflowing and remnants of mayhem on every countertop. And yet the tiny green light on the dishwasher signals completion . . . Well, full marks to you, fellas! I doubt my sister would have been so generous under the circumstances.

I flick the switch on the kettle before opening the fridge and encounter my second surprise: a mountain of brown paper bags stacked like bricks, the darkening patterns on each suggesting fresh produce inside. Who's fetched this? And where from? Especially given it's just gone half seven.

Buzz.

My mobile sounds in my pocket, announcing the arrival of a text. Here we go. The first of many from Mr Hart, I assume. It's been all of twelve hours since his last barrage of instructions. And I'm expecting the steady flow to turn into a tsunami in the coming days. Not that he's barking new orders in every text, it's more that he's simply never as organised as he likes to portray, so tends to drip feed. And he relies heavily on me. That seems to have been our deal for near enough ten years. He's the boss, the bigwig, and I'm the understudy, providing continual support and encouragement from the wings and tending to his every need. My job title might be PA, but I'm more like a runner-gofer person behind the scenes, pandering to his every whim. And the line between what's work and what's not is non-existent.

Unusually for me, I ignore the text. And suddenly the task in hand, a gut-buster breakfast, holds an all-new interest.

'Please help yourself, but mind the dishes – they're piping hot!' I say, gesturing towards the spread lining the centre of the dining table. 'Though how we've wangled this lot, when the local stores aren't open yet, I don't know!' Everyone hurriedly grabs a seat and sets to as if there'd been a rationing of food since yesterday's pizza fest.

'I went jogging earlier and came across a guy delivering trays of chilled produce to the local deli on the main street. The store assistant said they didn't open till nine, but I didn't have any cash on me anyway. So, I asked the driver if he'd any going spare for a cash sale. I explained where we were staying and asked if he could nip in when he drove past. This is the result – all fresh, he assured me,' explains Affie. He makes it seem as if questioning delivery drivers is a daily occurrence. Then, offering me a beaming smile, he adds, 'Thank you, Kate – this looks terrific.'

'Look at you bringing home the bacon for the ladies,' jests Carlos, reaching for his orange juice.

'Were you too busy sleeping?' quips Selena, giving him a sideways glance.

'Were you?' retorts Carlos, as quick as a flash, clearly irritated.

Paisley politely smiles to smooth out their snappy exchange; she's present but not herself. Joseph looks none too clever either. I note the distance between them – you couldn't choose seats further apart.

'Oi! Dig in and not at each other,' I admonish, surprising myself with my spontaneous wit.

'Look who's talking tough!' mutters Selena, helping herself to slices of black pudding.

'Not at all. I'm simply not putting up with a sparring match each morning – you aren't going to spoil my breakfast. Anyway, you need to eat, clear and clean up ASAP, as we're heading out.'

'Today? Us?' asks Paisley, coming to life.

'Clean?' asks Selena.

'Yep, you pair. We're in this together, remember? I'm not carrying the can for all three of us. I've upheld my end of the bargain! I've done the cooking – you can do the scrubbing!'

'This could prove interesting,' says Carlos, turning towards the other fellas.

'Oh, give over. My older sister's hardly going to put me out in December during my birthday week – think about it, Carlos.'

'I might!' I correct her.

'Whoo! Burnt – right there!' laughs Carlos, snapping his fingers as Selena's jaw drops at my remark.

Chapter Fourteen

Paisley

I flick through the TV channels in search of something to hold my attention while I hide away in the snug. Selena and Kate are busy getting ready upstairs, and I've got ten minutes to kill. Bumping into Joseph is the last thing I need after surviving last night, and breakfast. Hopefully, Kate's bright idea of a surprise day out will lift my mood and we can begin enjoying our staycation. Though what she's so happy and skippity about is anyone's guess – you'd think she was off on a school outing the way she darted upstairs to get ready. But maybe she was just keen to avoid Selena's endless moaning about clean-up duties. Or maybe it was Affie's generous praise after her gut-buster breakfast proved itself nameworthy that energised her so?

A cute nappy advert fills the screen and I react instantly, like a gamer shooting zombies, my finger manically prodding the remote button. The screen blanks before the next channel reveals three highchairs being road tested. My finger reacts again, only to reveal a giant tub of milk formula with a blurred image of a woman breastfeeding in the background on the next channel. I give up and kill the screen, leaving myself staring into the void. How many times a week do I do this? – it's fast becoming my new habit in the last eighteen months. Never did I think I'd become one of those women that avoid so much in life because it triggers them. I can honestly go from being in the best mood to being in the worst, my doldrums lasting all day, simply by seeing a specific image of a newborn. Dodge them as I try, their cute bubble lips, chubby fingers and tiny pinkies litter my world like land mines. Never did I think I'd burst out crying in the middle of the high street on seeing the revamped window of Dreams bed centre, but I was that woman. I used to pass it twice a week and each time I had to avert my eyes from that cute baby picture plastered across their main window. Not to mention the prams, pushchairs and toddler nursey groups walking past me crocodile style on their way to the local park. The pain is endless, and each day is an assault course trying to avoid all the beautiful cherubs that will most definitely trigger my emotions, which will then set me off down a path where all I wish to do is dive under my duvet and hide for a month.

Anyway, it'll do me no good to sit here and mope. I need to switch to my professional mind-set, where by simply donning my uniform I'm able to switch between my private world to my vocation in life. I'm able to cope with anything baby-wise then. I consider myself a safe pair of hands, caring for these tiny babies as if they were my own. The same visual triggers surround me and yet, strangely, I'm able to distant my emotions, as those special babies and their parents need me. I suppose this partitioning of my emotions is no different to how the other emergency services cope when it comes to balancing what they see every day and their private lives. The focus is away from me, you see, as they need my expertise, my knowledge and my observations.

Peeling myself from the sofa cushion, I head towards the kitchen in search of further distraction. But as soon as I open the door, I wish I hadn't; Joseph is positioned at the table reading the paper.

It's too late to backtrack, so I meet the challenge head on. 'Do you still see Jamie and Jen?' I ask, trying to sound blasé and hoping to remain on a neutral subject as I head towards the kettle.

'Nah. Do you?' He looks up from the sports pages.

'No. Not since . . . I thought they chose you over me.'

'I thought likewise.'

'Despite him being your best friend from school?'

He nods before speaking. 'Ah well, proves they didn't like either of us that much.' We each give a polite laugh as the truth hits home.

'I really thought they liked me,' I say.

'Sadly not. Clearly, we were both phased out.'

'Jen's blatant flirtations with you were always cringeworthy – those late-night drinking games became embarrassing; as if the rest of us didn't exist.'

'I never noticed.'

'You must have.' I seem to have forgotten about wanting coffee.

'I swear. I wasn't interested in Jenny.'

'Weren't you?'

Joseph gives me that look, his dark eyes framed beneath his heavy brow.

'Are you for real, Paise?'

'I'm just saying it as it is. Was. Anyway, Jamie saw it. I'm surprised Jen hasn't contacted you since we split up.' The kettle begins to boil behind me.

'Are you joking, Paise?' His horrified expression is not complimentary; Jen wouldn't feel great if she could see this reaction.

'She dropped enough hints during that week we spent in Bulgaria.'

'No, she didn't.' Joseph grimaces as if I've said the most ridiculous thing ever.

'She did!' A flame of annoyance reignites deep inside me. I'm as pissed off now as I was back then, when she wore that little red dress and laughed so loudly at his jokes in that hyena-like way of hers. She never laughed like that normally, when we used to meet up for coffee.

'No way! Jaime was like a brother to me – he never mentioned it, not once.'

'He mentioned it to me, on more than one occasion,' I say. Joseph's jaw drops wide. 'It unsettled him.' I cock my head in his direction, as if silently driving home my point.

'What? You honestly thought I'd crack on with my best mate's wife?' he says. 'Bloody hell, you've got such a high opinion of me.'

A wall of silence falls between us. I shuffle my stance, not sure whether to leave the room or not. Joseph refolds his newspaper.

'Anyway, that's in the past now, so why let it rattle you?' he says finally.

'I'm not rattled,' I say, clearly rattled to the core. 'I'm just saying how it is – because I have no reason not to nowadays. Back then it probably wouldn't have been a wise move, given how attentive she was towards you, but now . . .' I shrug, as if to prove how little it matters to me now.

Joseph starts to laugh.

'What's so funny?'

'But now . . . but now I might well take her up on the offer, even though I was never interested in the first place?'

'Why joke about it, then?' I snap, irked by his reply.

'Because that's what us single guys do, apparently. Once we have an ex-wife, we chase our mate's . . . no, correction: ex-mate's wife, just because we can. What's the world coming to?'

'You should know!' My comment hits the bull's eye. Joseph's smile vanishes, and he looks hurt by my insinuation. I shouldn't have said that.

'You're absolutely right. Men like me, who dally around outside of their marriage, know exactly what the world is coming to – yep, of course we do!' Joseph looks around as if seeking his own distraction from the reopening of old wounds. When he doesn't find anything or anyone else, he shrugs before adding, 'Anyway, I'll leave you to it. I'm taking up too much of your time. Enjoy your girls' outing.'

Chapter Fifteen

Mid-morning

Selena

'Gather round, please. I promise I don't bite,' announces the young woman, donning an unfashionable but necessary hair net and white lab coat. I smile politely as the three of us reluctantly shuffle forward, creating a semi-circle alongside a family of three as we await her introduction. The excited daughter is jigging about on the spot but firmly tethered to her father's hand. 'Welcome to the Chocolate Box. My name is Tanya and I'll be your chocolate host for today.' As a marketing nerd, I flinch a little. I can't argue with the nature of her role or the glorious materials of her craft, but I would definitely object if any boss wanted me to go with 'chocolate host'. That's not a title anyone wants on their CV. Even Willy Wonka had better sense regarding his Oompa-Loompas.

I fix my gaze on Tanya as she continues her clearly well-rehearsed welcome speech, because I mustn't catch Paisley's eye. Otherwise we'll end up giggling like a couple of immature schoolgirls. And Kate will be majorly peeved if we embarrass her in public, as she definitely doesn't do immature giggling. We do, though.

'We are expecting some more guests to join our party, so if I could ask that we wait a few minutes, that would be wonderful.'

We stand silently before her, each wearing a logoed Chocolate

Factory pinny over pristine white lab coats and dinner-lady style hairnets, patiently awaiting the late arrivals. Beside us is a horse-shoe arrangement of stainless-steel tables upon which are numerous spatulas, plastic moulds for reindeers, and an array of dishes containing colourful but edible decorations. I deduce from this that we're making our own festive reindeer; next week's participants will probably begin the Easter egg season, I suspect. I've also spied the giant chocolate fountain in the far corner of room, and clocked the nearest shelving display, which it's hard not to drool over. I can imagine sampling each decorative box: Turkish delight, coffee caramels, strawberry creams, mint creams, nougat, honeycomb ... How embarrassed would our Kate be if I launched myself at the neatly stocked shelves and began tearing off the cellophane wrappers, as every nerve of my body is twitching to do? Already, within seconds of our arrival, I'd pressed my nose flush to the window, desperate for them to open up early just for us. I wanted to smell, lick and all round indulge. Frankly, I wouldn't mind being locked in here after hours. Heaven on earth!

Not that I'd say I was a chocoholic. Yes, I consume slabs and chunks whatever the season, festive or otherwise. But a chocolate *lover* is how I'd term it. And yet I have no true lover in life. Mmmm, which can I live without the longest?

'Could I wash my hands while we wait?' asks Kate, gesturing towards a row of sinks a distance away.

'Good idea,' says Tanya, more casual now her opening speech is out of the way. As usual, Kate clearly trying to save us from wasting time and wants to get our chocolate experience up and running efficiently – organising others is her thing. Paisley and I follow her lead.

'Who in their right mind is late for a playdate with chocolate?' Kate whispers, as I roll my sleeves up and she double pumps the wall-mounted soap dispenser.

'Exactly. We, meanwhile, arrived ten minutes before our booking time, thanks to you,' I reply. But that's my sister. She can knock up a decent cooked brekkie and arrange an outing in the time it takes to decide what outfit to wear. Google it, book it and enjoy – swift, efficient and secure. But I was thrilled when I learned of her booking.

'Them, that's who!' scowls Paisley, pointing a wet hand towards the large display window overlooking the pedestrian walkway. Carlos and co. are casually sauntering across the forecourt towards the entrance, clearly in no rush.

'Urgh! Of all the places they could go, they walk into *our* chocolate factory.' The sentiment escapes before I could mute it.

'That's bloody great,' sighs Paisley, drying her hands. 'Day two of scuppered plans.'

'Sorry we're late,' says Joseph to the chocolate host. 'A slight problem held us up.'

'Like not wishing to attend,' moans Carlos, staring at us three, before offering a genuine smile to the family of three.

'Be nice, ladies,' mutters Kate, before speaking up. 'Hi fellas, didn't expect to see you here.'

'Not my choice, believe me.' Carlos is shaking his head as he takes in the industrial stainless-steel surroundings of the factory, the glass partition separating us from the shop, and the huge vats of chocolate.

'Please tell me you're several hours earlier for your chosen session and not the missing trio making up our session?' I ask, knowing the answer but chancing my luck.

'Apologies, but we are the three,' says Affie, directly to Kate, as if she'd spoken.

'Ooof,' I sigh, and turn to Kate, 'can we not cancel and organise this for another day?'

'No. We're not leaving. We booked first,' snaps Paisley, throwing daggers at the three men now donning their lab coats.

'Welcome, gents,' calls Tanya, her flat introduction tone returning.

Joseph offers his usual head nod in our direction and Affie seems to be blushing slightly. At least they have the decency to look slightly embarrassed, whereas Carlos clearly doesn't give a monkeys about cramping our style.

I don't wish to appear selfish, but why can't they give us a chance to enjoy ourselves on an all-inclusive girls' week away! How a chocolate tour comes under the umbrella of enjoying a boys' week of TV sports is beyond me. Joseph doesn't particularly like chocolate, if I remember correctly. He's more a savoury person. Though, given Paisley's taut expression, that detail is providing little comfort now.

'If you three gents wouldn't mind donning your aprons and hair nets before washing your hands? And for the gent with the beard, Affie, is it? You'll be needing a beard mask too,' explains the session leader, gesturing towards various boxes while speaking.

'Nice accessories,' mutters Carlos, nudging his buddy. Affie touches his beard protectively.

'Sorry. It's a health and hygiene requirement when handling food,' explains Tanya, sounding genuinely apologetic.

Chapter Sixteen

Paisley

I keep my eyes on our chocolate host. I can't look up, as Joseph keeps staring at me, his dark eyes scrutinising my every breath. It's my own fault. I should have done the sensible thing and simply left when the boys filed in. Or, better still, continued to walk when I reached the garden gate yesterday afternoon, rather than agreeing to this shambles. How ridiculous am I? Sharing a festive-holiday-come-birthday-staycation with a man I vowed never to put asunder. In hindsight, I was far too eager to agree to such vows. I don't even know what 'asunder' means, but I definitely promised it. I've proof on a wedding video. And it's a good thing the said video is actually digital, given the number of times I have played it while sitting alone, with the curtains drawn, accompanied only by my 'friends', Ben and Jerry. And a spoon. Be it a teaspoon, soup or tablespoon, maybe even a serving spoon – whichever I grab first. I gorge myself to chase away those negative feelings of sadness, low self-worth and isolation – spoon by spoon I try to make myself feel better, but without success.

Oh God, now he's come to stand beside me. Go away, Joseph. Go, go, go! And bloody take your new mates with you. I don't like your new haircut, your trendy aftershave – who even puts aftershave on to visit a chocolate factory? Carlos probably, but not the Joseph I know. Bloody hell, *knew*! The Joseph I once knew. I won't pretend I know this one. I took my vows with a heart filled with joy and love and hope and everything that is good in this world. I believed in them. I wanted them. I upheld them. I lived by them each and every day that we were man and wife. How on earth did my life come to this? As man and wife, we stood before an altar, which seems like a joke now I'm standing here beside him watching a woman explain the importance of the cocoa bean.

As Tanya, our chocolate host, passes around the nugget of goodness for inspection, as Joseph casually hands me the oblong brown nugget – I've never felt so lonely in my entire life. Who would have predicted it would come to this during that celebration with the four groomsmen, six bridesmaids, a page boy and flower girl, followed by a reception in a ginormous marquee – wasn't that enough to signify our devotion to one another? Obviously not!

I'm the innocent party. As lily white as lily white can be. Not a spot or blemish of gossip to stain my character. It might sound all goody-two-shoes but I'm proud of how I've conducted myself, head held high, with dignity intact and squarely in place. Apart from that ridiculous show of opening the garden gate yesterday!

'And this, ladies and gents, is the basic raw ingredients for the chocolate that you know and love,' explains Tanya, grabbing another handful of beans from the nearest hessian sack among those piled against the wall. 'You'd need about 400 beans to create a pound of chocolate. Fifty per cent of all cocoa is currently grown in the Ivory Coast and Ghana. The bean is valued throughout the world for its glorious oils, texture and final product. Chocolate, in fact, is considered higher than a basic food, more as a potion for love.'

A potion? Oh, is it now! Not in my sodding book! I snort, clearly louder than I expected, given that both Selena and Kate turn around to look at me. I apologetically wave away their concern. Never have I read in any of my multitude of self-help 'Get over your divorce in 30 days' books to just buy a sodding bar of Dairy Milk and be done with it!

'Do you remember the hissy fit you threw when my brother ate your birthday chocolates that year?' asks Joseph, leaning in to whisper to me.

I say 'no' primly, but I vividly remember the wailing and tears involved when I realised he'd eaten the entire box.

Tanya ushers us towards the ginormous vat of warm choc- olate. I'm mesmerised by the mechanical paddle rhythmically gliding through the rich brown liquid, creating a deep swirl and fold effect before repeating the manoeuvre over and over. I could watch this all day. I fight the urge to dunk my head into that vat and slurp. It would definitely make me happy, I think, and silence my inner demons before they have a chance to resurrect. I just can't cope with this whole situation. It's absurd. I take thee, Joseph Lefroy McLoughlin – an absurd name, I always thought – as my lawful wedded husband. To have and to hold until this day forward, when we inspect a cocoa bean in each other's company and then casually pass it to a third party to inspect. How ridiculous can life get? I promised to bear him children, yet here I am tentatively taking a bean from him as if it were the most delicate object in the world. Yesterday, I thought I was being mature and zen when I agreed, but this ... this is simply crazy. I can't function like this for an entire week. Much like breakfast this morning, I suspect staying entirely mute is the only way not to allow things to slip out. Joseph keeps glancing at me. Dream on, mate.

I've been thrown into a life that I never wished nor hoped for, which seems to now include watching a chocolate host pulp the warm cocoa bean between her fingers to paste. That's pretty much the same state I was in after Joseph left. Maybe I should take note of her talk, and apply the same principles to my own life, hoping that it too can become as sweet as chocolate, once blended with other ingredients.

'Are you OK?' Joseph keeps checking on me.

'Me? I'm fine. You?'

'Perfectly well, thank you.'

I want to say – I bet you sodding are, with your new haircut, your swagger and your new best buddies. Life must be a bloody dream! But instead I smile sweetly and sniff the cocoa bean before passing it to Selena.

Chapter Seventeen

Selena

I'm lost in a world of milk chocolate, busying myself filling a piping bag with dollops of the warm satiny-smooth chocolate, when I feel something land on my face. I instinctively wipe and check my fingertips: milk chocolate. How in heaven's name did I manage to daub my own cheek? Ridiculous. I lick my fingers – can't waste the good stuff! I return to filling the piping bag. I've got some big ideas for decorating my Christmas reindeer with swirls of thick chocolate along its neck, adding a sprinkle or two of edible glitter, a decorative candy shell or two and a garland of candy sweets – I can picture it in my head. If our chocolate host wants us to have a mini-competition, then I'm in. So far my inflated ideas of my chocolatier skills are a total mismatch to the reality, but nothing that can't be bridged with hard work and determination. Sure, my efforts so far don't match the image in my head, but only because I didn't realise piping bags were so troublesome. It's not as easy as those pros on the telly make it appear. My imagination has conjured up a chocolate reindeer worthy of prime position in Harrods' Christmas window. The reality, however, looks more worthy of a child's craft session at nursery school. Yet I'm having the best time. Still, it's a good job other creatives are deployed to produce the ads my muse conjures up, as there's no way I'd have collected the professional accolades I have otherwise. I've got the brain, and bags full of self-belief when I tackle any promotion, but even at my most deluded I know I don't have the skill set to go it alone. Nah, I delegate left, right and centre, ensuring I have the best bods surrounding me, and together we get the job done. Boost the sales, smash the predicted goals and win the shiny coveted awards that line my mantlepiece.

Plop. A spot of chocolate lands on the arm of my white coat. I did it again. Get a grip, girl! I need to be more careful. I glance up and notice Carlos smiling inanely at me. What's he looking at? Isn't he missing his TV sports schedule yet? Isn't it time for a beer refill? Clearly not, given that he's faffing about scraping his mixing bowl with a large serving spoon. The others are all heads lowered, engrossed in their own fabulous creations. Even Affie, who's still wearing his beardy face mask. I thought he'd have snuck off by now. I would have. Lord knows whose idea it was to follow our example, though Kate swears she didn't mention booking tickets while cooking breakfast. I've a good mind to ask our chocolate host for the precise time of their booking, see if we were indeed first this time!

I carefully position my reindeer so it's standing squarely before me, gather the ends of my bulging piping bag and twist, forcing the contents towards the fine nozzle. This is going to be superb, the best of the lot. The owners are going to want to clear their current window display and put my reindeer centre stage for the remainder of their festive season. In fact, it'll be so good they'll probably want to extend their festive decorations way past the twelfth night. Possibly until the end of January! Though, on second thoughts, I'd like to take it home. Unless I make two reindeer stunners, if my talent can stretch to that. I might never eat this masterpiece but save it as an ornament for my kitchen cabinet. Or keep it in case of emergencies, when only chocolate will do. Not that my life has much stress nowadays. Once you kick dating to the kerb, so to speak, you have very little worry in life. Men: the source of all that is bloody evil, be it dating disasters, divorce or babies. You can't live with them and yet most women can't sodding well live without them! Thankfully, I've finally learned how. So has our Kate. Though Paisley would give her right arm to have a decent loving man back in her life, I suspect, as I know she still craves a family.

I roll my shoulders, working out the tension, and focus on the job in hand. I'm going to do my very best to create a swirling mane ... plop. Three splatters of chocolate land in a neat line up my sleeve ... how the hell? I couldn't have created that by accident, given the direction of the splatter pattern. I look around but am greeted by nine bowed heads. And yet ... Carlos' shoulders are shaking uncontrollably as he attempts to suppress a belly laugh. Aha!

'I suppose you think that's funny?' I say. Everyone stops working and looks up.

'Sorry? Are you talking to me?' He acts the innocent.

'Yes, you. You're flicking chocolate at me. Stop it!' I show my splattered sleeve as proof to the group, who then turn to Carlos. Tanya shakes her head, while the father of the family looks away first, uninterested, and suggests his daughter remove the unicorn horn she's added to her festive reindeer.

'Why would I do such a thing?' ask Carlos, still battling laughter.

Why indeed? The others don't seem interested in my chocolate woes, so I return to my task, preparing to pipe the world's best and most intricate decoration.

'Oi!' shrieks Kate. 'Whoever did that, stop it!' She's staring at the three guys. A splatter of chocolate ruins the front of her clean pinny.

'Here, Kate,' says Affie, quickly offering her a paper towel from the nearest wall-mounted dispenser. 'Guys, can we stop this stupidity now – it'll end in tears.' The family of three are blank faced and exchanging glances with each other. I imagine they're wishing they'd booked another time slot. I'm sure the awkward vibe between us three is rather spoiling their chocolate experience. Tanya looks alarmed. Joseph and Carlos each protest their innocence. I shake my head at Kate, offering commiserations that her overall have been splattered too. Of our party, only Paisley remains pristine in white. Though given her faraway expression, she's not exactly with us.

'Oi!' The father suddenly shouts.

We look up to see a huge splattering of chocolate running across all three of them, like a chocolate strike through. For the two adults, the splatter is across their chests, but the girl has a direct hit splattered across her face, cheek-nose-cheek, much like Adam Ant's nose stripe back in the day. She looks delighted, however, until she picks up on her parents' frosty glare.

Affie takes one look at the situation before roughly snatching the large metal spoon from Carlos' hand and growling something at him. I watch in admiration as Affie steps forward, offering the child a paper towel to help her clean up (which she seems a little reluctant to do).

'Ooops, sorry, folks,' says Carlos. 'I didn't mean it to get you.'

'Didn't you? Are you sure about that?' The father lifts his spoon from the nearest mixing bowl and furiously thwacks it in Carlos' direction, sending a flurry of chocolate splatters flying about his head and shoulders.

'Hey! I said I was sorry. It was an accident,' protests Carlos, wiping chocolate from his face, but then, quick as a flash, retaliating in the father's direction. Unfortunately, it lands in the mother's hair instead and droplets spray everywhere.

'Oi, you got me too that time!' hollers Joseph, clearly peeved.

Carlos holds his hands up in surrender, as a thick dollop of milk chocolate flies across the tables, smacking him directly in the mouth and nose.

'Cut it out!' he snaps, clearly not amused to be on the receiving end.

I never imagined I'd get a direct hit first time!

'You started it – not so funny now, is it?' I chide, pretty pleased with my shot.

'Ladies and gents, please, please . . .' demands Tanya with some urgency, her hands flapping.

We all mutter a soft apology. I'd quite forgotten she was even there. We resume our activity in strained silence, just a busy bunch of tourists happily decorating our reindeers with coloured sprinkles. Until a dollop of warm milk chocolate lands in my hair, which was freshly washed only this morning, igniting round two.

Carlos hasn't learnt his lesson, so thinks it's highly amusing.

'Yeah, yeah. We all know how much you performers love your body art and melted chocolate, Carlos. Parading like peacocks, delivering a repertoire of nifty but oh so intimate dance moves, but I am *not* a willing member of your screaming audience!' I scoop a dollop of precious chocolate from my large metal bowl and thwack it in his direction faster than he can defend himself.

'Funny that. For a moment there I thought I recognised you from the front row of last week's performance!'

He might have started this, but I will end it!

Chapter Eighteen

Early Afternoon

Kate

'I've never been so embarrassed in my life!' I say, as we head inside the Queen's Head pub in search of much needed gin. Three double gins with a splash of tonic, ice and a slice are most definitely necessary right now. I'm so het up I don't care whether they stock any trendy fancy pants tonic water or not. I'm counting on a big slug of gin to help me wipe the disaster we've just left behind from my mind. It was hardly the fault of our chocolate host, but swifter intervention, and possibly a police taser, might have at least prevented things from escalating so quickly.

My fury has grown with every step along the main street from the chocolate factory and now we're standing in the centre of the pub's noisy bar area. Our surroundings are traditional in every sense, with a red tiled floor, leaded-glass windows and a low beamed ceiling. Slightly unusual but nostalgic paintings of dogs line the walls, and wooden bench seats edge the room, with sturdy oak tables positioned at regular intervals. Paisley's busy securing a quiet one for us among the festive revellers.

Buzz. My phone vibrates in my jumpsuit pocket, much like it had throughout our chocolate experience. I ignore it. I'm supposed to be on a break. Psycho-boss can wait for a change. I've completed my task list, arranging everything he and his brood might need for a larger-than-life, ultra-fancy engagement party. Now I'm on my own time until I choose to answer.

Selena stands beside me. Her hair is pulled back into a bobble, but smears of chocolate are visible at each temple. Carlos, Tanya and the small child definitely came off worse. Selena's reaching for her purse, but I know it's a gesture and she'll assume I'll get to mine first. I'm no longer offended by my sister's 'little sister' habits – they're par for the course for us at this point. She has her faults, but I can't blame her for playing her part to my 'big sister' act. We come as a pair and have perfected our intended roles in life. It just wouldn't work if the roles were reversed. I retrieve my purse from my handbag, which contains everything but the kitchen sink, from a natty nylon bag in case I purchase additional goods, sunglasses, wine coasters with corporate logos, spare change for parking, hair bobbles, hair grips, even a CPR mask – 'in case I come across an emergency'. Nothing is essential, apart from my purse, but everything else is 'just in case' – which sums me up pretty well. I'm an organised person who thinks ahead. Though on this occasion my emergency stock of wet wipes proved futile and utterly useless when it came to the end result of flying chocolate.

'I've never seen a child fully coated in milk chocolate before,' says Selena, attempting to lighten the mood.

I need gin quicker than this bar man is delivering it. Thankfully Paisley has secured a spot and settled at a decent table where we can regroup, calm down and decide on our next step for this birthday week.

'Nor me. Though I think your apology was lacking in sincerity, given that you caused the ruckus.'

'I never – he did! You heard what Affie said yesterday – Carlos' always acting the fool! Well, today, he picked the wrong person and took it too far.'

I say nothing. I refuse to argue. Especially when the barman has just appeared before me, eager to serve. I swiftly order before continuing my conversation. 'Yes. He started with the flicking, but, Selena, you goaded him about his work. What the hell did you expect him to do? Lie down and take it?'

'Actually, I think that's their go-to thing when lashings of warmed chocolate appear on stage. If he's that touchy about being a stripper, he should find an office job! I was only joking – there was no need to lose the plot and start lobbing chocolate at me.'

'In front of a child – how inappropriate, Selena.'

'I forgot she was there, OK? She wouldn't have noticed anyway ... she was too engrossed with her unicorn creation. I thought the father was going to have a coronary when that bowl was tipped over her.'

I shake my head, trying to erase the image of a chocolate-covered child. 'I can't imagine that Tanya will be hosting any more tours today – she'll need a lie down after our session.'

'Probably a shower too.' Selena barks with laughter but stops when she catches my glare of disapproval. 'Sorry. But you've got to admit it was funny.'

Buzz. There goes my phone again, vying for my attention. The barman returns with our drinks. I wish I'd ordered triples now, given how I'm feeling.

I give her daggers. Love her as I do, at times my sister's off the scale. When pitched against the likes of Carlos, her competitive streak is sure to make an appearance, and then she'll do battle until she has won.

'You've got the devil in you today,' I mutter, pushing a glass into her hand.

'Why, thank you. My big birthday week is definitely off to a flying start – be that milk, dark or ruby chocolate with added glitter sprinkles.'

'Could you take that to Paisley. And, please, behave yourself in here, Selena.' She's crossed a line but hopefully that's the last of her high jinks for one day.

Selena does as I ask for once. Pity she didn't thirty minutes ago. I've never been asked to leave anywhere in my life, be it a bar or a nightclub. I never imagined I'd be barred from a chocolate factory by a chocolate-covered employee. I did offer to help clean up, but Tanya's boss was having none of it. I hope that nice little girl doesn't take a leaf out of my sister's book regarding behaviour. Having witnessed two adults do battle with a vat of warm chocolate, her belief in grown-ups, fairy tales and unicorns may have been a little bit skewed. If she were mine, I'd arrange a counselling session, just to be on the safe side.

I'm starting to relax by the time Selena collects our third round. The pub has a warm, welcoming atmosphere and the festive cheer is flowing freely. Much like the chocolate had earlier. I smile, finally able to appreciate the funny side.

'Do you remember that sleepover when you snuck half a bottle of vodka out of Dad's drinks' cabinet and ended up puking all over the duvets and each other?' I ask, glancing at the other two and doing my best to forget about the multitude of text messages stacking up in my phone.

'I don't think that was us!' retorts Selena.

Paisley begins to giggle.

'I think you'll find it was! You woke Mum up with your noisy antics – she was *not* amused with the pair of you.'

'When I got back home I was grounded for a week,' says Paisley.

'Really? I don't remember that. How old were we?'

'About fifteen, I think. We drank it neat . . . urgh!'

'No way! Sorry, but I've never drunk pure vodka,' states Selena, sitting up in agitation.

'We did, I swear. Swigged it from the bottle, as you'd forgotten to smuggle glasses upstairs,' corrects Paisley. 'Kate's right. Your mother stripped the beds in the middle of the night and put a white wash on.'

'It was probably the racket you were making with your giggling and squawking that gave you away – you were totally out of it. Dad thought you maybe needed a trip to hospital, but Mum was so mad with you both she literally forced water down your necks and then plied you both with black coffees.'

'She wouldn't let us sleep, would she? She made us walk around the lounge.'

'Are you sure I was there?'

'Yes!' Paisley and I say in unison.

Silence descends, allowing us each to savour our fresh drinks before Selena gives me a cheeky grin.

'What?' I ask.

'Affie seems nice,' she observes.

'He does.' I shut her down. I know her game.

'Well?'

'Well, nothing, Selena. This week's about you and your big birthday, nothing else.'

'But if something more comes of it, then yay! Maybe . . . that's simply a bit of good fortune.'

'Is it now?'

'Don't try telling me that you haven't noticed how attentive he is. Didn't you see how obliging he was during the chocolate decoration or how he stepped in to help that little girl?'

I shrug. I figure I can play along with her chatter without committing myself. He certainly moved like lightening to provide paper towels from the dispenser when I needed them, though. Not to mention the frequent glances across the tables when we were decorating our reindeer.

'I reckon you've got lots in common: a quiet disposition with a strong sense of self . . .'

'Mmmm,' I mutter. Yeah, and both of us have to put up with bloody idiots accompanying us through life.

'Mmmm nothing, sis – what are you waiting for?'

Now, there's a question. I keep my own counsel.

'You of all people should be ready to start venturing out there. It's not as if you haven't enjoyed your hibernation after your divorce. You've probably enjoyed it a little too much, doing your own thing every weekend, visiting places and expanding your horizons. Maybe this is perfect timing for the new year ahead?'

I'm listening. I'm hearing what she says. I'm even somewhat in agreement. Have I the heart to seek something new at this stage? Or am I protecting myself by remaining as I am? I'm content right now. I'm comfortable in my own skin doing as I am – so why change? Just for change's sake? Nope, that's not enough. Not after Cody's behaviour, with all that running up debts and outstanding IOUs. To think I nearly lost the roof over my head because of his gambling addiction. Never again. It would take a lot for me to trust someone. My love life can wait for another time, another week – definitely not the week of my sister's big birthday bash. She's not wrong, though. I have been focused on looking after myself, taking time to readjust to my status in life. I've visited no end of new places, travelled, explored. So, yeah, if the right man came along, I wouldn't be in a rush to refuse some decent company – a few nights out or interesting conversation added to the mix of my daily routine.

'But?'

I look up, startled by the ongoing line of questioning.

'Sorry, but what?'

'I sense there's a "but" coming . . .'

She's got me on the metaphorical ropes and her instincts are right, but I don't have to elaborate, because doing so will make me sound shallow. I purse my mouth, as if internally locking it down and refusing to answer. I'm not one of those superficial people, but I have certain preferences, one biggie being a natural attraction towards an individual. Nothing forced. Nothing constructed or feigned. I need that instant 'zing' of chemistry that occurs between two people. I don't need nice guys telling me how nice they are – I need 'zing'. That silent and stealth-like 'zing' that sneaks up on you when you're least expecting it. I accept people for who they are and can overlook the modern obsession with 'ick' factors, but ... a man bun? Nope. The no-socks is one thing, but the hair, nah – I can't see past it. Which clearly makes me a bad person. I'll hold my hands up: I am far from perfect. But surely instinct counts for something? And my instinct recoils without a conscious thought. I've probably got plenty of 'ick' qualities myself, qualities that others, namely men, will have recoiled from, but I accept I'm not everyone's cup of tea. I'm Kate. Uptight, stressed out and usually more interested in my to-do list Kate. My need to assist and organise, my role as a people pleaser, a helper, all align with my big-sister attributes, which others must find annoying. My ex-husband certainly did – Cody even tried to list them as grounds for our divorce. Thankfully he was saved by our irreconcilable differences, at the root of which was his gambling addiction.

'It's the man bun, isn't it?'

My eyes widen. She's got me.

'I knew it. The no socks doesn't help either, but can't you look past the hair? He seems a great guy.'

'Selena!'

'I'm only asking,' she continues.

I laugh. My God, she truly rushes in where angels fear to tread. Only my little sister.

'Oh, to be more like you and simply say it how it is in life,' says Paisley. She's barely strung a coherent sentence together these last two days. Not that she needs to explain to the likes of us; we'll accept her without question even when she retreats into her own shell. We understand why. I'm sad to see she has that despondent expression again, the one she wore for the majority of last year. When nothing in life interested her, nothing seemed to bring her pleasure and no one could make up for the hurt and pain she'd suffered. It's as if the empty void has returned along with Joseph McLoughlin.

'Believe me, you don't want to follow my lead – it gets you into no end of trouble. But I'm right, aren't I?'

'You're right. There. Does that make you feel better? He seems a decent sort, attentive, aware and balanced, when compared to the other two, and I wouldn't mind getting . . .'

At that very moment the pub's main entrance swings open, and in walk three familiar figures. Freshly washed, spruced and decked in clean clothes, they're ready to enjoy a quick jar in their current local.

'Oh, great!' Selena grumbles. Then she hollers, 'Is the sport channel cancelled today?', unconsciously touching her chocolate smeared hairline.

'Behave yourself,' I admonish her, catching sight of how pale Paisley has become.

Chapter Nineteen

Paisley

'I see Kate and Selena still have your back,' says Joseph, thumbing over his shoulder towards the bar, where our next round is being taken care of by Kate. Behind her stands Carlos, waiting to buy the guys' next round. The other two have disappeared, separately but together, in search of toilets. Leaving us two sitting awkwardly on neighbouring tables, yet facing one another, with little to distract other than meaningless chit chat. The alternative is silence. We've lived through silence before: immediately after his confession, during his suitcase packing session, and finally at the joint meeting with the solicitors to discuss our divorce settlement. I vowed never again, though at least this time there is the promise of a stiff drink, unlike the previous occasions.

The only free table had been the one beside ours, and so the three of them had settled themselves nearby, but this meant our conversation was punctuated by overheard snippets of their conversation, stuff like: 'Do you remember that time we had to rescue . . . ?', 'I don't reckon we'd have found that couple that night, if it wasn't for . . .' and even 'That call out was the worst because . . .' Not that us girls were listening, but you can't help hearing what is said close by, can you?

'Why wouldn't they have my back?' I say, answering Joseph's remark.

'No reason. Life changes, situations change and people move on – that's all. Is Selena OK about earlier?'

'What, the chocolate fight that Carlos started, you mean?'
'Yeah.'

'Sort of. She has chocolate smeared in her hairline, so please don't mention it, right? She wanted to go straight home, but Kate wouldn't allow her to. Though Kate's majorly ticked off too, so doubly don't mention it, otherwise she'll just be even more wound up that her planning went to pot.'

'Which *never* happens.'

'Exactly. Unlike yours. You planned to spend the rest of your life with me but accidently knobbed someone during a night out – not such a great planner after all, eh, Joseph? Maybe get Kate to plan your next marriage and you might have more success!' I'm better than this, but I can't help poking the bear.

'Paise, stop being so tetchy. I'm trying to get along, given the circumstances. Or do you want me to sit here in complete silence until a third party joins us to mediate? I can't make the bartender serve them any faster, you know?'

'Mmmm.'

'What? You think I could try a little harder to speed him up with the optics?' He calls towards the bar, 'Oi, mate, please hurry up – the ex-wife is not impressed with your performance.' Then turns back to me. 'There, did that work? No.' Several other customers turn around in their seats to stare at us. But mainly at him.

'Ha ha, you think you're so bloody funny, don't you? Well, you're not! I've had funnier moments with a verruca,' I whisper harshly, hoping no one clocks my tone. But couldn't I have come up with something better than that? Surely verrucas are tame compared to other ailments.

'Please don't bother, Paise – you've never mastered sarcasm.'
'I have.'
'When?'
'Since you left.' The words literally spit from my mouth.
'Congratulations. Your parents must be thrilled.'

There's a lengthy pause, and I just want him to drop it and leave me alone. But he's Joseph McLoughlin, so he has to keep going. 'So, how are the old buggers since I last saw them – George and his dragon doing OK, are they?'

I can't believe him!

'My father's fine.' I stall, knowing what's coming.

'Good to hear ... and his dragon?'

I don't attempt to soften the blow of my delivery. He can have it, both barrels, right between the eyeballs.

'My mum died seven months ago, if you must know. Cancer.' Joseph's jaw drops wide.

'Paise, I'm so very ...' Instantly he reaches for my hand to offer comfort, but I snatch it back, avoiding all contact. I don't want him to touch me now he's touched others.

'Save it! I don't want to hear it from you.' I wrap my arms about myself in an act of self-protection.

'I'm sincerely sorry. I didn't know ... no one said.'

I scrunch up my features, attempting to hold back the tears. 'Why would they? You're the ex-son-in-law and I don't think Hallmark stocks a condolence card designed for that.' When did I learn to be so venomous? Especially to the one I'd loved so much? But I hate him so much in this moment.

'Paise, come on now. You know that was always her jokey nickname – she was always alright with me. Until ... well until, you know – she wasn't.'

'When you cheated on her only daughter with some drunk slapper you picked up in town one night – yeah, that sounds like my mum being a total dragon.'

'Paise, please. This is no joking matter.'

'You don't say!' I wish the others would return to the table and save me from this conversation.

'I'm sorry. Honesty, I didn't know. I hadn't heard. How could I? I don't see or hear from anyone any more. I don't do social media or the snap chat stuff like you ladies do. I don't hear from my team mates, play footie or meet up with the old crowd like I once did. Our parents didn't keep in touch after we split, so how would I know? I haven't seen you since . . . well, there was that fleeting moment, but that was months ago. Do you seriously think I'm so awful I'd ask after her if I knew the answer?'

'It was March time. Nine months ago.' I hear my bland statement of the fact, and the thought of the time that's passed hits home, hard. A double whammy of sorts. One off-chance meeting in the car park of a sprawling shopping complex – he leaving, me just arriving. Ironic, I suppose. Nine long and painful months. Months filled with spring, summer and autumn and now wintertime. Nine whole months in which we could have had the dream of all dreams . . . instead we're sitting opposite each other awaiting a round of drinks in an unfamiliar pub, arguing about his reference to my late mother. What the hell! How did this become my life?

'How's your dad coping?' he asks solemnly, attempting to rectify his error.

'How does anyone cope once they've lost their life partner of thirty-three years?'

'Badly, I'd imagine. It's tough enough after . . .' His words fade but I get his meaning.

'Exactly. He's not good, but he's trying his best.' Much as I struggled to do some eighteen months ago and then had to repeat again after the bereavement.

Joseph nods, lost in thought.

'And your family?' I ask, trying to put the conversation on safer footing.

Joseph pauses before answering, a slight flush colouring his cheek.

'Seriously. I am interested. After all, they never did me any harm.'

'I know. I . . . they're all good, thanks – over the moon, in fact, as there's a grandkiddie on the way.' Joseph bites his lip. He knows the news will sting, deeply. And it does. My pain registers instantly. I swiftly rearrange my features, ensuring I convey the appropriate delight for others while hiding my own pain. A habit born of recent times.

'Ahhh, that's lovely, but which sibling . . . who's expecting?' My mind reels with his brother and sister's names. Last I heard, neither one was settled in life with committed partners.

'Anthony . . . and his new girlfriend – a little sooner than he'd hoped, I think. But everyone's on board now and looking to the future . . . and the little one.'

'Oh.' The word drops from my lips, plunging to the tiled floor along with my heavy heart. Why could Affie or Carlos not have stayed behind to bagsie their table. I could have mustered a conversation about football results, but instead I have to endure this. 'That's nice.'

'My parents were shocked at first – they'd only been together for a very short time, but these things happen.'

I'm narked. Majorly pissed off at the universe, all in the space of a heartbeat. How can that be? How can that happen for others? That was *our* plan. Planned and prepped and planned and . . . and dreamed of and . . . wanted and needed and . . .

'Yeah, it can happen when folks . . .' I can't bring myself to say what I really do want to say. The usual niceties. But my bitterness will spill out upon the floor tiles and someone will need to clean that mess up before others trip, fall and hurt themselves. How has it come to pass that Joseph McLoughlin will become an uncle before he becomes a father, a father to our child? How? Who planned that one? 'As long as everyone is happy and healthy – that's all that matters.' I literally force each word into existence to keep from falling apart right in front of him. 'Anyway, I must nip to the ladies.' I flee the table before my eyes can fill with tears. This was not the news I needed before New Year. In fact, this was not the news that I ever needed to hear at any time in my life. The McLoughlins soon having a lovely new baby in their family, but one that did not carry my DNA, was never supposed to happen. As selfish as that may seem, if our baby – Joseph's and mine – was never going to exist ... why the hell should any of them get a McLoughlin baby instead? The unfairness of it all breaks my heart all over again. I swiftly navigate my way through the crowded bar, my vision blinded by the surge of tears distorting my view. *When* is this sodding nightmare going to end?

Chapter Twenty

Selena

'What do you do for work, Selena?' asks Affie, leaning over to our table, clearly being polite and trying to include me in the conversation.

'I work in marketing, advertising . . . that sort of thing,' I say nonchalantly.

'Boring, is it?' ask Carlos. Mmmm, direct as ever.

'Actually, no. I, of course, find it interesting, but I've learnt from experience that others aren't so into the detail. Nowadays I don't tend to get into it unless people are genuinely interested. But that's fine with me. I love my job. I wouldn't choose anything else in the world to spend my time on.'

'I'm interested,' says Carlos.

'You'll regret that, mate,' says Joseph.

'Really?' I say, attempting to hide my disbelief. I still can't quite look at him properly, as I'm mad at him for what happened back at the chocolate factory.

'I'm not just saying that. Joseph here is clearly bored by the very mention of your work, but that's him.'

'I'm not. You forget I've spent years listening from the sidelines about this campaign and that campaign, and blah de blah de blah!' corrects Joseph, before sipping his Guinness.

'You didn't go blah de blah de blah when she organised a delivery of free products, did you?' points out Paisley, having my back as ever.

'Well, no, fair point,' acknowledges Joseph.

'Free stuff?' asks Carlos, his interest piqued.

'Such as?' asks Affie.

This is the moment everyone always shows most interest. Their minds whirr with the imagined glitz and the glam, but that's very different to the day-to-day reality of my industry. Their interest will dim as soon as I start listing the actual campaigns I've worked on, and then before I can even get going about all the things that still fascinate me after all this time, a certain something happens and I lose the crowd and they invariably drift away to another conversation.

'Come on, don't be shy!' urges Carlos.

'She's done some biggies, haven't you?' adds Kate, building up my part as only a sister would.

'I think so, but others . . .'

'Come off it, Selena! You can't get much bigger than the Christmas Guinness ad!' squeals Paisley, bursting with pride. 'How many times did we record it or report back when it was spotted?'

'Guinness? Bloody hell. You're up there, then,' says Affie.

'I've worked alongside some of the biggest names, if that's what you mean,' I say, a blush colouring my cheek. Why I get so embarrassed is beyond me. I've worked my ass off since leaving education and yet still I almost apologise when others realise where my efforts have been applied. I shouldn't be bashful, but I am, every time.

'Did you get freebies for that one, Joseph?' quips Carlos.

'I did, actually.'

'He did! Bloody cases of the stuff!' says Paisley. 'They filled the back wall of the garage for months on end.'

'I don't drink it, so I gave it away to someone who would appreciate it more,' I say, remembering his delight when the courier arrived.

'And very grateful I was too,' says Joseph, raising his Guinness glass in my direction. I return a smile, knowing I daren't look in Paisley's direction, as she hated the sight of it by the final few cases.

'Perk of the job,' I say, brushing off the episode as mere nothing.

'Spill, then – who else?' asks Affie excitedly.

'Like a secret lover, I don't kiss and tell,' I say, instantly regretting my coyness as Carlos' eyebrows lift.

'I'll tell you, then ... she's worked on campaigns for Sky Sports, Gillette, Cadbury's and Heinz,' says Kate, counting them off on her fingers. I smile. It's interesting to see which campaigns she remembers, and they're not necessarily the best ones I've done but the biggest named brands. 'There's others, many others, but ... my little sis has done us proud.'

'Ahhh, thank you.' I squirm under the spotlight of my sister's praise; it's rarely heard but deeply appreciated. 'Though when you love your job as much as I do, you can hardly call it work. I love pushing an idea and seeing where it lands.'

'What? As in TV adverts?' asks Carlos, sitting tall.

'TV and radio adverts, websites, internet banners, billboards, flyers in magazines, full-page newspaper ads – she's done the lot, haven't you, Selena?' says Kate, overflowing with pride.

'I loved the razor advert with the line-up of top-class footballers – each one standing before the mirror, their faces lathered up,' says Paisley.

'What I'd give to be sharing a dressing room let alone a pitch with those fellas. Can you imagine it?' says Carlos, glancing between Affie and Joseph.

'Razor sales went through the roof. If you find the right hook, the public are putty in your hands, give or take a few tweaks.'

'What are you working on now?' asks Carlos, leaning across the table, clearly wanting to hear more.

All eyes turn to me.

'I'm on my holidays ... much like everyone else,' I say, coy again.

'But afterwards, when you go back to the office – what then?' asks Affie.

'I'm heading up a brand-new campaign, which brings its own troubles. You gel with your old faithfuls and then get handed a new opportunity, but it needs fresh ideas, a new dynamic, as such. All in all, exciting times.' I glance around the table, hoping that's enough detail. 'Anyway less about me, what about the rest of you – what are your plans for the new year?' No one speaks. 'Kate? How's that psycho-boss of yours? Now, this gal deserves a medal for putting up with his antics for the last decade.'

'Still as psycho as ever – though I think his ego needs massaging more the older he gets,' says Kate, safely taking the conversation baton from my clutches.

Chapter Twenty-one

Kate

Paisley has offered to cook a late lunch for the three of us, and I'm not about to argue. Instead I grab the guest book and pen from the hallway table, pour myself a glass of wine and head to the snug for some quiet. Not that I probably need more alcohol, given our earlier drinkies, but it makes sense to marry the two together: an enjoyable read and a rosé. It sounds nerdy but I love flipping through strangers' comments about accommodation and the surrounding area in guest books like this one. You never know what you'll find in among all the 'beautiful cottage – a home from home' remarks and the generic 'best wishes from the Philips family from Pooley' messages. Sometimes there'll be a recommendation highlighting a local restaurant or a beauty spot worth visiting – it almost feels like a welcoming gift, from a stranger to a stranger. Plus, it's always fun to be nosey about complaints – if there are any.

Settling on the couch, my wine positioned next to me on the coffee table, I nestle into the corner, pulling a tartan throw over my legs for added comfort, and flip open the front cover. It's top quality: the book cover, the paper ... even the accompanying pen held fast with a loop. Just like every detail of this cottage, you could say. I read:

Thank you for choosing Lakeside Cottage, Hawkshead, for your holiday stay. We offer a blend of home comforts coupled with hospitality in an atmosphere of timeless elegance,

*within comfortable and stylish rooms and alongside un-
rivalled lakeside views of Cumbria.*

*We want you to enjoy every precious day of your stay,
so we pledge to you our service is guaranteed to meet your
highest expectations. Should you require any additional
help or information during your stay at Lakeside Cottage,
please do not hesitate to contact our local host, Josie Adams
(contact details are listed in the kitchen).*

*Please add notes or memories of your holiday to our
guest book, as it provides a true history of the many and
varied lives passing through this beautiful cottage.*

*Wishing you and yours the warmest of welcomes,
Mr and Mrs Campbell, Shetland*

I flip through the pages, eager to find any recommendations
that might satisfy our own interests. I shouldn't be feeling
guilty for taking my eye off the ball regarding organising the
little extras for Selena's big birthday bash, but I am. My little
sis deserves to have my full attention. No one else in life is as
dear to me as she is, yet I've been hiding a secret from both her
and Paisley. The engagement party. Selena, and more so Paisley,
will hit the roof if they figure out that I have stupidly arranged
everything for him: the live entertainment, free hospitality bar
and hot/cold buffet with cuisine from around the globe, as if
I were a party organiser and not just psycho-boss' PA. That
said, I've done it so well that I'm half looking at starting up
my own planning business and running it as a legit concern
between my lunch hour, coffee break and managed meetings.
But, for now, I'm on my time, so I take a huge sip of my rosé
before indulging further my nerdy appreciation for reviews
and comments.

Genevieve Garland, from Oswestry, wrote:

'*A week of self-indulgence enabling me to be myself! A fabulous stay with impeccable hospitality – excellent company, plenty of drama and a range of characters befitting a bestseller!*'

Lulu from Kettering wrote:

'*I came, I went and I bloody well conquered! I've left my fingerprints in numerous rooms and created fabulous memories in others. May you have the best bloody holiday of your life at Lakeside Cottage – I certainly did. Plus, I went home with the greatest souvenir of my life!*'

Martha, from Todmorden, wrote:

'*All you need in life under one thatched roof – clean bed sheets, an original scullery sink and a faithful Aga! On second thoughts, the old Aga beats the other two hands down!*'

Lowry Stephens, from Pendlebury, wrote:

'*A Christmas holiday to remember, forever and always. Though beware, if you hang the mistletoe above the newel post – it doesn't stop people from kissing! xx*'

I flip to the final entry and am surprised to find today's date, 28th December, beneath which is Selena's distinct sloping handwriting. I squint to read her one liner.

'*Delightful cottage: location, location, location! Superb!*'

I'm still lost in a delightful world of my own when the door bursts open and a frustrated Paisley enters, wearing a pair of quilted oven gloves, a tea-towel neckerchief and carrying a metal baking tray before her, upon which are burnt remnants.

'Kate, is this too far gone to be consumed?'

'Crisp. Burnt. To. A. Beyond. Recognition. – shuffle as you feel necessary. You decide, sweetie.'

'Personally, I think I could scrape the worst . . .'

'Nah. No one could salvage those, unless you're serving coal with onion gravy! Use the Aga, did you?'

'A first for me . . . as if you can't tell. I think I used the hottest oven. Kate . . . would you?'

I check my mobile for the time, not the number of texts. I did well clocking up twenty-three minutes of alone time with both Paisley and my sister in spitting distance. I peel myself from the leather sofa, placing the guest book on the coffee table for later. 'Remind me we need to write something witty for the guest book, otherwise we'll be letting the side down,' I say, tapping the front cover to emphasis my point.

'Fine. But first could you make something edible for dinner – otherwise it'll be coal and onion gravy after all,' mutters Paisley, feigning a woeful expression to gain sympathy.

Chapter Twenty-two

Selena

I'm standing, glass in hand, at the kitchen sink running the cold water tap – definitely in need of rehydration after our unscheduled drinkies. Carlos enters the kitchen carrying a huge bundle of prickly holly and ivy, so abundant he can't even see over the top.

'What are you doing?' I ask, filling the tumbler.

'Clearing away this festive crap. Why do you ask? What's it look like I'm doing?' he snorts, making straight for the split stable door to the garden.

'Is that from the lounge?' I ask urgently, pausing in my task.

'Yeah. From around the hearth, the mantelpiece, the doorway and picture frames.'

My jaw drops.

'What? If you haven't noticed . . . it's not Christmas any more. The housekeeper's taken the tree down so why she left all this festive crap everywhere is beyond me,' he says, as his fingers blindly grope about for the door handle.

'Don't you dare touch the hallway or the dining room or our snug!' I say, clearly irked that he didn't bother asking for our opinion.

'Phuh, if you girls want such fussy decoration, you're welcome to it. But this . . .' He wrenches the door open and launches the contents of his arms across the patio, with no thought for where it lands or who will clear it away. 'It's nothing but a distraction when you're trying to enjoy a game.'

'Bloody oaf,' I mutter, between sips of much-needed water. I've lost count of how many rounds we had, but I'm feeling the effects now.

'What did you say?' he asks, closing the back door, his task complete.

'Nothing,' I lie, continuing to drink but opening the fridge to hide my face in case it gives me away. I expect him to return to their den of testosterone and alcohol, but he doesn't. Instead Carlos' denim legs appear beneath my half-opened fridge door. I play for time by moving about bottles of wine; clearly, he heard my remark after all.

'Now, correct me if I'm wrong, but I'm sensing a distinct vibe that you're not overly impressed with the likes of me,' comes his voice.

'Me?' I swiftly close the fridge door and face him.

He continues, 'I understand why you've got your back up in relation to Joseph; you girls sticking together and all that business where their divorce is concerned. Affie, meanwhile, doesn't irk anyone, but me – I'm a different story. I think you've been nursing a pretty low opinion of me since the moment I stepped inside this cottage.'

'You've got some cheek! I could say pretty much the same thing. You described Paisley as nice.'

'She is.'

'You said the same of my sister.'

'I did.' His expression is deadpan.

He's not reading between the lines. He's clearly not hearing what I'm actually trying to say. I should swallow my pride at this point but I can't – so I plough on as if my life depends on it. I'm used to being the anchor of this group. The middle link in the trio chain, I like to think. I rarely find myself in this situation, as more often I'm sticking up for everyone else. It's rare that anyone has to fight my corner, whether it's needed or not. Usually I fight my own battles while protecting everyone else. Much like earlier, when this oaf splattered chocolate in my hair and ruined my crafting fun. That's the role I've adopted in life – the one everyone expects of me. Whether it be described as sassiness or simply being argumentative – they're referring to the same thing. It's that spirit inside me that never gives up, never fails to ignite, and engages with the world around me. But, if the truth be known, I get on my own nerves.

'By saying *that* you're implying that I ... that I am ... not.' The final word slips from my lips, sounding weak and pathetic.

Carlos purses his mouth, as if holding back his answer.

'So, Paisley's the nice one,' I continue. 'Kate's the organised one, actually ... as well as being nice, and I'm the nasty, scrappy one – is that it?'

He doesn't flinch. Doesn't correct me. Doesn't do anything other than breathe and remain silent. My brain is whirring, searching for something else to say. Anything. His insinuation, as I saw it, was that I couldn't possibly be liked, or hold favour, with anyone in the presence of the other two beauties. But I've met the likes of Carlos before. And he's wrong about me. So wrong that I have to prove it by somehow showing that I have equal kindness, flare ... a nice side.

Carlos continues to stare, watching me. He knows I'm rattled. That his silence is winding me up a treat. He knows we're cut from the same cloth. A tough, rough and ready material, hard wearing and durable, with a strong thread of bolshiness among the weft and the weave, like a flaw in the fabric, which constantly challenges others.

'If that's your opinion, there's clearly no changing your mind,' I say, and then a flash of inspiration: 'If you'll excuse me. Some of us have a little more respect for the festive season, given that it's our birth month.' My head tilt and a hard stare indicate it's wise he moves out of my path. Carlos duly steps sideways and I proceed towards the stable door. On opening it, I'm greeted by the sight of holly and ivy strewn everywhere. I've no gloves, no broom or container to put anything in, but still I step outside to begin picking up each sprig, attempting not to be prickled as I do so.

'What are you doing?' comes his voice from the doorstep.

'I'm rehanging these decorations elsewhere – away from your "sports lounge", so don't panic.' I haven't thought this through, so can't say any more, and surely actions speak louder than words. But Carlos doesn't know that. Though, on second thoughts, given his bemused expression, maybe he does.

Chapter Twenty-three

Paisley

'Who are you kidding? You didn't go from bar side to shagging!' Having consumed one too many gins at the local and abandoned my cooking duties, I should have offered to join Selena in her attempt to re-decorate the snug with Carlos' festive cast-offs. Truth was, I couldn't be arsed. It was unfortunate that, instead, my poor gin-addled judgement delivered me into the garden, raking over old coals with Joseph. It had taken all of three minutes for us to start bickering. 'You and she had numerous moments when you could have turned back from a bad decision. You linked up by flirting, then kissing, then left arm in arm, chose a suitable hotel, checked-in, then travelled up to the room, presumably by lift – surely at any moment during that time you could have spared a thought for me. Home alone in ignorant bliss! But no, you continued towards room number whatever, wherever, and went in. Still then the dirty deed couldn't ... wouldn't have happened straight away. Did you have a little drink from the minibar, maybe a shower, maybe a little chat, a reconnection of sorts, eh?'

'I think you've spent too much time obsessing about this,' says Joseph, repositioning himself on the wooden bench discretely positioned and so hidden from the view of the kitchen window, behind the sturdy brick outhouse.

'You think? I went to bed every night, sobbing and imagining you working your magic with another woman!'

'Paisley, please – don't do this!'

'Ha, very funny. I'd have said the exact same thing to you, Joseph – moments before you did the deed! But no. You and the trollop got naked and carried on without any regard for me. Did she even know about me? Sitting at home awaiting your return, ready to snuggle up in bed – all cosy and warm. Nope? You stripped. She stripped. Or did you undress her? Slowly and purposefully like we used to do with each other? Do you remember those nights? Or did you cheapen that memory with a re-enactment with her? Or did you rip her clothes off like there was no tomorrow? Living your best life outside of our marriage?' I'm on a roll, gathering speed and pace, and couldn't stop with my running commentary even if I wanted to. 'It's that that haunts me, Joseph – not the dirty deed itself. Each stage allowed you time to stop, collect your thoughts and think of us – but you didn't, did you? You couldn't have cared less. I was too trusting. You were too clever, sly, horny ... whatever you want to call it. Cheap and common – that's what I call it!'

He sighs heavily, as if he's heard all this before. Which he probably has, given as I've ranted it enough times to an empty home, so maybe the gist of it was carried on the wind to wherever he's been staying.

I don't remember this being the reason I ventured out into the garden. Wasn't I heading to check out the herb garden beyond the copper beech hedge? Clearly I was distracted, much like Joseph on his infamous night out.

'And then, afterwards – urgh. It makes me sick. You looked at her, she looked at you, and what ... some more pillow talk or did you have a little extra in the morning or go your separate ways? Did she ask if you could meet again? Did she nip out, dirty and unshowered, or did you? Was it awkward? Did you laugh at me – stupidly awaiting your arrival at home, hoping you'd had a good night out with the boys. When I think how much I missed you that night . . . I was literally on the doorstep waiting for you.'

Joseph flinches. I don't pause to let him speak. I lean in, feeling the magnetic force that was once a daily occurrence for us.

'Did you ever meet up with her again?' I finally ask the question that has haunted me for eighteen months.

'Who?' he says, his puckered brow displaying confusion, as if he hasn't been present the whole time I've been ranting at him.

'Her!' My lips spit the word.

'No,' he replies swiftly, a flicker of irritation replacing his confusion. 'Paisley, seriously. Are you joking me?'

'You might have. If she was worth us breaking up over, she might have been worth you seeing again, dating . . .'

'Dating?'

Great. Good enough to shag but not to date – nicely defined there, Joseph.

'Was she worth it?' My repertoire of nightly questions just keeps coming, I can't help myself.

'Paisley. Stop, please. How many times do I need to say . . .'

I jump in quickly, knowing all the answers he's ever given. 'It was a one-night thing. It was a mistake. It was stupid of me. I made a ridiculous error. It wasn't planned. It just happened.' I fall silent, my mimicry sounding ridiculous, even to me. Why do I still allow myself to be drawn in and get so upset by his behaviour? And now, even my own.

'And no, it never happened again or is it ever likely to. There, feel better now?' he finally says, standing up, signalling this conversation is over. 'Look, if we're to get through this week together under the same roof then, please, this . . . needs to cease. OK? If not, then I'll pack my stuff and be gone, because I didn't book a week away with the lads to be harangued for my past mistakes.'

I look up at him, hurt as always. Before me stands an older

version of the man I vowed to love for ever and ever, amen. How have we come to this? Once so close and now so distant.

'So, what's it to be, Paise?' I inwardly flinch, reminded of how deep this wound actually is. Dare I be honest and say 'I can't do this with you here. I can't sleep under the same thatched roof or see you across the breakfast table.' Or do I pretend, as I have for the last fifteen months, that I am stronger than I look and feel?

'You're right. We need to call a truce.' My voice sounds small and flat, like that of a chastised child. Joseph gives his usual nod and swiftly leaves the bench area, returning to the cottage. I stand there wondering why I've agreed to such terms even though I'm completely incapable of calling a cease-fire on my emotions.

Chapter Twenty-four

Early Evening

Kate

Buzz. My mobile sounds yet again from the coffee table. I play deaf, hoping that the other two follow my lead. I steady my face in a blank expression, awaiting the second reminder bleep; so far I've managed to cover-up my predicament. Not that I'm not reading psycho-boss' messages, I am. Thankfully, simple two line replies are all that's been necessary so far. Though that could all change if his daughter has yet another bright idea for her engagement party. We're too close to the actual date for any last-minute arrangements, but you never know with these people, as they're used to throwing cash at things and, of course, they get their way more often than not. I shouldn't have agreed to do it; I just can't help myself. I must have a chromosome purely devoted to organising that needs exercising more than my current life can put to use.

'So where did you find the tools and necessary equipment to transform our hidey-hole into a festive grotto?' I ask Selena, keen to distract by admiring her attempts with Carlos' cast-off decorations.

'Nothing much was needed, in the end – just a pair of scissors from the kitchen drawer. Though I doubt they're there for such a purpose. I did wash them afterwards.'

I casually retrieve my phone while Selena rattles on about

her unexpected floristry skills. Paisley is only half listening. I feel so sorry for her. As I know only too well, it's hard to come back from a divorce – to find your feet, to pick up the pieces of your life and plod on, especially when it wasn't truly of your choosing. To then have the git in question show up during your first proper festive holiday since the divorce is pure bad luck. Last Christmas doesn't truly count, given she was still in the depths of the initial shock.

'As I was saying,' continues Selena, 'I've no plans to move from this company for a few more years and so I'll probably be offered another promotion and then . . .' I tune out. It's not that I don't care, but she's all talk, for now. She's in a good position job-wise, bossing it by all accounts and gaining the accolades, receiving the recognition from the top tier and living the work-dream she wanted. Unlike me. I love what I do, love how I perform and the location. I can't even complain about the extra work I'm given, such as the engagement party. I simply dislike my boss' attitude, his psychological game playing. The daily put downs, the scapegoating he does when he needs someone to blame.

You know you've been too long in the same position when you're the go-to-person whenever someone forgets the name of an ex-colleague during the retelling of a funny anecdote. It's one thing if they casually ask you in passing while waiting for the lift, i.e. 'Kate, you'll remember the name of the woman whose father was a famous footballer – she worked the reception desk for just shy of a working week and had spent twenty-seven grand on a new kitchen for her bungalow. You remember?' It's another level when they send a runner down to ask you the question partway through their lunch break, to guarantee an instant answer. What's worse is that I can recall everyone's name and contact details instantly, from the Rolodex memory card in my head. Give it another spin and I can come up with any number of previous names and faces that have passed through the corridors of my workplace at any time over the last decade. Even some from before my time.

Buzz. Another text. I glance over to see if I can glimpse a word or a turn of phrase on the screen.

Looking up, I find two sets of eyes watching me intently.

'What?' I say, feigning ignorance, but I know.

'Back with us, are you? Or are you planning how to discreetly answer all those dammed text messages that Mr Psycho-boss is sending you?' asks Selena, glancing at Paisley, who gives a grimace of agreement. Clearly they've been discussing things.

'Well . . .'

'Cut the crap, Kate. We know you too well,' Selena continues triumphantly.

'Do you now? Well, do you know that I think . . . I think you've over done it by decorating this joint,' I gesture towards the holly and ivy. The tiny snug is far too small to accommodate all she's crammed into it. 'It's like sitting on set for a film-adaptation of *The Chronicles of Narnia*. I'm half-expecting Lucy and Mr Tumnus to walk through the door at any minute,' I say, attempting to distract from her lecture. 'In fact, you've left just enough space in the corner to accommodate a small lamppost.' I feel a bit mean, mocking her efforts, but I need to head her off. I have no feasible excuse to be doing what I'm doing for my boss, except that it's a dammed sight easier doing it than not doing it. I figure, if I don't, I'll just have it forced upon me in the end as an emergency job, with a much smaller time window for completion. That's how things usually work if I don't work them in my favour from the off.

'Was I wrong, then, to salvage what I could? He simply lobbed it all out of the back door and onto the patio, with little thought for who was going to clear up the mess afterwards. Self-centred, if you ask me.'

There's a pause before Paisley speaks.

'I like it. It feels as if I'm sitting in a cosy den in a winter wonderland forest – all that's missing is a few strings of fairy lights,' she says, much to Selena's glee.

'Please don't encourage her!'

'And if you can't have what you want for a big birthday, then when can you?' adds Paisley. Though I notice her face drops as soon as she says it, clearly thinking back to her own big birthday back in September. Bless her. There was only one thing Paisley would have wanted and there's no chance of that happening in the near future, or rather not until she's more settled in life.

'Anyway, are you spilling the beans or am I to guess what on earth he wants now? Maybe he's asked you to organise a special post-Christmas delivery for his attention only . . .' says Selena, adding a saucy pout to underline her innuendo.

'Stop! For the love of God. I beg you!' I don't want any of her smutty jokes sticking put in my head in relation to my boss.

'So, fess up, otherwise we'll start recalling ick moments of yesteryear,' says Paisley, recovering her poise.

I send her a well-practised smile, much like the one I gave on dishing up our emergency dinner of steamed salmon, boiled potatoes and veggies earlier, after binning her coal and gravy Aga disaster.

'What about the time he asked you to collect an item from the gents' toilet?' says Selena, her memory kicking in. I certainly don't need a reminder of that particular event.

'OK. Stop! I beg you.'

'On an entirely selfish note, you are *my* sister so I should have one hundred per cent of your focus on my big birthday bash week.' I wince. There are times my nearly thirty-year-old sister can demonstrate she's as self-centred as a six-year-old.

There's a lengthy pause, which I'm not willing to break, so I take a sip of my wine.

Paisley comes to the rescue. 'Did you hear the fellas earlier in the pub comparing notes and talking about their missions?'

'I did. It sounded dire,' says Selena, reaching for her wine glass from the coffee table.

'Can you imagine your collective memory of your friendship being someone else's worst nightmare – stuck on the side of a desolate mountain awaiting help?' says Paisley, giving a little involuntary shiver.

'Urgh! Could you imagine being out there right now? In the wind, fog and fading light, and knowing you are stuck until someone, anyone finds you? I'd literally die of fright,' I say, catching Paisley's matching shiver.

'Christ, could you imagine seeing the likes of Carlos bounding towards you out of the mists and knowing that ... well, just knowing that you're safe ...' says Paisley, getting panicked at the thought of a dilemma.

'Then he could provocatively strip for you before he carries you down in a fireman's lift? Bloody hell, what a sight that would be,' interjects my sister. 'Free of charge too!' She falls about laughing. Paisley and I exchange a fleeting glance, but can't help laughing a little too. Though it feels wrong to be making comments about his physique – I wouldn't want them joking about our natural assets over there in the lounge, between football matches and snooker games.

Bang on cue, there's a tapping at the door and we turn expectantly to greet the newcomer.

Carlos fills the doorway. He's about to speak, but on noticing the decoration appears taken aback. 'Ladies, it's like a woodland lair in here. Are you three witches maybe plotting the demise of us fellas with your potions and brews?' he asks, his gaze landing upon Selena.

'What do you want?' she snaps, clearly not willing to entertain his take on her efforts.

'Joking aside, it looks quite festive in here – that is, if spending your evenings surrounded by damp woodland was your desire. Personally, I'd prefer the roaring log fire that we'll be having later, but hey, each to their own.'

'Carlos. Again, what do you want?'

'Affie fancies some wine . . . so could we?'

I'm about to answer but take a fraction too long.

'No. You pulled this stunt yesterday by sending Affie. You fellas have enough booze to sink a battleship but each night you fancy our stuff. I think not, otherwise are we to expect Joseph to come knocking tomorrow night? Nah. Don your boots, brave the night air and go fetch your own from the local Co-op,' says Selena, turning away as if to dismiss him.

'Is she for real?' asks Carlos, turning to Paisley.

Paisley's eyes widen, indicating uncertainty.

His gaze moves on to me. I shrug. Selena's remark seems a bit petty and mean, but I get where she's coming from. Second night, second request – is this going to be a week-long thing?

'OK, tell you what, we'll buy a bottle of wine from you girls. Name your price.'

I shift in my seat; this is swiftly becoming uncomfortable. Paisley does likewise.

'Erm, no,' comes the reply.

His mouth drops wide.

'We'll pay double the price, how's that? I'll give you cash . . .' he digs into his jeans pocket, retrieving a fold of notes from his wallet.

'Nope. Sorry, no can do.'

'Lady, you can be one mean gal, do you know that! For someone whose livelihood depends upon the portrayal of symbolism and depiction of hidden meanings . . . all this,' he swirls a hand gesturing around the cosy room '. . . might have provided you with some enlightenment. Clearly not! Catch you later, Kate, Paisley.' In an instant he is gone.

We sit in silence. I'm eyeballing Paisley, not daring to speak for fear of the wrath simmering away on the opposite couch.

'He's got a fecking nerve,' spits Selena, her gaze drifting towards the greenery around us.

I want to remain neutral, but equally feel the need to smooth things out too. It's a bottle of wine at the end of the day. I go to get up, and Paisley goes to do the same.

'Look, I'll go and sort . . .' she says hastily.

'I was about to say the same,' I add, uncurling my legs from beneath me.

'Bloody typical of you two – they're grown men. Let them sort themselves out for once in their lives. Did you see him splatter chocolate in my hair earlier? It might as well have been a declaration of war.'

'It's not worth the bad feeling, Selena,' I say, knowing she won't take kindly to me breaking rank.

'Look at how much fresh food Affie bought for breakfast . . . a bottle of plonk – it's of little consequence to us,' urges Paisley earnestly.

Selena shakes her head, sips her wine and stares mutinously at her glorious decorations.

'I'll be back in a minute,' I say, taking that as a green light to nip out and deliver a peace offering to the sports lounge.

Chapter Twenty-five

Paisley

'It doesn't just go because you've divorced someone, you know?' The topic reverts to me on Kate's return. I presume our supplies in the fridge are now minus another chilled bottle.

'What are you saying, Paisley?' asks Selena.

'All those feelings, that overwhelming sense of love – it doesn't just die with a decree nisi. However, earlier in the garden, I agreed to a truce, as if everything is hunky dory.'

'But he broke your trust.' Selena looks up at her intently from her mobile screen.

'I don't need reminding, thanks.'

'But surely you're not saying what I think you're saying. Are you?' asks Kate, her brow furrowed.

I shrug. I've no idea what I'm saying, to be fair. It might be the drink talking, as I've had a fair amount more than I usually would today.

'A shrug doesn't cut it, Paisley – not with a question such as this,' says Selena. As ever, she's annoyingly right.

'It's that whole thing of meeting so many people in life, getting along with some of them, bonding with others, gelling or not, as the case may be, but then you find that one person. Boom! An instant connection! And you feel you've known that stranger for a lifetime yet you haven't ... because you've only just met. But the more you speak, the more you realise that you're caught within their magnetic field, with your head spinning, your feelings building, and you have to admit that no one has ever made you feel that way before.'

'But they will in time,' offers Kate.

'But they haven't, Kate. And I've met thousands of people in my life, yet only one man made me feel like Joseph does . . . did.' I quickly correct myself.

'You need to give it time, Paisley. The last year has probably been your toughest. You'll meet someone new and boom! Life begins again,' says Kate, gesturing the said boom. She's trying to be encouraging, but I know she knows the reality of life after love as much as anyone.

'How many have you met?'

'Me?' Kate prods her own chest.

'Yes, you, Miss Boom-life-will-start-over-again. I'm not talking nice guys, OK guys or we-get-along guys . . . I'm talking the full works: chemistry, connection, morals and aligned values – keeper-guys.'

Kate's expression fades a little. 'Phuh! If that's your requirement, then two . . . maybe three at a push.'

I glance at Selena, who's clearly thinking. 'One or two, no more,' she offers.

'See. I've met just the one guy. I met him when I least expected it. We had chemistry, we connected. I loved him, I married him and I ended up divorcing him, but . . .' I fall silent, I can't find the right words.

'You still feel that way?' asks Selena.

I nod. I have no other answer.

'Wow!' whispers Kate.

'Shit,' mutters Selena, her phone screen still illuminating her features.

'So, what do I do?' I ask, glancing between the pair of them. 'Somehow, I don't reckon a "boom" and life restart is my answer.'

'Only you can answer that,' offers Selena, returning to her phone.

'In that case, I'm stuffed! Because despite his actions, the love hasn't died – I only wish it would,' I say, holding my drink aloft. 'What's more unnerving is that neither the chemistry nor connection has faded either.'

'Even though he proved his morals were, shall we say, slightly skewed compared to yours?' says Kate, pulling a face to lighten the mood a little.

'Maybe. Were Cody's morals aligned with yours?'

'Urgh! You've got me there. I think our morals *were* once aligned, but his addiction took him over the edge. With his secrets and lies he behaved in a way I never could. Though I'm unsure if he even realised that part of it until it was too late,' says Kate. I've never heard her admit that before. Before now, she's always side-stepped Cody's issues.

'But you've got to admit, Joseph's definitely grown up in the last eighteen months,' I continue, relieved to have shared my thoughts.

'Certainly matured, definitely grown up,' adds Kate reassuringly.

'He bloody needed to,' says Selena, rapidly flicking her mobile screen. She suddenly looks up. 'Are we done with Joseph?'

I love Selena to bits, but there are days her lack of tact, style and grace comes across as overly bullish. Kate shakes her head in amusement.

'Why? What's of interest on your phone?' I ask, knowing she's been consumed by something online.

She doesn't waste a heartbeat. 'That cheeky git has basically implied that I have no goodwill, loyalty, determination or growth! He can feck right off with wanting more wine where I'm concerned. But I bet you delivered a bottle, didn't you?'

'I did. It was spiteful not to,' says Kate, eyeing her.

'It hardly broke the bank, did it?' I say. 'And I don't remember him saying anything like that.'

'He did. By referring to the holly and ivy decorations . . .' she swirls her hand dramatically, gesturing towards the walls and ceiling. 'It says here that holly traditionally represents peace, goodwill, fertility and eternal life. And ivy is fidelity, immortality, devotion, loyalty, growth, determination, protection and healing. He reckons, or rather is suggesting, I haven't any of those qualities! Phuh! I've got them in abundance, boyo!'

'The symbolism of each complements the other rather well,' I say, looking at the festive decorations with fresh insight.

'I see ivy as a weed. A real pain in the arse once it takes hold in your garden or brick work,' says Kate, 'I pulled all of it out when I moved into my current house – I didn't want it causing me trouble in years ahead.' Likewise with Cody – there was never talk of him returning to the fold; Kate ripped him out root and branch. I'm unsure what happened to him after their break-up.

We both look at Selena, quietly pondering her interpretation of Carlos' remark.

'He clearly knows more about nature than you'd imagine. But don't let him get under your skin, Selena. Forget about it. It's just not worth it,' I say, suspecting Carlos has equally misjudged our Miss Selena Smythe.

'Mmmm, like poison ivy – he's not worthy of the irritation, more like,' she chunters.

'Here we go! I knew it wouldn't take long,' says Kate, peeling herself from the sofa. 'I'm grabbing a refill. What are you fancying?'

I smirk, thinking her choice of words could potentially be classed as a Freudian slip. 'Not sure, but I suggest yours might be Affie.'

'Stop it. I mean wine-wise.'

'Can we open that nice sauvignon blanc – the one that was advertised on TV by . . . What?' says Selena, seeing Kate grimace.

'That's the bottle I gave to the fellas.'

'Blood great! These are my birthday celebrations and I'm the bugger that's doing without! Thanks a bunch, sis. No worries – I'll have whatever is open,' huffs Selena, returning her focus to her phone screen while Kate and I exchange a rueful smirk.

Chapter Twenty-six

Selena

'How was my sauvignon blanc – crisp and fresh, was it?' I ask, entering the kitchen to find Carlos making a toastie in one of the many chrome-gadgets lining the kitchen's countertop.

'A tad acidic and too dry for my liking, if I'm honest,' says Carlos, buttering his bread on both sides. Somewhat heavy-handed but each to their own. 'I much prefer a pinot, to be fair. Slightly fruitier and more rounded in body – but hey, beggars can't be choosers now, can they?'

'I fear not. Especially when it cost them naught.'

He stops buttering his bread and turns, butter knife in hand, to catch me watching him, before saying, 'It'll cost us for sure – nothing in this world comes for free!'

'Really?' I mutter, irked at the way he's acting as if he's teaching others a life lesson.

'Do you not find that? That there's no such thing as a free lunch.' Every nerve in my body wants to roll my eyes and dramatically huff and flounce from the kitchen. He's sounding much like my father did when I was about fifteen years of age, for God's sake. I fight my reactive urge, grit my teeth and the moment passes. Though something about the way he looks at me intently implies he's guessed at my inner dilemma. I want to say something glib about the awful job he's doing with the toastie, but I don't. I put my dirty glass into the dishwasher and close the door.

'Earlier, you didn't actually say which advert you'll be working on when you return after Christmas,' says Carlos.

'Didn't I?' I say, feigning ignorance. Great! This guy's going to prove to be one of those genius brains that remembers every damned detail in every sodding conversation. A habit that can bite you on the arse should you deviate from the truth by even half a degree. I've met people like this before, and they jump on every discrepancy you might make when retelling a story as if it were a police interrogation.

'No.' He resumes his buttering, giving me another sideways glance as I remain silent.

'Oh.'

He's almost too patient for my liking. Deliberately silent, carefully crafting his snack by layering the ham and cheese, all while analysing my response, probably even counting my breaths per minute. This feels like he's testing me. A bit like Mr Psycho-boss seems to test my sister.

'So … ?'

'So, you're interested in what I do for a living?'

He nods, eyes fixed upon his snack making. He's waiting and I can't think of a single bloody thing to say, which is unlike me. I am usually a motormouth. Bright ideas and one-liners usually burst from me at speed like someone on one of those panel shows. My brain rarely has time to put itself into gear as my mouth takes over.

The toastie maker's bottom plate sizzles as he gently manoeuvres the buttered bread tower into place. My mouth waters. I could really go for a freshly-made toastie, though obviously with less butter than he's applied. Surely that there is a heart attack waiting to happen.

'I've never met anyone who creates stuff for TV. The sort of thing that mere mortals like me see ten times a day between programmes or, let's face it, whizz through on fast forward.'

I don't need reminding. 'That's actually one of my bugbears – no one watches the adverts like they used to.'

'That's because we're all rushed for time. I want to binge-watch programmes rather than be delayed by nappy commercials.'

'Which makes my work harder. Don't you feel you're missing out on the enjoyment of TV by doing that?'

'Nah. I'm missing out on a load of naff adverts, which many of them are nowadays. Surely you'll agree there? What's with that new washing powder advert suggesting all blokes are gormless? I don't understand the thinking behind some adverts – surely the whole point is snagging the audience's attention and persuading them to part with their cash?'

I shrug. 'They're not all as enticing as mine, but hey – pay me dough and I'll create fabulous for anyone.'

'You're not picky, then?' he asks, bringing the top hot plates of the toastie machine down and trapping the buttered bread in between. I note that he's misaligned his creation and the pinched crusts hang over the edge, exposed and naked. I'd pick those off and eat them while waiting, but he's a guy, and maybe guys don't do such things.

His question tweaks a nerve. Has he just switched our conversation topic, dropping the advertising thread and landing on my personal life? Guys like him think they're so clever, having cross-purpose conversations with subtle innuendos, trying to trip you up.

'I'm definitely picky. Too picky, some might say.' My tone is nonchalant, as I want to save face if he's trying to be clever. 'So picky, in fact, that others assume I'm left on the shelf, overlooked, and class me as unapproachable.'

Carlos pulls a face, turning to look over his shoulder. I automatically touch my hair as if the remnants of smeared chocolate are still there, despite the thorough wash and blow dry earlier.

'Sorry. I thought you just said "pay me dough and I'll" ... ?'

Shit. I did. He's not playing mind games – he's sticking to facts and straight questions. I'm the one who's changed tack. Backpedal quickly, Selena!

'Actually, what I mean is: pay me my worth and I'll create "fabulous" for whatever product I'm assigned.'

'You're assigned products! I thought you'd choose and pitch for what you fancied working on. Sorry, I misunderstood.'

'I do!' My tone is gaining edge. There's a little more insistence than I intended, but this guy is unknowingly winding me up a treat. It feels as if everything he says has a double meaning. I feel like I'm performing a conversational gymnastics routine, jumping through hoops in an attempt to show myself in a good light. Or, alternatively, just trying my hardest to avoid confirming whatever low-brow opinion he currently has of me.

'I'm confused. Are you assigned products or do you choose which products you want to represent?'

'I choose,' I say defiantly, hopefully ending this hoop jumping conversation like a pro gymnast, with a flourishing but secure landing without a single wobble or telling back-step in sight, before adding, 'I've been in this game too long and have too many successes under my belt to be thrown any old product.'

Carlos nods slowly. His unwavering gaze suddenly breaks and he returns to his task.

'So . . . what's next?'

And there it is. I thought I'd finished the assault course of hoop jumping, but sadly not.

'Something a little different for the New Year – I'm heading a new group for a focussed one-off campaign.' It's a line I've repeated so much in recent weeks it almost feels like a cliché. I wanted a challenge. I opted for a challenge. Every career needs a moment of madness when you force yourself out of your comfort zone and greet an opportunity head on, doesn't it?

'Beer? Chocolate? Razors?' ask Carlos, his interest piqued further with each suggestion.

I'm pleased he's remembered each of the biggies.

'Well ...' I'm stalling, as I don't really want to think about all the challenges I'll face when I return to work right now, but if needs must.

'Selena! There you are!' cries Paisley, barging into the kitchen, before adding, 'I've been calling you from across the landing for God knows how long. I thought you were upstairs.'

'I'm here,' I say, stating the obvious.

'I can see that now. Anyway, Kate's got something to show you. Now, you don't have to agree, but it would make things far easier if you do. Right?' says Paisley, holding the kitchen door wide open and beckoning me, clearly on strict orders from Kate.

'Right ... I think,' I instinctively reply, before offering an oh-so-casual 'See you' in Carlos' direction.

'Yep, laters,' he says, eyeing us both before muttering, 'You're good.'

I'm about to slip through into the hallway when my brain registers what he's said. I whip around like the time-obsessed wolf in the children's game. 'Sorry?'

Carlos gives me a wide grin as he lifts the upper hot plate to check on his toasties. 'You heard.'

Chapter Twenty-seven

Kate

It takes ages for Paisley to fetch Selena, so I distract myself by sorting through the chocolate goodies I purchased earlier, which are now spread across my duvet. My original intention was to only buy certain bars, but given the mess and mayhem created by their chocolate fight, I felt obliged to overspend to compensate and bought every flavour, filling several large carrier bags. I have mint-cream chocolate in every size they produced, for example: six, twelve, sixteen and twenty-four chunk-sized family bar. The same goes with the Turkish delight, coffee caramels, strawberry creams, nougat, honeycomb – each in an assortment of dark, milk or ruby chocolate. Hopefully, my chocolate splurge will last me until Easter. As long as it went someway to saying 'sorry' to the owners, as my repeated mumblings seemed inadequate.

'Knock, knock!' My bedroom door opens, revealing two smiley faces. At last! I pat the billowy duvet to indicate that they should join me on the vast four-poster, just like back in the good old days of our youth. Back then, we could all easily fit onto Selena's single bed, surrounded by a tangle of hair driers, curling tongs and other styling paraphernalia, all of which were deployed to curl, defrizz and straighten, ready for a girls' night out.

'Step away from the calories, Kate!' hollers my sister, as they settle beside me.

'You can talk, after this morning's incident. You might have had a go about Carlos, but I saw you having a sneaky lick of some of the chocolate that landed on you.'

'It landed in my hair!' she bleats.

'Are you cracking these open?' asks Paisley, clearly over my sister's drama and eyeing the treats.

'Be my guest.' Both of them swiftly grab, snatch and retrieve different bars. I try to take stock but their manners have patently disappeared. I select a slimline strawberry-cream fondant in ruby chocolate, carefully breaking the silver foil to reveal the pale pink gloss beneath.

'Really, Kate? Ruby chocolate? Urgh, no. Dark chocolate for me – you can't beat it,' says Paisley, waving her half-opened bar. Selena's too engrossed with biting into hers. Silence descends as we savour the glory that such simple ingredients can muster.

'I was hoping we'd enjoy a nice gastro-pub lunch and a few glasses of bubbles after our chocolate factory experience, but ... that went to pot, didn't it?' I begin, breaking off another chunk of ruby chocolate. 'This is lovely, by the way.'

'Let's have a piece?' asks Selena, switching her attentions from her own bar.

I duly deliver and watch as she inspects the chunk before it disappears into her mouth.

'Don't crunch it – it's a waste. You're so uncouth at times,' I mutter.

'It's chocolate! It's meant to be enjoyed any which way I want. Don't spoil my fun!'

'Can you smell smoke?' asks Paisley, lifting up on her elbows, her nose frantically twitching in all directions.

'No. Just lovely chocolate,' I reply.

'Affie mentioned they were planning to light the log fire,' adds Selena, taking a good sniff. 'Given they're overgrown boy scouts, what's the bet it'll be viewed as an honour to build it.'

'There's no need. Apparently, the housekeeper has already

prepared the kindling in the hearth – it's ready and waiting. A simple match will do the job,' adds Paisley.

'I wouldn't be so sure – have you seen a group of men attempting to light a BBQ after a belly-full of beer,' laughs Selena, finishing her original bar and screwing up the papers.

It sounds awful to make fun, but she's not wrong: firelighters, testosterone and charcoal briquettes – hardly a winning combination. Hence my ex-husband's dangerous technique with lighter fuel, always guaranteed to destroy a pleasant summer afternoon as well as our neighbour's line of white washing.

'Anyway, as I was saying . . . I don't want another day to breeze past like yesterday and today has. It's no one's fault,' I swiftly continue, to avoid someone interjecting.

'Well, as I'm the star of this week's show – I was hoping that us three girls could . . .'

'The plans for tomorrow are already made, little sis . . . so listen up. Because you left the rental booking to the last minute, Mum and Dad hadn't any choice but to leave their present until the last minute too, so tomorrow you, accompanied by Paisley and me, will be enjoying . . .'

A sudden hammering on the bedroom door is followed by hollering. 'Ladies! Ladies!'

'What the hell is happening?' says Selena, scrambling from the bed to answer the door. 'Carlos, what's up, big fella?'

'Ladies, you need to make your way to the garden, please,' he says authoritatively, stepping through the doorway, addressing us each in turn.

'Woah there! No one enters my bedroom and begins by making demands,' says Selena. I hate to correct her error that this is my room and not actually hers.

'Selena, quit with the ego, and listen. This way, ladies!' His tone is such that Paisley and I both follow his instruction without quibbling.

'This is ridiculous! Ha, ha, you ruin our chocolate tour and now decide on a practice fire drill – all very funny, fellas! You're too safety conscious for your own good. If we can make this role-playing snappy, I'd appreciate it. Though I'd appreciate it more if I'd grabbed a bar or two from our Kate's chocolate stash,' says Selena, bring up the rear as we cross the landing and are ushered down the staircase. Carlos firmly closes my bedroom door.

We're halfway down the staircase when I glance up, through the wooden spindles, and see Carlos crossing the landing to swiftly open each of our bedroom doors and briefly inspect inside before closing each door.

There's a distinct smell of smoke tickling my nostrils.

'Only you guys could pretend to burn down a sweet rental cottage, complete with a thatched roof,' scoffs Selena. A thatch! Oh my God, there's a bloody thatch.

'What's going on, Carlos?' I say, stalling a little, conscious that I hadn't questioned his instructions. Carlos doesn't answer me, but silently ushers us downstairs. Buzz – there goes my phone in my pocket. Later, I think: I'll deal with you when I'm on my own. As needy as my boss is with this constant questions and demands, I can only do one job at a time. And now is not the time.

'Down you come, please!' calls Affie, beckoning us from the hallway, which has a definite smokey aroma with a misty grey swirl to the air.

'What's happening? Where's Joseph?' asks Paisley, a tinge of urgency to her voice.

'He's fine. He's . . .'

'Have you set the bloody chimney alight?' asks Selena, breaking rank as we file along. I watch as she sidesteps Affie's bulky frame to enter the lounge, through which a steady swirl of smoke is seeping.

'Selena!' Affie calls her away urgently. On cue, she can be heard frantically coughing.

'There's always one – come what may!' observes Carlos, instantly barring my path from following my sister.

'What the hell? Get out!' hollers Joseph, appearing from the lounge, his jumper pulled up high across his mouth and nose and man-handling my sister, who is bent double and coughing and spluttering. 'All of you – out now!'

We don't wait a second longer. Joseph McLoughlin clearly means business when he raises his voice. Buzz. My phone keeps reminding me that my boss hates being ignored too.

I take the lead, scurrying along the hallway and through the kitchen to stride out into the chilly fresh air of the patio. Paisley quickly follows. Selena slowly emerges as well, her eyes streaming, gasping for breath, and plonks herself down to sit on the garden steps. 'The . . . chimney.'

'Yes, exactly. The chimney is blowing back into the room not drawing the smoke up, as it should,' explains Carlos, as Joseph and Affie stand a distance away flipping through the cottage's emergency folder, searching for a contact number I assume.

'Surely you phone 999?' I ask, stating the obvious.

'We put out the fire out before it had chance to ignite whatever's blocking the flue,' says Joseph, throwing the remark in our direction, busy with his task.

'Joseph dashed the hearth with a bowl of soapy water from the kitchen sink, dowsing the flames. Though the water simply created a load of steam and even more smoke from the kindling, which filled the room. It happened so quickly. Relax, they've got it in hand,' explains Carlos, attempting to calm our nerves.

'And . . . here's me . . . thinking you'd set . . . the bloody room alight, Carlos . . . with your smouldering good looks and hot personality. Thanks for confirming . . . it's just a dead pigeon blocking the chimney,' splutters Selena, unable to resist a jibe.

'Stop it!' I snarl, embarrassed by her remark. Selena's way too familiar when it suits her.

'He started it, not me,' she snaps, gulping for air and wiping tears from her eyes.

'Sorry,' I mouth in Carlos' direction, though he appears to be smirking rather than offended. 'Could we still call the fire brigade?'

Carlos shakes his head. 'I'm not sure it's necessary, though you can't tell for sure what's needed until the smoke clears. Boy, that happened fast, though. One minute we're watching the match, the next I could hardly see the TV. It'll only take a spark or two to ignite a blocked chimney and . . .' His hands mimic a blaze before he goes over to join Affie, a short distance away.

We sit in silence, watching as Joseph dials the housekeeper and begins explaining; I can only imagine her reaction. I'm sure she'll be regretting us ever booking – it must feel like there's been endless aggro since the moment we arrived.

Affie drifts across the patio to join Carlos, their eyes cast upwards, randomly pointing at sections of thatch roofing around the chimney pot. I'm bracing myself, half expecting a wisp of smoke before a flash of fire appears, setting the entire roof ablaze.

'Fingers crossed our rental insurance would cover such a disaster if the roof catches. Not that I want to find out,' I say to Paisley, who's standing beside me.

'Are they joking?' whispers Paisley, warily scanning the bulky straw. 'The straw could be alight in seconds!'

'I know. Start praying for rain or snow, though I doubt it would save it,' I mutter, not wishing to tempt fate.

'I wish they'd hurry up and decide. I'm sodding freezing out here,' moans Selena, hugging herself.

I give her a black look, the one that I save for those special occasion when my sister truly does my head in.

'What? I am!' she adds, sensing my annoyance. 'If the fire brigade aren't needed, then what are we waiting here for?' she continues.

'Asks the woman who was hacking her guts up less than a minute ago,' says Carlos, overhearing her remark.

'Ha ha. Save your breath for you own funnies. Don't start hijacking my humour, thanks very much,' she retorts.

'Will you stop it!' I whisper furiously, before smiling politely at the two men, who are watching our exchange.

'OK,' announces Joseph, ending his call. 'Josie's going to contact the local chimney sweep and see what he says. She's asked us to keep a look out because the danger is that a thatch can smoulder for hours on end before it takes light. I'm sure we averted such a danger, but I'm not prepared to chance it. So, lads, who's taking the first shift out here?'

'Phew, bloody hell. You men are obsessed with your scout duties,' mutters Selena, standing up from where she was sitting. 'Are we heading back inside, ladies? I can hear the chocolate calling my name. All a bloody big fuss about nothing.'

Paisley follows her lead, while I hang back to offer the guys our thanks; I wouldn't want to sit outside in this chilly weather with the light fading fast. Hopefully, my apology covers my sister's lack of grace.

Chapter Twenty-eight

Paisley

'Don't you play footie any more then?' I ask, knowing that footie and his best mate, Jamie, were intrinsically linked.

'Not for ages. I picked up a shoulder injury when some clown attempted a dirty tackle, so had to rest up for weeks. I was advised to try gym exercises to strengthen the muscles and aid my recovery ... I'd started the trekking by then, so I didn't go back to the footie.'

'Wow!' I'm stunned.

'Are you shocked?'

'Actually, I am. You attended religiously, week in week out, Sunday matches, Tuesday practise session, Thursday's five-a-side, going to watch games every weekend, Monday night footie on TV – you were a dedicated fan, living it, breathing it.' I'd be ticked off at the extent of it and disappear to my parents' house for a cry and a moan. My dad never understood Joseph's obsession with the game, and felt it was all too much, despite liking and loving him as a son-in-law.

'Pretty much. Nah, all that has gone.'

A wave of sadness floods over me as old conversations resurface. I never wanted him to abandon his love of football, but simply ease up a little, so we'd have more time for us and our home and ... plans. When I think back to the arguments we've had because footie dominated his free time, you'd think I'd asked for the earth.

'You always said: "footie till the day I die and no one's stopping me – ever".'

A slight flush appears at his cheeks. 'That sounds like me. I'll admit it. I was a bit of a dick about it at times, if I remember correctly.'

'Never admit that, man!' interjects Carlos, walking in on our conversation.

'I was, Carlos. All she wanted was a bit of notice and some planning for the week ahead so that we could do other stuff, but I was no, no, no, you're not banning my football,' explains Joseph, which is exactly as I remember it too. I stay quiet but I'm warming to his honesty.

'Can't stuff happen at other times, then?' asks Carlos.

'Thing is, it could be family stuff, couple stuff or house stuff, but I'd come in from work and be straight out the door with my footie kit within the hour. Sometimes I didn't get back much before closing time. Other times the lads would venture out for a curry afterwards, or crowd around ours for a big match day.' Joseph pauses, turns to me as he continues, 'It couldn't have been much fun at times. Sorry.'

I'm too stunned to speak, so I give a slight nod and enjoy the moment, but I can't help but feel sad that this realisation has only come about after the divorce was finalised.

'I see,' mutters Carlos, his steady gaze flittering between us.

'I could have compromised but everyone else kept sticking their oars in. You know what it's like, the ribbing you get from the guys if you act all "under the thumb",' says Joseph. 'It's a bit too easy to listen to them rather than use common sense or listen to your own wife. And they'd all been married for longer than we had and ... well ... yeah, it's all crap advice really.'

I remain mute. All this stuff he's coming out with would have made such a difference to us back then. Why oh why couldn't he have had this light bulb moment back then ... when it mattered? It mattered to me, so much.

Chapter Twenty-nine

Evening

Selena

'How's Paisley coping?' asks Carlos, as I peeled the spuds for roasties, as per Kate's instructions.

'Good, I think.' I glance up and spot the lady in question out in the garden. I assume she's talking to her ex-husband, who's out of sight.

'Got over her initial shock, then?'

'I think so. We all have.'

'Tight, were they, as a couple?'

'God, yeah. Soul mates for sure, until well, you know . . . but hey, Joseph did what Joseph did, and Paisley responded how she responded.'

He eyes me cautiously, as if awaiting further details. 'Sadly, people do.'

'Do what?' I watch the length of potato peel lift slowly from the spud, revealing the pure white naked potato flesh underneath.

'Nothing. Forget it.'

'Sorry, you've lost me.'

'You were saying . . . oh, never mind, forget it.'

'Look. There's nothing much to say other than they were the tightest couple I knew, until he did the dirty on her. And then they weren't, and she was heartbroken. Still is, I think. There, is that what you were expecting me to say?'

'Not quite, but thanks for the summary.' There's a chuckle in his tone, as if I've said something funny. I certainly haven't nor did I mean to. I've stood by and watched my dearest friend go through hell over the last year and a bit. To see her withdraw again these past two days is a reminder of how delicate she continues to be, despite the progress she's made.

'What's you're issue?' I say, swilling the dirt from my next spud.

'Mine?' His gestures towards his chest, as if unsure who I'm talking to.

'Yes. You. From the very first moment I met you you've been all "way-hay", acting all bolshie and bigging yourself up like . . . like . . .' I know what I want to say, but I'll sound rude and aggressive, so I reel it back at the very last minute.

'Like you?' He gives me a sly grin.

'Me? It was you that started lobbing chocolate earlier – I would never have done anything like that. Our Kate's still fuming that you'd show her up.'

'I'll apologise, again. I wouldn't offend her for the world.'

'But you would me?'

Carlos shrugs, which immediately annoys me.

A lengthy pause follows, which makes me feel uneasy.

'What made you join the rescue team?' I ask, not wanting to pry but at least it changes the subject.

'I enjoy the great outdoors and had time on my hands. A couple of friends of mine came unstuck while out one day and they needed to phone through an emergency call. Thankfully, they were successfully rescued. Afterwards it got me thinking about the folk who'd rescued them – just ordinary folk giving up their time, expertise and their knowledge of the area to assist when needed. I suppose that appealed to me,' says Carlos.

'It didn't prove difficult with your weekend work?'

'My what? Oh, yeah, that. Well, sometimes, but I get some weekends off – it isn't performance after performance, weekend

after weekend. I'm not some cart horse you can keep flogging
on stage to entertain others – I have a life outside.'

'I bet it's busy during the summer.'

'The summer?'

'With hen parties and such like.'

'Yeah, of course. The heat can certainly get turned up on
nights like that.'

'Surely you do the same routine, though?'

'Sometimes. It depends on the interactions with the crowd.'

'Are you kidding me?'

'No. Some nights the audience can be lukewarm or tepid,
and other times the ladies are almost hot stuff, literally boiling
over – it's frightening. You think they're going to storm the stage
or something.'

I've witnessed such nights myself when dragged along on
hen-do weekends. I was a little frightened, and I'm not one to
scare easily.

'Have you ever been attacked on stage?'

'No. But I know guys who have been. Not a pretty sight when
an excited woman is waving her talons about when you're half
naked in the spotlight dressed in just a thong.'

'I can imagine.' I instantly blush, having pictured him in said
spotlight, quickly adding, 'Sorry. I can't, but you know what I
mean.'

Carlos flashes me a look, which only makes me more flustered.

'Not that I've been looking or checking you out, but given
your size and . . .' Stop talking, woman! What the hell am I jab-
bering on about? His ego will explode.

Carlos smiles. 'Which means you definitely have.'

'No. I haven't!' I protest, knowing that my blushes suggest
otherwise. 'I couldn't care less how big your biceps are – it's
the size of your heart that matters to the likes of me. Us. Us
women – all of us, that is.'

'Are you sure?' he says, close by now, playfully nudging my elbow.

'Yes. I'm sure. I should think you're sick to death of women ogling you and making suggestive remarks.'

'It can get tiresome.'

'I bet. If anything, you probably have an idea of what us ladies go through – all that sleazy talk, lewd suggestions . . . it's not nice. You're not some lump of meat, are you? Someone with nothing between your ears, some bimbo-bloke who dances because he has nothing else to fall back onto.'

'You've noticed that too,' he says, with a wry smile.

'Yes. I mean no! Well, of course I have.'

I need to stop talking, as I'm digging myself one hell of a hole.

'I'll take that as a compliment.'

'Good. Though it wasn't meant that way.'

He smiles again. 'Bye, Selena. Catch you later for another bout of blush and bullshit.'

The kitchen door closes on his final word. Did he just say bullshit? Me?

Chapter Thirty

Kate

I didn't expect to be the last one at the dining table, or that the guys were joining us, until I heard Selena announce 'dinner's served'. Before I know it, they've trundled through with their takeaway and beer, and joined us while we eat our roast chicken with all the works. I also hadn't realised people were switching seats either, which meant I was forced to take the remaining chair beside Affie. But did Paisley willingly opt to sit beside Joseph or was that masterminded by our Selena? That said, it seems Selena's sole intention is to verbally poke Carlos throughout the meal, even if it gives the rest of us indigestion.

'Have you always had long hair?' The question is out before I put my brain into gear.

'Not always, but in recent years, yeah,' replies Affie, smiling wryly as he picks up a strip of kebab with his fingers. I feel a bit uncomfortable eating with a knife and fork next to him.

'What's so funny?'

'You seem surprised by your own question, as if you didn't intend to ask me that,' he answers.

'Well, possibly not, but then why not?'

'Indeed, why not.'

'And the man bun?'

'Not a fan?'

'Err, I wasn't asking for a particular reason.'

'I liked the style when it first became popular, but I didn't have long hair back then. I figured a full set of extension was a bit much, so I grew it.'

I nod. My eyes glued to his prominent blond top-knot with tufted ends and elasticated bobble. His hair isn't sleek like a shampoo advert, but a messy frizzy style that needs smoothing from the roots before being drawn upwards. Granted, he's got a decent head of hair, it's just his chosen style that's bemusing. He's not a bad-looking guy in many ways: strong bearded jaw-line, heavy brow, clear skin . . . and yet the man bun – it ruins everything.

'Anything else?'

'Sorry?' I'm lost in my own thoughts. I blush, realising he was watching me watching him.

'No need to apologise . . . my mother's constantly questioning my common sense.'

'Does she not like the bun?'

'She hates it. My old fella even more so, but what can you do when you've a wayward son who does his own thing?'

'Refusing to grow up, is that it?' Again, the words slip out before I can think. 'So sorry, that came out wrong.'

'Did it?'

'Yes, it did. It's none of my business. No one tells me what to do with my appearance, so why should I do that to anyone else. It was wrong of me. I shouldn't have asked in the first place.'

'Kate.'

'What?'

'Stop apologising . . . I bet this "psycho-boss" of yours loves it.'

I don't understand.

'I bet it boosts his ego no end, with you apologising every hour of the day for your supposed errors – even for breathing, I should imagine.'

'I don't apologise at work.'

'I bet you do – it seems like second nature. You shouldn't feel it's necessary to apologise for being present, or be made to feel that way.'

I sit upright, totally uptight, unaware until now that I'd been leaning towards him. 'I don't feel that way. No one makes me feel that way. I do what I do because I want to do it, nothing more.'

Affie nods as he continues to chew. I glance at the others, seeking reinforcements, but they're busy yapping in their pairs.

'What? You don't believe me?' I ask.

'OK. No need to stress.'

'I'm not stressing, but you clearly don't believe me. I'm being straight with you, Affie – I apologise if I feel I've done something wrong, nothing more.'

'That's OK then. That's how life should be.'

'Good. I'm glad you realise.'

'Sure do.'

'Yeah, sure.'

'All I'm saying is that, if you were apologising for other reasons, then just know that you don't have to ... no one who knows you will think any less of you for simply being you.'

'Who thinks less of me?'

'No one.'

'So why say that. Now you've got me thinking that someone has said something against me.'

'On the contrary, Kate – everyone speaks very highly of you. Paisley, Joseph and even your little sister, which is most unusual as sisters go.'

I open my mouth to speak, but he jumps straight in with: 'What? Now you're going to apologise for that too?'

'Nooooo.'

'Mmmm, I suspect you were.'

'I'm no pushover, you know – I stand my ground when I need to.'

'I never said you were, but you constantly apologise for the world around you, which isn't your responsibility.'

'Sorry, but I . . .' My words linger, and Affie smiles a little as he chews.

The distinct yet magical sound of strummed harp strings fills the air.

'Is that my phone ringing?' asks Affie, breaking off from our conversation, quickly patting down his jeans pockets before looking about the dining room.

'Here you go, mate,' says Carlos, grabbing the ringing mobile from the nearest sideboard and passing it across.

'Thanks. Hello?' Affie stands tall, his tone of voice altering immediately. I'm startled by the change from relaxed and chatty to alert and ready for action.

'That's right. I am,' says Affie. 'What wrong?'

We continue to eat in silence, staring as Affie heads purposefully towards the doorway. As he nears the door, his shoulders drop, his head cocks and he stops dead before turning around to face us again, his eyes wide, startled. You can see the cogs whirring as he listens intently to whoever is calling.

'His daughter,' whispers Carlos, in explanation.

'I should think it's her mother, actually,' offers Joseph, eyeing Affie carefully.

'He's got a child?' The question falls from my lips without thinking.

'Yes. He is an actual adult – quite the grown-up, in fact, despite the hair bobble,' jokes Carlos.

'Sorry. That came out wrong,' I say, blushing at how judgemental I sound. 'What I meant was . . . he hasn't said.'

'He doesn't always – unless it's necessary,' says Joseph, 'She lives with her . . .'

'Are you joking me, Juliet? I said weeks ago that this week was booked. I changed my summer plans when you said it didn't suit and now, now that I'm here – you're saying this! Are you for real?' We all turn in unison as Affie's voice lifts. A tinge of annoyance fills the air and there's a lengthy pause before Affie speaks again. 'So, what are you actually saying?' His brow is deeply furrowed, his gaze fixed a little way ahead, as if staring at the person on the other end. His head begins to nod, slowly at first, before it grows in frequency and then becomes a bounce-like action. 'OK, then. How?' Pause. 'Look, you've sprung this on me but I'm all ears ... so what are you suggesting?'

Paisley gently taps my shoulder. 'Kate, stop staring.'

'Sorry. I was ...' I have no idea why I'm mesmerised by this instant transformation, all triggered by a ring tone. Much like Pavlov's dogs, Affie's reaction was instinctive. Fascinating to witness. He forgot he'd been talking to me instantly.

'So, again, what are you saying?' he asks the mobile, his head shaking slowly and deliberately.

'The answer is "yes" from us, if she's asking the usual,' offers Carlos, after a swift glance towards Joseph.

'Yes to what?' asks Paisley.

Joseph twitches his eyebrows in response.

'Look, Juliet ...' Affie turns to the guys, his free hand lifts in a half shrug, only to be met by reassuring smiles from his buddies. 'OK. OK. It appears to be no problem, so yeah, whatever you're saying. What time?'

'Sorted,' observes Carlos to Joseph.

'What's happening?' asks Selena, before draining her wine glass in one final gulp.

'I'll let Affie explain,' says Carlos, nodding towards him as he finishes his call.

'Look, I didn't know ... but Juliet reckons ... Juliet's heading on up to Edinburgh for New Year.'

'Don't worry about it, lad. You know what our answer will be,' says Carlos.

Us three girls exchange puzzled looks before Affie turns to address us.

'Ladies, I've got a big favour to ask . . .'

'They'll be fine about it,' interrupts Joseph, nodding towards us three. 'If not, they'll need to reassess their own request for a favour from us.'

'My daughter needs to spend some time here, with me.'

There's a split second before we all react simultaneously. There's no need for discussion – of course it's OK.

'There's plenty of bedrooms going spare, Affie, so stop panicking, man. It'll be fine,' says Carlos, without waiting for any of us ladies to speak.

'I know, but this always happens, doesn't it?' He's clearly well used to having to imperfectly juggle his responsibilities. 'Juliet didn't have Edinburgh plans before we left for here. I know that for a fact.'

'Well, she has them now!' says Joseph. 'How's the little one getting here?'

'Her grandad is driving up and dropping her off later . . .' He sighs with relief. 'Thanks, folks.' Affie takes a final look at his phone screen before addressing us three women. 'Sorry, ladies, but Mia's always on her best behaviour. You won't know she's even here.'

'She's a cute little kiddie-wink,' says Joseph. 'She wears hair bobbles too, just like her dad.'

'Exactly. What's the saying? Ugly bull, cute calf,' jests Carlos.

'Slightly harsh, Carlos,' I say.

'No. He's right – she's a little beaut,' adds Affie, biting his bottom lip and retuning his mobile to the sideboard.

'How old is she?'

'Just six.'

'And the ringtone?' asks Selena, pulling a quizzical face. 'Is that "When You Wish Upon a Star"?'

'Her favourite Disney lullaby as a baby – it reminds me of those early days.'

'Ahhh, that's cute,' says Paisley, clearly melting at the mention of lullabies.

'That tune saved me on many a night when she wouldn't go down. On which note, does anyone mind if I switch bedrooms for one of the doubles with single beds – it'll be late by the time she gets here. I don't want Mia waking during the night in a strange house and strange room without me there and being disorientated.'

There's a chorus of 'of course, Affie', 'do as you wish' and 'there's plenty of choice', and he responds with a wide smile.

'Thanks, guys, I owe you one. Right, I'm done with food,' he says, waving a hand at the remnants of his kebab. 'I'll nip upstairs and get mine and the babe's room ready.' He's gone in a heartbeat, and something deep inside me a twangs at hearing his eager footsteps pound up the staircase.

Chapter Thirty-one

Paisley

Before poking my head into the lounge, I tidy up my make-up and run my fingers through my unruly hair. 'Joseph, could I have a quick word?' I'm surprised to find they've each commandeered a specific sofa to sprawl across, and note the beer bottles within easy reach on the coffee table, among the debris of crisp packets and Pringle tubes.

I don't wait for an answer, but walk towards the kitchen, expecting he'll follow. I flick the switch on the kettle and prepare to lay down some rules. It's not fair to anyone to wing this, and certainly not Selena, who just wants to enjoy her celebrations. I know only too well how it feels not to enjoy a big birthday, and I'm not having that happen.

'So, what made you decide to volunteer?' I ask, filling the silence as I make tea for the girls.

Joseph sits himself down at the table, but looks surprised – he's clearly expecting a bigger question.

'Seriously, I'm interested.'

'I believe you. I wanted . . . no, correction, *needed* something to take me out of the house at weekends. I started off by hill walking, which proved beneficial for both my head and my health, and my involvement grew, so soon the majority of my weekends were filled with planned treks and outings. That's how I met Carlos. One thing led to another and he happened to mention that they were recruiting volunteers to help out in

North Wales. The Snowdon area is particularly busy, given the number of tourists each year. I wasn't convinced it was for me, but thought it was worth a try. As it happens, I loved it.'

His features become lighter, almost glowing, while he's talking. The smile I knew so well for so many years returns. Gone is the look he shot me a few minutes ago.

'You're really enjoying it, aren't you?'

'Yeah. You never know what you'll be called to. One day might be a father and three children out climbing in a fog, another maybe a hen party tackling a climb in stilettos.'

I burst out laughing, 'Yeah, right, because that happens.'

'I kid you not, Paisley. Stuff like that happens more than I care to recall. And the rescued party always say the same thing: "we were told there was a path to follow!"'

My laughter feels like old times. Those moments we shared as we enjoyed a large glass of red while cooking, or when attempting DIY together, or just relaxing in the bathtub, just the two of us. That long forgotten sound seems so familiar, yet its loss pulls deep inside of me, and I feel a longing for those days. Carefree, conventional and committed.

'I'm not kidding. Burning blisters, aching arches and twisted ankles – you name it, they sit down and wait for emergency help to arrive. Some even ask if we're going to call the helicopter to collect them, as if it were a regular taxi service.'

'You're pulling my leg!'

'I'm not.'

I continue to laugh, while admiring his ability to start afresh and dedicate himself to something new and worthwhile.

'I couldn't do it,' I say, partly to him, partly to myself, as I pour the boiling water into three mugs. 'There must be some awful injuries sustained and desperate people in need of rescuing?'

'Sadly, yes. But you take the rough with the smooth. I'm not out there rescuing on my own. The team works together to support the casualties and each other. For much of the time I'm simply a strong bod carrying a stretcher after someone else has had the difficult task of tending to a nasty injury or physically manoeuvring themselves down a precarious drop to make contact or identifying . . . well, yeah, identifying.'

I fill in the blanks. How very sad.

'Nope. I couldn't do it. Well done for volunteering and showing up when others need you. I can only imagine the sheer panic they must be in – some of them, at least – making that initial call.'

We both fall silent then, exchanging an uncomfortable look, as if apologising for getting along too well, given the circumstances. 'It almost felt like old times then,' I say, unable to help myself, and for which I could kick myself.

But then he says sorry, which irks me more. Whether it was his need to say sorry that ruined the moment we were having or my reference to our past, we've killed the moment. Instantly, we return to being two strangers standing in a kitchen, looking for any excuse to return to our respective friends.

'Best get back to it. The next footie match will be on soon,' says Joseph, standing up and collecting a folded newspaper. He pauses before asking, 'We're good, yeah?'

'Yeah. All good.' I give a hearty smile to reinforce my words, then watch him hastily leave.

A wave of sadness washes over me. There's so much I want to say, intended to say, and yet between our discussion of his volunteering and my tea making, had it all been said? I silently congratulate myself for not going further than I did. I feel exhausted and we're just two days in of five. Though, once I get home, I'm almost tempted to rewatch our wedding recording, because *where* in our vows did this situation get addressed? I remember the 'to have and to hold', the 'till death us do part', but never the 'to apologise and scurry' vow. Back then, never in a million years did I think we would end up like this.

'Here we go, a fresh cuppa. But I refuse to do the late-night toastie treat like your father used to, ladies,' I announce, entering the snug with a tray laden with mugs and a half-finished packet of biscuits, which might, now I think of it, belong to the fellas.

'I think I'd have preferred another . . .' Selena raises her empty wine glass, and grimaces. Was I supposed to be a mind reader. I'm clearly not, given the state of affairs in my own life.

'You angel,' coos Kate reassuringly, depositing her empty glass on the coffee table in favour of my fresh brew. 'Biscuits too.'

'Yep, pinched from the guys, I think, but after this morning's antics they owe us one,' I add, silently debating whether I should mention my little chat with Joseph. Get their opinion, say, or at least a fresh insight. Might as well. 'I've just spoken to Joseph . . . while making the tea. I reckoned I ought to clear the air.'

Two shocked faces stare back.

'Don't look at me that way. I need to know I did good. Played it fair and acted like the bigger person . . .'

'I'm sure you did, but . . .'

'There's always a but . . . isn't there?' I mutter, regretting my decision to share.

'Sadly, it's usually the important bit.' Kate is as sensible as ever. Selena makes an effort to stand, collecting her empty glass for a refill and ignoring the tea.

I sink back into my chair. Maybe I shouldn't have tried to smooth things over? For a split second I actually felt better about our situation, but now, on receiving this lukewarm reception, I wish I hadn't bothered. Joseph has returned to his sports marathon and I'm no better off. One nil to him, no?

'Maybe we could do something away from the cottage tomorrow?' I suggest, changing the subject. Away from the guys, is what I want to say, but I can't bring myself to sound so mean. Selena nods as she skirts the coffee table, heading for the door.

Kate taps the side of her nose. 'I've got that sussed, young lady. You pair need to be up early and dressed for the day, as we'll be leaving as soon as breakfast is sorted. Are you listening, little sis?' Selena acknowledges her with a slight grunt, nearly out the door.

'Sounds good. Will the chef be ready?' I jest, matching her lighter tone.

'You cheeky mare!'

'Only joking, babe.'

'Nothing would ever get sorted if it wasn't for you,' offers Selena, from the doorway. 'My organising never goes right.'

'Though Affie's no slouch either, given he got all that extra produce,' I say.

'How is Affie getting on with his preparations?' asks Kate, gingerly sipping her tea.

I eye her cautiously before speaking, 'Is there something I've missed?'

'Not at all. Just asking as his little girl is supposed to be arriving in the next hour. I was just wondering—'

'I was just wondering . . .' I mimic. 'I'm sure he'll get his act together before the little one arrives. Do you care to know how Carlos was? Or Joseph?'

'Are you OK with her arrival?' Kate eyes me over the top of her steaming mug.

I shrug. I'm grateful for her thoughtfulness, but I'm not sure how to explain how I'm truly feeling, as I don't know myself.

'It's OK not to be OK with it, Paisley. I get it's a lot to ask of you.'

'But is it?' I say, attempting to brush the whole thing off.

'Of course, we don't want you bottling things up and . . .' Her words fade, not daring to say aloud what they all think.

'I think I'd have been happier with a little more notice. Mia's arrival coming on the back of the McLoughlin family baby news hasn't helped, but then it appears no one had warning of that little delivery, so who am I to expect one. So other than that—' My sentence is overshadowed by the jangling of the doorbell chimes. It must be the front door's bell-pull.

Kate puts her mug down and jumps up as if she's the one in charge.

'Are you going out to greet her?' I ask, surprised she's getting involved.

'No. Of course not, but there's nothing wrong with being ready – Affie might need our help. There could be items that the mother hasn't packed or forgot in a rush. It'll be easier all round if we play our part – remember the boys did us a favour by allowing us to share the cottage, otherwise we'd have been out on our ear the very first night.'

'I can hardly forget, under the circumstances, Kate,' I reply, tartly.

Selena's head and shoulders appear around the door. 'Mia's arrived. Are you coming to say hello?' Before she disappears, I notice her wine glass is virtually brimming with rosé.

Kate hesitates, then stands, making for the door, 'Are you coming?'

'I'd best show willing – otherwise something might be made of it.'

'Paisley, it won't. Though, if you've managed to put one ghost to rest with Joseph, maybe a second one might be in order.'

'Eh? What ghosts?' I follow Kate's lead, deciding to linger at the rear. A blast of cold air greets us in the hallway, as an older gentleman waves an uncomfortable hello from the doorstep as Affie pulls his trainers on.

'This is the gang, Roger. The three ladies are Kate, Selena and Paisley – friends of friends, as such.'

We all say hello, including the other two fellas, who are

standing in the lounge doorway. I suspect they don't want to lose sight of the current match, but know what is expected of them.

'She's in the car, lad. Flaked out in the back – she's slept all the way,' says Roger, having acknowledged our presence, while Affie heads out to collect her.

We loiter awkwardly, not saying much, simply waiting for the arrival of a sleepy child, with tousled hair and a creased cheek.

'Coming through, and straight up the stairs we go!' whispers Affie, coming back in. In his arms is a wrapped bundle, a tuft of blonde hair is visible and a pair of bare feet dangle at the other end. In a heartbeat, they are in, up and gone, and yet the image that lingers is one of protection and pure love. How wonderful to be safe in her father's arms and carried up the stairs, still wrapped in a blanket like a giant cocoon. My heart melts, my throat clogs and I swallow deeply, vainly attempting to control my emotions. As I glance away from Affie, my eyes meet Joseph's. I look elsewhere in haste. The last thing I want right now is another conversation full of regrets.

Chapter Thirty-two

Sunday 29 December 2024

Kate

I head downstairs to be greeted by lyrics of 'Frostie the Snowman' blaring out from the record player. Framed in the kitchen's open doorway is the appealing sight of a girl-daddy performing the daily ritual of plaiting his offspring's hair. Even though said jiggling pyjama-ed child is impatient to be off playing.

'Morning,' I say, smiling at each of them, my heart melting a little, before passing through towards the kettle area. 'Seems Daddy has hidden talents,' I observe. Affie's daughter giggles and jiggles some more – not quite what he needed her to do. She's tiny in comparison to him, which makes the juxtaposition seem cuter still. I don't remember my own father doing anything other than brushing our hair at most, but modern dads have certainly evolved.

'Morning, Kate. Mia, this is Kate, a friend of Joseph's,' murmurs Affie, his nimble fingers clasping strands of blonde hair as he pauses to make the introductions.

'Hello, Mia,' I say to the little girl, who whispers the faintest of hellos in return, before acting all bashful.

'As a young lad, I never imagined I'd have to learn such skills,' jests Affie, finishing off the plait and stretching an elasticated bobble over his fingers in order to secure his handiwork.

'Or excel at such tasks,' I say, observing the neatness of his hairdressing.

'Exactly. There'd have been fisticuffs in the playground had anyone even suggested it and yet . . .' he pauses, a flush coming to his cheeks as he neatens the remaining ends, '. . . I'm quite handy with a tail comb and hair grips.'

'Us girls will know where to come from now on.'

'My speciality is a fancy French plait with colour contrasting ribbons – but only on high days and holidays,' quips Affie, turning Mia around to get a look at the end result, adding, 'There you go, little madam.' He affectionately nips her nose between his fingers before she skips off in search of her socks.

My heart melts, again.

'Practise your technique on your own mane, do you?' I add, flicking the switch on the kettle.

'Oh no. I couldn't possibly work a French plait and ribbons into mine. Have you ever tried it with your hands working back to front in a mirror – totally beyond me, that's another level.'

He's quite funny, without Carlos here to steal the spotlight.

'Coffee?' I ask, as I begin my prep for today's cooked brekkie.

'Please. Though I'll get out of your hair – ha ha, see what I did there?'

'Yeah, a definite dad-joke.'

Affie beams as he collects his hairdressing equipment, stashing it neatly in a quilted bag.

Despite the noisy chatter in the kitchen, I hear my phone bleep in the other room.

'Could someone watch this bacon for me while I nip . . .' I don't elaborate but merely gesture towards the door.

'Sure,' offers Carlos, stepping forward and taking the spatula from me. It can only be psycho-boss. Now what does he want? Surely everything is in hand? He'd better not have changed his mind about the colour, the size or the timings of anything. I head for the snug, expecting to find my mobile where I left it on the coffee table. Instead I find Paisley, looking confused and clutching my mobile.

'Argh, there it is,' I muster, reaching for the device.

'Uh-uh,' she says, snatching her hand away. 'Your boss is texting you?'

'Is he?' I say, feigning surprise, while attempting to retrieve my mobile from her.

'Kate, what's so urgent that he constantly disturbs your holiday?'

'Lord knows. Pass it here and I'll see.' I can't exactly rugby tackle her to the floor, so I attempt to maintain some dignity and stand still in front of her, open palm awaiting the delivery of my phone.

'Kate?' Her tone has edge.

'Paisley?'

She drops the mobile into her lap, leans forward and takes hold of my outstretched hand. 'Kate, what's going on?'

'Nothing. Why? Why should there be anything going on? You've got the wildest imagination, haven't you? Can't a boss forget a detail and contact his PA? Surely the quickest solution, given everyone else at the office seems so sodding useless.'

My words spill into the void rapidly forming between us. Paisley's face slowly morphs from concern to panic.

'Oh, my God. What are you and him up to?'

'Me? Him? No! Nothing,' I stammer.

'So why . . .' she gestures towards her lap.

'He's not great with organising stuff, you know that. How many stories have I told you over the years? Loads. Why would anything change just because I'm on holiday? He's not, is he?'

'But you are, Kate!'

I flinch, as she hits the bull's eye.

'So, what are you organising?'

I could do without this.

'Shall I fetch Selena?' she asks, knowing it'll force the issue.

'Don't be mad, but I've organised his daughter's engagement party for the thirtieth.' I wait for the words to register.

'Tell me you are joking?' Paisley's face screws up in disgust. 'Seriously? Can't his wife and daughter sort that out?'

I shrug. 'I've organised the whole shebang – party, location, food, booze and novelty entertainment.'

'Such as?' asks Paisley, forcefully.

'The fiancé is into birds – so they want the engagement ring delivered Harry Potter-style, via a swooping Hedwig.'

'Christ, how the other half live,' mutters Paisley. 'An engagement ring and a marriage proposal isn't enough – the actual delivery has to be staged, on cue and organised by the bride-to-be's father. Or rather his PA! That sounds so fancy pants lush having a fully fledged party-organiser on speed dial – especially when you don't pay for her time, effort or energy! Though good luck with your future marriage, young man. Psycho-boss father-in-law will be cheering you on from the side lines come your wedding night, I'm sure.'

'Stop it!'

'Or you might be assigned that task too, Kate,' scoffs Paisley.

'Anyway,' I say, hauling the topic back, 'he's just nervous, that's all. Surely you can understand that?' I add, hoping to gain some understanding.

'Nope. Get your own family to organise your daughter's big day rather than the rent-free skivvy at the office.'

'Paisley, can I have my phone, please. It'll only be a small thing, I'm sure, and I need to get back to the breakfasts.'

'Kate, no.'

'Pretty please? We can talk about this later, but right now . . .' Paisley thrusts the phone at me, clearly frustrated, and I quickly retreat with it to the kitchen, knowing this conversation isn't over. Though I really hope she doesn't snitch on me to Selena.

Today of all days. I'll never hear the end of it. I unlock and retrieve the message.

'Is there a cake ordered?'

Phew! Is that it! Simple and easy. My fingers dance across the screen, supplying the answer instantly. I smile at Carlos, and take back control of the spatula and the pan of sizzling bacon.

Yes. Cake delivery timed for six o'clock at the venue. Baker happy to decorate the cake table/trolley for surprise delivery.

I quickly press 'send', put my mobile down on the countertop and return my focus to the task in hand: serving breakfast.

'I hope you guys are hungry, because I've been a little heavy handed with the bacon,' I announce, turning from the stove and coming face to face with Paisley, who's glowering at me. She's joined the hungry gathering at the table. Only my sister is missing. Joseph is watching Paisley carefully, Paisley's watching me.

'I'm starving,' calls out Carlos, readying his line-up of condiments from the cupboard in preparation.

'And me,' says Affie, grabbing the pile of paper serviettes to take through to the dining room.

'I reckon I could eat a scabby donkey,' adds Carlos, before heading after him, armed with squeezy bottles.

I grab the plates warming in the Aga, which are slightly hotter than I'd like, but swiftly begin dishing up, praying that Paisley doesn't go on the attack and drop me in it. I can explain. He's not taking advantage, if that's what she's thinking. No, I wouldn't let that happen, after all these years. I've got him sussed, I swear.

'I mean it, Kate – he's taking advantage of you,' states Paisley, firmly. At this, Affie and Carlos stall, midway through the door.

'Mr Psycho-boss has got her organising his daughter's engagement party while on her holidays,' Paisley elaborates for their
benefit, but more to make the point to me.

'His wife never has time to organise such things. He's told
me over and over how much she hates missing engagements
because all her time would be swallowed up chasing suppliers
and assessing catering options, and all the million and one little
things.' Even to my own ears, it's a weak defence.

'Or so he says,' mocks Affie, standing in the doorway.

'No, honest, it's just the way it is. It's just easier this way.'

'In that case, what a clever man he is. He has the best of both
worlds – a wife at home and you to run his errands outside of
the home. Hell, he's a bloody genius!' says Affie. To my relief, he
leaves it there and heads down the hallway, calling out for his
daughter to come through to eat.

I turn back around to tend to the bacon, but something deep
inside twangs like a harp string at the exchange between father
and daughter. I know Paisley's still watching me, however; I can
sense it. Have I really been working unpaid and unappreciated
overtime for decades, as she claims? In my head I thought I
was being helpful. Efficient. Using my talents. Organising others
that couldn't, but maybe Paisley and Affie are right. Is my inner
need to help others so skewed that I'm being manipulated? Am
I being used?

Chapter Thirty-three

Selena

I'm eager to start the day, especially given that there's a promise of doing something different on the cards. Not that I'm complaining about the previous two days, but things hadn't gone quite how I imagined. Not that I'd arranged any of it, other than rental of this cottage – and that failed to go as planned. I've no idea what Kate is organising, but given it's my big birthday, I bet it'll be doubly good. Even if it is on behalf of my parents. Everything Kate does is good. Something that her psycho-boss latched on to a long time ago and has used to his advantage ever since. All we need to do is ensure no mean boys get in on the act and wreck our experience this time. Not that I'm giving Carlos the satisfaction of knowing that he wrecked my chocolate treat, but clearly he did. Worse still is that he messed up my hair! He reminds me of Jez from work. All ego, glib remarks and with his eyes constantly on the prize of a winning campaign, all the while scrutinising everything that I do, for fear I do it better than him. Which I will, and always will do, but I could do without the waste of energy spent constantly watching my back every time Jez is within earshot or snooping around my team. There's a definite Jez kind of feel to Carlos. In fact, there's such a Jez feel about him, he's probably more Jez than Jez could ever be.

I clomp down the staircase two at a time, like a child eager for cartoons. God knows how suitable my shoes are for today's excursions, but Carlos interrupted Kate's info session and she didn't reiterate specific clothing. I figure a jumpsuit and wedges are suitable for most outings. Though if Kate wears her jumpsuit too, I'll have to change. With her leggy, slender frame, I'll look like a plumber's mate-cum-apprentice in an unflattering boiler suit in comparison.

I can hear the happy chatter of voices before I reach the dining room. I hope it all relates to my birthday plans, but it's probably more down to Affie's little girl, Mia.

'Morning!' I announce, finding I'm the last to join the throng and my breakfast plate is already waiting.

In among the chorus of 'mornings' from the adults comes a tiny 'hello' from the new addition. There she is: the cutest little girl, still dressed in Disney pyjamas, with blonde hair tied back in a plait and a smattering of freckles, digging into her bowl of Frosties.

'Good morning, little one. I'm Selena. The loud one. I'm guessing you're Mia.'

'Yep, that's me.' Her sweet voice matches her bright smile. Affie proudly looks down at her, affectionately sweeping away a stray sticky-up section of hair from her forehead.

'Nice to meet you . . . and if these boys get on your nerves any time during your stay, Mia, just shout and we'll come and rescue you from yet another football match or whatever it is they're watching in the lounge. OK?'

'It's *How The Grinch Stole Christmas*,' volunteers Mia, glancing up at her father.

'Are you serious, fellas? Isn't she a bit young?' I ask.

'Oh, but I like the Grinch,' says Mia, proudly looking up at her father. 'I always choose it at home.'

'See, Selena, the child has taste,' offers Carlos, leaning down towards Mia to loudly whisper, 'Mia, Selena doesn't get the plotline, unlike you, so don't let on. She'll be jealous.'

'Seriously, Affie. Don't force feed her such scary stuff. The language, the violence, the bloodshed, killings and don't get me started on the F bombs!'

Then the truth dawns – I've waded in without thinking it through yet again.

'Oh no, wrong film. That's *Die Hard*, which guys try to make out is a Christmas film, when it is clearly not a Christmas film. Probably your favourite, Carlos?'

'Selena, give it a rest,' mutters Kate, offering me a freshly poured tea. I get her drift and resolve to pipe down and shut up. I'm not trying to start an argument at the breakfast table. It's a bit early even for me to start rattling the first cage of the day.

'Anyway … You're welcome to drift our way, Mia, if these chaps get on your nerves. Especially this one.' I point at Carlos, which makes the little girl giggle. She's clearly met him before. 'So, Kate, where are we going today?'

'I suggest you eat your breakfast before the eggs congeal and maybe grab some toast before it is stone cold, because I can promise chilled bubbles, which you won't want to enjoy on an empty stomach. All courtesy of Mum and Dad,' explains Kate.

'Or, rather, *we* won't want her enjoying bubbles on an empty stomach,' adds Paisley. 'It's never a pretty sight.'

'Exactly,' says Kate. 'Anyway, you'll know when we need to leave, that's all I'm saying. We'll be travelling in style.'

'In style?' I say, liking the sound of this, and confident she'll have planned my outing to the nth degree.

'Where are your parents?' asks Joseph, finishing his breakfast just as I tuck into mine.

'Well, because it took madam here so long to make up her mind about what she wanted to do, she left them little choice. So they've ended up doing their usual Christmas holiday in Lanzarote, where they have a holiday home. It's an annual thing. They hate the British weather, so they disappear for six weeks every winter and return in February,' explains Kate, as I chomp through my lukewarm breakfast.

'Nice work if you can get it,' whistles Carlos, wiping his near-empty plate with a slice of buttered toast, collecting the remnants of egg yolk.

'Exactly. They were actually hoping a certain someone would join them in order to celebrate,' continues Kate, staring hard at me. 'But given her lack of plans until the last minute, they've come up with a great idea to mark the occasion. I'm only hoping she appreciates it.'

'Oi! I always appreciate everything,' I mumble, through a mouthful of food.

'Nah, even I can tell that's a whopper,' scoffs Carlos, shaking his head.

'What do you know?' I retort.

'I can tell.'

Joseph interjects. 'Anyway . . . before this pair start sparring again . . . I've had a message from the lovely Josie regarding the hearth in the lounge . . .' He reaches for his phone and starts running through his messages to find the right one.

Bang on cue, someone raps firmly on the front door, making several of us jump.

'I'll go, because *that* might be perfect timing,' says Joseph, stuffing his phone into his jeans pocket and making his way towards the hallway. 'And then I won't need to explain.'

'You don't look anything like Dick Van Dyke.' I'm watching as the engineer pieces together sections of extendable tubing. There's no neckerchief, no flat cap and definitely no fake Cockney accent. There's not even a long-poled sweeper's brush either, just a load of dust sheets, a large vacuum pump contraption and said extendable suction tubes.

'You don't say, love. I've never heard that before in my thirty years on the job,' he mutters, clearly not impressed.

'I feel robbed,' I say, more to myself than him. I'm hanging about, awaiting the promised signal to leave for our outing. Kate's not spilling, and I'm half convinced that I've already missed it. Paisley seems nonplussed either way. I've a nagging feeling she'd be happy to stay put and maybe even do something boring like watch footie all day in the lounge.

'So you do this role permanently?' I ask, trying to make conversation in the face of my disappointment that technology has denied me a true Mary Poppins experience for my big birthday.

'No, love. I tend to linger around outside the park gates for the majority of the day performing as a one-man-band and playing to the tourists and creating a few chalk drawings on the pavement in-between the rain showers.'

'You're making fun of me.'

'Yes, love. Clearly, I'm joking. Talk about perception and reality. I hate to disappoint, but even a job like mine has moved on with technology.' He's rolling his eyes a bit as he stuffs his length of tubing up the hearth flue.

I crouch down beside him and try to see what's up the chimney, despite it being tricky.

'Careful now, Selena. We wouldn't want you getting sucked up the flue,' comes Carlos' voice from behind me.

'Ha ha, as if.'

The chimney sweep shakes his head as he continues to thrust the tubing up the chimney. 'If I had a pound for every time someone said something like that, I'd have been retired by now. And my father a decade earlier than he actually did.'

'Personally, given my marketing expertise, where perception and reality are my forte, I'd suggest you start playing on the fact that your customers would like to experience the so-called perception of your role and not the true reality. You might find there's a bigger market for such things ... as I can't imagine there's much call nowadays – given you're so readily available in attending our flue disaster at just gone half eight of a morning.'

'She's here all week, mate, if you fancy returning for another lecture about your job and possible sidelines. Or would you fancy a coffee while your work?' says Carlos, giving a jaunty nod in my direction.

'Coffee, please. And some quiet would be nice.'

Carlos laughs, before heading out to make coffee.

Cheeky bastard. What the hell does he know!

There's a sudden noise. Carlos stops near the doorway, turns around and, like me, stares at the hearth, as if that's the source of the din.

'Not me, love,' says the chimney sweep, switching his machinery off.

The door opens, nearly knocking Carlos aside, revealing a hurried Kate.

'Quick, Selena, come on – this is us. Or rather you,' she says, beckoning me frantically to follow her.

Chapter Thirty-four

Mid-morning

Kate

Selena didn't even get the chance to catch her breath. I literally pushed her out of the cottage, having thrown her jacket at her, slung her handbag over her shoulder, grabbed a set of door keys, then dragged her along the cobbles. The noise was still deafening. There was no hope of explaining what we were about to do so it was better that she see for herself. As we drag her by her wrists the short distance along the lane, our hair begins blowing in every imaginable direction, and her look of shock and growing apprehension deepens. My stomach was swirling and twirling – but at least I knew what was in store, having had some time to get my head around the idea after our parents gave me the full details. But to know nothing until you saw the helicopter in the neighbouring field must be quite some shock. There in front of us was a sleek black machine, its rotatory blades swirling, with the half-crouched co-pilot awaiting our arrival. Every blade of grass, bulrush and hedgerow around had been disturbed by this beast that had landed beside the water. Selena's mouth fell wide open.

'No way! That's not for us?'

'Yes way! For you, Selena! Happy birthday from Mum and Dad!'

'Bloody hell, I'm not sure I can do this,' shouts Paisley, even though I'd debriefed her some twenty minutes ago. I daren't say anything earlier, in case she went all wobbly and ruined the surprise. Bless her, she's had enough to contend with this break and we're only on day three.

I can't hear what the approaching guy is trying to say, but his outstretched arms are gesturing for us to bend down as we approach. That said, given the size of those whirring blades above our heads, surely it's instinct to duck.

Selena's mouth is yawping away but I can only hear every other word.

'My ... God ... How ... Bloody ... Hell ... Amazing ... Save ... Ass ... My ... Life,' she's screaming, which I think is a good reaction, but I'm not hanging around to find out. I follow the guy's frantic instructions and head towards the open rear doors. As we reach him, he hands us each a set of bulky earphones, just like the ones he is already wearing. We all gratefully grab a pair as we clamber inside.

I dive across the wide seat, Paisley slides in next, and then Selena, so she gets to sit by the door. I pull the bulky defenders over my ears and look towards our goggled pilot for direction. He's giving us the thumbs-up gesture, along with a winning smile. The meet and greet co-pilot is beside us, indicating our seats' safety harnesses before the door slams shut, and he does a double check on the locking mechanism before hopping into the front passenger seat. It all happens so quickly our Selena has barely had a chance to close her gaping mouth.

The co-pilot turns around in his seat and indicates to our defenders before he begins to speak, and then his voice comes through the headphones clearly.

'Hello, ladies. How are we today?'

We all nod, somewhat stunned.

'My name's Tristan and our pilot today is Matt.' Matt gives us another big smile and a thumbs up before turning back around to begin flicking switches on his dashboard. Tristan reaches for a clipboard of notes from the front dashboard and so begins a short safety drill.

'Selena, we believe this is a surprise gift from your parents, so shall we let you in on the itinerary for today's trip? We are going to soar up into the skies, allowing you to enjoy a unique view of the surrounding countryside that is our beautiful Cumbria. Matt's then going to head out towards Lake Windermere, which isn't far away, then take a swift turn, taking us towards Coniston Waters, at which point we are going to be landing nearby, enabling you ladies to enjoy a visit to Brantwood, the beautiful historical home of John Ruskin, the writer, art historian and art critic. And I believe that Kate has a few further birthday surprises organised too.'

I nod frantically, enjoying the sheer thrill evident upon my sister's face. And yet – buzz goes my jacket pocket. We're squashed up against each other, so Paisley feels it vibrate against her thigh, and gives me a hard stare. I give a weak smile in return, in an attempt to pacify her, but it's not going to wash.

'But first, buckle up, sit back and enjoy the ride, ladies!' announces Tristan, turning forward again and joining the pilot in the pre-flight checks.

I check my harness buckles again, purely through nerves, and then sit back to enjoy my sister's delighted expression. She keeps looking from me to Paisley and back again, blown away by our parents' gift.

I turn to my right-hand side and stare out across the lake and the wild meadow that sit behind the cottage but then the warmth of Paisley's hand wraps around mine and gives a tight squeeze. I smile and see she's holding Selena's hand too on the other side. You can't beat moments like this.

We scream in unison as the helicopter begins to wobble and lifts up. I didn't expect that, and neither did Paisley or the birthday girl, given their wide-eyed expressions. In a heartbeat, we've left the ground behind. Selena leans around Paisley to tug on my arm, gesturing outside. I crane my neck to see through her window and spy three men and a little girl, who's excitedly jigging about, all looking up and waving gleeful goodbyes into the sky.

'How small does the cottage look now?' I ask, trying to distract from the second buzz occurring inside my pocket and avoiding Paisley's stare.

'Bye bye, Lakeside Cottage. This sure beats a rerun of *The Grinch*!' Selena's voice is coming through loud and clear through my headphones.

'Sure does!' I yell, unsure if I've just deafened everyone with my enthusiasm.

'It feels like we've got a date with Ant and Dec plus a jungle full of celebs!' adds Paisley, excitedly.

'Not quite, but we can dream!' says Selena cheekily, as the helicopter sweeps high into the grey winter sky, the stunning patchwork of earthy shades and vast stretch of shimming water glistening below. I bet this view looks glorious at the height of summer with swathes of green and yellow stencilled below. 'Who'd have thought Mum and Dad would even think of something like this!'

I smile; such a treat, I feel, simply matches the high flyer that she has always been.

Silence descends. The immense noise of the rotatory blades makes it easier to indulge in our own thoughts rather than attempt to talk. I feel overwhelmed by the sheer beauty spread beneath us as far as the eye can see. It's such a privilege to see the world through the eyes of a bird in flight – what a truly glorious spectacle.

'It's huge! And busy!' cries Selena, minutes later, as the helicopter swoops lower over the rippling waters of Lake Windermere. The noise from above makes the tiny people below glance up in surprise: some wave, most stare, as we fly by.

'The lake is just over eighteen kilometres in length, so we won't be travelling its entirety today, but you can appreciate its natural beauty and importance to this area from up here.'

'I never imagined so many people would be out on the water – there's so many ferries and small boats. Look, there're canoeists over there,' yells Paisley, clearly forgetting we can hear her perfectly well via the headsets.

'It's teaming with visitors every day, regardless of the weather or time of year,' adds Tristan, turning around in his seat again. 'Walkers, hikers and mountain bikers swarm here. If you're a fishing enthusiast, you're spoilt for choice, with pike, perch, roach and even salmon and sea trout in certain seasons. This stretch of water is brimming with life, in and out of the water.'

'And it's the largest, yeah?' asks Selena, sounding interested, which surprises me, as she's not one of nature's natural enthusiasts.

'Yep, the largest lake in England. Though not the UK,' confirms Tristan.

'Fancy trying your hand at canoeing?' I jest, unsure if I'm seeing a new interest take hold. Though if her chocolate skills are anything to go by, it'll probably be another disaster.

'Phuh! Not on your nelly. But I admire anyone who's prepared to don a wetsuit and enjoy the elements to that extent. I'll stick with dry land, thanks. Unless it's a waterfall. Now they mesmerise me.'

'Stoke Ghyll Force might interest you, then,' says Tristan. 'A pretty little waterfall with a steady flow and within walking distance of where you're staying. Head north from your cottage – you can't miss it.'

'Actually, you could and many do,' quips Matt, the pilot. His first comment since welcoming us.

I take note, knowing we might need a back-up plan if the weather turns, scuppering my current plans.

'But, for now, we're going to take a sharp right and cut across towards Coniston Waters, where I believe you ladies have a booking at the beautiful Brantwood.'

'We do,' I say proudly, noting that Selena looks confused but also pleased as punch, what with all the treats that are coming thick and fast. She makes out she's all brash and untouchable, but she loves a bit of TLC and having attention lavished on her.

We spend the next fifteen minutes in stunned silence as the beauty of the Lake District passes beneath us – quaint villages gathered around tiny greens or church yards, narrow roads twisting like satin ribbons strewn between ancient hedge-rows and streams. The only interruption on our scenic journey towards Brantwood is the odd comment via the headsets from Tristan.

'And just below us is Hill Top. The cottage and gardens belonged to Beatrix Potter, author of the Peter Rabbit books. The lady was big on conversation and left us a great legacy. She was big on conservation, you see. She owned fourteen farms in total and literally helped save our local breed of Herdwick sheep from dying out. Now, that's a must if you've time to visit – we locals owe her so much.'

I duly note these details too, but given Selena's lack of maternal urges and total absence of interest in children's literature, I'm not sure it'll be to her liking. I've got my doubts that our chosen destination will be up her alley either, but choices were limited, given how late all this came together.

Suddenly an impressive house comes into view, nestled among the trees. Its peach-coloured walls give off an Italian villa vibe, which is exaggerated by leaded windows that overlook sweeping lawns that run down to the water's edge.

'We're going to touch down here, ladies. We've been granted per-mission, so don't panic,' says Matt, skilfully doing his manoeuvres.

'Can I ask that everyone stays seated and allows me to assist once we're safely landed,' adds Tristan.

Selena's face is a picture: her eyes are wide, and her mouth nearly as wide. The glow of sheer excitement radiating from my sister brings tears to my eyes.

Chapter Thirty-five

Early Afternoon

Paisley

'Whose house?' I ask, sounding pretty stupid. Kate sounded so assured as she talked about 'the famous art critic, art historian and writer' as the uniformed waiter delivered our afternoon cream tea on silver tiered cake stands to our wrought-iron table set beside the choppy waters of Coniston.

'Ruskin. John Ruskin.' Kate looks at me, clearly surprised by my ignorance.

'Nope. Never heard of him,' I admit, reaching for a delicate cucumber sandwich. Selena shrugs too, adding, 'She had me at Hill Top with Beatrix Potter. I've at least heard of her.'

'Which is a shame, given that we're sitting on Ruskin's lawn enjoying some chilled bubbles,' mutters Kate, reaching for an egg and cress.

'See, if we'd nipped to Hill Top for afternoon tea and sat among her cabbages, I'd have had no need to ask who,' I blurt, relieved that Selena's in the same boat as me.

'Ignorant. The pair of you.'

'And you aren't? You only know because you booked it. Alright, tell us about the studying you've been doing then? Clearly you've read up on him, as that's so you,' prompts Selena, sitting back, her champagne glass in hand.

Kate blows out her cheeks, exasperated.

'He's of the Victorian era, a great man recognised by Queen Victoria herself. He met Wordsworth . . .'

'Now, him I know,' announces Selena, gesturing with her near-empty glass. 'He gave me GCSE nightmares, what with his daffodils.'

'Funny that, because there's a swathe of daffodils here, come the spring, and our other option was visiting Wordsworth's grammar school in Hawkshead village,' says Kate.

'So why are we here then? Or didn't that justify Mum and Dad's chopper ride?'

'It's closed at this time of year, otherwise . . .'

'Oh, great. You picked my birthday celebrations, paid for courtesy of my parents . . .'

'*Our* parents.'

'OK. Our parents. But you picked based on the likelihood of them granting permission for a chopper to land and not based on my interests? Nice one, sis,' bleats Selena. 'I suppose the cabbage patch at Hill Top wasn't large enough for a helicopter?'

Kate swallows hard at the ingratitude. 'Look, this is beautiful. A stunning location. Right by the water's edge with grand views on all four sides. What more could you wish for when eating a cream scone and sipping your bubbles? Just be grateful that . . .' She stops dead and begins to nibble her sandwich, as if she hadn't been speaking.

'What? Be grateful for what?' asks Selena eagerly.

'Nothing.'

'That you haven't got your daddy's PA organising every last detail of your celebration, unlike some we know?' I say, reaching for another scone.

'What?' squawks Selena, clearly confused.

'No. That wasn't what I was about to say.' Kate gives me daggers across the table.

'Sorry, but what?' asks Selena, again. 'Out with it.'

I remain quiet this time as Kate briefly outlines and plays down her starring role as engagement organiser for her psycho-boss.

'You had better be kidding me, Kate!' mutters Selena, clearly disappointed. 'You are a sucker for punishment!'

'It explains all the text messaging – which we'd picked up on,' I add, confirming what we, me and Selena, had previously discussed.

'It was hardly taxing, I organised her engagement-do in between arranging your surprises, there's nothing to it!'

'Urgh, Kate! I don't want to hear about it ... them ... your psycho-boss and his sodding family. This is meant to be my big birthday!'

'OK, Drama Queen! Just be grateful that Carlos isn't here bugging the hell out of you. Though I'd have welcomed his presence – *he* knew who Ruskin was,' offers Kate, skirting Selena's annoyance.

'I bet he bloody didn't,' scoffs Selena.

'He did, actually. He knew all about the gardens and who'd designed them. I mentioned it in passing after breakfast. Which surprised me somewhat, but still, you only know what you know and he knew about John Ruskin.'

'Joseph wouldn't,' I add.

'No. Affie didn't either.'

'But Carlos did?' asks Selena cautiously.

'He did. There's more to him than meets the eye – far more than nice skin and decent cheekbones.'

'Is that all you've noticed? His skin and cheekbones – how about his breadth and brawn?' I ask.

'All I can say is how nice it has been without those pesky boys cramping our style!' says Selena, holding her crumbling scone aloft.

We all fall silent, eyeballing one another as we continue to nibble our tiered treats. I suspect we all have the same thought; how can anyone be so bright yet be in his line of business? Though, as it has been for days, my mind then strays to Joseph.

'I hate to be rude and change the subject but ...' I can't help myself. 'Seeing him, hearing him, watching him, just knowing him ... this hurts me more than what he actually did,' I say, my words gushing like a forgotten tap. Selena and Kate exchange a glance, which I can't ignore despite wanting to. 'What?' There, I've said it aloud. Now who's the fool?'

'You're no fool, Paisley. I think you've been brave these last few days even sticking around. I wouldn't have wanted to re-enact this scenario with one of my exes and I've never been married to any of them,' offers Selena.

'Nor me. I feel guilty for talking you into it the other day, but you're a braver woman than me. I certainly couldn't share a roof with Cody. One of us would have been arrested by now.'

'Exactly. See, you're doing great, despite what you might think, Paisley.'

'Believe me, I'm not.' I have to tell someone and its best its these two rather than him. 'What if I made a mistake. What if every guy has to grow up, as it were, before he realises what he actually wants in life? What if we were supposed to work through the issue and be stronger afterwards?'

'Work through his cheating?' Kate sounds dubious.

'Some couples do, don't they?'

'Forgive him at the time, you mean?'

'Yeah. Forgive him. Be as angry as hell, that he's done me wrong, hurt me, cheated on me, ruined our wedding vows ... but over time, could we have got through it? Moved on. Stayed together and ...'

Kate is open-mouthed and staring.

'Are you joking?' asks Selena. 'You've dragged yourself through hell and back and now you're suggesting there was a way through for you guys. Because I don't remember you saying anything of the sort at the time.'

'I know it sounds ridiculous. It cut me to the quick. I never dreamed he'd act that way. But what if we weren't truly on the same page back then?'

'I can't believe I'm hearing this,' mutters Kate. Selena shakes her head, then faffs with the champagne bottle and refills our glasses. I know she's heard me talk it all through a million times but still. Not like this.

'I get it. You've both seen all I went through, and you've both been there for me. But what if . . . I'd reacted differently? I was always going to blow my top, scream and wail about the hurt, but what if, afterwards, when the dust settled, I'd asked him to come back? We'd taken it a day at a time? Slowly rebuilding what we had, instead of busting it apart. What then?'

'No one can answer that,' says Selena. 'Not you. Not him. No one.'

Silence descends. The wind whistles in off the water and we each shiver, despite out outdoor jackets. Though the weight lifts from my shoulders a little, and my mind is lighter now that I've said it aloud.

'OK, let's run with that scenario. He left that Sunday morning, and he spends a week at his mother's, just like he did initially. Then let's say you asked him over to chat and you both decided he was to move back in . . . into the spare room, whatever you thought best. Let's pretend you both went back to the basic routines while tackling the issue of what he'd done. You focus on the job routine, family routine – the basics of day to day . . . are you saying you think that, over time – be it six months, nine months, a year – you'd have been able to forgive and forget the cheating incident? Resume your relationship, as was?' asks Kate, working through it.

'Who knows?'

'What if you'd done that and he'd done it again . . . that he'd continually led you down that road, doing the dirty on you each time he was out?' Selena's eyeing me cautiously. She's watching me like a hawk, bless her.

'I'd have had to finish it and call it a day, but did I finish it too soon? Could we have made it through? And, right now, life would be so different, wouldn't it?'

'It could. It might. Or you could still be going through hell with a cheating husband at your side. I get where regret comes from – each and every one of us knows that feeling – but think about it, Paisley. Could you honestly say you'd have been able to trust him on a night out again? A boys' weekend away, such as this? Never wondered where he is or who he's with when he's late home from work? Your mind would have been in turmoil, second guessing every move he'd made following that little indiscretion.' Selena shakes her head again before continuing. 'That would have torn you apart.'

'Exactly, but you've hit the nail on the head right there, his "little indiscretion". You're forgetting . . . he told me. I heard it straight from the horse's mouth the very next morning. He sat me down and he told me what he'd done. Confessed, as such. Now, does that sound like the actions of a bloke who is prepared to travel that road time and time again? I think not.'

'I couldn't imagine it, to be fair, Paisley,' says Kate. 'Forgiveness is one thing, but without solid trust in a relationship – what have you got? You're flogging a dead horse.'

'Madness, if you ask me,' agrees Selena. 'Could you imagine it? You'd be pacing the carpet, questioning every move – you wouldn't want that, Paisley. Life's tough enough as it is.'

'Should I not have given him a second chance, then?'

'Nah.'

'Nope. He doesn't deserve one,' says Kate sternly.

I shrug.

'Have *you* needed a second chance in your marriage or have you managed to stay faithful?' asks Selena.

'You know I have.'

'Well, then. Would he have given you a second chance if you'd been the one to mess up on a night out?'

'Probably not. We both knew how each other felt about such tricks.' Not the nicest of the conversations that we'd had while getting to know each other, but a necessary one nevertheless. It had been triggered by the news that a friend of a friend had embarked on a lengthy five-year affair when the truth had finally came out.

'There's your answer, then. I think you need to quit beating yourself up and get on with enjoying yourself. You've done yourself proud these last few months, so why let this hamper your progress and get in your head?' says Kate.

I fall silent. I thought they'd get my drift, understand where I was coming from, but all they seem to be interested in is ordering a second bottle of chilled bubbles.

Chapter Thirty-six

Late Afternoon

Selena

'What did you think of Brantwood?' asks Carlos, the second we return to the cottage from our helicopter jollies. I've being dying for a cuppa all day and yet now, clearly, he's going to bug me while I make a brew.

'Lush. Though I wouldn't want to live there. But it seems pretty palatial and the grounds are beautiful . . .' I say, watching his reaction. 'Despite the time of year.'

'Really? Not to Your Highness's liking, then?'

I eye him cautiously while lining up three mugs. My cogs whirl and I'm unsure how to play my next move. It's as if a magnetic charge is spanning the gap between us. The air feels electrified, almost as if the static might zap at any second, causing us both to snap back and shake our limbs at the painful sizzle. What is it with this guy? Is it his confidence? His bolshie attitude? Or that ego of his that allows him to say whatever he's thinking?

'Our Kate reckons you knew a thing or two about the previous owner, Ruskin.'

He nods. The git.

'Go on, then, brain-box — what do you know and how?'

He laughs, before shaking his head and changing the subject.

'You'll only be needing five mugs — Affie and the little one

have been out all day.' Then he returns to the original topic, 'An
education, my dear girl – it's a wonderful thing!'

'Not at the school I went to.' I carefully pour the boiling
water into the waiting teapot, a bit miffed that he automatically
assumes I was making everyone tea.

'Nor mine, but hey – reading, learning and studying – it does
you the power of good in all respects. The gardens probably
didn't look their best, but return in summer and you'll have seen
some spectacular beds of geraniums, and hollyhocks galore on
either side of the gravel walkways leading down to the harbour.
One section is a blaze of yellow daffodils come the spring-
time – it's truly worth seeing. All designed by Ruskin's cousin,
apparently . . . she . . .'

It's now my turn to smirk – he's lost in a world of his own.

'What?' he says, noticing my bemused expression. 'You reckon
because I do what I do that I can't possibly have a decent level
of intelligence? Is that it?' he challenges.

'Did I say that?'

'Not in so many words, but, yeah, your expression did.'

'Noooo. I'm curious, that's all. You come across as so laddish
with your beer cans, your sports obsession, the blokey banter,
and yet you were the only one who knew what our Kate was
yapping about. Highly offended she was earlier when I hadn't
a clue. Nor Paisley.'

'Just proves that appearances can be deceptive. Surely you
recognise that as a marketing guru?'

I pull a face as I swish the tea bags in the steaming pot.

Carlos says nothing further. I turn around to check he's still
there. He is, which is slightly embarrassing, as he sees me looking
for him.

'Time to come clean methinks.'

I look up again sharply as his remark hits a nerve.

'What with?' I ask, trying to play dumb.

'Your fancy New Year campaign. What fabulous luxury is it this time? Straight up, out with it. No dodging or diving the question – name your product,' says Carlos, as I open the fridge in search of milk. That's not what I thought he was asking about, but he's right about me playing coy.

'Lard,' I say, closing the fridge door.

Carlos roars with laughter, 'Yeah, right! Pull the other one, it has bells on it!'

'I'm not joking – lard. I'm quite looking forward to it, actually. I chased the lard campaign and won it hands down, beating our competitors. It might not be everyone's cup of tea, but I wanted something I could get my teeth into, so to speak. Though not literally, of course. Urgh, that would be gross!'

'Lard? The white greasy stuff?'

'That's the fella.'

'Lard? No way,' says Paisley. She and Kate have tracked me down in the kitchen, probably wondering where their tea tray is.

'Lard – the creamy white pork fat that you buy in slabs, like butter,' I say. 'Can you all stop saying "lard", please. It's freaking me out the way you all say it with such disgust.'

'Jesus, Selena. Is that your next campaign? You're already doing that marketing thing – you'll be going all M&S sultry tones on us in a minute,' giggles Paisley.

'You can all laugh, but when I win an ad campaign, I win at an ad campaign. I'm promoting it to the hilt, with everything I've got – there's no half measures with me. You know that. Nobody will promote lard better than me. No one!' I have no idea why I felt the need to reinforce my point so much, but it's true.

'Why? Don't tell me there was competition to pitch for that?' asks Kate, grimacing.

'God, yeah. I worked around the clock to perfect my pitch and came up with a winner. Now all I have to do is deliver the same energy and creative ideas for the actual campaign and then I will be a shoo-in for promotion. I'm not planning on being side-lined or stepped over by the likes of Jez and his team.'

'Go on, then – pitch lard to us,' teases Carlos, settling back against the larder door, waiting.

'Yeah, right,' I retort, batting his suggestion away.

'Serious, like.' He smiles in such a way that it comes across as a dare. I don't do dares. Not usually. I see it as a weakness that anyone should take the bait in order to prove themselves on the spot. I'm not some one-trick pony here for other people's entertainment.

'She won't,' interjects Kate, noticing our exchange and sensing trouble brewing. 'She keeps her cards close to her chest, does this one.'

'It's larrrrrd,' mocks Carlos, assessing Kate before returning his attention to me.

'What she said.' I point towards my sister, grateful for her input, before carefully pouring out the teas.

'I don't think I've ever bought any,' pipes Paisley, her expression verging on repulsed.

'Never?' I ask. This could be enlightening.

'No.'

'Haven't you got a half open pack stashed in the top of the fridge? Everyone has, surely?' asks Kate, looking around the group.

'Why would I?' says Paisley, adding, 'It's pork fat, right?'

'Yep, bang on,' I confirm, showing a slither of knowledge. 'Rendered from pork – it's a highly saturated fat.'

Carlos stands stock still. 'You aren't joking, are you? You've done your homework.'

'Lard companies need to promote and win over consumer interest just as much as the chocolate, razor and drinks industries. It might not be "top drawer", but I like Kate's concept: top-notch fridge stash.'

'I didn't actually say that, Selena,' groans my big sis.

'Anyway, I wanted a new challenge. The big glossy companies are great, but I've done so many they all become a much of a muchness after a while. Whereas this bad boy has a tricky reputation and I hope to turn that around with some strategic thinking and creative shebang!'

'Who even eats lard nowadays?' Carlos says, pulling a face. 'Do you?'

'Sometimes. When I'm making a Sunday roast. You can't have decent Yorkie puds without piping hot lard spitting in a bun tray, can you? Nor decent crumbly pastry, a traditional fry-up or proper deep-fried chips either.'

'No. Maybe lard's the ultimate in perception verses reality,' suggests Carlos, with a grin.

Mmmm, maybe he's right . . . though I won't be bolstering his ego with a confirmation.

Chapter Thirty-seven

Kate

'Hello, we're back!' calls Affie, as we hear the front door slam. His heavy boots resound on the wooden floorboards, along with a pair of tippy-tappy footsteps trotting to keep up. 'How are we all?'

I turn from the sink to be greeted by his beardy face poking around the kitchen door, Mia's beaming smile poking around the edge too, but much lower.

'Hey, Affie, my man, good day?' asks Carlos, coming alive at the kitchen table, where he and Joseph had plonked themselves, both clearly bored by whatever events are currently being screened in the lounge.

'We've had a good day, haven't we, Mia?'

'I made a chocolate unicorn!' announces the child, thrusting a plastic box towards Carlos with as much enthusiasm as he'd lobbed chocolate in Selena's direction yesterday.

'That's nice,' says Joseph, filling in for Carlos' initial silence, possibly as he recalls past poor behaviour.

'Lovely that. A unicorn, you say?' says Carlos, smirking up at Affie.

Affie pulls out a chair on which to lift and settle his child.

'And did the nice lady get the collywobbles on recognising you?' I ask, busy peeling enough spuds to feed an army. I'm now regretting my decision to offer to cook for everyone tonight, but it made sense as we need an early evening meal due to another booking elsewhere this evening.

'Ah, well, she didn't let on, if she did.' Affie shakes his head at Carlos, who gives a nonchalant shrug.

'Full marks to Tanya,' I say, retuning to my task.

'We went for a long hike before that, though, didn't we?'

'We caught the bus,' announces Mia.

'Yes, at one point we did, because someone's little legs couldn't cope.' Affie makes big eyes at the guys before swiftly continuing. 'But what did we find?'

'A big waterfall,' says the child.

'We did. Though it wasn't as big as I thought it would be,' adds Affie. 'Pretty, though.'

'Oh, look at that reindeer – I have one just like it,' observes Selena, appearing in the kitchen doorway just as he finishes speaking.

A chorus of 'it's a unicorn' fills the air before offence can be taken by the smallest party.

'Sorry. A unicorn – I should have guessed. When I was your age, I loved clowns. I always begged to be surround by brightly coloured clowns – the trend nowadays is definitely unicorns, though.' She joins them at the table asking, 'So, you're not barred then?'

'I'm not, but I think you pair probably are. Tanya was good, but she was twitching when the large vat of warm chocolate was shared out at the demonstration table. I felt the need to apologise, but I didn't.'

'They've been to see the waterfall that Tristan mentioned earlier,' I say, moving the topic along for fear of unrest.

'Have you? I'd have been interested in that,' says Selena.

'More than Ruskin's house and gardens?' asks Carlos, a bit bewildered.

'Yep. I like free flow, I like fluid thinking – waterfalls are my kind of thing – whereas man-made harbours and a swathe of potential daffodils in spring – urgh! The very thought triggers

me and reminds me of good old Wordsworth and GCSE English,'
says my sister.

'You said that earlier and I'm not sure you're remembering
it right,' I say.

'I *am* right, so don't go squashing my memories. Anyway . . .'

'Kate, your bloody phone keeps pinging . . . here,' announces
Paisley, entering the kitchen and handing me my phone.

'Thank you, I think.'

'Who's texting you?' asks Selena.

'Mr Psycho-boss. I told you why.' I glare at Paisley for throwing
me under the bus in front of everyone.

'Seriously?' asks Selena, instantly annoyed.

I read the text, and shove the mobile into my pocket. Yet
another random question, one which I've answered numerous
times already. The cake will arrive tomorrow.

'Seriously, the guy creeps me out,' says Paisley.

'Me too. What about the time he asked her to collect an item
from the gents' toilet?' says Selena.

'I remember that,' says Paisley. She's caught the attention of
the others now, and what seems like a sea of quizzical male faces
stare, awaiting more details.

'Go on,' urges Carlos.

'As Selena said, he asked me to enter the gents and collect an
item from the second stall from the door . . .'

'And you went into the gents?' asks Affie, lifting his hands,
ready to cover Mia's ears.

'Sure. I gave a shout through the doorway and made sure all
was clear beforehand,' I say, over my shoulder, not wishing to
turn around and meet their gaze.

'That's not the worse part,' mutters Selena, grinning like a
Cheshire cat.

'So, you enter . . . then what?' urges Carlos.

'I gave the cubicle door a push and collected said item,' I say, sticking to basics.

'And what was it?' Carlos persists.

'His mobile? I've done that several times and had to dash back before it got swiped,' says Joseph.

'His wallet?' asks Affie.

'Nope. His business card.' I turn to watch as my answer registers with each of them.

'A business card?' Carlos' holds up his fingers, gesturing the usual size of a card.

'Hmm-mm.'

'Are you joking? He was doing his "business" on the lav while staring at his own business card?' asks Affie, looking baffled.

'Yep. It was propped on top of the tissue dispenser – where he said it would be.'

'Nothing else?' asks Carlos.

'Nope.'

'I hope you washed your hands after delivering it back to him,' offers Paisley.

'Scrubbed them,' I confirm. I've retold this story countless times, or rather our Selena has.

'I'd have been embarrassed to have admitted such antics. How narcissistic is that?' says Affie.

'I'd have been more embarrassed propping it on the lav roll holder in the first place to admire while I ...' say Carlos. 'Did he thank you when you returned it?'

'I simply placed it on top of his afternoon post pile, so not specifically.'

'Urgh! How gross,' says Carlos.

'That's my boss for you, ladies and gents.'

'Literally gents! And still, he isn't pleasant to you, is he?' says Selena.

I don't respond. Selena knows the answer, so why fish unless it's purely to out me before this crowd.

'Look at her, she's still prepared to defend him every time . . . it's unreal, Kate,' says Selena, a whine creeping into her tone.

'Do you enjoy your work?' asks Carlos, sensing the friction between us sisters.

'I do. As hard as it may seem to understand for some people.' I turn around to stare down my little sister, 'I wouldn't be there otherwise.'

'So why the game playing – what's all that about?' asks Affie.

'That's just him. He's never been any different from day one, but I can handle it.'

'Phuh! Not always,' mutters Selena.

'OK. So it gets to me down at times, but the majority of the time I can handle it,' I protest, determined not to lose this argument for the umpteenth time.

'I couldn't . . . and wouldn't, do it,' says Selena.

'Good job we're all different then, isn't it – I wouldn't put up with Jealous-Jez at your place, but *you* do.' There, I've said it.

'He's nothing to worry about! Just a dick who thinks he's king-dick,' she snaps back.

'Excuse me, ladies, but little piggies have big ears!' says Affie, quick as a shot.

'Woooo, ladies, it's the festive season – goodwill to all men and such like,' interrupts Carlos, glancing between us and then at the child. 'There'll be no handbags at dawn, thanks very much.'

'Yep, and certainly not in front of . . .' Affie nods towards his daughter.

'Sorry' we both mouth, before we each send an ultra-bright smile in Mia's direction. Sisters – united in an instance, as it always has been.

'Tell us more about psycho-boss. Does he get you to do errands other than toilet duty collections?' asks Carlos, sidling to the fridge to grab a round of beers. Affie stands to make a glass of squash for his daughter.

'Yep, birthday, Christmas, anniversaries – ridiculous stuff he's spotted on the TV – you name it, I can usually source it.'

'An ivory letter opener?' says Carlos, testing my claim.

'Really?' I say, grimacing at the very thought.

'OK, not ethical, but how about a full set of NatWest piggy banks?'

'Too easy. There's loads on eBay or at auction houses. You'll need to try harder than that, Carlos,' I jest, returning my attention to the stove.

'I will. I'll come up with a request that you can't fulfil.'

'Yeah, right. As if that'll ever happen.' I pause, then announce, 'This will be done in forty minutes.' One by one, all three men and a little lady exit for the sports lounge. One man in particular is on a mission. I hear the kitchen door softly close.

'He's got you there – challenge on,' says Paisley.

'I'm not worried. I doubt he'll suggest the impossible. And I've never failed yet. Maybe a tight squeeze on occasion, with the deadline looming, but I've never failed to produce the goods,' I add. But I'm still miffed that she mentioned my boss and the text messages.

'Along with gift wrapping them, labelling and tying it all up with ribbon. You'll do the same for Carlos – when the time is right, no doubt,' mutters Selena, getting up to grab fresh wine glasses from the cabinet.

Chapter Thirty-eight

Early evening

Paisley

'Anyway, he pulls a large bird's nest down the chimney, along with a dead pigeon, and the smell was atrocious. I'm surprised we couldn't smell it on arrival,' explains Joseph, as if we need such details around the dining table. Thankfully, I notice Mia's not listening, too busy eating her dinner, which is a blessing.

'They're supposed to be good luck, aren't they?' asks Carlos, scraping his dinner plate.

'Dead pigeons?' mouths Affie.

'No. Chimney sweeps crossing your path. Like black cats, I believe.'

'I've got a black cat called Zebedee,' I say, without thinking.

'You've got a cat?' asks Joseph. 'You don't like cats.'

'I do now.' I glance around the table at three men and a little girl, who's greedily enjoying herself. Kate and Selena had finished some time ago and disappeared upstairs to ready themselves for tonight's celebratory excursion, so aren't here to back me up against Joseph.

'No. You don't,' he says forcefully.

'Excuse me!'

'Paise, you cringed every time my mother's cat used to enter the room. Admittedly, she's a Persian — a huge fluff ball, really, nothing more. But you hated her.'

'That was then.' I smile forcefully.

'So, what's changed? I remember the time you freaked out just because Tinkerbell rubbed herself against your leg. All hell broke out during Sunday lunch. My mum . . .'

'Argh!' I try to head him off.

'Don't argh me for reminding you. You virtually turned the dining table over, along with a whole roast dinner and trimmings!'

'*Full* trimmings, Joseph – not just "trimmings".' I mimic his mother's description.

'Is that a knock at my mother?'

'Does it sound like one?' How ridiculous am I being? Or is it him?

Silence.

'To be fair, it sounded like one to me,' pipes up Carlos, clearly not reading the room as we sit, gaze lowered, attempting to finish our meal.

'Who asked you?' I snipe, annoyed for letting myself down, yet again.

'Sorry, I was just saying.'

Joseph gives an annoying smile and it feels like point scoring. He can sod off too, though I'm not going to say that because it'll look childish. With the silence lingering, I pick up my plate of cheesy mash pie, lovingly prepared by Kate, stand and excuse myself, heading towards the snug, purely to save face. And to have a little cry, if needs be, while I finish eating my meal. I doubt the girls will be long in getting ready and coming downstairs.

I flick the light switch on and am about to close the snug door when I hear Carlos say, 'You get it, don't you?'

'Oh, yeah. I get it alright. Trouble is . . . what's the answer?' comes Joseph's voice.

'That, my boy, is up to you,' says Carlos.

What's that supposed to mean? Me? He gets me? Or my

comment? Or my change of lifestyle since I kicked him out? Or my silence? Yeah, he *totally* gets my silence. Good. Joseph McLoughlin, you're *meant* to understand my silence. I'm glad we understand each other so well, having been through what we've gone through, and all because of you.

I settle on a couch, use a sofa cushion as a tray and continue to eat what remains of my dinner. Each mouthful has lost its enjoyment, tasting bland and barely necessary – much like each day of the past eighteen months.

Why did everything have to change for us? Why couldn't he have gone out with the boys, enjoyed himself and returned home to me and our marriage? But, no, I faced an entire night pacing the house, phoning around the hospitals desperately waiting his return. Only to hear those infamous words after his key sounded in the lock, once they'd been left on the radiator shelf, as was his habit. 'Babe, can we chat – I've got something to tell you.'

How I wished he'd never said anything. Never gone out. Never come back . . . ever.

A huge tear rolls down my cheek and falls from my jaw onto the edge of my dinner plate. The quicker this week finishes, the better it might be for me.

Chapter Thirty-nine

Kate

'What are you saying, Selena?' I whip around from where I'm sat at the dressing table, my make-up brush suspended in mid-air.

'Back off with hogging them both!' She's reclining on my bed as if she owns the joint.

'Are you joking me?'

'No. You want it all your own way, as always.' Her head slowly turns to watch me; I'm hoping my shocked reaction is clearly visible.

'I do not!'

'You do, Kate – nothing ever changes, even on my big birthday break.'

My mouth drops wide.

'Don't come at me with that. You're working them both to see which fits the bill for you. The man bun might grow on you. Carlos' gobby attitude might quieten. I get it, I've done it before with guys – but not when my sister was keen on one of them.'

'You say it as if I'm scheming against you.'

'Aren't you?'

'No! I bloody well am not!' I pause, before adding, 'It hurts to think you even think that of me. I'm your sister. And on second thoughts ... care to enlighten me with which one you think you're interested in, because we know your thoughts on Carlos.'

She shrugs, as if my question means nothing.

'Who's caught your eye, then?'

'Maybe Carlos,' she murmurs. 'Though his brash nature puts me off slightly, but hey?'

I smile; she's oblivious, clearly.

'You do know you have the exact same stinking, rotten, bolshie attitude, which rubs everyone up the wrong way, don't you?'

'He might. I haven't.'

'Yeah, you have. So, I wouldn't keep mentioning it.'

'No. *He*'s bolshie, I'm simply direct – there's a difference, Kate.'

'Not from where I'm sitting. Two peas in a pod, more like.'

'That's a good thing in life.'

'Not necessarily,' I say, knowing I thought my ex and I were a good match, and look how disastrous that turned out to be.

'I think we could get to know each other if . . .'

'If what?'

'If you stopped butting in each time we're attempting to have a conversation and forge some common ground.'

'Me? Barge in? More like you messing it up.'

'I don't. I never mess up with guys.' Dare I count the ways and occasions! I could do. And Paisley more so. Sadly, she's downstairs still, finishing her evening meal.

'All the time stomping your great size sixes into every topic and trampling across any progress you might have made. Do I need to remind you it was you who started the chocolate fight? Though you'll say it was him.'

She scowls at me. I relent and playfully scowl back at her. Typical Selena, can't take her own medicine when it's dished out by others.

'Can you just back off a little and give me a chance? Let's just see what happens,' she finally says.

'I was simply being sociable, nothing more – if that's what you're alluding to.'

She pulls a face, her get-out-of-jail card since childhood whenever we've found ourselves locked in sisterly battle. Not that we're locked in one now, of course. I'm not interested in Affie *or* Carlos. Or Joseph, come to think of it. So, I'll do the right thing and back off. It appears that the 'no guy' rule for this big birthday week, as declared by Selena herself, has been long forgotten.

Chapter Forty

Evening

Paisley

Our footsteps echo as we stride along the desolate High Street. It's as if every building and house is watching our every move, until we're in sight of the high-walled boundary from which the church overlooks the entire street. It's shadowy bulk looms skywards to greet the stars. Its stained-glass windows give a deaden stare, like a forgotten corpse from times gone by.

'I don't like this,' I moan, linking arms with Selena, hoping she'll save my skin if needs be. 'You just know that some sidekick actor-friend is waiting ahead, dressed as a ghoul in a rubber mask, ready to jump out and scare the living daylights out of us. My anxiety is going through the roof.'

'You've got an overactive imagination – it's harmless tomfoolery, that's all,' she replies, oozing common sense to sooth my nerves. It doesn't work.

'We're on a sodding ghost walk. What the hell did you expect?' mutters Kate.

'I know, but still. Even pretend spooks will spook me regardless of how much warning I am given.'

'You'll probably make that daft noise you always make on waltzers, roller coasters and at scary nightclub bouncers.'

'Do you remember that time we were thrown out of the Black Orchid club for dancing on tables and taking the micky out of the caged dancers?' I ask, suddenly brightening at a random memory.

'I miss those days,' says Selena.

'Do you? I don't.'

'Nor me,' adds Kate. 'I certainly don't miss queuing for the ladies for half an hour only to find no bog roll or having to save my new suede shoes from water damage by side stepping the floor puddles. Nope, I'm grateful that they're long gone.'

'Agreed,' I say, as we approach a huddled crowd standing in the middle of the street ahead.

The wall of bodies parts, providing a human corridor through which a guy dressed in an undertaker's top hat, with a flowing mourning veil and natty cane, steps forward. 'Good evening, ladies. An evening of spooks and screams is before you, if you'd care to join the mourners.' His cane glints in the lamplight as he dramatically gestures towards the gathered mortals, dressed, like us, in cosy puffa jackets, but looking as equally nervous as I feel.

'Do you need to see our tickets?' asks Kate, offering her mobile screen.

'Ooooo noooo, not necessary. No one would be fool enough to gate-crash my ghost tours. They might find themselves becoming a victim as I conjure up the local spirits,' he says, his ghoulish made-up face peering down at her. Goosebumps ignite along my spine and I shiver.

'I'm not liking this. I'm scared,' I mutter to Selena, snuggling in close to her shoulder.

'He's a true performer – I'll give him that,' replies Selena.

I gulp, taking in his deathly pale features, his extravagant dress and his theatrical mannerisms. I've had enough ghosts from the past returning to haunt me this week, thanks. Though I daren't utter a word for fear I'll bring further attention to myself.

'Ladies and gentlemen, please walk this way,' announces the guide, and leads away, his jaunty step enhanced by his natty cane.

We move off behind him, and he swishes the cane to ensure no one is level at his side. 'I *literally* meant walk in the same manner as me – tall, proud and daring to meet the ghoulish ghosts of the past eyeball to eyeball, without the need to blink! Now, please, I beg you: walk this way!' His voice lifts in an operatic manner as we all change our gait to walk with a fraction more swagger and self-confidence. Frankly, if I do meet a ghost, I'll be cowering within a split second.

'Now he's a *true* showman!' whispers Selena, adding, 'Unlike some I could mention.'

'Stop it!' hisses Kate. 'Especially after the lecture you gave me while we were getting ready.'

Clearly I've missed something? What lecture? Who, what, when and where? I'll ask later.

We follow the leader from the main street and around the corner to a sweeping pathway below the looming church. The moonlit sky plays havoc with my eyesight – all I can make out is us the gathered huddle, a gated driveway and a pitched roof suggesting an entrance to the church graveyard. God forgive me, but I swear if he takes us through that gate I'll be bricking it and might possibly cry.

'This way, folks,' he instructs, pointing his cane to show the way. My heart sinks.

'Is he serious?' I ask Selena, who's striding forward, clearly up for whatever is in store.

'Come on, he's larking about. Nothing bad is going to happen to you, is it? Or is it!' She shouts the final few words, causing the majority of the group to turn and stare at us, as she's rattled them as much as she has me. 'Sorry, folks, I didn't mean to . . .'

'Come on, you pair – stop pratting around and keep up,' scolds Kate, who has wandered ahead, alone among strangers.

'Now this beauty is our parish church – in the olden days it was said that . . .' We crowd around as the guide takes time to elaborate on one of his practised ghost stories. I'm not listening. I can't for fear of hearing something that will chill me to my bones. I'm not one for scary stories at the best of times, and it doesn't help that I've come face to face with the ghosts of my own past these last few days. Even Scrooge wasn't thrown in at the deep end; he had fair warning – unlike me.

'Quick march! Remember that at this time of night the ghosts and ghouls are coming out to play among the graves, so please be respectful towards our sleeping dead. No playing hide and shriek – we'd hate for one of you to trip, fall and join their merry throngs rather than remain with our group!'

'My God, slightly morbid or what?' I chunter, not liking his tact regarding the health and safety warning.

'It's a ghost tour! What the hell did you expect, one of Mia's fairy tales? "Once upon a time in the land of Nod"?' quips Selena, linking arms again as we trudge up the sloping path towards the looming church.

Chapter Forty-one

Selena

We're huddled around a Victorian grave, with the guide shining an eerie torch beam onto the swirling script etched into the masonry, when the church clock strikes ten, causing us all to jump from our skins.

'Ha ha, gets 'em every time!' cackles the undertaker, waving his cane at head height, which makes his veil swirl wildly.

'Clearly his favourite moment of the ghost tour,' I whisper to Paisley, who jumped more than anyone.

'Not quite, young lady,' calls the undertaker, overhearing me, 'we're far from finished yet.'

'Great! I can't wait,' mutters Paisley.

'Let's gather our thoughts, say a prayer for our dearly departed, and lift our spirits,' he continues. 'Come on, ladies, join me – because we all know demons are a ghoul's best friend. Get it?'

'Sadly, yes, but I'm too freaked out to laugh. Sorry,' apologises Paisley, clearly embarrassed to be singled out from the crowd.

'Now, listen carefully ... because I'd much prefer you only spook when spoken to! Ha ha, the old ones are always the best!' crones the undertaker. 'We're not going the long way around the street, past the clothes booootique, or Royal Mail's ghost office, but rather along this back path, down the narrow slope and into the grammar school. Follow me!'

'Oh, great! Just want I wanted – Wordsworth after dark and

not a minute too soon,' I mutter, staring at Kate, as we hastily follow him.

'How was I supposed to know where the ghost tour actually went? It says the grammar school is closed, but clearly he has special access for his tours,' Kate replies. 'The website stated "around the village" . . . and so far, he's stuck to the script.'

'Gather round, folks, gather around, closer . . . closer . . . not that close! Don't trample me to death!' hollers our ghoulish host, as we stand before a large white building sideways onto the street. Several people are using their phones as a torch, which picks out the details in the leaded windows staring down at us, as if passing judgement on our future fate. I sense mine already: a deep longing to escape, a dread of poetry and keen desire to avoid anything connected to daffodils. Or maybe this knee-jerk reaction of mine is purely down to the poor teaching inflicted upon me back in secondary school?

'The key, please?' calls the undertaker. A lady steps from the crowd to do the honours with the old wooden door with its decorative metal hinges depicting leaves and flowers, complete with a sturdy handle and aged lock.

We're led into an open schoolroom, where bit by bit the detailing and decoration is eerily illuminated by the torch light. The wooden desks with their built-in benches are lined in rows, facing what I assume is the front. Stained ink wells, piled school-books and a faded globe are revealed in sections of light. The light from my mobile follows the lintel above the leaded win-dows, highlighting the phrase 'Books we know are a substantial world both pure and good'. I nudge Paisley and point. 'Well, that's good to know.'

Kate tuts loudly.

'Ladies and gents, if you've travelled these parts, you'll have heard the tale of the Claife Crier, a wailing monk wandering the shores of Windermere seeking to save the souls of immoral women. You'll have heard of the bride from Armboth, who mysteriously drowned on Halloween, the night before her wedding. But what you might not know is that, here in Hawkshead, we have our very own home-grown ghosts, who reside in this very school room.'

Someone at the back makes a ghostly 'oooooo' sound, which sends a titter of laughter through the school room. The guide quickly reclaims our attention. 'It's no laughing matter, because if they're present tonight, they'll be standing none of your nonsense!' With that he thwacks his cane down hard on the nearest desk, making us all jump for the umpteenth time tonight. 'They've stood no nonsense here since the year 1585, so be warned.'

Bang on cue there's a flapping noise and a further thwacking sound, but from what I can see in the murky light, the undertaker is standing stock still, his head bowed as if in honour of the ghosts surrounding him.

'The headmaster's cloak ... his footsteps ... his cane ... can you hear him striding upon the floorboards?' calls out the undertaker. The glass pane in the nearest cabinet door begins to rattle, and instantly the atmosphere changes and there's a definite chill in the air. The wooden floorboards creak some more, the flapping of fabric as it circles us causes others to turn their heads, as if watching someone striding the room.

'The shadows – look,' whispers a man, pointing to the movement visible upon one wall.

'Oh Lord, I'm not liking this,' says Paisley, burying her face into the shoulder of my jacket to hide her eyes.

'Paisley, can you smell that smell?'

I hear her sniff loudly, before whispering, 'No, what?'

'Daffodils, I swear.'

Chapter Forty-two

Kate

'I swear to God, I've never been so embarrassed in all my days,' splutters Selena, trying to retell her ghost story about smelling daffodils on our return to the cottage. The guys stand around the kitchen in various positions: Carlos leaning against the fridge, Affie at the countertop and Joseph settled at the table. I make tea, and Paisley stands staring at the back of Joseph's head.

'Though when I fainted they soon switched the electric lights on. And I'm grateful to the lady that delivered first aid. She was an angel.' Paisley blushes, recalling the scene.

'The sodding undertaker wasn't much use, was he? He went to pieces as soon as you hit the floorboards – shocked the rest of the party,' adds Selena, giving her bestie a sympathetic smile across the kitchen.

'As long as you're OK, that's all that matters,' I say, wishing Selena would give it a rest. That's when I picked up on the vibe of the menfolk. Carlos hadn't made a wise crack, Joseph was simply nodding, and Affie was positively smouldering, given his creased brow. 'Mia in bed, is she?'

'Yep, went out like a light,' says Affie, picking at his fingernails. Carlos and Joseph remain schtum.

'What's wrong with you fellas?'

Paisley and Selena quickly glance at each of them before the penny drops for them too.

'There's been a bit of an incident, shall we say,' answers Affie, clearly choosing his words carefully.

'You might call it that,' mutters Carlos, shifting position as if ready for action.

'Are you three alright? You seem a bit edgy?'

'Did your match not go as you'd planned? Did you lose a bet?' asks Selena.

'I wish,' mutters Affie, still picking at his nails.

'Is no one going to say?' asks Paisley, clearly unsure how to proceed.

'Someone left a pair of scissors lying around ... and Mia decided to play with them ... and only at half time did we discover that she'd ...' Affie looks up and regards Carlos steadily.

'It wasn't me. I keep telling you that!' insists Carlos, gesturing his hands wide.

'And?' I ask.

'She's cut her hair,' adds Affie, grimacing a little.

Us three women automatically cringe, gasp, our hands fly up to our mouths or faces to self-comfort.

'How bad is it?' I ask.

Affie shakes his head.

'It wasn't me,' insists Carlos. 'How can you know she didn't find them in any one of these drawers?'

'There was a pair ... in that first drawer.' Selena gestures as she explains. 'I used them when decorating the snug.'

'See! Thank you, Selena. He's not believed me all evening.'

'How bad, Affie?' I ask again. I wince as he mimes the overall effect – super short.

'No!' mutters Selena.

'I've put her to bed, but first thing tomorrow she'll need it sorting – Juliet will hit the roof.'

'Juliet? You nearly went through the roof when you found her,' adds Joseph.

'It was the bloody shock. You girls might understand a bit more, but she was proud of her efforts – God knows why ... there was hair all over the floor,' he says, gesturing around the table. 'I don't know how we'll fix it, but she can't go to school looking like that after the holidays.'

'Did she cry?' asks Paisley.

'By the time I'd cleaned up and was readying her for bed, she was sobbing.'

'Don't worry – we'll sort it. How many times did you cut your fringe as a teenager, Selena? And always lopsided,' I say, attempting to be reassuring.

'Every other month, once it grew out from the last disaster. Don't worry, Affie – we'll take a look in the morning and do a tidy-up,' says Selena, probably not wishing to dwell on her own hairdressing misery.

'Thank you, I'd appreciate it.'

'And me ... because I had nothing to do with scissors lying around,' adds Carlos. 'It isn't nice being accused of something you didn't do, Affie.'

'That's probably because you're the only one prat enough to leave scissors out!'

'That's nice. Cheers, mate! The perception of me might not be great, but the reality is that I have more up here ...' he taps his temples, '... than others may realise, so think on. And on *that* note, I'm stating my innocence one last time.' We watch as he slopes off towards the TV, his shoulders a little less square than previously.

'You've offended him good and proper,' says Joseph, once the door is fully closed.

'He'll brush it off.'

'I'm not so sure. He sounded genuine,' I say, not wanting to see a divide between the guys.

Chapter Forty-three

Late evening

Paisley

'I never understood why you did it, anyway.' I've followed him out to the rear garden for a breath of fresh air once the others had drifted from the kitchen or retired to bed. Joseph turns to look at me, taking in my expression, and then looks away unconcerned, as if I'd asked him the time. My heart rate keeps leaping around, fluttering away beneath my ribcage. Finally, the one question I never dared to ask becomes the only question to slip from my lips. Surely I have a right to know, to understand the logistics of my life, despite not playing the hand myself and the end result being orchestrated by others.

'You're really going to go there?' he mutters, his chin dropping as he stares at his feet. Interesting choice of words. Ironic, given his behaviour that night.

'Yeah. Maybe it's time.' What the hell?

His face lifts sharply, he turns to me fully, and stares, taking in my features. He gives the tiniest of nods. I'm unsure if it's in agreement or in the knowledge that I'm clearly bluffing. I sense my subconscious starting to strap my emotional armour into place ... This wasn't the plan when I agreed to us sharing this holiday cottage. This was never the plan, for me to sit alongside the one man in my life who I have ever truly loved, the man I married and divorced, and to ask to hear the details of his infidelity, the infidelity that wrecked and ultimately destroyed us. Destroyed me and my world. And for what? One sordid night of hot dirty sex? He threw us away for that! My anger flares deep inside. The flames consume my innards, as if twisting and leaping, reigniting the old wounds.

'What do you want to know?' he asks, his voice measured and calm.

'I want to know why.'

'The big question.' He sits back, takes a deep breath and exhales almost immediately. 'I could sit here and make every excuse under the sun, feign ignorance, pretend basically, but the truth is I was tired. Tired of us. Tired of our life. The routine. A daily existence that revolved around one thing – plans for a family. Gone were the days we'd laugh and joke, have fun, act up, play stupid, get pissed and fool around. Instead each day was filled with set routines, charts, temperatures, readings, calendars, questions from your mum, worried looks from my mum, jovial back slaps from my old man – my dad never used to do that until you announced we were trying for a family. Christ, the guy rarely hugged me, but then suddenly feels it necessary to be offering me weekly back slaps as commiseration, as it appears there's "a problem". Christ, I felt pressured every time we went around for Sunday lunch. How many times did that lull between the main course and my mum's apple pie become tense and tetchy as those present gave us a minute or two to make an important announcement? Every week – it was ridiculous. That wasn't what I wanted.' His words spill out, with little breath or pause in-between, and I hear his pain. I can virtually see his pain in profile. Still.

'I didn't mean for that to happen. It just did.'

'You didn't think it through, despite us talking it through no end. You shouldn't have told people.'

'People? They're our family, Joseph.'

'Still. It was private to us.'

'So, I wasn't allowed to share? I think that's a bit much – we both come from close families.'

He snorts.

'What, you don't come from a close family now, is that it?'

'But there's close and there's close, Paisley. Our decisions were simply that – our decisions, but . . . because of your announcement, we had to hear everyone else's opinion on our decision.'

'They were excited for a grandchild!'

'It was too much, Paise.'

'Are you joking me! You knob some trollop just because I'm too much trying to plan the conception of our child, hoping to provide them with the best start in life! Are you bloody kidding, Joseph?'

'Paise, your mother gave us a wedding present of a bale of baby towels, adorned with a fluffy teddy bear and a box of folic acid, for Christ's sake! Who even does that?'

'She was just eager to be a grandparent.'

'No, Paise. She overstepped the mark and interfered in our marriage from day one by trying to force our hand on the subject. It was supposed to be *our* decision to have a child – no one else's.'

'She apologised for that.'

'Not to me, she didn't!'

'Well, she apologised to me.' Though I don't specifically remember her doing so.

'From the very beginning of our marriage, we didn't have chance to enjoy ourselves in those early days . . .'

'Come off it, Joseph – we'd been together for four years before we married. We got married with the intention of starting a family. My entire existence changed.'

'I didn't ask you to do all that,' he retorts.

'I know. I chose to do all that I did, as I wanted to ensure that we could have the best chance of having a healthy baby.

What did you do ... oh yeah, you gave up alcohol. Until the night you didn't?'

'Is that what's triggered you? Seeing me drinking alcohol with the boys?'

'Are you serious? I don't give a flying frig how much alcohol you and your boys pour down your necks. You're missing the point, Joseph. I didn't just want a baby with just any guy. I wanted a child with the one man that I had a true connection with and had committed myself to. That was you! I wanted you to be the father of my children. The end goal wasn't simply a bloke and a baby – it was us! Us as a family unit.' His bulky frame sags as my words hit home. I don't let up.

'I don't even know why we're having this conversation – our plans are long gone,' I say. I'm exhausted. My energy spent. My relaxed vibe long gone. If the truth be known, I want home. My home. My own four walls, where I can hide and find security without having to put on a brave face for a second longer. Where the tears can flow, and the rest of the world can get on with things while I fill each day with just getting by. Getting by without Joseph, without a child, without the life I had once believed was to be mine.

'Here we go again. Do we have to do this?' mutters Joseph.

'Yes, I do. Because I'm the one that was left bereft by your actions. I'm the one that still doesn't understand how or why you did that to me. To us! You trashed everything we had ever worked for, planned for and had discussions about. If you hadn't wanted a family in the first place, why did you bother leading me on and saying you did? It would have been easier to have remained unmarried, just living together – it wasn't that bad. We were happy. We each knew where we stood. Each of us knowing the ultimate commitment was on the horizon but that, should either of us decide otherwise – we had options. We had options right up until our wedding day. At least, that's how I saw it. But afterwards, nah! Some guys go crazy on their stag nights or in the lead up to a wedding, but you, Joseph, you decided that seven months in would be the perfect time. After four years of dating. We didn't even make it to our first wedding anniversary! How embarrassing is that?'

'Why must you keep going over the same details?'

'Because I'm like a broken record trying to fix myself. The stylus in my head is stuck in the grooves and this sorry state of affairs keeps going around and around, morning, noon and night. You've no idea what you've done to me, Joseph. The one person I trusted the most in this world and you did me over the first chance you had.' I fall silent. I'm spent. Sitting on that wooden bench, staring around at the mid-winter garden surrounding us, surveying my emotional litter strewn about our feet. I'm not sure if I have the energy to drag my sorry ass back into the kitchen to get some warmth or whether I prefer to simply sit here and cry. Joseph has a clear choice: remain or leave. Ironic, he had that choice on that fateful Sunday morning too. Back then, he chose the latter.

'Paise, you were verging on obsessional,' says Joseph, raising my heckles again in an instant.

'Well, apologies if I wanted the best for our child.'

'What child – it never happened.'

'The one we were planning! If you'd read any of the books and literature that I brought home, you'd know that planning and prep are essential for a health pregnancy, baby and delivery – but, oh no, you were too busy to read.'

'You made it so regimental, so orchestrated, so scheduled . . . where was the passion? The natural connection we'd always had and enjoyed. The thrill of us? You killed it.'

'You slept with another a woman!'

'Because in a moment of weakness I was stupid and sought affection elsewhere.'

'What a pathetic excuse!'

'Really? You try being me when all you're wanted for is a dedicated five days each month, then have to cope with the tears and sadness two weeks later. It was exhausting, Paise.'

'So, it's all my fault? I knew it would be. I'll shoulder the blame for everything despite staying faithful to my husband.'

Joseph's shoulders slump before he speaks. 'What should have been the nicest time during our marriage was turned into an emotional minefield. Didn't you feel how distant we were? How stagnant we'd become?'

I can't believe what I'm hearing. 'Good job we didn't conceive, then, isn't it? We'd now be fighting like cat and dog over a toddler.' Tears spring to my eyes and glide down my cheeks. 'I'm sooooo happy that you found your freedom from such a worthless marriage and an undeserving wife, Joseph. I hope you'll be very happy when you find your perfect match, and you can have a natural conception without pre-pregnancy planning.' I'm in the throes of ugly crying now and I can't stop.

'Paise. Please don't. I'm going to leave you in peace for a while,' he says, standing up and gesturing towards the kitchen door. 'I'm happy to chat later, if you want, but, for now, I think we both need some space.'

'Space,' I repeat, in a sarcastic tone.

'I get that you're still hurting – you're justified in everything that you say, but a week of this and neither of us will be still standing ready to face a new day let alone a New Year.'

I raise my eyebrows, as if challenging him – but that's why he's taking the upper hand and calming the situation down. He knows, if he doesn't, I'll be all guns blazing for round two ... then three and possibly four. There's only one person worse than me with this tendency to get locked on, and that's Selena. When she gets going, you better run and take cover! I'm not quite on her level, but nearly, which is probably why we understand

and support each other so well. I doubt I'd have survived 'that' Sunday morning without Selena dashing around to comfort me, along with a gallon of hot steaming tea. If the truth be known, I wouldn't have survived any morning since if it wasn't for my best friend. There have been mornings when brushing my teeth seemed like a challenge and a half, if I'm honest, but that's what friends do. I'd do the same for her, if necessary. They stay by your side, stick around and support you when others flee the scene.

'I-it's f-f-fine. I d-d-didn't really want a baby with you anyway!' I regret the words the second they leave my lips. I don't mean it.

'In that case, it all turned out for the best, then,' he says, as the hurt lands squarely on his shoulders. 'Better luck next time, eh?'

I blink and he's gone, the kitchen door closing quietly behind him.

I laugh hollowly, as if delaying my own reaction to that whooping lie I've just told. 'If only that were true.'

Chapter Forty-four

Selena

The kitchen is warm and snug, thanks to the old Aga and the muted lighting provided by a few cabinet spotlights. I sit at the kitchen table creating my own party decorations while Carlos sits opposite, swigging his bottled beer. Everyone else is watching a late-night film in the lounge, armed with snacks and drinks. I'm conscious that neither one of us has spoken for a while, as I'm focusing on cutting lengths of string, ready to create a birthday balloon arch, while he's absently peeling the paper label from his bottle.

'I don't know how you do it,' he says, breaking my train of thought.

'Do what?' I ask, without looking up, continuing to slice with a huge pair of scissors – I presume the ones Mia had helped herself to from the drawer.

'You know.'

'Eh? I've no idea.' I glance up from my task to meet his direct gaze.

He's now staring, his thumbnail still annoyingly picking at the paper label while he chews at his top lip.

I stop cutting the string for fear of slicing my fingers.

'Come again?' I say.

He smiles, before he lifts the bottle to his mouth and takes a long swig, his dark gaze not leaving mine.

What the hell is he on about? I wait, sensing he's clearly miffed with the lads and has probably been building up to saying something for the entire time that I've been snipping string.

'I said "I don't know how you do it".'

'I heard you the first time. Sadly, I have no idea what you're referring to, which is why some clarity would be nice.' My tone is slow and purposeful.

'I've been watching you these past few days. Personally, I think it's blatantly obvious, but clearly others have missed it,' he says, placing his now empty bottle on to the table top beside the condiment set.

'What are you on about?' I ask cautiously, holding the scissors aloft. I might as well play along. I've a decoration list as long as my arm, but, hey, a mind game here or there won't go amiss if I can still crack on with my tasks. He's bluffing. Carlos knows nothing.

'You can barely look at him, flinch when he speaks, and your tone when answering him is nothing short of an ice queen.' His steady gaze takes in my reaction.

I freeze, my gaze fixed on his. My breath snags in my throat as his words register and replay inside my head. Stay calm. No sudden outbursts. Or erratic comebacks. He's simply fishing, casting his net wide and hoping for the best. I grimace and shake my head.

'Do you still fancy him?' His tone is deadly serious, his gaze unflinching.

'Ehhh?' I stare back at him. What the hell! The penny drops. Dropping in a manner that feels like something has come crashing down inside my head like a weighty boulder rolling down a rocky mountainside. I can feel the flying debris being thrown in all directions as it gathers pace and continues to plunge towards impact. My expression clearly gives me away.

'Ah, there it is. Caught on, did you?' he says, as a flicker of something crosses his brow.

The scissors clatter to the table, the blades lie dangerously open wide. My mouth goes dry. My stomach drops by a mile. And I simply stare. I shouldn't answer; I should act dumb. Attempt to play for extra time. But I have a feeling that won't cut it either. I should, could and would do a lot of things if I have the chance to, but given his relaxed expression, Carlos has thought this through. He's clearly not bluffing. He knows what he's doing. He's obviously been watching, putting two and two together, and come to the correct damned answer of four. So what choice do I have but to answer?

'No.'

His chin lifts, as if surprised. 'I honestly expected you to follow your gut reaction and lie, or continue to feign ignorance. Fair play to you for answering.'

I don't reply, just stare. I have no idea where he's taking this. It's like being caught in the act doing the worst thing you could possibly do, but worse, given that I didn't get caught at the time. But now, a near stranger is sitting in judgement after just three days of meeting me. I don't know which is worse: the fact that he's spotted something or his ability to air my dirty laundry to my nearest and dearest tonight, the night before my big birthday.

'Stop it!' I muster. 'This isn't a joke.'

'Bloody right it's not a joke. For one poor soul, it would be the be all and end all of everything she still holds dear in her life. And for him . . . well, I bet his heart nearly fell through his ass when he saw you standing there. Let alone his ex-wife.'

'There's so much more than you'll ever understand. What do you want?'

'Me? I don't want anything.' His eyebrows have shot up into his hairline.

'Come off it, Carlos. We wouldn't be having this conversation if it didn't serve a purpose. At least be honest . . . I have been.'

'Have you? Have you really?'

'As honest as I can be.'

'Wow, that's a line and a half, given the circumstances!' His words linger. I'm swathed in guilt; for once I have no witty comeback with which to end this conversation.

I hate myself for how I behaved. I hate the lies, the continued deceit and the hurt my actions have caused. Actions that Paisley would never have committed if the tables were turned. Ever. Yet I succumbed to the highest of temptation, and broke the girl code. Regardless of my situation and pain, I should never have sought comfort where I did. What's worse is she's been dealt consequences that I couldn't have imagined at the time. The loss and pain she has endured because of me . . . Sure, it takes two to tango, but the blame lies with me, purely me. Because, despite his promises, his vows, his commitment to their love and till death us do part, I was the one from whom she never sought such a vow, never needed to – a girl instinctively knows her bestie will have her back, come thick or thin. There's no need for a forty-minute ceremony defining your commitment. Instead, it's built week on week, year after year, as young kids and teenagers. By the time you reach your twenties, you know who you can trust. Who has your back. Who you could bet your life on. And that's what kills me. I've always known I could trust her with my heart and soul – and yet I failed to protect her heart during a drunk dalliance with her husband . . .

'You can say, you know – I know you're regretting it.'

'You don't know me! You know nothing about me!'

'Don't I? Are you sure?'

'I'm damned sure. You've known me all of three days, so don't go giving me the "I know you" line. Save it for those that'll swallow such nonsense.' There's no way he'd understand the pain I endured or the depths to which I fell.

'You can barely stomach being in the same room as each other – I know that much.'

He's got a point, so I don't react. I don't need some clever arse reminding me what I did. I've punished myself enough over the months since and regularly self-flagellate both emotionally and mentally whenever I feel even remotely happy in life. That's probably what my constant stalling has been linked to. I deserve the life I have. Or lack of it. To be nearing thirty, fearing the emptiness like I do, and the prospect of it continuing, as penance for the harm I've caused to my dearest friend.

Silence lingers, as if it's pulled up a spare chair and sits observing us, staring back and forth across the salt and pepper pots.

'So, when are you going to tell her?' I ask, dreading the answer but needing to know.

He shrugs. 'What makes you think I'll tell?'

I pull a face. Who's he trying to kid? He has the ammunition, so it's only a matter of time before he uses it.

'Have you spoken to him?'

'Why would I do that?' Carlos pulls a quizzical face.

'Because you're mentioning it to me,' I say, stating the obvious.

Instantly he looks away.

'Are you going to?'

'Nah.' His attention returns to the table and my pile of string worms scattered about. I watch as he plays with one piece, singling it out from the pile to manipulate it into the letter 'C'. 'It's the ultimate in your perception verses reality, though.'

I'm not liking this. What is this guy up to? Who was it who said three people can keep a secret, but only if two of them are dead? Until this moment, I'd never dreamt that, despite the passing of time, the number who knew our wretched secret would ever increase. The plan was to forget the terrible thing we did, ensuring that Paisley was harmed no further by our utter foolishness.

Carlos continues, 'Firstly, what would I gain? Secondly, Joseph doesn't deserve that shit being reignited during this holiday. And, finally, but most importantly, Paisley doesn't need that type of hurt when she's been through what she's been through.'

My mouth falls wide. Did I just hear him correctly?

'What's that about me?' asks Paisley, appearing bang on cue in the hall doorway, clutching an empty wine glass.

'We were discussing online dating and Selena here said you might be up for trying it. I was just saying you can probably do without the time wasters after what you've been through,' says Carlos, as quick as a flash. I hold my breath, unable to speak.

'Too right! I am definitely not going down that route,' confirms Paisley, wagging her index finger in my direction while heading for the fridge.

'Just a thought,' I say, giving Carlos daggers once her back is turned.

'Are you two not coming through to be with the rest of us?' asks Paisley, retracing her steps with a brimming wine glass.

'No, I want to get this balloon arch made,' I say, lifting the lengths of string for her to see.

'Why didn't you just buy one? It's far easier,' she asks.

'I can make one for a fraction of the price. Anyway, I've already bought the balloons – though someone needs to blow them up. I suppose it depends which individual is filled with the most hot-air around here.' I daren't look at Carlos, knowing he's scrutinising my every word, reading what he can from my interaction with Paisley.

'Good luck. Though I'd have bought it for you as a birthday treat if you really wanted one that badly.'

I shake my head. It's unforgivable how I've repaid the one person who would always have had my back, regardless of the situation, by hurting her in the most unimaginable way.

We both watch as she saunters from the kitchen, none the wiser.

'Thank you,' I silently mouth.

Carlos shakes his head slowly, before whispering, 'I didn't do it for you, but for her. She deserves only the best.'

'She does. Better than me – that's for sure.'

'Mmmm,' hums Carlos, sounding rather judgemental. 'Kate said she could deliver me anything, but even she can't deliver the truth on this topic, can she?'

I shake my head. Boy, if only he knew the full details. Not that I'm seeking sympathy, mind you. I doubt anyone wishes to hear my side of the story.

I collect the scissors and resume cutting. Though now there's a deep sense of foreboding niggling deep within me about how long I have until my own bubble bursts.

Chapter Forty-five

Monday 30 December 2024

Paisley

'Morning,' he says, coming into the dining room first thing as I attempt to stick a shimmery birthday banner to the leaded window.

'Morning, Joseph. This week's passing so quickly, we'll be heading home before we know it!' That sounded fake and weird. Why didn't I stop at 'morning'?

'Are you OK?' I half-turn at his question. He stands stock still in the middle of the floor, watching me attempt to press Blu Tack blobs to the window.

'Yeah. You?' I cringe. How can he be nice to me after I said what I said last night?

'I suppose.' Joseph drops his head as he fiddles with his pocket. Silence isn't the answer. I need to put this right.

'I didn't mean what I said. I was being selfish and wanting you to hurt some more.'

'Job done, then – you were bang on the button.' Joseph doesn't look up.

'You know how desperate I was for a family . . . so desperate I destroyed us, as you said.'

'Paise, you didn't destroy us – I did that. You had a dream and I messed it up for the both of us.'

'You'll laugh, but there are times I wished you'd never told me,' I say, cringing. 'Did it ever cross your mind not to say?'

'No. I knew that I had to tell you straight off and deal with the consequences,' he says, his gaze finally meeting mine. 'You had every reason to kick me out and do what you've done since. I made my bed and you've certainly made me lie in it.'

I nod. He looks so woeful. I avert my gaze, purely to distract my thoughts. The archway of dancing balloons crafted by Selena last night catches my eye.

'You'd never have trusted me again if you'd found out – you'd always said that, ever since we met. Be it weekends away with the lads, nights out or Sunday lunch drinks – it would have been a nightmare for both of us. Constant arguing, always anxious, always wondering. That's no kind of life.'

'And this is?'

His gaze is fixed upon mine.

'This is better than that . . . isn't it?' His voice is soft, tentative in tone.

I shrug, unsure.

'I honestly don't know. If I could remove that Sunday morning, and the week that followed . . . if I could go back and . . . I don't know. Maybe see it for what it was. I'm not saying ignore what you'd done, but see it differently instead of kicking you out, changing the locks, the solicitors' appointments, the road to divorce paved in just seven days – who knows?'

Joseph is static, like a mannequin. I hope he's hearing the truth behind my words. 'At times, I just wonder . . . that's all.'

'I gave you no choice other than to start divorce proceedings.'

'But you signed. Without hesitation.'

'What was I supposed to do?'

'Fight for us, Joseph. That's what you were supposed to do.'

'What, like you did? You wouldn't talk to me, answer my calls or arrange to meet me. I collected my clothes during a set time window, with your mother standing on the side lines, starring as I moved around my own home.'

'Oy, that's not fair!'

'No. You're right, it wasn't! You could have given me ...
us ... time to talk. Yes, the dust needed to settle, but to change
the sodding locks within what ... four hours? Now that's a low
blow, Paisley.'

I flinch as I recall how my parents talked me into that task.
Initially, I was in such a state, such an emotional wreck, that
I couldn't think straight, so needed their advice and support.
And they called the locksmith. Which went against my better
judgement, but I hadn't the fight in me to argue. To them it was
common sense. 'You lit the fuse on the biggest emotional bomb
of my life, Joseph.'

'Do you think I don't know that?' he says. 'I'm sorry if my
confession hurt – I thought it best. Or better than acting like I
wasn't at fault.'

'Fair play to you,' I say, noting his gaze doesn't leave mine.
Is he trying to get the upper hand regarding brutal honesty and
self-flagellation?

'What?' asks Joseph, studying me.

I stare blankly at him; I'm not answering, I don't need to be
too honest.

'Nothing. Just interesting to hear, that's all.'

'You don't believe me?'

'I do, actually.'

'Why the ...' He waves his hand before his face, as if that
describes my actual expression.

I shake my head, feigning a lack of understanding.

'OK. I get it.' He gives a low laugh, more to himself than me,
which instantly gets my back up.

'You get nothing,' I mutter to myself. I'm edging towards
another sparring match, straight out of nowhere, without true
cause or reason. How dare he turn up all 'I've grown up', 'I'm a
better man', 'self-reflection has done me the world of good' – all

very tabloid talk-show style, with high-brow drama and low-brow morals.

'Are you brewing for an argument, Paisley?'

'Me? Phuh!' He knows me too well.

'You seem narked, despite my honesty.'

'Not me. I'm fine and dandy.' Dandy? What the hell?

'Dandy, eh? Well, that's good to hear. Anyway, I'll get out from under your feet, then, if we're fine and dandy.' Joseph stands tall, collects his coffee mug, and bids me goodbye with a weak smile.

Bastard. He has absolutely no idea what he has done to my entire world. I put all my eggs into his basket, as they say, and what thanks did I get? He smashed the bloody lot in one drunken night with some cheap hook-up. That's what you get for being one hundred per cent faithful in a marriage. Broken hearted and left for what? He didn't even go off with the woman he chose over me. Not that I'd have wanted that either. To know that he had found his new soul mate in life while I'd stupidly misplaced mine would have killed me. Soul mates, phuh! What a waste of time that phrase is! I need to take a leaf out of Joseph's book and grow up, mature, develop and ... move on. I'm instantly annoyed with myself, though whether it's about the realisation that I need to change or that I'm using my ex-husband as the measure for such a reflection, I'm unsure.

The dining room door reopens and Joseph appears again. He looks at me, concerned.

'Paise, are you sure you're OK? Because you looked as if you were having a bit of a moment then,' he says.

Shit! 'I'm fine. Absolutely fine, thank you. Never better!' I bleat, now with a gregarious smile plastered in place.

'And dandy, I hear you.' Joseph gives a curt head nod before disappearing once more.

I'm fooling no one, not even me. Least of all my ex-husband, who knows me so well.

Chapter Forty-six

Kate

'Can everyone not react, please,' calls Affie, before coming in. 'Smiley faces would be good.'

I swiftly exchange a glance with Paisley, who's busy faffing with the breakfast teapots. 'It must be bad,' I whisper, before plastering my grin in place.

The door opens, revealing an anxious daddy and a tiny, pyjama-clad Mia, clinging to his thigh.

'Good morning, sweetheart – how did you sleep?' I ask, turning from the grill pan.

Mia's bottom lip protrudes further than normal. She turns her head to hide her face against stonewashed denim. I bite my lip on seeing the extent of her handiwork, chunks of missing hair one side, with choppy sections on the other. Affie's hand gently rests on her nape, his fingers softly tracing her skin.

'Mia, Kate asked you a question,' whispers Affie.

Her sad little face reappears and a tiny voice stutters, 'I dreamed of a unicorn.'

'Did you now? I wish I had.'

'And me,' adds Paisley, stirring the pot.

'What will you be wanting for your breakfast? Frosties like yesterday or egg and soldiers?' I ask, as Affie draws out a chair and plonks himself down, the upset child cradled on his lap.

'Frosties, please.' Her eyes are downcast and her smile has gone. I see Paisley gulping, coping with her own reaction to the child's sadness. We've all been there; a tragic hair day and your inner being can't face the world. 'And after breakfast shall we have a playtime pretending to be at the hairdressers?'

Mia looks up at her daddy for an answer. Affie gives her a tiny nod, before Mia nods too. The tiniest of smiles reappears.

'Good, good. Leave it with me. We can rescue anything with a bit of magic,' I say, more to Affie than the child.

The kitchen door bursts open, revealing a daring diva in an emerald gown, dressed up to the nines, with hair coiffed and full make-up. 'Ta dah!' she announces, flinging her arms wide. 'I don't mind what the rest of you are wearing, but this is me for today!'

'Happy thirtieth birthday, my darling!' I squeal with excitement at her entrance and match her enthusiasm.

'Look at you, all made up with no place to go!' giggles Paisley, bringing the teapot to the central table. 'You certainly don't need Kate to work her magic with playtime at the hairdressers, do you?'

Chapter Forty-seven

Selena

'I'm head of the table today, thank you!' I announce, sweeping through into the dining room.

'Seriously, have we got a whole day of this?' asks Carlos, finding his seat at the furthest chair from mine.

'Hopefully not. Fingers crossed she'll be bored come lunchtime and want to calm down and enjoy the birthday treats that we've organised for her,' says Kate, with an air of mild frustration. A buzz sounds in her pocket. That bloody phone – does it ever stop buzzing?

'Oy, less of the cheek, please. This is my day and I'm going to enjoy it any which way I can. I have no idea what you did on your thirtieth, Carlos, but you, Kate, spent the day in Vegas, so please give over with the eyeball rolling and such like.'

'You could have had Vegas too, if you'd made your mind up earlier and booked flights. But, oh no, typical Selena. Always last-minute-Larry in life.'

'Thank you, I'll take that. As long as I'm not last-minute-Larry at work, then I'm happy!' I announce, reaching for the bottle of champagne that I'd left in here prior to making my entrance in the kitchen. 'Everyone for bubbles?'

Kate shakes her head before disappearing to fetch our now-routine cooked breakfast. Buzz goes her phone for the umpteenth time this holiday.

'Is Mia allowed some fruit juice in a big girl glass?' I ask Affie, eyeing her plastic tumbler.

'She can. But you'll be very careful, won't you, darling?' he says to his daughter.

Bless her, such a punky haircut like that, I'd be needing more than fruit juice and my sister's skill with scissors to help my recovery. I swiftly pour the little girl some apple juice and pass her the large crystal glass. 'Both hands, I think.'

'Carlos?' I say, tentatively, knowing this guy now has more power than I'm happy with or used to, despite my birthday bravado.

'Go on then, if I must.'

'Don't force yourself to please me. Seriously, it won't be wasted if you pass.'

'I'd hate to offend you on your birthday,' he quips, holding his glass aloft.

'Why break a habit of the week?' I jest saucily, in return.

'Can you pair give it a bloody rest,' mutters Paisley, taking her plated breakfast from Kate. Buzz. Buzz. Buzz.

'Kate, will you switch your sodding phone off? Today of all days, I don't want to hear it!' I holler, as I'm pouring the champagne. Carlos' gaze flickers up to meet mine as I fill his glass. I've seen that brooding look before, and plenty of other times in my life too . . . I rarely react, but if given the chance, I might just. Though, on second thoughts, it didn't end well last time, did it?

Chapter Forty-eight

Mid-morning

Paisley

Breakfast proved to be a lively affair. Selena insisted on chilled champagne to accompany our usual cooked breakfasts. Her determination to make a toast between the rounds of toast was amusing, though slightly over the top, given that she'd insisted on standing at the head of the table framed by her DIY balloon arch. What was it she said? 'I don't need a big crowd around me, simply the people I love dearly. So, let's enjoy ourselves by making lasting memories, because the last thing I want today is a big hullabaloo of sheer nonsense!' Then she'd opened our gifts. My gift of a diamond bracelet was met with floods of tears, which was not the reaction I was expecting. A diamond for a true diamond, as my gift card said. She's not the most sentimental of us three, as a rule, but it was nice all the same. Kate was overcome a couple of times too. I think she's found it hard this week, juggling the likes of the rental mix-up and Selena's big day plus her boss' demands. But, surely, today puts an end to all her stress too.

'So, where is madam sitting to have her hairdresser's appointment?' I ask, playing up to my role and hoping to put both Mia and Affie at ease.

'In the kitchen, I think,' says Kate, adding, 'I've found a large cape-cum-table cloth in the scullery that can cover her shoulders. Plus there's no mirrors until the final reveal – just like TV.'

I drag a kitchen chair into the centre of the floor, which Mia happily climbs onto as her daddy takes a seat at the table too and Kate dramatically unfold her makeshift cape and knots it loosely around the child's shoulders.

'Is madam comfortable?' asks Kate, standing behind the child and exchanging a glance with the anxious father, who's clutching his fresh mug of tea.

'Yes, thank you,' comes the tiny voice.

'Let's see what we're doing today.' Kate begins to comb lengths of butchered blonde hair. 'I used to play hairdresser with Selena's hair all the time when we were little. One time she . . .'

I'm lost to a world of my own. This, this is what I wanted. The family life of nonsense and mishap, of everyday stuff and magic moments that create memories. As I lean against the kitchen cabinet, on-hand as a hairdressing assistant, I feel a pang of something deep inside my chest. Jealous that Kate gets to do this. Kate's not into kiddies, not that maternal even, and yet here she is doing what Kate does best – sorting out a situation. Admittedly, not her situation to sort, but still she dives in just as she always does. Kate being Kate, fixing a problem and delivering the goods for others. Bloody hell, why couldn't *this* scene be in my kitchen, with me combing, smoothing and snipping the precious locks of my own child?

Selena comes in, interrupting my train of thought, champagne glass in hand, her slinky gown held ankle high to prevent her tripping. 'This looks like a mighty fine salon. Are there any free appointment for later today?' she asks, joining in the fun.

'Believe me, you haven't time for any more appointments today of all days. You'll see later. We've organised more than enough surprises for you today,' explains Kate, her magic fingers making order out of chaos.

'Do you mind if I nip out for some fresh air?' I say to Kate, gesturing towards the back door. 'I think the bubbles have gone to my head.'

'Sure. I think this is in hand, if we go pixie-style cut all over,' she says, glancing between me and Affie, as snippets of blonde hair drift around the child's shoulders.

I don't hesitate and head out. It's a lie, but what's a lie among friends. I close the rear door, cross the patio and am up the stone steps heading for the bench hidden behind the brick outhouse. A moment to myself is all I need. To sit here and enjoy the peace and quiet of this overwintering garden with its bulky archway, its herb garden and fairy stepping stones. Letting my thoughts drift and resettle, my emotion flow if necessary, and to regather myself ready for the remainder of the day. It wouldn't be fair on Selena if I became all emotional and stole her thunder on her birthday.

Minutes later, I hear the back door open, and I sigh. Can't I have just a minute alone? In a cottage this size, you wouldn't think it'd be an issue, but it has been since our arrival. I plaster a smile on my face, half expecting Kate to appear around the side of the outhouse. Instead I hear male voices drift from the patio area.

'What are you supposed to do? Spill your guts before your ex-wife, hoping against hope that, in the blink of an eye, she rethinks the situation and gives you a second chance? Yeah right, like that's going to happen!' says Carlos.

'It might.'

'Bullshit, J. There's about as much chance of her taking you back as pigs flying. Seriously, man, have a word with yourself.'

There's silence between the pair.

'Come on, man – move on,' says Carlos.

'What if I can't?'

'You must.'

'Why?'

'Because somewhere out there is a bright shiny-new future waiting for you. With no untimely reminders or bullshit lurking from the past. No flippant remarks or emotional baggage that instantly takes you right back to your worst days. Or nights. A brand-new relationship from which the new you can start afresh rather than being constantly berated for your flaws and the clanger you dropped one night while drunk. *That* is why!'

'But what if . . .'

'Man, she has seriously screwed with your head this week.'

'*She* has a name!' Joseph's tone has edge.

'Sorry. Paisley has seriously screwed with your head,' repeats Carlos, slowly, conscious he's treading on eggshells.

'I get where you're coming from, I do. But if the shoe were on the other foot – I'd probably be telling you to go for it.'

'Really?'

'Yeah, because, for all the shite we've been through, there's no one other than Paise for me. And I've known that all along. Since the day we met. Even on the day she kicked me out. I know – I knew – that fact. I've always known that. I was just stupid in not listening to my own bloody self on realising it. I trashed what we had despite knowing exactly what I had.'

'There's no helping you, in that case – if you know what you've gotta do, then the likes of me won't have the words to stop you.'

'I know – thanks for your honesty.'

I hear the back door close behind them.

Chapter Forty-nine

Selena

From upstairs in my bedroom, I hear the door chimes sound, then my sister hollering like a fish wife, which is not her usual style.

'Selena! Selena! Answer the door – there's a delivery for you!'

I don't hang around. As beautiful as their gifts were at breakfast, I'm hoping for many more surprises. Though not much will beat the diamond bracelet from Paisley or a classic solitaire necklace from our Kate. Though the circular blue commemorative plaque stating 'Selena Smythe: daughter, sister, best friend, advert chick, sometimes witty!' seems slightly off the mark; I'm more than witty, much more! Does it truly depict my entire existence? A condensed life? I'd hoped for a little more in the years ahead. So it probably won't be gracing the exterior wall of my home.

I race to the top stair before checking my pace, as otherwise I'll trip head over ass, given the length of this hemline. I peer down the staircase and see them all gathered in the hallway: another reason for an elegant entrance. Through the small bev-elled window in the cottage's front door I can see the distorted features of a delivery lady.

'Hurry up! We've got a game about to start,' urges Carlos, clearly forced into attendance by my sister's nagging.

'Don't rush me,' I warn, as I slowly descend.

'For the love of God, she's in her element today,' says Affie, clearly much more relaxed after my sister's handiwork on Mia's hair, who now looks ultra-cute.

'The world and his wife are under strict instructions to follow her every command, I believe,' grumbles Carlos. Joseph says nothing, but lingers in the background.

I reach for the door latch, a welcome smile in place, acting up even more now I realise it is rubbing Carlos up the wrong way. Not that I've forgotten what he said last night. But dare he act on it and spill the beans? – he'll be seeing another side to me, if he does. For now, I'll keep it light.

I open the door.

'Hello, love. I've a delivery for a Miss Selena Smythey,' declares the lady, holding a white cake box in front of her.

'Smythe. Selena Smythe,' I correct her – clearly a typo at the bakery. 'I am she.'

She pushes the cake box into my waiting arms and then attempts to offer me a stylus with which to sign an electronic screen. I clutch the box, gesturing for our Kate to do the necessary. 'Kate Smythey – would you do the honours, please?'

Within seconds, the door is closed, the bakery lady gone, and so I lead the gang, including Carlos, into the kitchen to reveal what I am dearly hoping is a decent-sized cake. It feels weighty. I'm hoping for a fruit cake rather than a sponge. Though I'm fussy about icing – too thick and its inedible and too thin and you're denied the enjoyment of a proper sugar-rush. I place the box on the table as the others gather on the opposite side. I clap my hands excitedly, anticipating the big wedge of cake to come – a corner piece, I think, for maximum icing.

I lift the cardboard lid. Then stare straight at our Kate. She smiles, clearly proud of her handiwork. I lift the lid again, purely to check. And drop it closed a second time. I've no idea how many glasses of champagne I've had today but this can't be right!

'Mmmm,' I say, not getting the joke.

'What, are you not liking the colours? I did ask for pink and lilac, but specified a sophisticated design, not anything garish and girlie,' says Kate, looking worried.

'The colours are fine,' I say, unsure what else to say or do.

'Bloody hurry up, will you? The match will have kicked off by now,' moans Carlos, checking his wrist watch.

'Oy! Hold your horses, mate – you'll be wanting some of this cake later,' says Affie, clearly on Team Girls after this morning's emergency rescue for his daughter.

I stare at each of the men in turn. I have no idea where Kate's head is, but I'm pretty sure she's being a bit brazen to expect any of the three to deliver the essential goods today, going by the cake. Despite my sparkling charm, my excellent choice of dress for this occasion and the delights of the past few days, I think she's pretty off target. Joseph – no. Affie – maybe. Carlos – perhaps, if he can soften the attitude.

'Will you let us see the sodding cake, for crying out loud!' wails Paisley, impatiently.

'She's doing it on purpose so I miss the match kick off,' chimes in Carlos.

'I don't know which guy you're expecting to step up to the plate. Or maybe you're expecting one of them to take one for the team, Kate, but I think this might be a bit of a long shot even for you to arrange on my thirtieth!'

'What?'

I whip off the cake box lid, revealing a beautifully decorated square cake, iced in pristine white, with fancy swirls and decorative flourishes in each corner, intricate detailing piped on each side and highlighted in gold, and, in swirly scrolled script: 'Congratulations on your engagement!' running from corner to corner.

I look up at their expectant and stunned faces. Only Mia seems delighted to see a cake so big.

'Count me out,' mutters Joseph.

'Noooooooooooooooooooo!' wails Kate, for approximately ten minutes, until Carlos thrusts a bottle of his finest chilled beer into her sweating palm.

Chapter Fifty

Kate

'Noooooooooooooooooooo!' My voice rings out as my mind goes into melt-down mode. The emails, the phone numbers, the orders, the payments and the sodding addresses. Who? What? When? Where? But more importantly – how? How the bloody hell has this mix-up happened?

If Selena's received his daughter's engagement cake, and she hers, then the upside is that at least I stuck with a traditional message in coloured icing, announcing 'Happy 30th birthday, little sis!' I was so tempted to order the giant saucy nun cake, declaring 'Don't make a habit of this, sis!'

No wonder my boss has been texting all morning – buzz, buzz, buzz all through breakfast. When Selena insisted I silence my phone, even the vibrating 'buzz', I was grateful for the excuse. But now I'll have no choice but to reawaken the device and take a look at the stream of incoming messages, none of which I'll want to answer. I've been ignoring psycho-boss' frantic texting throughout Selena's present opening, her self-indulgent mini-toast and the hairdressing role playing. Argh! To think of the time I've spent organising each cake delivery!

'What are you going to do?' asks Paisley, removing the bottle of beer that Carlos had thrust at me and replacing it with a hot mug of sweet tea.

'I'll apologise to him. I'll apologise to his daughter . . . but, if that order is wrong, then maybe other stuff may have got caught in the crossfire of email confirmations and such like too?'

Carlos reclaims his bottle beer. 'It can't be that bad, surely? A slight mix up with the cake addresses – what's the worst that can happen?'

I sink into my chair, imagining the worst that this day could potentially bring. Images flood my mind. 'I'm screwed come new year – I'll never live this down!'

'There's only one thing to do, then,' says Affie. 'Phone the suppliers and check the delivery addresses, pre-empting and correcting any errors that might occur later in the day.'

Bless his soul. He makes that sound so easy. I give him a weak smile for his efforts. If only life were as simple as that.

I take a swig of my sweet tea, stand tall and take a deep breath. 'Time for action. Who's in?' I ask. I reach for my phone and flip through to my contacts. 'Paisley, phone this number and ask if the birthday cake has been delivered.' I show her the screen and she instantly begins dialling on her mobile. 'Affie, same here. Ask them to confirm the delivery address for this item.' I turn to Carlos. 'You really don't want a task, do you?'

He shakes his head. 'I have football to watch. I'm sure whatever ends up where will be enjoyed by those present.'

'I like your honesty, Carlos.'

'Come on, Mia. We've got a match to watch. And if and when the cake gets cut, can we order two big pieces for the lounge, please? Thank you!' With that, Carlos disappears, taking Mia by the hand, saying, 'So, Mia, there's a blue team and a red team and we're . . .'

'Who am I phoning?' asks Joseph, stepping up to the plate.

'Thank you. You're a good bloke, despite your faults.' I show him my phone screen and he retrieves his mobile and follows the example of the others.

'Hello, what about me?' calls Selena, her emerald dress sparkling under the kitchen spotlights.

'My God, Selena, I'd never hear the last of it if I gave you a task on your big birthday. Be off, go drink your bubbles and prepare yourself – the rest of your day could get a bit freaky!'

'We all have our off days,' offers Paisley.

I look at her blankly. Not me. I have never had an off day. Not until today.

Chapter Fifty-one

Afternoon

Paisley

'Paisley, can I have a word?'

I look up to find Joseph, coffee in hand, striding across the patio towards my bench. I can hardly say no, so simply smile blandly in reply. He looks agitated. That same pinched look he sometimes had during the days of our marriage whenever he was trying to figure something out, steeling himself to address something he'd rather not address. This looks like business.

'Are you OK?' I ask, watching him take the stone steps two at a time. He gives his habitual nod before plonking himself down beside me, his body turned square to face me. 'Are you sure?'

'Look, I'm sure you'll agree that this hasn't been the easiest of weeks. I firstly wanted to apologise for the discussion we had about your mother ... I truly didn't know. I would never have been that insensitive if I had. You know that, Paise – you know me. And then the situation at the chocolate factory. I couldn't believe they'd behaved like that and I didn't want to stand my ground and sound all gruff and cross, but I was, deep down. It was good to see you enjoying yourself, and that pair of prats ruined it for you. Then, afterwards at the pub, we sat there all tetchy and cross ...' His shoulders drop, as if the words had been holding him up. 'Look, you're the last person in this world that I should ever feel that way about when seated opposite, and yet ...

I was . . . we were . . . and Paise, it's not right, babe. All this . . . the things we've said to each other this week – it's simply not right.' Finally, he draws breath, before quickly adding, 'Do you agree?'

'Hold your horses, Joseph – I wasn't expecting a day-by-day analysis,' I say, holding my hands up as if protecting myself from further details.

'Sorry, I . . .'

I reach to touch his forearm. 'I get it. The thoughts swirling and whirring . . . until they flood your mind and block out every other thought.'

'Precisely.' He snaps his fingers and points in my direction. A new gesture that I've never seen him do before. Maybe another trait of the newly-created Joseph, the post-divorce Joseph, to go with the different friends and daredevil interests.

'I know.' I stop myself from saying more and spilling my own thoughts regarding this week.

His eyebrows shoot up to his hairline. His mouth twitches, as if daring to ask.

'You do?'

'Yep, you're not the only one to have dug deep this week regarding us. There's been loads of moments . . . I mean, some moments when I've had to stopped myself from mentioning, correcting, retelling a memory, restarting an arguing that should be long-forgotten, and yet it has risen to the surface as if were yesterday.' I continue, despite feeling a deep blush rush to my cheeks, 'And . . . yeah, not the week I'd envisaged. Most certainly not the birthday week Selena was hoping for, though in other ways . . .' I daren't trust myself to continue further.

'Paise . . . if there's something you need to say, then you need to say it.' He urges, leaning forward. It's as if we're magnetised. 'We need to say it.'

I roll my lips inwards, as if gluing them together for my own safety. And maybe his. I can't. I won't admit anything. What happens if my words fall flat? If he doesn't say what I need him to say? I need to survive this week, return home and press my internal reset button. My original default factory settings are probably long gone, but my hard-won resilient attitude, my positive outlook and my allergic reaction for all things Joseph McLoughlin needs to return ASAP. I can't believe that my skin hasn't come out in blotchy hives from top to toe given how I'm feeling during this break. So I say nothing.

'Paise.' One single word ignites a past me locked deep inside. Like a smaller Russian doll that's buried within. I feel her react. I sense her instant response to his voice, that fractured line of communication which can't be severed and yet is no longer available 24/7. 'I messed up. I have never denied that fact. But if there is any way you are feeling anything that I'm feeling, then . . .'

'No!' I say, interrupting his flow.

Joseph flinches.

'No?'

'No. Nothing.'

He winces and moves backwards a fraction, as if the force field between us has faltered.

'I can't deny that seeing you, being in your presence all week, has affected me, but . . .'

'Don't say "but", Paise. Please,' he says softly, reaching for my hand. I snatch my hand back, as if burnt by skin-on-skin contact, but in reality I'm scared. Scared what'll unravel inside. Staying mute is the only way not to allow things to slip out. He falls silent, watching me. He can see through me, I know he can. Nothing has changed between us, despite the divorce. From that first moment we met, way back when, he could read me like a book, turning page by page. The first person in my life who was able to that, which is why he rocked my world the way he did, and then rocked and ruined my world in the way he did.

'Stop thinking, Paise. Go with your gut . . . your heart . . . not what your head is telling you to do.'

I shake my head, not to say no but to clear my thoughts.

'Please. I messed up big time. I ruined the best thing that ever happened to me . . . there, I'll freely admit it, Paise. You and me – we were solid.'

'Until you ruined us.'

'I know. Which is why I admitted it the very next morning. I knew I couldn't lie to you, hide it or undo the damage I'd caused. And every day since that day I've regretted how I behaved.'

'Regretted telling me?'

'No. Never. You needed to know. I needed to tell you . . . The life I wanted to protect and keep precious was ultimately the life I destroyed for us both. I can't tell you how much guilt I've felt. I've relived it each day since. Until this week. This week has been the easiest week since that Sunday morning. Paise, I breathe differently in your presence – I'd forgotten that.' His words fade, his gaze intensifies and my breath snags in my throat.

Where do I go from here? Why does life have to be so painful? So tough? No one ever warned me I'd have moments like this. No one prepared me for how tough love could be.

'W-what are you asking m-me, Joseph?' I stutter, grateful that I can't put it clearer than that.

'Us. I want us back. This week could be the restart of us.'

I watch motionless as the man I vowed to love for ever delivers the words I had longed to hear him say. Question is, can the woman I am now accept this as his truth? Or is it simply an emotional blag, lining me up for another gigantic fail in life? One that guarantees that, a year from now, I'll be back to square one: hurt, vulnerable and not coping – relying on Selena and Kate to get me back on my feet for a second time.

Chapter Fifty-two

Selena

There's a rap-a-tap-tap at the front door, and everyone sitting around the kitchen table instantly looks my way.

'Is that for me?' I ask Kate, unsure if she maybe wants to check first.

'I've absolutely no idea! Why don't you go and find out?' she says, her demeanour flagging as she's clearly rattled by the mix-up over the cake.

I'm up like a shot, leaving the kitchen gloom behind me and heading to answer the door. I relish the luxurious weight and shimmy of my birthday gown skimming my ankles with each step – shame I can't walk around like this every day.

Through the door's bevelled window I can see the distorted image of a guy with a bulky white shape at his shoulder. Could it be a parcel? A surprise gift from my parents on top of their helicopter ride – surely not? That would be really spoiling me. Maybe a flower delivery? A huge bouquet of white lilies, white roses and eucalyptus leaves, say – my favourite. Or a balloon delivery, as that's also popular nowadays. Though wouldn't Kate have had something to say about my DIY balloon arch project, if that were the case?

I automatically say hello as I open the door, and before the sight on the doorstep has chance to register in my brain. Bloody hell, an owl! A youngish man is standing there with a huge owl. Bloody big claws! Even bigger beak! 'Are you OK there?' I ask.

'Sure. I'm looking for Selena Smythe,' he says, as calm as you like, as if unaware that he has a bird of prey perched on his forearm. The owl's white mottled head swivels around to the right, rotating far more than it seems natural to, and its orange eyes fleetingly glare at me in passing. It looks like a Potteresque-Hedwig sort of owl. I'm uncertain of the breed, but I'm guessing snowy maybe, given its appearance.

'I'm she,' I say, stepping backwards awkwardly, somewhat in awe of this feathery creature being so close.

'Happy birthday! Harry here is eager to deliver your birthday wishes!' announces the owl guy, casually glancing towards the bird. Something I'd advise against, given a beak that shape could peck out your left eyeball before you'd have a chance to holler.

'Could you hold on for just one minute?' I ask, unsure if he needs to speak to Kate first before delivering the goods.

'Sure.'

I turn, leaving the door wide, as it seems rude to close it, and head to the kitchen again. I get partway along the hallway before shouting for my sister. 'Kate . . . there's a guy on the doorstep with an owl!' I say the last bit as I pass through the kitchen door, in time to witness my sister's horror; she's still seated, but her head is in her hands and she's groaning loudly. 'Yeah, I don't think this present's for me. Not quite my bag, but a lovely gesture all the same.'

'Let's have a look!' Carlos dashes off to check it out, closely followed by Affie and a tentative Mia, while I wait to see what Kate says next. I'm not about to wish an emotional breakdown on my sister, but if this owl wasn't meant for me then her planning has definitely gone to pot in a big way. And, secondly, I'm rather interested in learning what my gift actually was and where it currently is. Though I suspect it's heading towards a posh engagement party.

'Noooooooooo!' She cradles her head, and then balls her hands into tight fights, snagging her blonde hair. Her knuckles are deathly white with the force. 'No. No way is this happening to me! This never happens to me! Never! Ever!'

'Kate, it doesn't matter – I'm happy with the owl delivery, but maybe you should consider warning . . .'

Kate stands up with such force that the wooden chair topples backwards and clatters to the floor. She's upset, more than upset – which is understandable.

'Let me see,' she says, ignoring the chair and striding from the kitchen. I follow her, unsure what she'll say or do, but the owl is possibly enough to tip anyone over the edge.

'Wow! Look how beautiful . . .' says Carlos, gently stroking the chest of the bird, while Affie awkwardly holds Mia up at shoulder height and a little closer than I would consider safe, given that the bird has no restraint, hood or safety gear.

'She's ten years of age and named after a boy wizard, but she's a gentle soul . . . is this the lady who booked?' The handler clocks Kate fast approaching.

'The owl? Yes, and I take it you have the others too?' she asks, abruptly.

'They're still in the van – quite secure. My assistant is on standby for when you give your instructions about where we're to set up and fly.'

'Fly?' I'm unsure if I'm hearing him right.

Carlos, Affie and I turn to look at Kate; her complexion is drained of colour and her mouth is working overtime but nothing is coming out.

'Yes, fly. That's what was needed, but not here, elsewhere,' stammers Kate.

'Many, many miles elsewhere, sadly. I'll explain . . . there's been a slight hiccup with the delivery addresses and possibly the greetings message too,' I add, from over Kate's shoulder. I don't want to get too close. 'She's just wracking her brains for how to sort out the situation – she might be a minute, so bear with us.'

The guy nods.

We all stand about in anticipation. Our Kate's masterplan mix-up is more than slightly awkward, and I can't see how this could possibly work out in anyone's favour. I just hope that who-ever has the gift intended for me isn't too peeved with whatever lands at their party.

'I'm happy with an owl,' I say, hoping to ease the tension.

'Really? You think this is OK?' Her tone is off and I can see she's rapidly losing control. 'Well, let me tell you, if you've been delivered the owl, then the engagement party has a bunch of five clowns about to arrive, with instructions to gambol and run riot with squirty cream, party poppers and oversized feet ... which certainly isn't what they're expecting. Especially as the happy couple particularly wanted the ring box delivered in a unique manner. So, cheers, Selena – I'm delighted that you're happy ... because I doubt they will be!' She finally loses it on the final words and bursts into tears. Her shoulders begin to shake vio-lently. Bang on cue, her phone buzzes yet again.

'Excuse me,' I say to the owl guy, before leading a tearful Kate back towards the kitchen, calling back over my shoulder, 'Carlos, can you help the guy and his assistant set up in the front garden so they can do the necessary there?'

'Sure thing. Bloody hell, this is going to be quite something if this bird flies like she ought,' answers Carlos, clearly oblivious to my sister's distress. Where is Paisley when I need her? Probably still having a conflab with Joseph in the garden. I'm reluctant to interrupt them, as they look engrossed. I peer through the kitchen window and catch sight of them sitting on the wooden bench. They look cosy. Connected, even. I stand at the sink unit watching them, which feels a little like I'm spying, but I'm certainly not trying to. I watch as his hand gently strokes her cheek. Paisley's head tilts a little, her expression softening. She looks content. Then slowly they move closer together, leaning in for what looks . . . they're kissing!

Chapter Fifty-three

Evening

Kate

The kitchen door opens and I don't recognise the man standing there. I glance away, but then a delayed reaction tells me to turn around. An attractive guy with startling blue eyes, a bulky frame and no socks is there in front of me, but . . . sporting a freshly shorn blond cut. This can't possibly be Affie – there's no man bun insight!

'Kate.' The voice is his.

'My God – w-what a t-transformation!' I'm unable to hide my surprise. 'Sorry to stare, but bloody hell, man – why have you not done that before now?'

'Thanks, but that's not quite the reaction I was expecting.'

'Well, forgive me for not recognising you immediately, but I'm lost for words – it's like one of those TV makeovers.'

'I've only shorn my hair and shaved my beard off.'

'Your beard – of course, it's gone too.' I hadn't realised he was fresh faced as well. It's almost as if I was blinded by his crew cut.

'It certainly has!' Affie rubs a hand over his chin, as if it feels strange to him too.

'And why, may I ask?'

'Well, maybe Mia's not the only one who needed a change of appearance, ready for the new year.'

Really? How lovely. That doesn't sound like a blokey thing. I pull a face to indicate I'm not buying it.

'You don't believe me?'

'Nah. You fellas don't appear to go in for the new year, new me regime in the same way us girls do.'

'Are you pair going to hurry up or what?' hollers Selena, dashing through the kitchen and interrupting, saving my blushes.

'We we're just . . .'

'Wow, you scrub up well!' she shrieks, starring up at Affie, her eyes agog and mouth wide. 'Bloody hell, I might look at you with fresh eyes.'

Affie is taken aback – me even more so. What the hell is she doing? I thought she said her interest lay elsewhere?

'Selena, do you mind?' My words are out before my brain is even in gear. Affie performs a double take in my direction, which maybe suggests he's understood more than I intended him to. 'Don't embarrass the guy. You wouldn't like it if he made such a fuss when you reapply your make-up, would you?' I'm back pedalling at breakneck speed and I'm not sure it's working. Affie continues to stare at me.

'True, very true. I can be a wreck in the mornings and the fellas have been kind enough not to point out my own daily transformation, but bloody hell, Kate – have you got eyes in your head?'

'Are you lot sorted or are you going to stand about goggling Affie's newly revealed chin all evening,' jokes Joseph, standing in the doorway. 'Some of us are waiting out here for the party to begin.'

I'm grateful for Joseph's interruption. Selena is beyond embarrassing.

'I'll be through in a second. I need to speak to Carlos first,' I say, heading along the hallway towards the lounge.

I find him, lying on the sofa, remote control at his side, with yet another beer in hand.

'Carlos, can you do me a favour?'

'Me? Sure. I'm liking the sound of this,' he retorts, giving a cheeky grin.

I return to the kitchen at breakneck speed.

'Here.' I thrust the ball of rolled up socks at Affie. 'They're clean.'

'They're not mine,' he says, staring at my offering.

'I know. They belong to Carlos and he's being the friend of all friends by allowing you to borrow them.'

'Why?' he asks, his brow furrowing deeply.

'Because.'

'Because?'

'Your sock situation freaks me out. OK, there, I've said it. Now you've kindly sorted out the hair situation – boy, what a difference!'

The penny drops. His gaze lifts from the socks to my face.

'Really? Hair and socks – you're a demanding woman, Kate.'

'I am. And proud of it, so thanks for noticing.'

A wry smile eclipses his whole face. Affie takes the offered socks, takes a seat and slowly unrolls the pair, his gaze repeatedly flickering upwards to meet mine.

Chapter Fifty-four

Selena

I rap on the dining table with a clean dessert spoon, though it's barely audible over the noisy chatter and the sound of the Eighties vinyl playing in the hallway. But finally the noise quietens down and my guests cease talking.

'I'm not one for speeches, but . . .' I say, as a groan fills the air. 'I'm not, honest! But still, I'd like to thank you all for coming this evening. I'll be honest: everyone knows I've been dreading this day for the entire year and, now it's here, it doesn't feel so bad!' A cheer goes up in certain parts of the room, while Paisley and Kate smile warmly. 'Honestly. These two will tell you I've done everything possible to avoid making plans, answering their suggestions or even discussing the possibility that I am about to reach the big three zero. But here it is . . . and I've arrived. Though, if the truth be known, its only down to the support of these same two beauties that I've made it this far.' I turn towards my best friend and my sister, raising my glass in their direction. 'Ladies, I can't thank you enough for simply believing in me when I had absolutely no faith in myself. You've trusted me when I wouldn't have graced myself with such an honour. Dried my tears when life has hit the skids and been there every hour of the day whenever I've had an emotional wobble. Be it a bad day at work, a crazy hair-raising scheme or simply another disastrous date. You've been beside me every step of the way. So, tonight isn't just a birthday celebration but also a celebration to honour these two ladies. Simply put, you're the longest and strongest relationships in my life and for that I love you both dearly. Can you all raise a glass in honour of my girls, as without them I would never have made it this far.' There's a shuffle of bodies and a clinking of glassware as each of the guys follows my instruction, and I raise my glass, adding, 'To Kate and Paisley.' A chorus of male voices repeats my words, and both women blush profusely, muttering their protests at being placed centre stage, both unsure how to respond or whether to raise their own glasses in reply or simply accept the gesture.

'Enough of this nonsense!' declares Kate at last. 'I just want to thank my baby sister for continuing to be the giant pain in my ass that she's always been. It has taken a year of nagging, cajoling and constant hint dropping regarding her big birthday but, thankfully, finally ... we have arrived. Personally, I can't wait until tomorrow when her sodding birthday is over and done with. I'll feel guilt-free for the first time this year! Lord knows what we'll be doing for her fortieth, but I now know the nagging needs to start far earlier than a year in advance if she's to shift her ass into gear. I might start dropping hints at about thirty-five! So, please, raise you glasses ... to my naughty little sister – a mighty pain in the ass, if ever there was one! To Selena.'

I cringe. I can't deny that every word she says is true. I'm no angel. I've never claimed to be, but still: 'pain in the ass' is not necessarily what you want to hear said aloud in public. My gaze drifts from my sister only to settle directly upon Carlos, standing beside my buoyant balloon arch. He's obviously still clocking my every move. His dark stare has intent, touched by a knowingness clearly absent in the others. Or am I overthinking it and his attention is purely in the nature of any celebratory toast? I stare at the floor instead, as if embarrassed by my sister's rambling. I'm not, though. I simply can't abide the weight of his scrutiny, which feels too much in this moment. I take in the freshly decorated room, the sparkling glasses lined up on the sideboard, the fresh delivery of flowers, the engagement cake sitting centre stage, courtesy of my sister's messed-up planning. Then I check to see if he's still watching. Bang! He is. His mouth twitches, as if supressing a smile, or is it a knowing smirk at my irritation? Though if he can see how awkward I'm feeling at this precise moment, then surely my sister can? I divert my gaze towards our Kate, who's happily sipping her drink and looking as if she's finished embarrassing me for the moment.

'Cake! Cut your engagement cake!' cries Carlos, with the enthusiasm of a five-year-old, forgetting we've all eaten numerous pieces throughout the day.

I reach for the ribbon-bedecked knife and hold it in front of me.

'Oooo, sis, my speech wasn't that bad, surely!' cries Kate, staggering backwards, hands raised as if protecting herself.

'Ha ha, very funny.' I attempt to cut some more slices. The others gather around, jostling for position. I never know where to cut a birthday cake, so I opt for plunging the knife blade in right the way up to the hilt, then slowly drawing the blade downwards, feeling the firmness of the fruit cake beneath my knife, much like you see newly marrieds doing. A wave of sadness crashes over me. I suddenly cringe, feeling as if I'm posing in a disjointed wedding photo. Me, the solo bride – without a glittering ring, without the adoring husband, cutting into a phantom wedding cake and smiling for the camera. Another reminder of my current status in life. Instantly, the idea of continuing with the task at hand, cutting slices and serving them to my guests, feels tarnished.

My painted smile still in place, I withdraw the blade, swiftly offering it to my sister to finish up for me.

'Bloody great! I'm assigned this task too, am I?' says Kate, taking over my duties. 'Everyone for cake, yes?' There's a raucous cheer and I sidestep the table, neck my bubbles and make my way through the bodies towards the kitchen for yet another refill.

'Here.' Carlos is one step ahead of me, so reaches the fridge door before I do. 'Let me get that.'

'Thank you, but I can manage.' His frame blocks my path.

'I don't doubt that, Selena. You manage everything – that's quite clear to see,' he says, without pausing for a reply. I have no choice but to allow him to select the chilled bottle from inside the fridge door for me. 'May I?'

I offer him my empty glass without a further word. It's not that I'm upset about the cake cutting scene, per se, more that once again I've self-sabotaged my own special moment. Worst still, I sense that Carlos has twigged too. So now I'm getting his pity, which he probably thinks is necessary, to smooth my raw nerves and bolster my ego. Wrong. What I could do with right now is a few minutes to myself in total silence while my brain gets a grip and disseminates fiction from my reality. I am a singleton of thirty years who frequently trips herself up in relation to self-belief, motivation and self-worth – that's it. And I live in a world where every other woman can slice her own birthday cake, while I rely upon my big sister.

'Sometimes it's nice if you allow others to assist rather than having to do everything for yourself,' he says, filling my glass. I watch the bubbles flow without looking up. 'There you go, birthday girl!'

'Thank you,' I say, still looking at my glass, 'but you don't have to make a fuss. I'm quite capable.'

'I'm not making a fuss – simply showing an interest.' My gaze instantly lifts to meet his. A gentle smile confirms I didn't mishear him. 'But if that isn't welcome, then I'll change tack and, yep, you'll manage just fine pouring your next drink.'

'Carlos.' His name slips from my lips quite unexpectedly. 'That . . . was rude of me. Sorry.'

'No worries. Here ... cheers. Believe me, I'm getting used to your ways after this week.'

'Cheers, Carlos.'

And just like that my world becomes a little bit brighter.

Chapter Fifty-five

Paisley

'Can you believe this is happening, Joseph? If anyone had suggested this just five days ago, I'd have laughed my socks off and called them insane,' I whisper, snuggling into the warmth of our seated embrace within the snug. The twinkling fairy lights and festive garlands provide a calming effect along with the mellow warmth from the muted lamplight. This room feels like a cosy underground burrow – the outside world has faded away and our existence feels magical in this tiny indoor garden of sorts. It's a new beginning for us: one man and one woman.

'Not really, given your reaction last Friday . . . this . . . us . . . would never been my prediction but, hey, things change.'

'I'm embarrassed to think how hostile I was towards you. When I stormed off, I was ready to leave for home. Honest I was,' I say, looking up at the underside of his jaw line.

Joseph's expression cracks into a broad smile. 'You made a poor attempt at opening the gate – I thought you were about to pull it from the hinges.'

'Don't laugh. I nearly did.' I fall silent as Joseph drinks his beer and the jigsaw pieces of our world settle, nestle and align. Each negative feeling slowly melts away. Fingers crossed this continues, but I'll accept this, right here, right now, as the picture of us. One I can hold on to.

How can life change in a matter of days? How I'll explain such a turnabout to my father, I don't know. He'll be shocked to the core to hear the news. Though given his current sense of loss, he may have more understanding. Maybe this is how our story was meant to be? Some couples have a straight road of happiness from A to B, whereas ours involved a major obstacle and a divorce before continuing on our path together. There's no instruction booklet for how this weird and wonderful life is supposed to be lived, walked or travelled. Maybe, one day, we'll look back on our troubles and see them instead as milestones within our relationship. We grew. We matured. We developed as individuals. We returned to each other. Returned, renewed and what . . . remade our vows – is that where this might take us? Remarrying the same guy isn't something I ever imagined doing, but then I never imagined being apart from my one true love either. Let alone divorcing him only to reconnect on a mini-break during the bleakest week of the year. I want to laugh. Cry. Shriek with joy. I feel safe, secure and protected in his presence. How is this even happening? Nothing needs to change from this moment forth. Nothing can ruin our sense of togetherness; this renewed sense of us.

'Are you OK?' asks Joseph, his voice softening to murmur in my ear. His warmth, his strength, his very being igniting memories of old deep within me.

'I couldn't be better,' I say, knowing that I could stay like this for ever. Sharing his space, this level of comfort with Joseph. My Joseph. Nothing to hide. Nothing to fear. Nothing else matters but what we have right here, right now. Living each day. I won't play it cool with him, I'll be cautious and yet upfront. Honesty – always the best option in life. 'If anything, being here proves that nothing will change how I feel about you, Joseph. Let's take each day as it comes and build from there.'

'I agree. If we can put the hurt aside, and focus on what we have, then maybe we can rebuild. We both made mistakes but that's all in the past, Paisley.'

'It is, but only one secret remains, so tell me.' The words slip from my lips before my brain is in gear.

'Tell you what?'

'Who was she?'

There's a moment's pause, a hesitation before he speaks, 'Uh-uh, we don't need to go back there.'

'I'm not. I'm being straight up and honest. I can take it.' I twist beneath his arm to look at him face to face, before continuing, 'If we're going to do this, we need a fresh slate, no secrets, no hidden issues – if we'd have been entirely honest beforehand and communicated better about our fears and worries, maybe we wouldn't have got in such a mess. You just said we both need to try to rebuild.'

Joseph shakes his head. 'Some things are best left in the past.'

'You're not prepared to try, are you?'

'I am. I will.'

I relax back beside him and stare at the ceiling. 'How is this ever going to work when that chapter isn't closed.'

He doesn't answer.

'I can cope with knowing, honest. I'm stronger than I was back then. Then I'd have been out to seek revenge, but not now. What's done is done.'

Joseph seems unmoved, clearly not convinced.

'I understand, I do. The basics of life don't change. You spied a pretty girl, had a few drinks, a flirty remark here and there, and our sorrows, our tensions coupled with laws of attraction and, boom, before you know it – things happened. I get it.'

'So there's no need for details, then.'

'If we're to start afresh, there's a need for honesty. I'm a big girl. I can handle it, Joseph. I promise.'

'Selena,' he whispers, barely audible.

'Selena what?' I reply softly.

'Selena,' he repeats, dolefully.

I'm staring intently at his face: his eyes look sad, his jaw tense, and that pulse at his temple flickers.

Selena's friend? Selena's co-worker? Selena's boss? Did she introduce you to her? Then my brain suddenly gets what he means. Selena!

Selena, my friend, my confidante, my supporter, my life-enhancing near-as-damn-it sister?

Now that's honest!

I jump up from our snuggled position to a standing position, staring down at him. His arm is still in situ, cradling an empty space. He doesn't move an inch. His gaze fixed on mine, a blank expression giving nothing away, his beer bottle in the other hand. My heart is racing, my mind too. A montage of images flicker and flood my head. I thought I'd be fine, that I could cope with knowing, but this is reality. Gone is the younger brunette I'd once imagined. Gone the tipsy shop girl, the attractive bar girl or a jilted woman seeking revenge for one night. With one word my world has changed, again. Gone is the man I was speaking to seconds ago. Gone the warmth and tenderness of the past few hours. Gone are the fuzzy dreams that were floating around just within my grasp. Gone, gone, gone!

Chapter Fifty-six

Selena

Affie appears in the kitchen doorway, two glasses in hand, heading for the fridge.

Carlos gently touches my bare upper arm, as if guiding me. 'Let's move along, so others can reach the booze, and maybe later we can have a chat.'

'Has Mia gone down for the night?' I ask Affie, looking for distraction.

'She has now. Though she put up a fight and a half, begging to stay up late,' says Affie, pouring him and Kate drinks, as we all drift towards the doorway.

I hate to appear needy because I'm fine just as I am. But to have Carlos take an interest in me, after several days of disappointment and feeling out of sorts makes me feel quite chipper.

'You're allowed to smile, you know,' prompts Carlos, as we move across the kitchen.

'Are you seriously going to piss me off again, having just implied you're showing an interest?'

'No. Especially not given that it's your big birthday.'

'Let's find a seat and you can talk some more about the interest you have in this wonderful woman you've got your eye on.' I'm pushing my luck a bit, but, hey, I'm allowed.

'Wonderful woman, eh?' I'm conscious that his hand remains resting upon my bare skin. The warmth from his touch is radiating through me like a mini heat wave in December.

'Sorry, is that not what you said, because that's what I clearly heard!' I say, arching an eyebrow in response.

'Did you now? It's always nice to know you have selective hearing before we get anywhere, because I'd hate you to get the wrong message and have to explain myself more than once.'

'Wrong message? Are you joking? You've been as guarded as they come since we met, so the fact that you're saying you're interested comes as a surprise to me – today of all days!'

'Come on. Let's go and chat in the lounge – it'll be far quieter in there.' His hand drifts from my upper arm around to the middle of my upper back as he guides me away, along the hallway. I notice the snug door is closed tight.

I gingerly push open the lounge door, relieved to find it empty and in pitch darkness, the TV screen blank – which is most definitely a first for this week.

'Here, let me get the lights,' offers Carlos, stepping around me to fumble with the nearest lamp. The mellow light instantly bathes the lounge in a warm glow. I feel similarly aglow. Not that I'm letting on to Carlos at this stage of the game how much I'm interested to hear about *his* interest. Is he actually going to make his move after nearly a week of us dancing around each other? I take a sip of my drink, half expecting that I know what's about to happen. And for once in my life I am going to allow this to happen, as it happens. He can spread his compliments thick and fast. I'll happily listen, soak up the good vibes, answer any questions he might have and even return a compliment or two. But this gal isn't falling fast for no clichés, no practised one liners and certainly no pretty boy vibes, despite his clear skin and good cheekbones. And she certainly won't be wobbling at the knees and falling over herself to align with any first date plans. If I'm free that night, then I'll be free. If my planner says I'm busy, then count me out. Those days of that over-obliging young woman I was before are gone, long gone. Now I've hit my thirties, my dating needs to be mature, managed and memorable.

'Have you had a nice day?' he asks, settling beside me on the couch. Not what I was expecting, but I'll go with it.

'I have. Lots of surprises . . . none more than this one!'

'Really? Earlier in the week I sensed that you might be showing some interest in me, which is why I've been open enough to say something. I wouldn't have chanced ruining your birthday with such an off-hand remark otherwise – we can't have the birthday girl upset on her big day . . . or night.' He rakes his hand through his hair. 'I wouldn't have said if I hadn't picked up on a definite vibe from you. I'm not that sure of myself – despite what others may think of me.'

'Are you not?'

Carlos pulls a face, as if baulking at the very idea.

'The first time we met you had more front than Blackpool pleasure beach. With your comings and goings with your boxes of beers, your flippant remarks and plans for a boys' week of sport. Was that not the real you?'

'It was given the situation. But this . . .' He casually gestures between us. 'This is far from that scene. On Friday, you were literally some woman giving us grief about the cottage being double booked and, in hindsight, were probably sensing that your plans were about to go belly up. Much like I was. You were definitely more vocal with your opinions and, in response, I was more active with my task of moving my belongings in to start my break. Same energy but expressed in very different ways. You're more ballsy and out there with your remarks, I'm wary without the snap judgement.'

My mouth drops wide. Cheeky sod. 'Are you saying I was rude?'

'Not much, but you definitely showed attitude, which wasn't the best light to frame yourself in. Whereas me, I've seen all that before. That was more like the younger me, which is why I probably see through some of your actions to the person beneath. Don't look so shocked. I have a sensitive side too.'

He's right. By standing my ground in any situation, I simply portray a typical guard up, barricades raised, defences securely in place kind of woman and then, slowly, if people earn my respect and I feel safe, said barricades are lowered. No haste or rush but steadily, an inch at a time. And if they can't be bothered to hang around long enough for the boundary to be lowered, then that's their look-out, not mine. Though I am the one left hurting when guys have upped and offed because they've felt my defences were simply too high to even bother attempting to scale. Or they've tried to find a quicker root inside by hammering a door down or sneakily trespassing where they weren't initially invited. Was that their impatience or my surly attitude? But how do you lower your boundaries, if all you've ever known is heartache, cheating, miscommunication, struggles and tears? Because try as I might to meet a nice boy, that is what I've been met with each time, regardless of how much time I've spent getting to know them better first.

'Wow, you're deep in thought. Are you weighing up your own behaviour or mine? Because, if the truth be known, and we had a video recording of that meeting, I dare say neither of us came off pretty well as a first impression.'

'So why are you interested now, then, if the first impression was dire?'

'Over the last few days I think I've seen *you*. Or more of the real you, I should probably say. And not the front that you hide behind.'

'Front?'

'Come off it, Selena. You accuse me of having front . . . at least own your own bravado. You wear it like battle armour.'

'Me?' My voice lifts by an octave and surprises even me.

'Yes, you. Oh, look, someone is interested in me. Someone is getting close. Someone is asking questions about me and my world – they're prying! Let's pull my armour on, and fix my protective helmet in place, strap it on real good, so I don't get hurt in battle. Yes, believe it or not, that's you!' Carlos even performs the bloody actions, as if to demonstrate buckling up, pulling on etc.

'I assume that move was my protective face guard?' I say wryly, having watched him get dressed into invisible armour.

He stops, realises what he's doing.

'Ah, I'm glad you see you have a battle on your hands, Carlos. I like a trier . . .' I stand up. 'Anyway, if our cosy conversation is done, and we've hit the mickey-taking, bantering stage – then excuse me, as I have birthday cake to eat.' He can save his banter-boy behaviour for the boys, I want a man who knows the boundary between me and his buddies. In two strides I reach the lounge door, which opens unexpectedly from the other side, almost knocking me backwards.

'Is Selena there?' demands Paisley, her voice is urgent.

'Yeah, here I am. I was coming out to join you.'

'Good!'

My heart stops. That one single word – its tone, its delivery, its depth of meaning does not sound right for Paisley.

'Paisley?'

She turns her stricken face to me and I know that of all the birthday surprises that I had been secretly hoping for this year . . . this is not one of them.

'I'd like a word!' Her tone is sharp, prickly and with a hint of venom threatening to surface.

'What's up?' I say as casually as I can muster. It's the stupidest thing I could ever have uttered to the one woman I love second in life to my big sister.

Chapter Fifty-seven

Kate

'What's up? You actually have the audacity to ask me what's up? I think you've known for a while what's up!' I hear Paisley's raised voice in the hallway, so move to stand in the doorway of the dining room. Paisley pauses to draw breath and appears to grow in stature to deliver her final line. 'Because you were the sodding cause of it all!'

A wave of sickness lifts from my stomach. She didn't just say what I thought she said, did she?'

'Shit!' mutters a male voice from inside the lounge.

Paisley barges through the lounge doorway, forcing my sister to step aside to get out of her way.

'Shit, you say? I'll give you a word of advice, Carlos: I'd keep your nose out of this "shit", as you so eloquently put it, because you haven't got a sodding idea what it's about!'

Affie moves to stand beside me in the doorway, his hand reaching for my shoulder.

'What's going on?' I whisper to him.

'I've no idea. Carlos and Selena were talking in the kitchen when I collected our drinks, but this ... nah, haven't a clue,' replies Affie, slowly shaking his head.

'Ahhh, well, that's where you're wrong!' I hear Carlos reply. I might only be able to see Paisley's back, but I know her expression is frozen, because her shoulders certainly are. Within the space of a heartbeat, it feels as if the air is sucked from the cottage. In the blink of an eye, the truth dawns and I understand everything that's occurred in the last eighteen months. And it's all going to come to a head, today of all days!

Selena's gaze finally shifts towards me. Her face drops as she realises that I've heard, and that I now realise the truth too.

'My God!' The words slip from my lips before she has chance to speak. I've seen my sister respond and react to a million and one situations growing up. The time she found her pet rabbit dead in its hutch. The morning we were told Granny had died in her sleep. The afternoon, as a teenager, when she was fired from her local egg delivery round. But never have I seen her react to my words as she just did. It was quicker than a heart-beat, faster than lightning, but in that tiniest measurement of time she knows that I know. Her brain registers my tone, my stance in the doorway and the sheer anger surging through me. I'm relieved when she doesn't utter that stupid phrase, 'what?', which would have been a metaphorical life raft for her to cling to while her brain stalls for time. She doesn't try to outwit me either, another trick of Selena's when she's up to her neck in it. Instead, she exhales a lengthy breath, as if she's held it deep inside since that Saturday night out many moons ago that ended in utter madness, and her nakedness in the presence of her best friend's husband.

Before my eyes, my little sister morphs from the woman I love dearly into a near-stranger, into that nasty piece of work that I imagined had done my good friend wrong. The sort of stranger you bump into around town on a girls' night out, and each time you see them, their history and the bad blood between you makes you cringe a little more than the last time. I don't know the woman standing before me. It's as if our shared DNA has just dissolved, leaving a blank sequence within the double helix chain. I stare at the features I know as well as my own and see a stranger.

In a flash, Selena darts for the staircase, her emerald hemline brushing each stair as she bolts for the sanctuary of her bedroom.

'Has she gone?' asks Paisley, coming out into the hallway to stand at the bottom stairs. I spot Joseph standing in the doorway of the snug, his shoulders slumped, his expression deadly pale.

'You've done it this time, Joseph McLoughlin. Well and truly done it,' I mutter, as Paisley climbs the staircase, trance-like, her tred laboriously heavy and slow.

How the hell do I give comfort to someone, knowing that my sister caused her heartache? I can only hope my presence will offer some support in easing her pain. Fingers crossed, I can do something for her. I sure as hell can't put it right!

'It takes two to tango,' mutters Carlos, once we venture through to the lounge.

'Exactly. He's hardly blameless, but right this second I couldn't give a sod about Joseph McLoughlin. Just his ex-wife!'

'And your sister?'

My God, to think this ticking time bomb has been there, hidden in plain sight, every day since Joseph confessed his dalliance and, here, today, tonight – it has blown up in our faces.

I go upstairs as well and burst into her bedroom without knocking, to find her sitting before her dressing table mirror. 'My God, Selena. What have you done?'

'Don't think I don't hate myself for my actions, but I've had to live with this guilt, all while supporting . . .'

'You selfish bitch!' I holler, unsure how to contain my own venom. 'Take a good long look at yourself in that mirror!'

'Kate?'

'How dare you even say such a thing, when you and he are responsible for breaking that girl's heart.'

'As if I don't know that!'

'Do you? Do you really?'

'Of course I do. You'll never know how many times I've wished I could turn the clock back and make this all better for her, for him, for me ... but I can't.'

'Too bloody right you can't. My God, when I think of all the time you've spent supporting her – is that what this was all about? Supporting her to ease your own guilt?'

'No.'

'I need to get away from you.'

'What?'

'Sorry, Selena, but I need time to think this through. You didn't think you could spring this confession on me and then have us sit for a tête-à-tête, did you?'

'No, but ...' She looks crestfallen.

'But what?'

'You're my sister.'

The words hit me hard, somewhere deep inside my chest. I inhale deeply. If this comes out wrong, then there'll be little chance to put it right later.

'I *am* your sister, but right now that's eclipsed by my devotion and care for Paisley.'

'Kate ...'

'No!' My tone is sharp. 'And now, given the circumstances, I need to go and check on my friend.' The rage within me is boiling over, as I attempt to hold it together knowing the distress that Paisley will be feeling. I have never experienced such anger in my life. I can't believe the woman before me is my sister. My own flesh and blood. Why on earth did she behave like that? *How* could she behave like that? I stride from her bedroom; there's nothing else for me to say.

I cross the landing, almost tripping over my own feet to reach Paisley. I have no idea what to say to her, but my need to say something, do something is overwhelming. Something ... anything that might ease her pain.

'Knock, knock, only me,' I say, opening her bedroom door. My attempt at bright and breezy falls flat on seeing her dishevelled frame curled foetal-style upon the bed. She looks tiny. 'Hey, sweetie.' I dash towards her, my arms outstretched, knowing words have failed me but having someone beside her might help just a little. Sitting on the edge of the bed, I gently brush aside her unruly auburn locks to reveal a pale waxy complexion and sore, red-rimmed eyes. Her appearance has gone from a healthy fresh glow to almost transparent with the upset. She doesn't move, answer or register my presence.

'I can't justify her actions, Paisley. I have no understanding of how and why this has happened. Just know that I am here for you.' There's nothing else to say. Nothing that will ease her pain. Nothing will correct the wrong that has been done to her. She's cold to the touch, so I pull the corner of the duvet over her legs. She doesn't flinch, as if she's so deeply buried within herself that nothing physical is registering. I stand, make my way to the large windows and gently close each curtain, blocking out the world, as if this day doesn't exist. It feels like the right thing to do, to calm her senses, allow her to simply be and breathe without the glare of the world witnessing her pain. I don't offer words, or food, or excuses. There's nothing to soothe her pain or erase her hurt. I know, I've been there. The only difference being that others clung to their clichés – told me to pull myself together, get up, get out, go show the world you can survive, be yourself and face the day. I didn't want to do any of those things. Worse than didn't want to – I simply couldn't. I wanted to lie on a bed and silently grieve for what could have been. What might have been, had everyone played their part differently in my stage show of a marriage. Sadly, there was no one to guide and direct us, the two actors abandoned on stage and caught in the spotlight while everyone else stood and watched. I return to her bed, and gather her into a bear hug. And squeeze. Her damp cheek is on my shoulder and the hiccupping continues for several minutes before it softens to rhythmical shallow breathing. I have all the time in the world, if she needs, to sit here in silence. I won't cajole her, attempt to buck her up; I'm just here to offer my undivided attention and presence.

Two hours pass without a word being uttered. Paisley has shifted position within my arms, enabling more physical comfort for the both of us without hindering the emotional comfort. The clock has continued to tick, moving her away from the moment of impact but without the ability to distance her from the pain.

'Paisley, you probably won't feel like much, but how about something to eat and drink?'

Paisley shakes her head.

'Nature still needs looking after,' I add, knowing we can't bring ourselves to think about the basics in life at times of stress. Yet the usual routine is still essential at any age. 'Some toast and tea?'

Her gaze lifts to my face, her heavy lids flicker in protest, but I persist.

'Here, let me fetch a tray.' I ease my arm from beneath her frame and slide from the bed. 'Is there anything else you'll be wanting?'

Paisley shakes her head. I'm not prepared to push her, as I know how exhausted she is.

I leave the bedroom, closing the door quietly behind me. I can't hear a sound. You'd be hard pressed to know others were in the cottage too. Or maybe they aren't?

I head downstairs to find Affie and Carlos sitting in the kitchen.

'How is she?' asks Carlos, turning around in his seat.

'As you'd expect when you hear your husband cheated with your best friend.'

Affie's eyebrows lift in response.

'Where's Joseph?' I ask, grabbing the kettle before reaching for the cold tap.

'Out. Walking, I think,' says Affie. 'He didn't want our company, so we let him go.'

'Good. It keeps him out of my way.'

I secure the kettle lid, replace the lead and flick the switch on. When I look up, Affie is studying me.

'What?'

'And Selena?'

'I don't give a sod where she is!' I snap, clearly rattled by his suggestion.

'Sorry, but you've asked where Joseph was and so . . . I thought.'

I think before answering. 'Right now, I hold her responsible for whatever happened between them – not him.'

'It takes two to tango,' mutters Affie, just as Carlos had said before.

'Maybe, but the bond she's broken is far greater than the vow he made.'

Affie blows out his cheeks, as if stunned by my response.

'Do you not agree?'

'Personally, I think its six of one and half a dozen of the other – but, hey, who am I to comment.'

I don't reply, as I've too much to say on this matter.

Chapter Fifty-eight

Tuesday 31 December 2024
Middle of the night

Paisley

'You've no idea what you've actually done!' My dignity and serenity are all gone in a heartbeat, regardless of it being three in the morning. I couldn't lie awake practising my lines any more, so when there was a knock at the bedroom door, I answered. Selena pales. I continue, 'Not the slightest idea of the damage you have caused.'

I'm fair minded enough to know she didn't do this single handed, but still, she's the one currently standing before me, so can take the full force of my emotions.

'I never meant . . .'

'Don't!' I snap. I can't bear to hear it.

'He doesn't care about me. He has only ever had eyes for you, Paisley.'

'Until he had eyes for you!'

'No. You're wrong.'

I pause, and sarcastically ask, 'If that's the case, how do you end up in a hotel bedroom, naked with my then-husband?' She physically baulks at the question. 'Go on, I'm interested to know.'

'Paisley?' Her tone is flat, almost begging for me to falter and cease.

'What, you think I'm being unfair to ask such a question?'

She shakes her head.

'Don't get me started on how you could even think of supporting me through the last eighteen months, knowing that you were the actual cause of it. My God, when I think back to how many times I've cried on your shoulder and you had the audacity to comfort me. By Christ, you must have been laughing your bloody socks off!'

She bites her lip and has enough decency to lower her head in shame. This isn't what I want, though. I want her to make an attempt at excusing herself, hear her overflow with remorse for her actions, have her apologise for the hurt, and witness the huge gaping wound that has been unceremoniously ripped open inside me. I never expected drama such as this during our week away. But then fate has dealt me a trump card to beat all, throwing the three of us together, so maybe this was meant to happen? A cathartic process in which we spill the beans, dish the dirt and bury the hatchet. Hatchet – I'd sodding swing for her if I had one close to hand.

'Look, I'm going to leave you in peace. I wanted to check on how you were and see if I could . . .'

'What, make amends? Ease my pain? Or pick up from where you left off with Joseph?'

'No! Paisley, I thought I could try to explain the huge frigging mistake I made. I hurt my dearest friend, ripped her sodding life apart and left her in a state that is beyond anything I even recognise as her!'

'Feeling guilty, are we?'

'You'll never know how much I hate myself for what I've done to you.'

'Oh, diddums!' My answer sounds pathetic, even to my own ears. The figure standing before me is a shadow of her former self, both in physical stature and personality. Gone is the bright, bubbly, over-the-top marketing exec, replaced by a ghost of a woman who I don't truly recognise. She's certainly not the woman who has accompanied me through life since we were six years of age, every single step of the way until . . . until she wrecked my life and brought it tumbling down around my ears.

'I've nothing to say to defend myself,' says Selena, her shoulders slumping further, as if the final gust of wind has been taken from her sails.

'Well, that's a first!' I try to hold back, and fail. But I have no need to cause her additional hurt – she's managed that task all by herself. Or rather, with additional help from Joseph.

Selena takes on board my final remark, silently nods and heads towards the door – there's nothing else I want to say. There's plenty I could say, of course, but nothing more meaningful than I've already thrown at her.

Chapter Fifty-nine

Selena

I wanted the relationship Paisley has . . . had. That's the truth of it. The one ruined because of me. I feel so guilty for committing the ultimate sin against my best friend. As tacky as it sounds, she was his lobster, you know? Soul mate. Mate for life. He'll never find another as good as her. I'll never know how that feels. Never. I can't imagine any man speaking so highly of me as he does of her, or knowing that he cares as much as he does, and can admit he messed it up. I have no doubt he'll meet someone else, but not like Paisley. If he'd kept on the straight and narrow, they would be parents by now. Well, as much as you can ever predict such things.

Which is what kills Paisley more than anything. To think that was all she's ever wanted. To be a mum, but not to any baby, *his* baby. A planned-for, yearned-for baby with the man of her choice. Paisley wasn't settling for anything less in life. Other women, like my sister, dream of a shoe collection that requires its own room with a floor-to-ceiling shelving system. Not Paisley. She only ever dreamed of a family.

But Joseph ruined that for her, on one drunken night spent with some loose woman. Namely: me. And the shame of that night hits me anew every time I think of what a low life I am to have made a play for my best friend's man, purely because I was jealous of the beautiful relationship they have . . . once had.

I didn't want him, as such, but their situation, their bond, their trust, their united future. I wanted to know how that felt, even if it was only for the briefest moment. How could the likes of me ever possibly know what that was like otherwise? Happy birthday to me!

Chapter Sixty

Morning

Kate

I knock on my sister's door, half expecting to find she's scarpered during the night.

'What?' comes her steely, defiant reply from within.

I open the door and poke my head around. She's sitting in the wicker chair looking as guilty as sin, clutching her phone.

'I wanted to check that you were OK.' I keep my tone neutral.

'I'm OK,' she mumbles, turning around to meet my eye.

'Are you coming down to breakfast or do you want something sent up?' She gives me a sarcastic head tilt. 'I'm not trying to be witty, Selena, honest.' I'm simply trying to make the best of a difficult situation, for all concerned. Though I might draw the line at Joseph McLoughlin.

'I'll walk down with you, then.' Selena shoves her mobile into her coat pocket, draped over the arm of the chair. 'I can't see that the masses will be that chatty with me, but still I'll show my face and what will be will be!'

'Selena, please. She has every right to be angry with you. Christ, I'm fuming at you too, but more screaming and ranting won't solve anything, will it?' She doesn't reply, as there is no right answer.

* * *

'Morning, campers,' I say, on entering the kitchen to find a trio and a child drinking tea. We catch sight of Paisley's hastily retreating figure dashing from the room, her head lowered, cheeks blotchy. 'Same breakfast as yesterday, Paisley?' I call after her, without expecting a reply.

Selena gestures to her own chest, 'That's all because I came downstairs.'

'Stop it! Affie, was she OK? I didn't manage to speak to her earlier.'

'So-so, I think. I'm not sure she's slept a wink, but she's upright and dressed,' Affie says

'Which is all that matters,' I say, heading for the Aga and removing the top plate coverings. 'Selena, can you make me a cuppa, please?'

I notice both men shuffle sideways away from the kettle area, giving her plenty of space.

'Was she slagging me off?' asks Selena, causing both Affie and Carlos to flinch.

'Not quite, but . . .' begins Affie.

'No. She was singing your praises, Selena,' says Carlos, cutting off Affie's attempt at kindness.

'Ha bloody ha, Carlos. As if you know anything about it.' Selena begins sorting mugs.

'So why ask?' he retorts. Affie places a restraining hand upon his back.

'You talk as if you're involved, Carlos. I've news for you – you're not. I messed up. Messed up big time. Lost my best friend in the process and buried myself in all-consuming guilt. If you knew how hard I've tried in supporting her and making it up to her, you wouldn't be so quick to judge me.'

'Support? Are you serious, Selena? Was it support or was it sticking close by, ensuring you knew every possible detail?'

'You bastard! What the hell would you know?'

Mia flinches at the table.

'Hey, hey, hey! That's really not necessary, Selena,' snaps Affie, his brow creasing, bringing their conversation to a close.

'He . . .' Selena's voice breaks and tears spring to her eyes. 'He has no idea what it's been like for me. I made a mistake. And the likes of him just want to revel in the drama.'

'Me? Phuh! I'm out of here,' says Carlos, thumbing towards the door. 'See ya.'

'What is his problem?' asks Selena, the second the kitchen door swings shut.

I raise my eyebrows. 'Isn't it clear?'

'I'll leave you two ladies to it,' says Affie, following Carlos' route. 'Come on, babe. Let's take your drink to the lounge. Good girl.'

Once alone with my sister, I stare her down as I grab the fresh produce from the fridge.

'What are you looking at?' asks Selena, resuming her task.

'At you, lady. We can see the situation. You don't have to be so defensive when folk are trying to help.'

'Help? You call that help?'

I don't answer, yet am grateful for her vigorous tea-making activities for filling the silence. She's not hearing him or me. Regardless of how Selena thinks she's supported Paisley, ultimately it appears as if she hasn't.

'Why's he so bothered anyway? I don't see him having a go at his mate.'

'Joseph isn't protesting his innocence, unlike some.'

'I'm not protesting my innocence – I'm guilty as charged. But he's making out that I'm not feeling it, that I'm swanning around without a care in the world.' Selena turns to me with her final words.

Does she really need me to point out the obvious?

'Kate?'

'What?'

'Did you hear me?'

'Yep. Isn't it obvious?' I grab the grill pan and layer it with bacon slices.

A steaming mug of tea appears at my right hand, along with a quizzical look from my befuddled sister. 'He's annoyed that you've ruined the prospect of you and him before it's even begun.'

Chapter Sixty-one

Selena

'Count me out,' I announce over breakfast, which has been a silent and tense affair. All their heads lift at neck-breaking speed, but no one utters a word. Kate gives me a hard stare and Paisley quickly returns her focus to her breakfast plate.

'It'll be a good day out,' offers Carlos, braving his chance to speak. 'I've visited a climbing centre just like this elsewhere. It's a laugh, if nothing else.'

'Thanks, but I'm all out of laughs today,' I mutter, pushing aside my breakfast, half-finished. 'I'll catch you all later. Enjoy.' With that I stand and walk from the dining room. A little more dramatic than I'd intended, but then they were a little more silent than I was expecting. I stand in the hallway, unsure where I want to go. I hadn't thought this plan through. No change there. Could no one other than Carlos offer a few words? I get that everyone's mad at me ... us – yeah, it should be us, but it doesn't feel that way. I could do with more coffee, possibly an extra slice of toast, but I'll have all the time in the world to grab those once they've cleared out for the day. I can't stand here thinking, so I head back to my bedroom, for now.

I lie on my bed listening. It feels like one of those sick days as a child when you're faking it and only know you've been successful when your sister has left the house to walk alone to the school gate. I can hear them toing and froing across the landing, the pummel of feet upon the creaky staircase and the odd slamming of doors. There's little conversation between them: Kate's being extra perky, Paisley is feigning chat with both Affie and Carlos, but hasn't uttered a syllable to Joseph. I want her to utter many, many syllables to Joseph. Big fat, angry, heated syllables which means that she's dividing her rage between us fairly. Right now, she appears to be blaming me alone for the destruction of her marriage. Has he got away with it, scot free? Though, on second thoughts, a divorce, a sold house, uprooting himself partway across the county and a rebuild of his daily life probably doesn't count as nothing, but still . . . Paisley needs to treat us both the same.

'Knock, knock.' Kate comes in without waiting for a response. She lingers a little by the door, as if uncertain now her sisterly love has broken through her annoyance.

'Are you sure you'll be OK?' she asks.

'Yeah, sure. It looks like rain, so I'll stay cosy inside and have a day to myself.' I want to add that I'll lick my wounds, rediscover my self-respect and give my bestie a bit of space, but I don't.

'I'll probably get drenched, as my coat hasn't got a hood,' complains Kate.

'Borrow mine. I won't be needing it,' I say, gesturing from the bed towards the wicker chair where my coat is draped.

'Are you sure? You can always borrow mine, if you need to head out.'

'Sure. But I won't be going out.'

'Kate!' hollers Paisley from downstairs.

Kate bites her lip, gesturing over her shoulder.

'I get it. Go to her.'

'I'm mad at you, but I still love you, Selena,' whispers Kate, rubbing my arm in an awkward fashion.

'I know, I'm mad at me too. Be gone before she has to come looking for you.'

Kate grabs my coat, blows me a kiss from the door and is

gone. I lie, listening to them rallying themselves with coats and keys – I can hear Mia's excitement – before the front door slams shut and I imagine the tiny latch falling into place.

Their footsteps resound upon the cobbles, the car doors slamming and their engines roaring signal their final goodbye. Silence. I lie still. My gaze travelling around the bedroom. So, what am I to do? I feel as guilty as I did back then. I deserve it just as much, of course, but somehow her nonplussed treatment towards Joseph is grating me. How can she stomach sitting in a car with him right now? Though they've probably gone in different vehicles. I bet my name is mud either way. I rock myself to standing, and plod back downstairs.

I hear a knock at the front door. I'm hoping against hope it isn't the others returning early and go investigate. I relax on seeing a familiar face, distorted by the tiny bevelled glass, as I approach.

'Sorry for disturbing you, but I wondered if everything was sorted regarding the chimney smoking?' says Josie, bashfully, as I open the front door. 'Not that I was expecting an immediate update, but these things play on your mind, don't they?'

'It's us that should be apologising, Josie. We should have said – that was rude of us. Come on in, don't stand on the doorstep,' I say, beckoning her in.

'I don't want to intrude,' she says hesitantly, before entering.

'Not at all. The others have gone out for the day – it's just me here.'

'Oh!' Her surprised tone punctuates my armour.

'All alone like billy-no-mates,' I mutter, on closing the door.

'By choice?' she asks.

'Not entirely, but it's probably for the best,' I say, widening my eyes in fake joviality.

'Like that, is it? I'm sure time will heal,' says Josie, glancing at the row of near empty coat hooks.

'I doubt it,' I say quietly to myself.

'I don't know why I said that,' corrects Josie, watching me intently. 'I don't believe time does truly heal us, but it certainly moves us forward and away from the moment of upset, which can sometimes make it easier to cope.'

I'm about to answer, but her words have hit my emotional bull's eye, causing my eyes to brim with tears.

'Oh lovely, I never meant to upset you . . .' she says, reaching for my forearm to offer comfort. 'I have a habit of saying whatever comes into my head only to . . .'

'You haven't. Honest. It's just me . . . I'm not good . . . it's just . . .' I'm trying to stop the tears, but it's too late as a torrent of them run down my cheeks. I frantically dash them away with the back of my hand but they keep coming.

'Here.' Josie offers me a folded white tissue from her handbag. 'It's clean. Now sit yourself down.' She gestures towards the staircase and I follow her instruction, settling a few steps up from the bottom. 'Whatever has caused your upset, I'm sure things will seem a little brighter after a cuppa. I'll go and put the kettle on, sweetie. You stay right there.'

I want to correct her – I'm the one that has upset the apple cart. I want to say don't trouble yourself, but nothing comes out except for more heart-wrenching tears, which are probably long overdue.

'Here you are. Now, mind yourself – it's hot,' says Josie, offering me a mug of tea and holding the sugar bowl ready in her other hand.

'T-thank y-you,' I hiccup, dutifully taking the mug and helping myself to sugar before she settles below me on the second tread, her own mug in hand.

'Now, I don't claim to have answers, lovey. But I know upset when I see upset.'

I nod, repeatedly.

'Yesterday, after my birthday celebrations . . .' I begin to explain the events: the bubbles at breakfast, the mistaken deliveries, the exciting birds of prey, the wrong cake, my disappointment about the clowns – which takes all of ten minutes. I'm in two minds whether to spill the beans about my indiscretion with Joseph. I can see she's listening in that non-judgemental way, gaze soft but steady and focussed. I feel safe, so I admit it when I reach that point in the proceedings. I feel obliged to mention Paisley's distress on hearing the truth at last, coupled with the weight of my embarrassment and stupidity. After which I fall silent, as if spent and empty of tears, sipping my tea – awaiting her response, I suppose.

'Oh lovey, you must have been hurting very badly. Clearly, you weren't yourself that night.'

'Sorry?' I can hardly believe my ears.

'Forgive me, but to have a lapse in judgement such as that there must have been other things . . . other situations affecting you.'

'You're right – there was!'

'Much like when my parents were aging, the pressure of constant caring around the clock ate away at me – I really wasn't myself for a while, a long while really. I got quite down about things and, well, you cope the best you can, but sometimes situations sneak up on you and you end up doing things you'd never dream of doing. It's a coping mechanism, you know.'

My tears erupt once again, surprising even me.

'Now, then, whatever it was, you mustn't suffer in silence.'

'But I have. I have for so long because I can't tell them. I can't say. It feels like an excuse, when it really isn't, but they probably won't listen or see it that way. Everyone's so angry with me, but really, deep down, I know if I'd said they might have offered help.'

'Hindsight is such a wonderful thing – we rarely get chance to put things right, though. Maybe this is your time, your chance to speak freely to Paisley, your sister or even Joseph – help them to understand your position a little better.'

'I can't,' I sob, knowing it'll break Paisley's heart. And the thought of me keeping secrets will break Kate's too.

'You can, my lovely. There's nothing you can't say, you just have to choose your words carefully, the manner in which you share and pick the right moment to explain. I'm sure the hardest part is starting the conversation . . . the rest will follow, honest.'

I shake my head as a fresh wave of tears spills over my lashes.

'What's the single most important detail you'd want them to know about from that time . . .' she says, patting my forearm, as I frantically dab the tissue to my face.

'Six m-months before that night . . . the n-night w-with Joseph . . . I lost a baby.'

'Oooo, Selena, I am sorry.'

Chapter Sixty-two

Mid-morning

Paisley

Having watched the instructor's demonstration, I lay the contraption on the ground in order to untangle the harness before stepping inside, as though it were a cat's cradle, before awkwardly working the canvas loops up each leg and tightening them securely around my upper thighs. Black strapping accessorising and an orange jumpsuit is really not my look. Great! I must look hideous from the back. I get that safety equipment is necessary, given that we'll be swinging from trees and, as the company branding says, 'Monkeying Around' at height. Something tells me that my then-husband already managed that some eighteen months ago.

'I doubt you'll have any blood supply to your legs if you pull them that tight, Paise.'

'If I should fall from this tree canopy, it probably won't be an issue, will it?' I retort, trying hard to cover my fear of heights. I give an extra tug to each strap just to make sure Joseph knows I don't take advice from him, not any more.

'Pin and needles it is, then,' he mutters, turning away to speak to Affie, who's busy helping young Mia with her harness.

'Mmmm, my choice.' My narkiness is pure fear. I'd much prefer to have stayed behind at the cottage, but alas Selena snatched that option.

'Ready?' asks Kate, enthusiastically bouncing over, clearly delighted at the prospect ahead.

'No. Not really, but still.'

'Oooo, come on, you'll be safe once you're clipped on to the safety ropes – though these are hardly flattering on your ass, are they? Look.' At which Kate turns around and wiggles her ass in my direction, much to Affie's amusement. She's right. Kate looks five dress sizes bigger, in billowing orange with tight strapping defining each bulge.

'I suppose. But you know this isn't my thing,' I mutter.

'Don't you get a sense of security simply by wearing a harness?' she asks, pulling at her strapping.

'Not really.'

'It's hardly going to break on you, Paise,' adds Joseph, rejoining our conversation.

'Mmm, funny that. My safety harness in life seemed secure and safe, yet was cut free when it suited others – it leaves a lasting memory.'

'Touché,' Joseph replies as my meaning lands, before turning back to Carlos.

'Was that really necessary?' whispers Kate.

'Why not?'

'Come on, snap out of it. Tomorrow we'll each go our separate ways and next time we book a holiday, a cottage or a spa break away, we'll check his lordship isn't booked, I promise.'

'That knot . . . the one that sat just here,' I pummel my breastbone to demonstrate, and she nods, 'it's back, and probably bigger than ever, given the week I've had. How am I supposed to keep doing this, Kate? Tell me that?'

'I don't know, lovey. I think you've braved it out this week far better than I ever could alongside my ex. And as for my . . .'

I raise my hand to stop her. Right now, I can't think about Selena – words simply fail me.

'I get it. Let's just get through today and tonight, and see what tomorrow brings.'

'A new year, a new me!' I bleat sarcastically, knowing it couldn't be further from the truth.

'You think?'

'Ladies, are you listening?' calls Affie, gesturing towards our instructor, clearly eager to proceed with our adventure among the tree tops.

Chapter Sixty-three

Selena

After Josie leaves, I wander through the cottage, from hallway to dining room to lounge, with a newfound sense of freedom at having the place all to myself. I'm emotionally drained and yet feel physically lighter after our chat. My grief should never have become a secret. I can't thank Josie enough. Her timing was near-perfect – she saw what others had failed to see. The weight of my secret has disappeared, leaving a void that I decide I need to fill with activity. I can play music as loud as I wish, especially as there are no neighbours to bother. I could even cook a top up on my breakfast, given that I cut it short due to the chilly atmosphere. I could open a bottle of something expensive and drown my sorrows or ... for my second day aged thirty, I could ... I stare around the lounge, hoping something grabs my attention. And it does. The scenery beyond the panoramic window, distant rolling hills, a low blustery sky in swatches of grey and dark blues and open space begin to call my name. I will head out on a solo jaunt. Be at one with myself surrounded by nature, tend to my emotional wounds and return in a better state of mind. Put myself back on an even keel, as it were. Sounds like the maturity of a new decade might be showing itself.

Returning to the hallway, I spy Kate's flimsy jacket, the one she offered me earlier, the one I said I wouldn't need 'as I'm not going out'. No hood, no thermal lining and probably no waterproofing, if it should rain. I'll be soaked, unlike Kate. Beside it hangs a second coat, bulkier, hooded and possibly hiding a thermal lining and much warmth. They'll never know.

I roll the elasticated cuffs back to reveal my fingers, zip and press stud my way from knees to chin – I must look a right sight, but I don't care. I care that I'm warm. I won't be seeing the locals again, so why pretend I'm bothered about my appearance.

My phone? I haven't seen it all morning, not at breakfast, not while lying down, not since … urgh, I shoved it into my coat pocket first thing this morning, when Kate knocked on my door. Ah, my coat – the one my sister is currently wearing. Ah well, it'll be a quiet day without that bad boy!

I snatch a set of keys from the hallway table and set out on a mission.

It takes all of twenty minutes to reach the centre of the village, a further ten to walk through, reaching the far side of the pretty main street. I can't remember the last time walking brought me so much pleasure. No music in head phones, nor phone distraction, nothing other than a slight breeze on my skin and the sights and sounds around me. The rhythm of my pace feels like a heartbeat thumping under foot, steady and strong, as my head fills with thoughts which are chased away by each sudden new sight, be it a shop frontage, a hedgerow or a signpost – I'm dipping in and out of reality at my own speed. I no longer hate myself for causing such upset. I no longer despise my former self for poor judgement or attempting to show penance by supporting Paisley to get herself back together over the last year and a bit. It was never about me, never. Though, likewise, it was never about Joseph either. It was purely that I wanted and needed that security, that bond, that reassurance that life would be OK … in time. The future they had in each other, the emotional investment – that's what I wanted. I was simply too stupid and impatient to wait for it to arrive. Instead, on a drunken night out, I indulged in what wasn't mine.

How I'd kept the baby I lost a secret from my nearest and dearest, I'll never know. After the shock of the pregnancy test came panic, quickly followed by bewilderment and, finally, acceptance. Then sudden loss. How cruel can life be? I coped by living a split existence: on-stage, off-stage. In public, I learned to smile and perform the basics of my job and attend to family. Alone, behind closed doors, I unravelled, unable to function other than to sleep and grieve until my next public performance demanded my energy. Which explains how I could be so understanding when Paisley needed daily support. I couldn't have left her side despite being the cause. I knew what could happen to her, where she might end up emotionally, physically and mentally. I couldn't make amends, but I could ensure she was safe.

It wasn't as if I was pregnant within a loving, committed relationship, but in a new situation where we were getting to know each other and things went too far, too fast. He didn't care. He wasn't interested in the news. Not that that surprised me, rather it confirmed that I was truly on my own. I could handle that. What I couldn't handle was losing what I never knew, and yet had instantly loved. That – that I couldn't handle.

Once lost, how do I explain my weeks of turmoil? How do I relive all the false smiles I used to hide the truth from the two people I was closest to? How did they not see? How did I not share? But I didn't. I figured it was best not to say. Best to keep quiet. Continue my life as it was, as it had been, and attempt to cope. Ha, cope. I didn't cope. Instead, I spiralled down towards the dark depths of beyond, becoming a walking, talking shell of myself, feigning life, laughter and love to those around me. I certainly wasn't living. Inside I was dying. But when do you tell? How? Recalling the misery you've experienced when your bestie is desperate for a baby and that's all she can now talk about? That wasn't going to work. And your older sister has her own issues too following her divorce, and you're using every ounce of strength to breathe, let alone explain the darkness that surrounds you. Despite seeing them as regularly as ever, our connection drifted as I distanced myself emotionally, hiding within the safe parameters of supporting them. I kept myself hidden. And no one noticed. And that's the hardest thing to acknowledge – they didn't notice my smile was a mask behind which I crumbled. My work was my only salvation, so I ploughed my effort into the hours in the office until I'd return home and face my reality.

I smile. How is all this making sense now? For eighteen months I've owed Paisley an apology and clear explanation, yet nothing had come to mind. Now, plodding along in an oversized coat, which had better not belong to Joseph, I finally have a lightbulb moment. A wave of renewed vigour surges through me; I might even go in search of that waterfall that was mentioned a day or so ago.

Chapter Sixty-four

Afternoon

Paisley

'Paisley, come on. You can do this!' yells Joseph, as I stand six metres high up, on top of a tree stump that is barely wide enough to place both my boots side by side. I cling to a suspended knotted rope as if my life depended upon it. I'm going to be sick. And at this height above the forest floor, an unexpected waterfall is not going to be a pretty sight.

'Paisley, you're quite safe!' hollers Kate, who has successfully left her stumpy platform moments ago, for the safety of a sturdy tree house, so can afford to smile and is offering encouragement to those left behind. The three guys, a small child and our instructor stand behind her, yelling similar sentiments regarding my safety, courage and my inner strength. Bugger that last one – I've used all my reserves getting though this last week. I'm not listening to their motivational chatter any more. I've switched off to their yapping. I want them to stop. I want this to stop. I'm not moving. Better still, they can't make me! I'll stay here for the rest of my life, clinging to this knotted rope – I'm sure it won't rot anytime soon. I can happily co-exist alongside nature for the foreseeable future. I want the whole damned world to stop badgering me into taking yet another step, be it here on this tree stump or life in general. I'm quite happy where I am. Let them go ahead, run off and chase their wildest dreams if they wish, but leave me here. I'm quite safe hanging on to this twist of rope, trussed up like a turkey in this damned harness and jumpsuit combo. What have I got to live for anyway? I'm single, divorced, childless, without a best friend, with the potential to lose my next dearest friend, given that they're sisters and we all know sisters eventually forgive and forget arguments. So, I'll be totally alone. I might as well stay here and live like a hermit for all that I have going for me.

'Can we carry on? Or do we have to wait for the entire party?' asks Carlos, posing his question to the instructor. The others glare at him. 'What? I'm only saying.'

'Go ahead. I'm fine here.' I shuffle my boots to prove my point, that I'm quite comfortable right here.

'Would you like me to come back and collect you?' asks Joseph.

'Are you friggin' joking! You are the last person I want coming back for me.'

'I meant in this activity – not in real-life, Paisley.'

'Ha ha bloody ha. You'd just love that, wouldn't you? Good old Joseph saves the day. Swoops in like Tarzan to save the damsel in distress,' I holler, more panicked by that prospect than I am at falling from this great height.

'I'll leave you, then.'

'Errr, I believe that's your style, no? But only after you've done the dirty with my best mate!' The words span the gap between me and them, startling our instructor, who looks away as if scolded by my words. Lord knows why . . . it wasn't him that they were aimed at. 'Don't worry,' I assure him, 'she hasn't attended this group booking today. She had the decency to stay out of my way and remain at home, unlike some I could mention.'

'Is that what you'd have preferred, Paise? For me to have stayed at the cottage and then you could have enjoyed yourself by swinging through the treetops and this . . . this giant leap of faith that you need to take now would have been nothing for you, if I'd been absent. I don't think so!'

Our instructor fully turns his back on us, as if embarrassed to be associated with our group. Not only is a woman stuck on the tree stump, but they're having a full blown domestic.

'You'd have probably been happier staying alone with Selena. You and her could have happily . . .'

'Don't!' yells Kate. 'Don't you even go there, Paisley.'

'Well, it's true.'

'No. It. Is. Not. True. Have you not listened to a word either one of them has said?' asks Kate, her temper overflowing.

'Can we not move on?' asks Carlos. Affie nudges him swiftly in the ribs to shut him up.

'Move on! How I would love to move on. Seriously, my vow of "death us do part" was sliced and severed eighteen months ago, and yet I find myself still being haunted by Joseph bloody McLoughlin,' I yell, in frustration.

'He meant with this task,' interjects Affie, politely gesturing over his shoulder towards the untouched course that awaits our party.

'Of course. You just go right ahead, just as in life everyone else can bloody well carry on. We'll all keep pretending that this shit show really isn't happening. And on this, the last day of the year too! Can you believe how lucky I am, instructor? I bet you would love to change places with me – it's all a bloody hoot. Because if all things had remained the same, I wouldn't be able to fit into a sodding jumpsuit of this size and would need a much bigger harness. I would be waddling around in maternity wear with folks constantly asking me "when are you due?", "do you know what you're having?" or "is it your first?" Instead I'm standing here, where I never asked to stand, staring at the rest of you continuing on your way, as if nothing has sodding well happened. Well, it did. And it happened to me! Because he couldn't keep it in his trousers when it mattered!' My rant finally ends, as I need to draw breath.

'I thought we were over the worst bit and could possibly be civil to each other, but oh no. You stand up there announcing this to all and sundry.' Joseph is narked too now.

'All and sundry? They already know! Everyone in my sodding life knows what you did to me.'

'So, what's the answer then, Paise? Tell me,' hollers Joseph. 'Because I sure as hell can't hang about here all day waiting for you to decide what it is that you want in life.'

'I wanted you. I wanted our baby. I wanted a future together. I wanted our home. The one we'd begun to build, filled with tiny babies and memories and fun and laughter. An everyday existence that other people might find mundane and unsatisfying, but I was actually looking forward to having all that with you. But you ripped up that family portrait and scattered my dream to the wind. And now, now, I have nothing that remotely resembles the dreams I once cherished. Because of you! And her!' I stop yelling at long last, empty of words and emotionally exhausted. 'Can someone just get me down from here. I want to go home,' I plead. I've never uttered a truer word in my life, apart from my wedding vows.

The instructor steps forward, radio in hand. 'Sure thing. Stay where you are. We'll get you down.'

Chapter Sixty-five

Selena

Finally, I found it. Stoke Ghyll Force waterfall, somewhat hidden and yet in clear view. I cross the wooden bridge to sit on a nearby rock and stare at the convergence of two streams combining into one. I ponder the force of the water, the amount, and the height of the drop. Birdsong surrounds me. Peace and tranquillity accompanied by the sound of cascading water. A rainbow effect glistens now and then as the flowing water catches what little sunlight there is. How beautiful nature can be. So pure and magical.

I'm not a spiritual person, not someone who believes in things I can't see, yet sitting here, mesmerised by the cascading water – I feel different. An inner peace brought about by the cleansing quality of water, as if my body and mind are renewed. Gone are the incriminations with which I was berating myself earlier. My heart feels lighter, my head seems less cluttered and my breathing calmer. Maybe a trouble shared is a troubled halved?

I never thought I would behave as I did. I have no plausible excuse, had no premeditated plan or legitimate reason for doing what I did. I simply forgot myself. Or rather tried to forget myself in the arms of a so-called stranger, as I certainly didn't think of him as Joseph. Which removes the ick factor in some ways, but still doesn't lessen the hurt and pain I've caused to us all. I say I, as I take full responsibility for what happened. I've known her the longest, stood by her since childhood – no husband compares to that length of dedication and love. Then I stuffed it up. Literally, overnight.

Maybe if I'd talked about my feelings regarding my own loss, unburdened myself of some of the grief and bewilderment, maybe I'd have had a different mindset that night. Maybe I'd have responded differently to his presence, rejected fleeting temptation and not chosen the path I did. Josie's right when she said 'you weren't yourself that night' – I certainty wasn't; that night being me was the last person I wanted to be.

I stand to find a closer vantage point to view the waterfall. If only I had my phone, I'd happily snap an image for my kitchen wall. I climb over the smooth boulders and rugged rocks to get a little nearer. It's risky, but I can climb a little nearer. Maybe a little higher.

Of all the details that make me cringe to remember, and there are many from that night, the worst was the next morning. I'd opened my eyes to bright sunshine spilling in through an unfamiliar window. I'd lazily stretched my legs beneath the duvet, toes pointed, knees locked and was about to welcome a new day when the memory of last night hit me like a thunder bolt. Sex. Hot sex. And . . .

I'd swiftly turned to view the other plump pillow beside mine and found my best friend's husband sleeping peacefully alongside me. I have never grabbed a pillow and rudely tugged it from beneath a sleeping head in my life, but that was my immediate impulse. Joseph's eyes snapped wide, took in my face and widened in panic. I leapt up, taking the duvet with me to cover my modesty, which was probably a little too late by that point. I don't remember the expletives – I simply remember his expression as he slept. Dark features, a stubbly chin and a transparent shadowy smudge beneath each eye. Is that the face she saw each morning? Those final few moments before our worlds came crashing down around our ears – I witnessed his final moments within a marriage. She won't ever believe me, but I saw so clearly his horror at seeing me where she should have been. We never cooked up a plan, created a feasible alibi or contemplated lying to her. We knew that neither one of us could ever undo the pain we were about to cause. I don't blame him for telling her of his error that night. I'm for ever grateful that he didn't name me, though.

Underfoot the surrounding rocks change from dry to wet as I get closer to the spray from the waterfall. The cascade itself is but a moment in time, despite the waterfall probably being centuries old. My boots slip and slide on the wet rocks. I wobble before regaining my footing and tentatively try again.

I don't know how I had the cheek to answer my mobile when Paisley called me in her darkest hour. I went to their house and acted as if I were totally detached from the scenario. I pretend that I don't understand why I did that. I tell myself a hundred times a day that I have no reasonable explanation. But I do. I don't wish to admit to it, but, firstly, I couldn't bear to witness her pain on hearing my side of the story. The truth. That I had done the dirty on her, behind her back, with her beloved husband. And he had had the backbone to come clean, but I hadn't. I was the lowest of the low for hiding the facts. I comforted her as if it were another woman, a stranger. I made her tea, toast and fetched tissues as she sobbed. I rubbed her back when she retched all over the bathroom and, later, dutifully cleaned up while she lay exhausted on her bed, still sobbing.

With every passing hour, I hated myself a little more, but when do you come clean and ask to back pedal as you've had a change of heart and need to confess? When? And it was all that bit worse when Joseph arrived and saw how underhand I was. I thought he'd squeal, but as angry as he was at my actions, he couldn't and wouldn't hurt her for a second time by giving me away. Our Kate always calls him a rough diamond, but I have a deep respect for Joseph McLoughlin, despite everything, because

I know how much he loves that woman. He refused to take her support away. No one took my original pain and grief away, but then I don't deserve it, do I?

The boulder rocks beneath my left boot, shunting my body off balance and causing me to stumble. My arms lift in a windmill fashion in an attempt to correct myself but I've overdone it, sending my body crashing to the right. It happens so fast. Argh! Knee. Hip. Shoulder. Head. Pain surges through my body as the sky fills my line of vision.

The pain from my right shin is excruciating, accompanied by a wave of nausea, which follows each time I attempt to move it. I instinctively reach into my right pocket to retrieve my mobile, but it's not there – just a half-eaten block of mint cake. Bloody great! I forgot this isn't my coat!

'Now what do I do?' I mutter in frustration, staring up at the patch of blue sky poking between the treetops. I have no phone. No one with me. No workable right leg – great stuff!

'Help!' I yell, as it's the only feasible thing to do. I just hope there's a kindly Samaritan in the area. Though given that I haven't seen anyone for an hour or so, I doubt it. There aren't any passing walkers, and the reason is obvious – it's New Year's Eve and every sane person I know is preparing for tonight's celebrations, not mooching around a sodding waterfall, clambering up for a better look.

A dart of colour catches my eye, as a robin red-breast lands upon the nearest bare branch.

'Mmmm, not what I was hoping for,' I mutter, as its beady black eye scrutinises me. Though what's the saying, 'robins appear when loved ones are near'? A sudden wave of emotion envelopes me as the sentiment hits home.

I feel hot. I feel faint. The pain is too much. I feel . . .

* * *

On opening my eyes, it takes me a second to remember where I am: waterfall, trees ... urgh, pain. The patch of blue sky has darkened somewhat, so I've probably been unconscious for a time. I cry for help, hoping someone is passing by.

No one answers my hollering, so I lie listening to the sounds of the waterfall and fighting the urge to pee. I need common sense if I'm to get out of this. I start creating a check list in my head. Am I bleeding? I can't bear to look, so reach my hand down along my right leg, feeling for a wetness, only to discover a misshapen bulky mass beneath my trousers, which I don't recognise as my leg. Busted, no doubts about that. But no sticky wetness, so I'm not bleeding. Though given the bulky shape, the lack of movement and the worst pain I've ever encountered, I can safely say I've broken my leg. Six to eight weeks in a cast was not on my new year wish list – but that isn't my biggest worry. That will be how the hell am I going to get down from here and save my skin before receiving treatment for my leg?

I should have listened to my inner voice when it suggested this was a bad idea. Maybe I should have endured a day alongside the others, hanging about and swinging from trees – I bet I wouldn't have injured myself there. Though, ultimately, it's Kate's fault. If she'd purchased a better coat with a hood attached, she wouldn't have needed to borrow my decent warm coat, which had my mobile nestled inside. Big sisters think they think of everything, even when they clearly don't.

The pain flares in my right leg as an unwelcome reminder. I'm stuck. Beside a glorious waterfall, upon a rocky mattress, with the afternoon sun drawing towards evening without a care for my wellbeing. The pain is unbearable. I need to distract myself, so opt for the easiest thing to remember: nursery rhymes. 'One, two buckle my shoe, three four knock at the door ...' I begin, muttering aloud.

I recite a string of childish rhymes but the pain remains

constant; my brain is working overtime now and I'm becoming increasingly frantic with panic. What if I lie here all night? What if no one thinks to search for me, given they're all annoyed with me? What if . . . what if I die out here, the day after my thirtieth birthday? That was *not* supposed to happen. I'm supposed to return to work in three days' time and launch a brand-new project.

I check my watch, and figure that another round of hollering for 'help' is needed. If I'm going to get out of this alive, I'm going to need to be methodical, just like our Kate would be. Surely there is someone else mad enough to be out walking along a desolate stretch of woodland in search of beauty, today of all days.

Chapter Sixty-six

Kate

The silence in our car is palpable. I keep my eyes on the road in front even though my head and heart wanted to stop following the guys' vehicle ahead of us and turn off the beaten track to disappear for a heart to heart with my friend. Though without the hysterics of earlier. Admittedly, I was both surprised and impressed at how quickly the team had attended and got her down via pulleys and hoists. But the raw emotion that was spilling out of her as she stood on that plinth is etched on my memory. I wish it hadn't happened. I wish we'd never gone, and I wish I'd realised sooner how near to breaking point she is.

'Paisley, are you OK, sweetheart? If you want me to delay our return, we can nip off someone quiet for a chat.'

'Nah.'

'Is there anything you want?'

She abruptly turns to face me, 'Other than what I stated earlier: a home, a husband and a newborn? Nah.'

We drive in silence for the remainder of the journey, watching the red taillights of Joseph's car ahead. Why didn't I see this coming? Isn't it the duty of a friend to see the warning signs on the horizon and take action? I'd seen nothing to alert me about how fragile Paisley still was and, worse still, I had no clue about the secret Selena was keeping. I'd clocked she'd suffered bouts of low mood and been slightly off kilter of late, but now I know why – her conscience was weighing her down. And yet she never confided in me! Do we ever truly know anyone? Ever see the pain they are enduring amidst the day-to-day grind of life? Never did I think a secret would cause such distance between the three of us. I'd imagined it was my fault for withdrawing into a world of my own while adjusting to my new post-divorce lifestyle. I should have taken more notice. I shouldn't have let them brush me off with a standard 'I'm OK'.

I turn the car's heater to a higher setting, switch the music to a soothing radio station and continue to drive, knowing all I can do is provide her with care and attention. There's nothing specific I can do or say that will ease her pain.

Lord knows what we'll encounter back at the cottage, but I'm hoping my sister has at least had a better day than we have.

Chapter Sixty-seven

Early evening

Selena

'Selena?' His voice is muffled, as if in a dream, but his sudden touch to my cheek and shoulder isn't my imagination. 'Selena, wake up! Come on now, come on.'

'Stop that!' I mutter groggily, as I focus blurrily on Carlos through half open eyes.

'Come on now. I'll keep doing it till you pay attention,' he says, as my hand takes a swipe at him.

'I've bust my leg.'

'No shit, Sherlock,' he says, with a chuckle.

The background to his blurry face is dark, not the azure blue of earlier. 'What time is it?'

'It's gone six, but we don't need to worry about that now. Can you move your toes on your left foot?'

'Aren't you going to ask about my pain first?'

'Nope. I pretty much know it's killing you . . . left toes?'

'Yes, I can feel everything – fingers and toes are normal on three limbs, so it's just my right shin you should be asking about. I fell.'

'From where?'

'That flat ridge there. I climbed up and was taking a look and stepped backwards to see if . . . well, it doesn't matter now. I fell and landed wrong.'

'Mmmm, very wrong, I'd say. Never mind, do you feel dizzy or sick?

'I did. I think I was sick earlier. How have you even found me?'

'Mmmm, I saw your ears prick up when Affie mentioned the waterfall and Kate recalled your interest when the helicopter pilot mentioned it. I figured it was worth chancing a hike up here while Joseph and Kate searched the surrounding lanes and the local village.'

I lie still, relieved to know that Carlos is near. I've no idea how long I've been lying here. How long they've been looking for me. But the sunlight has faded and the sky above has darkened to navy blue.

'Do you really think that little of me?' I ask.

'Sorry?' His eyes widen, as his hands gently assess my leg.

'Earlier in the kitchen . . . when you said . . .'

Carlos swallows hard.

'Look, I was trying to say that your behaviour since your dalliance, shall we say, looks pretty suspicious. Why would you cheat on your best friend and then stick close by in a feigned attempt to support her? It looks callous, totally heartless.'

I pause. This won't sound right, but I need to say it.

'I was trying to make up for my error of judgement and redeem myself.'

'By being the closest thing she has to a sister?' Carlos shakes his head. 'It would have been kinder to step away.'

'It looks rotten, doesn't it?'

'Yep, it does.'

'Brutal but honest. Thanks, Carlos.'

'You're welcome.'

There's more I want to ask, but don't. Can I redeem myself in anyone's eyes? Have I lost my best friend for good? How much longer am I going to be lying on this rock with an injured leg, which now feels somewhat numb, as if empty and lifeless.

'What's it matter to you anyway?' I mutter, sounding like a petulant child.

'Just because.' His gaze is averted from mine, his voice low and troubled.

'Because what?'

'Leave it, Selena.' He moves my right foot as he speaks. The pain reignites in my lower leg, proving it is still attached.

'Ouch!' I yell, through gritted teeth, instantly distracted.

'Sorry. You need to focus on this and face the consequences with Paisley later.'

'Did they argue all day?'

Carlos shakes his head.

'Pretty civil under the circumstances, to be fair. Though you did miss a cracking day out. Scampering around like children, we were.'

Great!

The pain shoots through my shin as a reminder of my current predicament.

'Ayyyy, how am I going to get out of here?'

'By the only means possible – rescue team.'

'No way! Please don't call them.'

'Why ever not? I can't move you unaided. There's no point me calling the guys from the cottage, as they haven't the equipment needed to stretcher you out, so I'll call the emergency services. Don't worry, this is what we do.'

'Carlos, I beg you not to.'

'It's not up for discussion. Though afterwards I will be interested to hear why you're wearing my other coat.'

He pulls his mobile from his jacket pocket and taps the screen.

'Hello, yes, emergency. Mountain rescue, please.'

Chapter Sixty-eight

Paisley

I hear Joseph's mobile ring, hear his startled response on answering, and pretend not to listen to his chatter by focusing upon the glossy magazine lying in my lap, which I've been pretending to read for an hour.

'Where did you say? . . . Seriously? . . . Good. And they're on their way.'

When I look up, I see that Affie too is blatantly listening to the call. Mia is cradled in his arms, asleep.

Kate appears in the doorway. 'She's not taken my coat, which she said she would if she needed . . .'

Affie raises a finger to his lips, before gesturing towards Joseph.

'I see. I get ya. So, we're not needed?' says Joseph, eyeing the rest of us, all suddenly poised for action. Even me, though I'm feigning a disinterested attitude towards my so-called once-upon-a-time friend. My ex-friend. Is that what happens in life? You collect a series of ex-relationships along the way?

'Where is she?' asks Kate, the second Joseph kills his call.

'She'll be OK. Don't fret, Kate. She took herself off to view the waterfall at Stoke Ghyll Force – it appears she's suffered a fall and sustained a nasty break to her leg. The rescue team are on their way, so we're not needed.' His final sentence is for Affie's benefit.

'Pity,' I scoff.

'Paisley, there's no need!' reprimands Joseph, before Kate can even speak.

But I can't help myself. 'Wouldn't that be ironic? My ex-husband wading in to save the life of my ex-friend, with whom he destroyed our marriage.' I can't help myself.

'Will you cut it out!' he snaps, the tension of the week finally surfacing.

'What do you want him to do, call the rescue team and persuade them to ignore the emergency call? Make her suffer purely out of a sense of justice?' demands Kate, angrily.

I flip my magazine closed. 'Actually, I wouldn't wish that even on her. If anyone knows what it's like to suffer pain – it's me! The likes of you,' I prod an accusing finger in Joseph's direction, 'destroyed my world with what you did, with her. And now you expect me to be happy that she's been found alive, despite a busted leg! Phah! No chance. And you,' I redirect my pointing to Kate, 'have no idea how the revelations of this week have undermined my sense of self. Destroyed everything it has taken me months to rebuild.' Kate goes to speak, but I continue my rant. 'No, Kate, even you can't fix this situation with a kind word, a phone call or a quick search on Google!'

'I wasn't about to try,' she confesses, seeking back-up from the two guys.

Affie slowly eases Mia from his arms and lowers her onto the couch, then sidles across to my armchair, before lowering himself to his haunches and taking my hand in his. 'Paisley, we get where you're coming from . . . it's a difficult situation all round. But you need to see that what Selena did back then means nothing regarding how she feels about you. You've heard her say how much she regrets her actions, and the reason why she behaved as she did. But it wasn't aimed at you – she was simply lonely and made a poor choice.' His steady blue gaze looks honest, there's no denying that. I glance from Kate to Joseph, who are both nodding. Affie continues, 'We hear your pain, but can you hear what hers was like?'

I snatch my hand back from his grasp; I don't want to hear common sense.

'She did me wrong!'

'She did. She acknowledges that fact, but you need to show some grace, Paisley. Now is not the time for you to desert her. She needs you just as much as anyone, if not more.'

I stare hard into his kindly face and see the truth. He's right. I don't have to lower myself to her standards, or lack of them, on that fateful night. I still have the right to be hurt, feel betrayed and yet still show grace towards her situation. Maybe her burden of guilt is proportionate to the depth of our friendship? Maybe or maybe not, but can I be the bigger person here? Can I forgive her dishonesty? I think I'm hurt more by her ability to stand by me in my darkest hour knowing that she caused it than I am at her doing the deed with Joseph. Her betrayal that night was simply one act, but to show up day after day, night after night, to soothe my tears, listen to my sorrows and still hug me feels so Judas-like.

'Sorry, but I can't stand here and simply wait for my sister to return,' says Kate, suddenly grabbing her handbag.

'There's no point doing anything else, Kate,' says Affie, reaching out to stop her departure.

'There must be!'

'The hospital, then . . .' suggests Joseph, 'There can only be one around these parts. Kate, you're not driving in your state. I'll drive.'

'I'll find the postcode while you ready yourselves – I'll stay put with the little one,' says Affie, pointing towards the sleeping child. I watch as they bustle around grabbing their belongings before heading into the hallway. What will I do, sit here and wait for news? Help Affie put Mia to bed? More second-hand news, as if I haven't heard enough that way in recent times. I throw aside my glossy mag and jump up, ready to join the party. 'Oi, wait for me!'

Chapter Sixty-nine

Late Evening

Kate

On arriving back from the hospital, I'm shattered – emotional but relieved to have brought Selena home with us. As Joseph drove towards the Westmorland General Hospital, I made a deal with the universe that if my little sister was just OK, without sustaining a head injury or life-altering injury, I'd forgive her anything. Just as long as she was still the brash brazen bugger that she's always been – the one we love so dearly. Despite her faults, I love her to bits. Thankfully, her broken leg looked worse than it actually was, so following the initial assessment and x-ray, a plaster cast was a belated last and final present for her thirtieth birthday. Not something she'd have chosen! And now she's settled in the snug, her cast raised on a cushion, so I have a few minutes to hopefully calm myself and breathe.

It's nearly ten o'clock as I take the stairs, heading for the quiet of my bedroom. A quick freshen up and a change of atmosphere from the stifling presence of others will do me good. The top stair creaks as I reach the landing, and I can hear the gentle notes of the Disney lullaby playing from Mia's twin-room and the sporadic murmur of Affie's voice.

Instead of heading for my bedroom, the tune draws me along the corridor. A stream of mellow light spreads out upon the carpet from the open doorway.

I gently tap on the open door, but he doesn't hear. He's lying prone on top of the duvet, fully dressed, with a sleeping child tucked under his wing. The lamplight throws a warm glow over them, creating a beautiful image. I'm spellbound. Affie is stroking her blonde fringe, following the soft curve of her temple, his index finger tracing the delicate line of her features, as if memorising every detail. He startles a little as he notices me leaning against the doorjamb, but doesn't stop.

'Hi,' whispers Affie. 'Is Selena OK?'

I simply nod. I'm too exhausted for anything more, and this gentle scene has made me too emotional to speak. I don't wish to break their spell with my tears.

Affie strokes her plump cheek, but Mia doesn't react; she's in the Land of Nod. I want to giggle as he slowly withdraws his chest and arm from beneath the sleeping child, who smacks her lips and murmurs as he moves away. He quickly places a finger to his lip, before pausing the music on his phone.

We don't speak until we reach the comfy sofa on the landing.

'That was so sweet,' I say, settling into the plush cushions.

'Maybe at that stage, but it's taken ninety minutes for her to drift off. Anyway, tell me how's it gone?'

'Selena's downstairs. She's got a plaster cast up to here,' I indicate my lower leg, 'and a set of crutches. Though Carlos was good enough to carry her in from the car. I imagine she's got a rough couple of months ahead of her,' I explain. Joseph sensibly and politely stepped back, ensuring that Paisley wasn't caused further upset by witnessing any unnecessary contact.

'Joseph mentioned you've had a rough couple of years,' he says, not shying away from an awkward topic.

I don't usually explain, but find myself doing just that.

'My ex-husband developed a problem with gambling after we'd got married. We'd been together for ages and even now I don't know whether he hid it well during that time or if it was the change of life and circumstance and then this issue kicked in. Either way, he became more involved and over time was betting larger amounts and would frequently lose to the horses, the dogs and his poker mates. It seems enough was never enough, and the problem just became unbearable to the point ...' I break off as the memories come flooding back. 'He gambled our mortgage payments and we ended up so far in arrears that the bank was threatening to repossess. I hadn't had a clue what was happening.'

'All behind your back?'

'Oh yeah. The lies told to cover-up his behaviour were immense. It ruined everything for us. We divorced and I set about rectifying the mortgage payments with help from my parents.'

'Sounds awful, Kate. But you're over the worst now, though.'

'And you?' I ask, not wishing to pry but wanting to know more.

'We thought we knew what we wanted, but neither one of us was happy in the relationship. We held out for as long as we could, but it wasn't fair on Mia. Living amidst tension is tough enough as an adult, and it certainly doesn't offer a secure environment for a little one. So we split. Mia was only three at the time, but she's handled it well, so far.'

'That's good to hear.'

'And tonight? You're OK now?'

I shake my head and sigh deeply. 'I'm wobbly at the minute, but just seeing you two so snug reminds me of how tight our bond as sisters is. I'll be fine as long as she is.'

'The last twenty-four hours have been a lot to process. Just sit with it for a while and let it wash over you a little.'

'That sounds odd but necessary.'

'It's what I do when we encounter nasty situations during rescues – let the mind settle then start again.'

'Start again, and what better time than at new year, which is only in a couple of hours' time.'

'I agree. Come on, let's make tracks downstairs – I'm pretty sure Mia's out for the count.'

I wait as Affie retrieves his phone, pulls their bedroom door a little further towards close, and we tiptoe downstairs to join the others.

Chapter Seventy

Selena

We gather in the snug, creating a tense triangular formation, sitting beneath a festoon of holly and ivy. Though there's nothing cosy about us sisters sitting either end of the same couch, and Paisley perched on the opposing sofa. For the first time this holiday, the main light is on, shining bright and startling, unlike the previous occasions with their mellow lamplight. The coffee table is bare of festive nibbles or cheese board and there's no alcohol.

Having returned from hospital, I'm deemed comfortable and am currently pain-free, but my body aches from the fall, my bruises are ripening in shades of blue and purple, and my plaster-cast leg is cantilevered up on top of the coffee table. The guys are elsewhere, probably enjoying a footie match, having brought this little gathering together. 'Be nice,' were Carlos' final words, which seems ominous, given the subject hanging over us.

Both ladies are waiting for me to speak, but I can't find the words. I haven't the knack Josie demonstrated earlier. I hate to add any more drama to this day than I have already, but needs must if they're to understand.

'I need you both to listen. I'm not seeking your pity, but simply for you to hear me out.' Kate and Paisley eye me cautiously before each give me a curt nod. I know what I need to say, but each word sticks in my throat. I could really do with a drink. It's their reaction I can't handle, though, rather than actually saying it aloud. 'Two years ago, I lost a baby.'

I look down, as I can't bring myself to meet their eyes, but both jolt in a sudden movement as my words register. I keep talking for fear of losing my nerve. I hastily deliver the basic details: my shock, confusion, decision and then utter grief, under which I felt submerged.

'That Saturday night, I spied a raucous crowd as my friends were leaving the bar. Familiar faces of old, laughing and joking and drinking. Selena-of-old would have been in the mix, centre-stage and lining drinks up at the bar, then knocking them back with the rest of them. But not this Selena, the one that now shied away from laughing, that felt guilty for lacking the maternal spirit and who wished with every fibre of my body to return to the woman I once was, within the arms of a guy who wanted me for me and nothing more. I never planned it. I never instigated it, and yet it happened. You don't want the details, I don't even want to think about the steps I took to get that far, but I did, we did. I've been sorry every moment since. I never meant to hurt you, Paisley. In that moment I simply wanted the security of a relationship. Or the illusion of one. One like yours.' I can't look at either of them right now, so stare at the skirting board and keep talking. 'I wasn't conscious that it was Joseph. I wasn't conscious that it was anyone in particular, which shows how far along the ledge I'd walked. Since when have I disrespected myself and body in that manner?'

'Never,' says Kate, tearfully.

'I agree,' adds Paisley, for which I'm grateful.

'I'm not asking for forgiveness nor pity ... just some under-standing that I wasn't myself that night.'

'Sounds like self-destruct mode to me,' offers Kate, wiping her eyes.

I shrug. I'm not making excuses. Not then, not now. I've nothing more to add, so fall silent.

Kate reaches for my hand, cradling it between both of hers.

The shock of her warm touch brings my gaze up to meet hers at last.

'And the guy ... the father?' asks Paisley.

'No one of importance in my world ... he's long gone.'

The silence laps between us like waves on a shoreline.

'I can't say that I understand, but I can see how bad things must have got for you. I'm sorry. You could have trusted me,' Kate says, her eyes brimming with tears.

'Selena.' Paisley's voice surprises me. Turning, I can see she too is broken. The darkened rings beneath each puffy tear-stained eye, her sallow complexion and unruly curls convey a picture of abject misery, one created by me. 'I'm so sorry,' she says. 'I suppose it never enters my head that you too have difficult times. It always appears as if you breeze through life untouched, unharmed and unbothered by events or people. I'm sorry I let you down when you needed me so badly.' She gulps back more tears on completing her speech.

'One of the hardest parts is that, in the blink of an eye, the due date came around, which knocked me sideways, and then just as swiftly I was reliving the events of the previous year: the test, the questions, the bewilderment and the loss. So now there's two additional dates on the calendar that send me into a wobble and which I can't forget. And neither do I wish to.'

'And nor should you have to, Selena,' says Kate, tears rushing down her cheeks.

'Which goes some way to explain my reluctance in making plans for my birthday. I suppose I was hoping that we'd be the same old trio as before, but, well ... it hasn't turned out that way, has it?'

'Oh Selena,' whispers Paisley, leaning forward, her outstretched hands spanning the gap between us.

There's a knock at the snug door. Talk about terrible timing.

'If they dare to ask for a bottle ... tonight of all nights,' mutters Kate, darkly.

'Only me,' says Carlos, pushing the door wide to enter, carrying a tea tray. 'I thought you might benefit from tea at half-time.' He gives a wry smile before placing the tray on the coffee table beside my leg.

'I'm not sure about your timing, but thank you – that was kind of you,' I say, glancing between the other two, both tear-stained, exhausted and in need of tea. That's the second time today I've been rescued by Carlos.

'What are you guys planning for midnight?' asks Kate, as Carlos hands around the mugs.

'Affie's staring at the TV having put Mia to bed. I'm hoping for a quiet one, in front of the TV with Jools Holland and his musical line up. You?'

'I'm going to bed in a while. I need to rest,' I say, sheepishly, not wanting anyone to talk me into changing my mind.

'Me too, I think,' adds Kate.

'Affie will be disappointed,' mutters Carlos, flashing her a knowing glance.

I watch as my sister considers his remark. I hope she changes her mind – she deserves to enjoy herself a little more than she does. Though I'm not about to start an argument with a chance remark.

'Paisley?' asks Carlos, offering her the third mug and awaiting her answer.

She shrugs. 'I'm undecided. I'll see how the night unfolds.'

Good for her. 'I hope it unfolds into a decent night, bringing new hopes, new desires and fresh beginnings,' I say, hoping she knows how genuine I am being, despite recent fallings out.

'Let's hope Joseph's staying up until midnight as well, then,' says Carlos, heading for the doorway. 'Selena, if you need help up the staircase, please holler.'

'Thank you, I will.' I feel myself blush a little, and Kate and Paisley totally notice.

Chapter Seventy-one

Nearly midnight

Paisley

'Can we talk?' asks Joseph, entering the snug. I'm sitting in here alone with my thoughts. Kate left a while earlier to assist Carlos with manoeuvring Selena up the staircase towards her bedroom. My half-hearted offer to help had been politely refused by all parties.

'Sure.' This could prove interesting.

Joseph closes the door, muffling the sound from the lounge's TV, before settling himself on the couch opposite. He's clearly not comfortable with my silence, but I'm not the one who asked to 'talk', so I'll be damned if I'm spilling my guts.

'I wanted to ask how you are? Now that you ... well, after knowing the truth and then hearing what she had to say too, and ...' He didn't say her name – interesting. Have I heard him say her name in recent days?

'You've got some cheek. How the hell do you think I'm feeling? I'm gutted. Can't get my head around the details. The lies, the deceit, the betrayal and now the cover-up ... people always reckon the cover-up seems worse than the actual deed, don't they? Well, they're right. It does!'

'Paise, I'm so sorry. I've caused all of this ...'

'No! You've both caused this. And now both of you expect me to listen to your anguish and then modify my own pain and anger in accordance with the details. I didn't do anything. Listen to *that* fact. I didn't deserve how I have been treated, regardless of your intention or situations. Yet I'm the one left feeling like this.'

'Don't you think I know that? It was you that insisted on honesty in order to start afresh – now look at the situation. I knew this would happen.' I watch as his shoulders rock back and forth with each word. His hands can't stay still, rubbing each other, raking through his hair and over his chin as he speaks. Anguish, pure and simple.

'I didn't expect you to say *her* name. I imagined it was a total stranger, but to hear . . .'

Joseph bites his bottom lip, then repositions his elbows on his splayed knees before clasping his hands, as if in prayer.

'Look, this is getting us nowhere. Are we going to spend the rest of our days searching for "another one" when "the one" we both truly want is right here?' His gaze doesn't leave mine. 'Is that what you want, Paise?'

I'm dumbstruck; with a single line he's summed us up completely. Is that what I truly want? To recover from this week away and then somehow find it in me to search for a new person to join my life? Or do I want to work on my forgiveness with the one man I've only ever wanted?

He quickly continues, 'Personally, I'd prefer to work on rebuilding what we had . . . have . . . rather than walk away at this point – especially given the week we've had. I know what I want, but I can't do this for the both of us, Paise. I can't carry the weight of future accusations, the renewed burden of guilt – I'm not prepared to spend the rest of my life paying for the mistake I made on one night. And, yes, I know I didn't fully explain, but I was trying to save you from the final hurt and humiliation.'

He looks emotional and dishevelled, with stubbled regrowth and waxy skin. I watch as the words pour forth from this man. Simple, no-nonsense sentiment that's hard to hear and harder to ignore. He's everything I ever loved or wanted. Can I truly overlook one night of madness for a lifetime of committed love? The festive decorations catch my eye as Joseph's words swim about my mind. The holly and ivy boughs looking decidedly vibrant with their luscious shades of green. I wonder how long they'll last before their lustre fades to mottled brown, before they become dried remnants of the season past. I can hardly remember what Selena read aloud about their symbolic meanings, except for fertility, fidelity, devotion and growth. Maybe it's a sign?

From the lounge the muted tones of a jubilant countdown begin in earnest: 'Ten! Nine! Eight . . . !'

'It's not going to be easy,' I say, unsure if I'm talking to him or myself.

'I know that, Paise. But surely it'll be easier than me living without you,' he says, reaching forward and taking both my hands in his. 'And no more secrets, I promise.'

'Five! Four!' continues the TV countdown.

I nod in agreement, my gaze fixed, holding his gaze, allowing him to cradle my hands and feel his reassuring squeeze.

'I want nothing more than to rebuild what we had, but with stronger foundations,' whispers Joseph, leaning forward and raising our clasped hands between us.

'And me.' We're so close I see his pupils dilate, his mouth relaxes as my breath catches in my throat and I anticipate what's to follow.

'Three! Two! Happy New Year!'

'Can I?' he asks, his gaze flicking to my lips.

'Yes.' In a heartbeat his lips are on mine, our clenched hands are awkwardly squashed between our frames as our troubles are forgotten in our tender but passionate connection.

The noise from the lounge disappears, the troubles and tense conversations from earlier melt away, and the joy that was once integral to me and Joseph ignites once more. I don't know when we released our clenched hands, but within moments his hand gently strokes the back of my neck as we slowly drift apart. Our foreheads remain in touching distance as I whisper 'Happy New Year, Joseph.'

'I'll do all I can for it to be *our* happy New Year!'

Chapter Seventy-two

Wednesday 1 January 2025

Kate

My mobile vibrates on the nearest counter top, and the screen flashes yet again as my boss attempts to call me. Yesterday I'd lowered the volume to silent in a poor attempt to ignore his repeated demands to call him back immediately. I can't ignore his calls any longer. I've done well to manage until now. Though, I certainly didn't plan on his voice being the first I hear this morning. I snatch up my mobile and press 'accept' call.

'Hello.' I set the phone down on the side on hands free, and continue to light the grill.

'Kate?'

'Yes.'

'Finally! Well, I have to say I'm not impressed with the manner in which you've conducted yourself in recent days. How many times have I had to message and yet you've ignored me. It isn't good enough, Kate. Not what I expect from the likes of you when I'm trying to get some clarity on what the hell happened at my daughter's engagement party. Do you know?'

'Know what?' My tone is admittedly surly. I feel like a teenager about to be grounded by a parent.

'The upset and embarrassment that you caused my family in front of all our friends, family and neighbourhood. A complete shambles, Kate – that's what you delivered. We'll be ridiculed for months after you showed us up with your shoddy organisation. My daughter was dreaming of a magical evening, but instead she had her engagement ring delivered by a bunch of clowns, and a cake that announced 'happy birthday Selena' – whoever the hell she is! My wife spent the evening in tears, and my daughter locked herself in a toilet cubicle, as she couldn't bear to face her own guests. Her fiancé was so taken by your promise of a bird of prey that he hasn't even presented her with the ring yet, as he was determined to incorporate the owl. You promised us the best engagement party, set the expectations high, as always, and yet delivered nothing but mayhem – utterly useless, Kate . . .'

From nowhere a male hand reaches around my body and taps my screen forcefully, cancelling the call. I whip around to find Affie standing there, shaking his head.

'Who the hell was that?' he asks, clearly not impressed.

'My boss – he was outlining . . .'

'No need. I heard enough. The guy's an out and out bully, Kate.'

'I can understand his frustration. I rarely make errors, but this time I totally screwed up.' I stare at my blank screen, shocked that Affie's silenced my boss. I'll really be in for it now. 'He'll call back. He won't appreciate being cut off mid-sentence.'

'He's welcome to call back, but not if he's gunning for you in that manner, Kate. He should question his own behaviour before addressing yours.'

'Thanks, but . . . ooooh, here we go!' I say, as my mobile screen springs to life with a second call.

'Hello?'

'Did you cut me off?' His voice is terse, but slightly calmer than before.

'Me? No.' My gaze drops in embarrassment, and I'm surprised to notice Affie's socked feet below on the red tiles. Interesting.

'Ah, well, as I was saying . . . a total embarrassment, Kate. The aftermath of which you'll need to start sorting out if we're to get refunds. There's no way my wife will agree to foot the bill for such a dismal evening. So I need you to . . .'

'Sorry. Me?'

'Yes, you, Kate. We're entertaining today – its New Year.'

I pause before replying. Affie's jaw has dropped.

'I'm quite aware of the date, thanks, and as such I can only offer my apologies again for how your night turned out. It was never my intention to ruin your daughter and future-son-in-law's engagement party, but I've plans for today . . . I'm busy with family and won't be able to make a start on contacting suppliers until . . .' He doesn't let me finish.

'I don't think so, Kate. I need to assure my family that this fiasco has been sorted and that the result I wanted is the one that's been achieved. You'll need to rearrange your free time for another time.'

I hear his words, but it's his selfish manner, his arrogance and contempt that strikes a chord with me. He couldn't care less . . . after all these years of dedicated assistance and support – it means nothing. I'd get more respect from those I've known for a lot less . . . my gaze lifts to Affie, who continues to watch me closely.

There's silence on the other end. I'd been too busy thinking to follow his demands.

'Kate? Are you still there?'

'No. I'm not entirely sure that I am. I think . . . I think I've just decided upon my New Year's resolution, and that's to find myself brand-new employment with a boss who respects his colleagues and who recognises boundaries within those working relationships. Thanks for calling, but please accept that as my verbal resignation. I will definitely put it in writing the first chance I have. Goodbye.'

I don't hear his reply, as I tap my mobile screen and abruptly end the call. After which I burst out crying like a child.

'Oh Kate, come here,' says Affie, wrapping an arm around my shoulders to console me.

'I c-can't b-believe I just did that!'

'Me neither, but I'm dead proud of you. He doesn't know what he's just lost.'

I slowly breathe out, in an attempt to calm myself, though the warmth of Affie's half embrace is helping immensely.

'Happy New Year to you both . . . oooh, sorry to intrude,' says Paisley, coming into the kitchen and eyeing us cautiously before seeing my tears. 'Kate, are you OK?'

I nod, fighting back more tears.

'She just told her boss to stick his job – or thereabouts,' explains Affie, whisking a fresh tear from my cheek with a sweep of his thumb.

'Wow! No more Mr Psycho-boss? Good for you! You should have done it years ago.'

I nod. I know she's right, but this really wasn't planned. I glance at my mobile screen – there's no incoming call, no text message, nothing.

'Bye bye to financial security . . . which seems slightly reckless.'

'There's more to life, Kate – and without putting up with the crap you've endured from the likes of him,' says Paisley, before adding, 'You've handled bigger issues in life.'

'You'll be fine. From what I hear, you've spent too long there anyway. A decent firm will snap you up first chance they get, no worries,' offers Affie, slowly unpeeling his comforting arm from around my frame. A little sooner than I'd hoped. 'Anyway, let's get you settled with a cuppa and I'll cook the breakfast.'

He manoeuvres me towards the nearest seat at the kitchen table while Paisley fills the kettle for a brew.

'Where's Mia? I ask, suddenly aware of her absence.

'Watching cartoons in her pyjamas – I didn't want her hearing the aggression coming from that chap,' says Affie, grabbing the grill pan and layering it with chilled sausages. 'Don't worry, she'll holler if she needs me.'

'How wonderfully reassuring to know help is always on call,' I say, more to myself than anyone. I glance up in time to catch Paisley's wry smile, and wonder if Affie heard, before he confirms with, 'It certainly is, Kate.'

Chapter Seventy-three

Mid-morning

Paisley

I made an extra effort to join the sisters in the snug after breakfast before packing my things to meet our departure time.

'How's the leg feeling?' I ask Selena.

'Heavy, thanks to this cast. It'll be a bugger getting around work on crutches, but I'll manage somehow.'

'I'm sure you will,' I add, grateful that we're at least being civil.

'I'm sure your lard campaign won't suffer if someone else takes over,' adds Kate.

'You have got to be joking. That's mine. I'm not passing this chance up for the likes of Jez – I'd never live it down!'

'You might have to if it proves too much, Selena,' suggests Kate, clearly treading carefully so as not to cause her upset.

'Not bloody likely. Lard is mine.' Selena's clearly back to her normal self.

The silence lingers so I quickly jump in.

'I've made us each a small posy from the festive decorations to take home with us,' I say, pulling the three bundles of holly and ivy from behind my back and quickly handing one each to Kate and Selena. 'It doesn't look much, but I'm hoping the sentiment will speak volumes. I'm not ready to open up about how I'm feeling, but I'm happy to pave the way towards better times together.'

'What was it Carlos said that time?' asks Kate, pressing her finger against the prickles.

'It wasn't Carlos – it was me that read it from the internet,' corrects Selena, pointedly, reaching for her mobile.

'I see you're feeling better – back to your usual self, is it?' quips Kate, as quick as a flash.

Selena ignores her sister and continues to list the symbolic meanings, just as she had the other day, before adding, 'Well, take what you will – there's something listed for each of us.'

'I thought that yesterday when I was chatting to Joseph. I'm hoping to take fidelity, devotion and growth,' I say, not daring to add fertility to the list, as it's a step too far at this stage. 'What about you, Kate?'

'I'm happy with goodwill, loyalty and determination, thanks very much. Anything else will be a bonus,' she says.

'I'm settle for peace, protection and healing,' comes Selena's reply. 'Though I won't say no to anything positive for the future.'

'Some counselling perhaps?' asks Kate, tenderly.

'A possibility – I'll see.'

We fall silent, each of us eyeballing the other two. It feels strange to have entered this phase, when we haven't previously encountered such awkward silences. And never imagined we ever would.

'Before you all start making plans on my behalf, I'll say that I've asked Carlos to drive me home because of this cast. So, Kate, if you'd be good enough to drive my car back, I'll follow with him,' announces Selena, taking a sudden interest in her festive posy. Kate smirks at me, without her seeing.

'What if I have my own plans?' jokes Kate.

'Have you?'

'Maybe.' Kate blushes while remaining coy.

'Spill the beans, please,' demands Selena. 'Otherwise I'll ask Affie straight out.'

'Shhh, stop. We've agreed to meet up in a few days for a quiet drink, nothing more – so don't spoil it for me.'

'Me? Spoil it?'

I remain schtum, knowing any remark from me might be taken too much to heart. This is the crux of the matter, as I'm now watching everything I say in a strained friendship where I never have before.

'Paisley, what are you plans?' asks Kate, shifting the focus.

'One step at a time for us, I think. I can't promise anything. I need time to process all that's happened and been said before I know for certain.' I daren't look at Selena as I speak, but I know she understands.

'I hope you manage to work through the difficulties and are truly reunited in time to come,' offers Selena. 'I genuinely mean that, Paisley.'

'Same goes for us three too. I've realised we'd been a little detached from one another prior to this break, and, well, in some respects maybe this week has addressed those areas. I hope we can reunite as we once were too,' says Kate, looking at each of us for agreement.

'I hope so,' says Selena.

'In time,' I quickly add.

Chapter Seventy-four

Selena

'I hate to think of the bad language and insults I hollered during my recovery at the waterfall. Affie says the rescue teams are used to it, though. That they understand the agony I endured,' I say, settling back on my sofa in the snug.

'You promise not to get tetchy and arsy if I'm honest?' asks Carlos, removing the last of the festive decorations from the fixtures and fittings, after we'd waved the others off.

I pull a face. Is he taking the mickey now.

'Seriously, I've never heard such language on a rescue, Selena. The air was blue. I winced throughout as they were stretchering you towards a waiting ambulance.'

'I wasn't that bad!'

His eyebrows shoot up, disappearing into his hairline, before he resumes with his task.

'And you attend accidents such as that each weekend?' I ask, watching his fingers busily working at the threads and wires secured to tacks and pins.

'Not every weekend, just the ones where I sign on for duty. Yeah, it's rewarding.'

'Phah! I can think of more rewarding ways to spend my weekends.'

'Such as?'

'Seeing friends and relatives. Being supportive when . . .' My words fade – I've hit my own sore point.

Carlos whips around to eye me warily.

'Nearly tripped yourself up then.'

'Paisley's got every right to feel betrayed. She thinks I found solace and redemption in attending to her needs, but, honestly, I didn't. If anything, seeing her shed so many tears for the home life that could have been tore me apart. There were so many times I nearly confessed and told her the truth.'

'Why would you do that?'

'To take what I deserved. She'd have felt better having taken her pain out on me rather than having a nameless faceless trollop to be angry with. It might have helped her.'

'And you?'

'I might have felt slightly better if that had been the case.'

'I doubt it.'

'What would you know?'

Carlos casts me a look while stripping boughs of green foliage from the nearest picture frames.

'Yeah, you're right – I know nothing. Bugger all, in fact. What's the saying "no sense, no feeling"? Yeah, that's me by all accounts.'

'Carlos!'

'No, Selena. You make out that I'm some yobbish brute, with his beer bottles, his quippy remarks, his don't-give-a-damn attitude, when actually the truth is I care about many things in life. I care about people. I care about others, full stop! I wouldn't give up my weekends to trek for miles and miles in the damp moorland searching for those that need help if I didn't care. You're making out I'm some heartless bastard. Well, I'm about as heartless as you are, Selena.'

'I'm not . . .'

'I know! Admit it, we're cut from the same cloth. Everyone describes you as brash, upfront, direct – yeah, right, all very polite, but it's plain and simple bolshie at the end of the day. Something you've called me from day one.'

'I haven't,' I mutter, knowing full well I have. 'Well, maybe once or twice.'

'And the rest,' he replies over his shoulder, while collecting the foliage into one huge pile.

'Please don't throw them from the doorstep like you did before.'

'I won't. There's a compost pile at the very top of the garden.'

'Pity you didn't do that the first time. I wouldn't have been narked enough to rescue and titivate in here otherwise.'

'Titivate? Is that what you call it? I don't believe you can titivate with *Ilex aquifolium*,' says Carlos, bundling the discarded decorations into his arms.

'The what?'

'Holly. But us gardeners, we prefer the botanical names.' He gives me a gleeful smile before heading out of the snug.

'What do you mean "us gardeners"?' I call after him.

Carlos' head and shoulders reappear around the door. 'Sorry to burst your bubble, but I lied about my stage performances . . . no can do, actually. I've been a gardener these last ten years.'

'You said . . .' My jaw drops wide at his audacity.

'Don't tell me you believed me?' he chuckles. 'Talk about perception versus reality – I was playing you up. The guys simply played along with my little joke.'

'I did. Seriously, I did.' I'm shocked that he'd pull the wool over my eyes to that extent.

'And now, you're relieved I'm not?'

'Why would I be relieved? It's not as if your job affects me.'

'I forgot that detail, though in some respects, if we continue to get along as we do, it might – now there's a thought.' On that note he disappears into the hallway, heading for the garden. He's got some nerve. He's cocky enough to be a performer, that's for sure.

I brood over his comments until he returns to the snug empty handed.

'So what was with flicking the warm chocolate then – I imagined that was your forte on stage.'

Carlos stares at me in bewilderment, before plonking himself down beside me. 'I do hope you're joking, Selena.'

'I'm not joking.'

'Wow! And here was me thinking we were getting along well. Well enough to see if this could go anywhere. Clearly not.'

'You were the one acting up – why do it, then?'

'To get your attention in a fun way.'

My cheeks burn deep crimson.

'I assume from that reaction I did, so there's a plus point.'

'There are better ways is actually what I was thinking,' I tease.

'Like this?' Carlos turns around in his seat, placing the crook of his index finger beneath my chin and gently brings my face to meet his. Our gaze locks, until my vision blurs and his warm lips touch mine. I'm lost in the moment and I feel a buzz of excitement deep in the pit of my stomach.

'That's a much better way of getting my attention,' I whisper, eager for more.

'I thought it might be.'

Epilogue

Tuesday 1 April 2025

Paisley

It takes an age to take the M4 towards Bath. Not that it's a bad road, more that the snaking traffic has a habit of stopping and starting each time the roadworks disappear. If only Joseph could have a free run and stay in one gear, we'd have been there by now.

'Will you relax? We're almost there,' says Joseph reassuringly. Clearly I'm not hiding my nerves all that well.

'It's OK Affie saying it's only ten miles from the M4, but if the motorway is snarled it might as well be a hundred.'

'You're right, but we've left the M4 behind us now, so we're on the last leg of this journey, literally minutes away. So take it in your stride, Paisley.'

I settle back, watching the local cream stone whiz past the car window. It feels like another world, another time in fact, given the amount of Georgian architecture that looms on either side. I'll admit I'm nervous. It seems months since our arrival out the front of Lakeside Cottage, ready for the week ahead. And then, within the space of a few minutes, we realised an error had been made and fate had delivered each of us a prospect that we hadn't planned. And, in all honesty, wouldn't have chosen. If I'd have realised, walking along that cobbled pathway towards my introductions with Josie, what the week held in store, I'd have probably turned and run. In fact, no probably about it. I glance at Joseph, and smile.

I'm eager to see the girls. Admittedly nervous at seeing Selena. We've made tentative steps over recent months to repair the trust ... our conversation feels relatively seamless as long as we avoid the elephant in the room. I'm still left seething when I think about my other half having seen her naked, but I have to close those thoughts down. Joseph actually wants me to seek help regarding my intrusive thoughts. Maybe one day I will. I'm just not ready yet. And it still eats at me to think she could offer comfort when she was the cause. Still worse hug, caress and soothe me, having done the same to him the night before, albeit under the pretence of lust and futile longing, but still. She did it, she went there and crossed a line I would never have crossed with any of her partners. Current, ex or potential, and yet she did. I still don't understand how. I have a better understanding of why, I suppose, when she explains her loss, the longing to experience and have what we had, but even so ... I couldn't have ventured where she did. Nor could I have hidden the truth afterwards for the whole eighteen months, all the while barely leaving my side. I don't know how she did that knowing she'd caused my pain. But she did.

No further, my brain tells me. I've learnt to loop back on myself at this point, almost like an endless car journey in which you need to steer clear of certain obstacles, knowing you'll snare yourself up and grind to an emotional stand still if you don't navigate properly.

It's the same game with me and Joseph. We're fine, hunky dory in fact, if we steer clear of certain topics. I can't say I've forgiven him. I don't think that's in my nature, but I'm learning to cope. To avoid those tetchy moments when I want to lash out and remind him what he did to us. The rest of the time we're getting along great. We've taken it right back to basics. We had to. From a simple kiss on a wooden bench right up until now, I can't be forced, rushed or pushed into anything that doesn't feel comfortable for me. Which is why today is a big day in many respects.

I'm not pretending that we'll make it back to where we were originally: dating, courting, marriage and home life. But we're heading in the right direction so far, though our beginnings seem firmer and more secure than last time – much like that cobbled path at Lakeside Cottage. I'm determined to lay a solid foundation that can last for eternity, or near enough.

'Here we are. Now that wasn't too bad, was it?' asks Joseph, pulling up alongside a row of neat terraced houses, identical in brick work and style, apart from the décor in the front windows. Number seventeen looks just as I'd imagined: neat, ordered and befitting Kate's new home.

'Long enough, given the motorway traffic,' I mutter, diverting my thoughts and struggling to keep my emotions at bay. I think I know what I'm about to walk into and I need to be prepared.

I'm barely out of the car, still collecting my handbag from the car's footwell, when the glazed front door opens and a happy skippity child dashes out to greet us.

'Aunty Paise!' she cries, her arms enveloping me, as if I'd been present since her birth and not just recent months.

'Hello, my sweet. How are you?' I bend to hug her tight and feel the excited wriggle of her within my big bear hug.

'We've got trifle, and cakes, and there's small triangle sandwiches – which I don't want, but I'm not allowed cake unless I eat them first,' announces Mia, grabbing my hand and dragging me towards the front doorstep. Behind me, Joseph retrieves my coat from the car's back seat and finishes securing the vehicle.

'Hello. Sorry, but she's been up at the window since long before you left home,' explains Affie, stepping through the gate to collect his daughter. Kate patiently waits on the doorstep, clinging to the doorjamb. They've taken a brave step in moving in together. Kate looks tentative and somewhat pale. I can guess why.

'Hello, my lovely, how are you?' she asks, her arms reaching for me as soon as I near her.

'We're good. Small steps, but good so far,' I whisper, within the confines of our doorstep embrace. I hear the lads back slapping and laughing behind, but its what's before me that I need to meet head on.

'Go through. Selena's already here,' says Kate, releasing me to gesture the way along the hallway.

I too feel sick. I take in a deep breath. I want this to work . . . for us all. I want everything to be alright and almost how it was before with my longest-standing, dearest friend. I don't know if what I'm hoping for will ever truly exist, but try I must. Otherwise my life will have a permanent gap, a hole where her love always sat. Our devotion to one another has been a constant since we were children. It's something that I'd never chose to lose from my life lightly.

I push the lounge door a little to reveal a brightly lit front room. Cosy couches, low coffee table and clean lines of décor – typical of Kate. There, on the far end of the couch, perches Selena. Looking totally uncomfortable, on the edge of the cushion, trying to hold it together. She's thinner than when I saw her last, but clearly relived to see me as much as I am to see her.

'Hi.'

'Hi.' My arms open wide to embrace the friend I've known for an eternity, not the woman who did me wrong. I keep reminding myself that one is more important than the other. 'How have you been?'

'So, so. You know how it is. I was good yesterday, but the thought of being here today . . . among you guys . . . Well . . . you know.'

'I do.' I drop my handbag down beside the couch and sit, patting her original seat beside me. I can't say too much – my emotions won't allow it – but she knows. It's a struggle for the both of us.

'I'll grab the drinks before we settle,' says Affie, as he and Kate drift in the wake of an excitable Mia, who's dancing and prancing around the lounge. Bless her, under the circumstances I'm grateful for the distraction she's providing.

'Is Carlos joining us?' asks Joseph, closing the lounge door.

'He is. But not for another hour,' says Selena, blushing some-what, which is nice to see and settles my nerves a little. 'He's busy working.'

'Stripping?' jibes Joseph, referencing his buddy's previous little joke on us girls.

'Ha ha, you boys are so damned funny, aren't you? A bunch of fools when you decide to play tricks,' retorts Selena, gleefully laughing at the reminder.

'Going well, is it?' I ask, wanting to take an interest yet not be too involved.

'Mmmm, it is. Though how I'm not so sure. We're both as brash as the other, can argue for England and our stubbornness is off the scale, but I'm learning.'

A ripple of polite laughter circles the lounge; we all get it.

'We're pleased for you both,' I hastily add, not knowing what else to say.

'How's tricks with you two?' asks Joseph of our hosts, settling himself in the armchair, as Affie prepares to leave us again to make the proposed drinks. Before anyone can speak, Mia does.

'Kate's having a baby!'

We all look at Mia, see her gleeful smile and slowly, one by one, turn our attention to the couple in question, frozen to the spot.

'Well, we were happy to delay the news till the kettle was on, but it appears that Mia's excited to share.'

Kate sighs, instantly looking a little more relaxed, if still delicate.

Affie gathers his arms around Kate's shoulders. 'Yes, we do have happy news, and we are indeed expecting a little one. And, yes, certain little piggies are thrilled at the prospect of being a big sister, to the point of having big mouths and ruining the surprise.'

I knew it. Why else would they have chosen to move in together so quickly. It wasn't just Kate's job hunting that spurred their plans, but bigger, more important issues. I feel the well of emotion lift within me. I want to cry. I'm so happy for them both, but equally disappointed for myself. One day I want to be the one delivering such joyous news. But, for now, I'll happily share the excitement at the prospect of Kate's new arrival.

'Mia, don't be so eager. I'll warn you now there could be trouble in store. In our family, the younger sibling is always the troublesome one!' announces Selena, with pride.

'Excuse me. Don't you mean the bolshie one?' jests Kate.

'On that note, I'll make some drinks. Mia, would you like to come this way and help, please,' instructs Affie, leading her with little choice from the room, allowing us adults to talk.

'I'll volunteer too,' says Joseph, jumping up and offering to help his buddy.

'Thank you, Joseph,' says Kate, waiting for the door to close before continuing, 'How are things, ladies?'

'I think you need to spill the beans first, Kate,' squeals Selena, eager to give her older sister a congratulatory squeeze. I take a deep breath, steadying my nerves, before hearing more about their happy news. I can do this. I can be happy for Kate, Affie and Mia. Admittedly, it would be slightly harder to cope with Kate's baby news if me and Joseph weren't getting along so well.

'There's nothing to tell really – I was as surprised as anyone. I'm blaming that tiny posy of holly and ivy that you presented me with,' jokes Kate, lost within Selena's bear hug while gesturing towards the dried posy arrangement lying on the mantlepiece. 'I'm sure I asked for goodwill, loyalty and determination and it seems to have delivered fertility and devotion. Not that I'm complaining – we're thrilled.'

'I hung my festive posy from the kitchen shelving unit with pretty ribbons. I've certainly been delivered peace, protection and healing, thanks to Carlos' continued presence and his expert knowledge on all things horticultural,' adds Selena, before turning to me.

'I separated my posy, carefully flower-pressing each stem and created a pretty pattern before gluing and framing it for positioning on my landing windowsill. So far, there's early signs of fidelity, devotion and personal growth,' I explain, supressing a coy smile.

'Wonderful. That gives me goosebumps, Paisley – I'm chuffed for you . . . both,' says Selena, with an encouraging smile. Clearly, she's aware of the poignancy of her reply. Just as I'm conscious of my actions leading me to truly forgive her.

'I'm happy that we had the chance to reunite at Lakeside Cottage in a meaningful way that has benefited us all, long after Selena's big birthday,' says Kate, reaching for each of our hands to offer a quick squeeze.

'And long may this continue, because despite the occasional upset – I can't imagine my world without either of you!' I quickly add, averting my gaze from theirs, as my eyes swiftly glisten with happy tears.

Acknowledgements

Thank you to my editors, Bea Grabowska, Kate Byrne, and Anna Hervé, plus everyone at Headline Publishing Group for believing in my storytelling and granting me the opportunity to become part of your team.

To David Headley and the crew at DHH Literary Agency – thank you for the unwavering support. Having a 'dream team' supporting my career was always the goal, and you guys make it the reality!

A daily 'thank you' to The London Writers' Salon at www.writershour.com, and the thousands of writers from around the world with whom I sit alongside in silence and write numerous times each day. We may not be together, but something magical occurs at each session! Thank you to P.L. Travers for creating and Walt Disney for filming my all-time favourite 'Mary Poppins'.

A repeated 'thank you' to Wordsworth – I couldn't ignore the young scholar of Hawkshead Grammar School, mesmerised by the beauty of the lakes and a swathe of daffodils. Though your inspiration came from your sister's account of Glencoyne Bay, Ullswater, while mine was from Brantwood, beside Coniston Waters.

A five-star 'thank you' to the various businesses on Main

Street, Hawkshead, in Cumbria, for welcoming a weary but excited author on her travels – I found good people, excellent food and a beautiful four-poster bed!

Unconditional thanks to my family and closest friends, for always loving and supporting my adventures, wherever they take me.

And, finally, thank you to my wonderful readers. You continue to thrill me each day with your fabulous reviews and supportive emails. I'm truly humbled that you invest precious time from your busy lives to read my books. Without you guys, my characters, stories and happy-ever-afters would simply be daydreams.

Make a date to stay at the beautiful Lakeside Cottage!

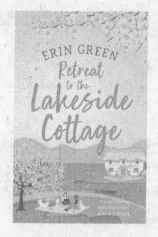

Available now from

Take a trip to glorious Lerwick . . .

Available now from

*A perfect feel-good read of friendship
and fresh starts, guaranteed!*

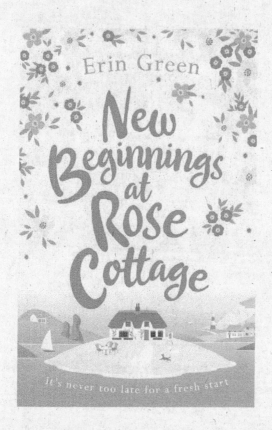

Available now from

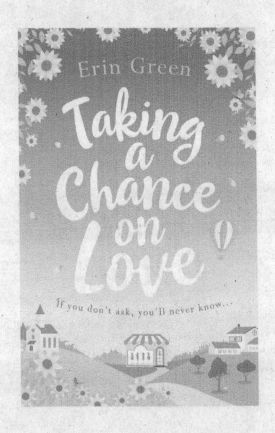